ARJUNA

SAGA OF A PANDAVA WARRIOR-PRINCE

ANUJA CHANDRAMOULI

PLATINUM PRESS

ISBN 978-9381576-39-7

Cover Design	Fravashi Aga
Editing	Abhijit Basu
Layouts	Ajay Shah
Printing	Repro India Ltd

Published in India 2013 by
PLATINUM PRESS
An imprint of LEADSTART PUBLISHING PVT LTD
Trade Centre, Level 1, Bandra Kurla Complex
Bandra (E), Mumbai 400 051, INDIA
T + 91 22 40700804 **F** +91 22 40700800
E info@leadstartcorp.com **W** www.leadstartcorp.com
US Office Axis Corp, 7845 E Oakbrook Circle, Madison, WI 53717, USA

For Veda Vyasa ~

the finest storyteller this world has ever seen

and the man who gave me the great love of my life

About the Author

Anuja Chandramouli is a full-time mother of two lovely girls, as well as a part-time writer. Her academic credentials include a Bachelor's degree in Psychology and a Master's in English. Having started out as a freelance writer with articles published in *Women's Era, Lonely Planet* and *The Hindu,* she currently works as an e-reporter and columnist.

Anuja is a self-confessed, big-dreamer, who is driven by an inner passion to contribute her mite to the great pool of human endeavour, thought, and wisdom. An ardent admirer of Veda Vyasa's *Mahabharata,* Anuja holds the Great Epic to be one of a kind, the Homers and Virgils of the world notwithstanding. Drawing her creative inspiration from the epic's timeless track record of sustenance through centuries of retelling, Anuja chose to debut as a storyteller with the immortal and eternally captivating saga of Arjuna, the *non pareil* hero. Putting together episodes from Arjuna's life (some well known, others relatively obscure), gleaned through years of painstaking research and then presented in a seamless narrative with the uninhibited panache and style of a 21st century writer, has been an immensely satisfying and self-actualising endeavour for this New Age Indian classicist.

Chandramouli can be reached at: anujamouli@gmail.com

Contents

Select Cast of Characters

KURU ELDERS

SHANTANU, King of the Kurus
GANGA, Shantanu's first wife
BHISHMA, Shantanu's son by Ganga
SATYAVATI, Shantanu's second wife
CHITRANGADA, Shantanu & Satyavati's elder son
VICHITRAVIRYA, Shantanu & Satyavati's second son
AMBIKA, Vichitravirya's Queen
AMBALIKA, Vichitravirya's second Queen & Ambika's sister
DHRITARASHTRA Eldest son of Vichitravirya & Ambika, born blind
GANDHARI, Dhritarashtra's Queen and mother of the Kauravas
PANDU, son of Vichitravirya & Ambalika
KUNTI, Pandu's first wife
MADRI, Pandu's second wife
VIDURA, King Dhritarashtra's advisor; born to Veda Vyasa & a maid
SANJAYA, King Dhritarashtra's advisor
KRIPA, *Guru* to the Pandavas & Kauravas
DRONA, *Guru* to the Pandavas & Kauravas

PANDAVAS, WIVES & SONS

YUDHISHTHIRA, eldest son of Pandu & Kunti
BHEEMA, second son of Pandu & Kunti
ARJUNA, third son of Pandu & Kunti
NAKULA, one of the twin boys born to Pandu & Madri
SAHADEVA, one of the twin boys born to Pandu & Madri
DRAUPADI, common wife of the five Pandava brothers
ULOOPI, a Naga Princess and Arjuna's second wife
IRAVAN, Arjuna & Uloopi's son
CHITRANGADA, Princess of Manipura & Arjuna's third wife

BABHRUVAHANA, Arjuna & Chitrangada's son
SUBHADRA, Yadava Princess & Arjuna's fourth wife
ABHIMANYU, Arjuna & Subhadra's son
UTTARA, a Princess of Matsya & Abhimanyu's wife
PARIKSHIT, Abhimanyu & Uttara's posthumous son
JANAMEJAYA, Parikshit's son
GHATOTKACHA, Bheema's son

KAURAVAS, WIVES & SONS
DURYODHANA, eldest son of Dhritarashtra & Gandhari
BHANUMATI, Duryodhana's wife
LAKSHMANA, Duryodhana's son
DUHSHASANA, second son of Dhritarashtra & Gandhari
DURMARSANA, a Kaurava
DUHSHALA, daughter of Dhritarashtra & Gandhari
JAYADRATHA, son of King Vriddhakshatra & Duhshala's husband

PANDAVA ANCESTORS
MANU, grandson of Aditi, mother of the *Devas*
ILA, Manu's daughter
PURURAVAS, Ila's son
AYUS, born to Pururavas & Urvashi
NAHUSHA, son of Ayus
YAYATI, Nahusha's son
YADU & PURU, sons of Yayati, forefathers of the Yadavas & Kurus

GODS, GANDHARVAS & OTHER CELESTIALS
SHIVA, the Destroyer
VISHNU, the Protector of the Universe
BRAHMA, the Creator of the Universe
PARVATI, Shiva's consort
KRISHNA, *avatar* of Vishnu; cousin to the Pandavas & Kauravas
PARASHURAMA, a warrior-Brahmin and incarnation of Vishnu
INDRA, King of the celestials & Arjuna's divine father

DHARMA/ YAMA, God of Death, Guardian of the Universe & Yudhishthira's father
VAYU, God of Wind & Bheema's divine father
VARUNA, presiding deity of water bodies & Guardian of the Universe
PARNASA, a River Goddess
DURGA, Mother Goddess
KUBERA, God of Wealth & Guardian of the Universe
AGNI, God of Fire.
SURYA, Sun God
ASHWINI TWINS, the divine fathers of twins, Nakula & Sahadeva
KAMA, God of Love
ANGARAPARNA, King of the *Gandharvas*
KUMBHEENASI, Angaraparna's Queen
CHITRASENA, King of the *Gandharvas*; skilled musician & dancer
URVASHI, an *apsara* and ancestor of the Pandavas
GHRITACHI, JAANAPADI, TILOTTAMA, *apsaras*

RISHIS & SAGES
VEDA VYASA, son of Satyavati & Sage Parashara; biological father of Dhritarashtra, Pandu & Vidura; author of the *Mahabharata*;
NARA & NARAYANA, ancient *rishis* reborn as Arjuna & Krishna
SAGE BHARADWAJA, Drona's father
SHARADWAN, Kripa's father
RISHI SVETAKETU, enforced stricter moral & sexual codes
SAMIKA, instrument in bringing about Parikshit's doom
SHRINGIN, Samika's son
SAGE DHAUMYA, *Guru* to the Pandavas
SAGE BRIHADASHWA, expert dice player & Yudhistira's coach
RISHI LOMASHA, accompanied the Pandavas on their *Teerthayatra*
YAJA & UPAYAJA, sages skilled in performing wish-fulfilling sacrifices
SAGE CHANDAKAUSHIKA, fulfills King Vrihadratha's wish for a son
SAGE DURVASA, sage who gave Kunti, the son-bearing *mantra*
BRIHASPATI, preceptor of the *Devas*

KACHA, Brihaspati's son
SUKRACHARYA, preceptor of the *Asura*s
SAGE NARADA, devotee of Lord Vishnu
SAGE VISHWAMITRA, a King turned sage
SAGE KANVA, a sage who pronounced a curse on the Yadava race
SAGE AGASTYA, one of the seven ancient *rishis*

PANDAVA SUPPORTERS
DRUPADA, King of the Panchalas; Drona's sworn enemy; Arjuna's father-in-law
DHRISTADYUMNA, Draupadi's brother & son of Drupada
SATYAKI Arjuna's student & beloved friend of Krishna
VIRATA, King of Matsya
UTTARA, Virata's son
SHIKANDIN, Princess Amba, reborn to slay Bhishma
MAYA, the architect of the *Asura*s

KAURAVA SUPPORTERS
KARNA, son of Surya & Kunti; raised by Adhiratha & Radha
SHAKUNI, maternal uncle of the Kauravas; Queen Gandhari's brother
ULUKA, Shakuni's son
ASHWATHAMMA, Drona's & Kripi's son
BALARAMA, Krishna's brother; whose favorite student is Duryodhana
JARASANDHA, Emperor of Magadha & Krishna's sworn enemy
KAMSA, Jarasandha's son-in-law
SHISUPALA, King of Chedi
BHAGADATTA, son of the *asura* Naraka; King of Pragjyotishapura
BHURISHRAVA, enemy of Satyaki
SRUTAYUDHA, King & mortal son born to Varuna & Parashara
SUSHARMA, King of Trigarta
EKALAVYA, Nishada Prince who joined the Kauravas to protect his *Guru*, Drona, from Arjuna
SHALYA, King of Madra; Nakula & Sahadeva's maternal uncle
KRITAVARMAN, King of the Bhojas

Prologue

Janamejaya, King of the Kurus, was a disturbed man, nursing a visceral urge for revenge that demanded requittal. He belonged to an exalted house. In his veins flowed the blood of none other than Arjuna, one of the mightiest warriors the world has ever known. The illustrious Parikshit, Abhimanyu's son and Arjuna's grandson, was Janamejaya's father. But he knew nothing of any of his ancestors – not even his father, who had been killed by the *naga* (serpent) Takshaka, while Janamejaya was still an infant. Even the last rites for his father had been conducted by the Ministers of State. They had then taken the baby who would one day be their King, and schooled him in all the subjects a future King needed to master in order to be an exemplary ruler. Young Janamejaya showed great promise of becoming a worthy successor to the throne and surpassed even the high expectations of his Ministers. When he finally sat on the Kuru throne, there was none to dispute the fact that he was a just and capable Lord.

When Janamejaya discovered the truth about his father's terrible death, caused by a potent curse and the deception of Takshaka, the Serpent King, fury and hatred transformed his usually benign countenance. He thought long about how he could avenge his father and destroy the snakes that had been his nemesis. The wise men he consulted advised him to perform the *Sarpasatra,* a *yajna* that would last twelve years and serve to seriously deplete the ranks of the serpents, if not destroy them entirely. In fact, he was told that Kadru, primordial mother of the snakes, had cursed those who had disobeyed her orders in her bid to enslave her sister, Vinata, pronouncing that they would be consumed by the sacrificial flames when King Janamejaya performed the *Sarpasatra*.

The information convinced the King that providence was on his side and he decided to go ahead with the *Sarpasatra*. The entire kingdom was in a state of feverish activity as preparations for the *yajna* went into full swing. Soon all was in readiness and the sages fixed upon an auspicious day to start the rituals. Janamejaya made an effort to concentrate as the sages began their incantations but he was feeling restless and allowed his thoughts to wander to all that he had been told about his own lineage.

Having grown up with glowing tales of the greatness of his ancestors, Janamejaya yearned to know more. His grandfather Abhimanyu, had died when he had been just sixteen and his great-grandfather Arjuna, had left with his brothers, so legend said, to begin their ascent to heaven, having placed Parikshit on the throne. About these great men, Janamejaya personally knew little, so it had become a habit of his to press older men for information regarding his illustrious forefathers. In this way he heard of the tragic death of his father, Parikshit...

One day, while out hunting, Parikshit had hit a boar but the wounded creature escaped. Knowing that a hurt animal was dangerous to the inhabitants of his kingdom, he went in pursuit of it. The search was long and fruitless. The King, separated from his retinue, was weary beyond endurance and drooping with thirst. But still he kept on till he reached the hermitage of the Sage Samika, who was then deep in meditation. Parikshit impatiently asked the ascetic if he had seen or heard a wounded boar. He also asked for water to slake his thirst. No reply was, however, forthcoming from the holy soul, who remained engrossed in his meditation. When his urgent queries were met with unresponsive silence, it angered the King. He helped himself to some water; then, seeing a dead snake in the vicinity, he picked it up with his bow and perversely placed it around the sage's neck. Having performed this foolhardy deed, he departed.

Shringin, the venerable sage's hot-headed son, heard of the incident and possessing none of the temperance or magnanimity of his father, immediately pronounced a curse on the impetuous monarch: 'Parikshit, the sinner who knows nothing of respecting his betters, shall be despatched to the abode of Yama by the Serpent King Takshaka, who, by the power of my words, shall claim his worthless life seven days from now'. Even the stoical Samika could not make his son retract his sinister curse, although he did send a messenger to warn the King.

Parikshit did all in his power to protect himself from the Serpent King. The soldiers of the royal guard screened and checked everything but the thin air that reached the King. But it was all in vain. Takshaka struck just before sundown on the seventh day. He concealed himself in the guise of a worm in a basket of fruit that he had his followers deliver to the King. He then emerged from his pulpy confines to claim his victim.

Janamejaya shuddered at the dreadful mental image of his father dying an agonising death. He felt heartsick over the tragic and untimely demise of his two immediate ancestors – his father dying an accursed death; and his grandfather Abhimanyu, who should have been there to raise him, being killed before he could lay eyes on his own son, let alone his grandson. Craving some solace, Janamejaya's mournful thoughts went further back – to Arjuna, the veritable jewel of their clan. Pride filled his being, spreading warmth from his toes to the crown of his head. How he would have loved to have known that mighty warrior...

It was while he mused thus that Veda Vyasa arrived at the *yajna* with his disciples. Janamejaya promptly came forward to welcome this most ancient of his ancestors and prostrated himself at the venerable sage's feet. Vyasa blessed him and when the formalities were completed, he took the seat of honour assigned to him, next to the King.

Janamejaya spoke up with childlike earnestness, 'Holy Sire! Pray tell me all about my ancestors. It has been reported to me that you have composed a poem, the very finest, about them. I yearn to learn every single thing about my great-grandfather Arjuna and his illustrious brothers. Tell me about the Great War in which they slew their cousins. Surely they would not have done such a thing without the utmost provocation? What was Krishna's role in the whole affair? It is believed that he was Vishnu incarnate and Arjuna was his most beloved friend, and that they achieved marvellous things together. Tell me every small, insignificant detail about Arjuna. What did he like? What did he think? Who was the love of his life? What were the events that led to his becoming the mightiest of warriors whom even the Gods dared not fight? Is it true that he was of divine origin, fathered by none other than Indra, the Lord of the heavens? Did he have a weakness? Is it true that he once died before his time and a Princess who loved him more than life itself, saved him? I want to know him as closely as if I were actually by his side when all the great events in his life unfolded. Tell me all there is to know of Arjuna!'

The young King's entreaties did not go in vain. The venerable Vyasa smiled to convey his approbation before replying: 'The time has indeed arrived for me to narrate the *Mahabharata* to you and through you, the world shall hear this wondrous tale now and forever. Lord Ganesha, while putting my words down as the divine amanuensis, blessed my endeavour and said that my poem would survive as long as the mountains stand and the rivers flow. Listen and become enlighted, oh King! I authorise my able disciple Vaishampayana to tell you the story of your ancestors. Through him you will hear of all those epochal events that transpired so many years ago. And your wish shall be granted – you will come to know Arjuna as well as you know yourself.'

In this way, with Vyasa's blessing, Vaishampayana began his narrative – and from the moment his first words were uttered, his audience was held spellbound. Janamejaya listened enthralled to all he said and every time Arjuna's name was mentioned, he savoured every last detail, storing them away in his memory to be retrieved and pondered over later. And this is what he heard about his famous ancestor...

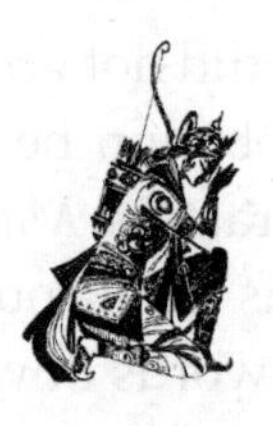

1
ARJUNA'S STORY

Arjuna was the son of Kunti Devi and Pandu, a scion of the illustrious Kuru clan. But unlike most mortals, he also had a divine father and the events surrounding his birth were mysterious and magical.

Pandu or the 'Pale One', was the second son of Vichitravirya and Ambalika, and the father of Arjuna. His own birth took place under quite unusual circumstances. Ambika and Ambalika were the wives of Vichitravirya. Unfortunately, Vichitravirya was afflicted by a wasting sickness and died young, leaving his wives childless. His elder brother, Chitrangada, had been killed even earlier by a belligerent Gandharva of the same name. Bhishma, the half-brother of the deceased monarch, was the sole surviving prince. He was also eminently suited to ascend the throne. But he had taken a terrible vow for the sake of his father, King Shantanu, forfeiting his right to the throne as well as his natural right to procreate. He thus refused the throne and also turned down the suggestion made by his stepmother, to marry his dead half-brother's wives and beget heirs to secure the Kuru line.

At this critical juncture, the Queen Mother, Satyavati, suggested that the young wives of Vichitravirya be impregnated by her other son, who was none other than Veda Vyasa. The famed sage was born to her of Sage Parashara, in her youth. Bhishma listened with wonder to her story and said, 'Mother, your wisdom is unparalleled. The scriptures have stated that one of the principle duties of a Kshatriya is to ensure that his line does not die out. If circumstances prevent him from doing his duty, it is recommended that his wife bear children with a worthy man who is the equal or superior of her husband and the offspring will carry on the name of the husband. The Kuru line will be eternally grateful to the noble Veda Vyasa if he would honour us by blessing Vichitravirya's wives so that they bear worthy sons.'

Satyavati summoned her son, who had already gained fame for classifying the *Veda*s. Vyasa dutifully arrived and stood ready to do her bidding. He agreed to help the Kurus and ensure the continuity of their line, provided Ambika and Ambalika were willing to accept him despite his unattractive face, unkempt appearance and unwashed body with its powerful odour. That night, Ambika was so appalled at the venerable Brahmin's appearance and his lack of hygiene, that she kept her eyes tightly closed throughout their time together.

Emerging from the bedchamber, Vyasa said to the anxious Satyavati, 'Ambika will bear a noble son, but he will be blind'. The Queen was aghast and begged him to father another child with Ambalika, as a blind man could hardly be expected to take on the mantle of kingship. Vyasa consented and went to visit Ambalika. The young lady masked her loathing of the unappealing Brahmin better than her sister had done, although the effort turned her pale and wan. Consequently, Vyasa foretold that the son born to her would be pale in appearance but a mighty warrior.

Satyavati was satisfied with her son's labours but just to be safe, she requested him to provide another son for the Kuru line. But by then

Ambika had enough and sent in her maid instead, dressed in her apparel. Vyasa was not fooled, however, and blessed the maid with a virtuous son. Thus were born, of three women, Dhritarashtra with the unseeing eyes, Pandu the pale one, and Vidura the wise.

Pandu was placed on the throne when he came of age. The young ruler was assisted ably by Bhishma in the considerable task of governing his kingdom. Pandu was a model ruler and undertook many military campaigns which expanded the boundaries of the Kuru kingdom and filled the royal coffers in ample measure. He had two good wives, Kunti and Madri. Life was good, and for a time it appeared that providence had only its bounties to shower on the young King. But flighty fortune was not a loyal mistress to Pandu. Storm clouds darkened the horizon, casting their pall on his future and signalling tumultuous times for him and his line.

One day, Pandu went out hunting to relax from the challenges of government. Lost in the pleasure of the hunt, his cares slipped away even as bloodlust warmed his blood and inflamed his senses. Suddenly he came upon a handsome deer sporting with its mate. Pandu took aim and let fly an arrow that flew true to its target and inflicted a mortal wound on the unsuspecting creature. As implacable fate would have it, the deer that lay in its death throes was in fact a *rishi*'s son, who was himself a powerful ascetic. He had taken the form of a deer to camouflage the act of love with his wife in the sylvan glade. Made to die violently at that climactic moment, he directed his vengeful wrath at Pandu and cursed him: 'Unworthy One! Since you saw it fit to take the life of an innocent creature at such an inopportune moment, you too, shall forfeit your life when you clasp your mate in sexual embrace'.

Utterly dismayed, Pandu tried in vain to placate the dying ascetic, pleading, 'Alas! I was only trying to capture my quarry, using the gifts of a hunter and a Kshatriya. Show mercy for I do not deserve such a fate!' But his pleas were in vain.

The deer-sage was adamant, 'It is not becoming of a Kshatriya Prince to kill his prey when it is at its most vulnerable and without the means to defend itself. Such deplorable conduct ought to be punished as an example to others who are carried away by bloodlust and forget to stay true to the dictates of *dharma*. You deserve your fate.' Thus spewing the venom of his terrible anger on the ill-fated Prince, he breathed his last.

Bemoaning the turn of affairs, Pandu decided to retire from kingship and become a wandering ascetic. He took to severe austerities to cleanse his soul of the debilitating misery and grief that threatened to overwhelm him. His two wives refused to remain behind and swore to follow him to the ends of the earth as their lives were irrevocably tied to his for better or for worse. Much to the sorrow of the royal household and the people of the kingdom, King Pandu left, never to return.

The life of an ascetic, despite the tremendous hardships involved, suited Pandu and his wives, far removed from the decadent luxuries and worldly cares of the court. However, Pandu still had one worry and it gnawed within him, destroying the very peace of mind for which he had abandoned all his royal trappings. He confided his distress to his wife Kunti, saying, 'It is my duty to produce worthy sons who will carry on my name, make amends for my sins and enhance my legacy. Manu himself has asserted that a man who leaves this earth without begetting sons, is derelict in his duty. It is truly unfortunate that I am unable to fulfil this one requirement essential for passage to heaven.'

'Let us pray to the Gods for a solution, my Lord,' said Kunti, unwavering in her faith in divine beneficence.

'We will pray. But I have given this matter much thought and I want you to bear my children by mating with a worthy man of your choosing. The scriptures condone this practice and so neither of us will incur sin thereby,' spoke the suffering Prince.

'How can you even suggest such a thing?' Kunti asked, repulsed by the suggestion. 'Not even in my thoughts could I entertain another man! I belong solely to you and death shall claim me before I allow even a man's shadow to touch me!'

'You must not allow emotions to cloud your thinking, Kunti. I am well aware that I am married to the most virtuous woman in the three worlds. But listen carefully to what I say. There is nothing wrong with what I suggest. In days of yore, women were not subject to the restrictions that have resulted in their leading such cloistered lives as they do today. They were allowed to move about freely and have as many partners as they pleased, marital status notwithstanding. It may seem strange to us with our rigid rules regarding sexual intercourse, but in those days, people behaved like the animals we see around us and were uninhibited where their bodily needs were concerned. Nobody considered such behaviour sinful, and passions like anger and jealousy simply did not exist. It was considered a natural and healthy practice in keeping with the original laws of *dharma*. And then things changed abruptly when the *Rishi* Svetaketu enforced new laws about morality and sexuality.'

'What happened to bring about the change?' Kunti asked, fascinated despite herself.

'One day, a Brahmin took his mother's hand in the presence of both Svetaketu and his own father and suggested that he be allowed to lie with her. Svetaketu was outraged, even though his father told him to calm down since women were allowed to indulge their sexual desires. Perhaps his own unresolved feelings for his mother, coupled with guilt, fuelled his resentment. Be that as it may, Svetaketu refused to be mollified. He decreed that henceforth women would be faithful to their spouses and practice fidelity. Failure to do so would be akin to killing an unborn child nestling in the womb. Straying men would also incur sin. Thirdly, a woman who failed to conceive, ignoring the wishes of her husband, would be guilty of the same sin.'

'Perhaps there is a solution to our dilemma, my Lord,' said Kunti, who had been listening thoughtfully.

An intrigued Pandu listened avidly as she, in turn, told a remarkable story. 'As a young girl, my father entrusted upon me the onerous task of looking after the sage Durvasa, for the duration of his visit to the kingdom. As you know, the sage is famed for his choleric temper, which he is quick to lose and the vehemence of his potent curses, which he is even quicker to pronounce. Having catered to every whim of the cantankerous sage, I earned his goodwill. Perhaps his yogic powers enabled him to divine what it was that I would need most in the future and he taught me an occult, son-bearing *mantra*. This enabled me to summon any of the Gods and bid them to bless me with a son. At the time, I was pleased to have carried out my duty without being cursed into oblivion and did not grasp the magnitude of the blessing. But now, I believe it can be the answer to our problem.'

Pandu was overjoyed with his wife's tale and pleased that the Gods had offered them a way out of their dilemma. It was decided that the *mantra* would be used by Kunti and Madri to bring forth sons as soon as possible.

Kunti, ever faithful to her husband's desires, acceded to his will and invoked the Lord Dharma first, who gave her a son who was his equal in virtue and rightousness. The boy was named Yudhishthira. Then Pandu and Kunti decided to summon Vayu, the Wind God. From his seed issued Bheema, the mighty Pandava Prince whose strength and great physical prowess became legendary from his boyhood.

The delighted couple, wishing for a warrior son who would be indomitable on the battlefield, performed penances for a year to please Indra, the mightiest of the celestial *Devas*, and their chosen leader. Indra was known to be a tad arrogant and despite the *mantra,* would not take kindly to being summoned to carry out the demands of mere mortals. But, having adequately propitiated the Lord of the heavens and incurred his goodwill, Pandu bid Kunti to call upon Indra for a son who would be endowed with his great valour and prodigious skill. And thus, Arjuna was born. When Kunti held this special child in her arms, the very heavens rang with divine voices singing of the magnificent deeds he was destined to perform and petals were showered on the newborn.

Pandu requested Kunti to teach the *mantra* to his younger Queen, Madri, who also longed to beget sons. Kunti acceded to the request and Madri invoked the Ashwini twins, who gave her the twins, Nakula and Sahadeva, both of whom were exceedingly handsome and intelligent.

Pandu was delighted with all five of his sons and was sure they would bring pride and glory to the family name. And among his divine progeny, Arjuna's star was destined to shine the brightest as he would go on to conquer the world with his incomparable skills as an archer and lay it at the feet of his brothers. He would gain eternal renown as a loyal friend, loving brother, beloved husband, doting father, talented eunuch, and powerful ascetic.

2
Early Days

Pandu's idyllic sojourn in the forest with his wives and sons was destined to be a short one. The boys thrived in the salubrious clime of the grove and diligently imbibed lessons from the resident sages, who schooled them in the *Veda*s and the basics of martial arts. Nearly fifteen years passed in this way. But on a beautiful, spring day, tragedy struck out of the blue.

Intoxicated by the heady charm of spring and his younger wife, Pandu gave in to his carnal desires and drew Madri to him, brushing aside all her pleas. The curse instantly took effect and Pandu breathed his last in his wife's arms. Kunti and the boys came on the scene and soon the sylvan quietude was shattered by their heartrending cries. Kunti sent the boys to inform the resident ascetics. Following their departure and in the depth of her grief, she gave vent to the jealousy and bitterness that possessed her on account of the preference shown by her husband to his younger wife, 'O Madri, you are blessed as our husband gave up his life for the forbidden taste of your charms. I only wish you, being aware of the curse, had shown more restraint and desisted from seducing our husband. Be that as it may, as the elder wife, I shall enter the funeral pyre with him and follow him to whatever lies beyond. I entrust you with the charge of looking after our sons. You cannot deny me this right.'

The devastated Madri disagreed, however. 'Beloved sister, since I am the accursed one responsible for the death of our husband, it is I who should enter the flames with him. This body of mine, which is responsible for the death of the one dearest to me, deserves to perish. Besides, you are nobler than I and will treat our sons equally, whereas I cannot be impartial. Everyone knows that Sahadeva, despite being from my womb, is your favourite son. It is only right that you live for their sake.'

Having said this, Madri entered Pandu's funeral pyre. Kunti did not stop her as she knew that the younger woman spoke nothing but the truth. And so it came to be that Kunti and the Pandavas lost two loved ones on the same day.

The sages of the forest accompanied the grieving Pandavas and Kunti to Hastinapura, where Bhishma and Vidura took them under their wings. The boys met their cousins, the hundred sons of Dhritarashtra and Gandhari, who were known as the Kauravas, and the other members of the royal household. The residents of the royal palace, as well as the citizens of the land of Kuru, warmed to the Pandavas immediately, impressed by their good looks and noble bearing. However, their Kaurava cousins, especially the eldest one, Duryodhana, took an instant dislike to them. The Pandavas, to Duryodhana's mind, were using their bereavement to worm their way into the hearts of their subjects and were succeeding in their design. People were already talking about how wonderful and noble they were. Duryodhana told his brothers that, in fact, they looked like the stray dogs that he was fond of stoning to death. He wished he could get rid of these five cousins the same way; but, the Prince informed his brothers, he would probably need a whole mountain to crush the life of the fat one called Bheema, whom he liked the least of the five.

Duryodhana's festering sentiments were not shared by anybody other than his brothers. Everyone else seemed to have been bowled over by the five young princes. Elder and Statesman, Bhishma, adored the boys and proclaimed the gentle Yudhishthira to be the very embodiment of *dharma*. He had similar words of endearment for the other Pandavas, especially the third one, Arjuna. Bhishma went to the extent of saying that Arjuna would perform such marvellous deeds that the world would never forget him or his achievements. It was particularly galling because Bhishma never showered such encomiums about Dhritarashtra's sons. In fact, whenever he laid eyes upon Duryodhana, he felt the need to launch into lengthy sermons about how he ought to conduct himself. All the Kaurava brothers shared Duryodhana's sentiments and so relations between the cousins grew increasingly strained.

Bheema's formidable physical strength and propensity to show off at the expense of his punier cousins, infuriated them, although it was done with boyish exuberance and not intended to injure anyone. Attempts were made on the young hero's life, spearheaded by Duryodhana. The Pandavas were deeply saddened. It was after one such nefarious attempt, when Bheema came close to losing his life, that Yudhishthira called his brothers aside and cautioned them, 'Duryodhana will not stop his scheming until he destroys us completely. We should be constantly alert from this moment on. It is important that we watch each other's backs and not relax our vigil for an instant.' The brothers heeded Yudhishthira's wise words and did their best to follow his strictures in order to survive in the treacherous vipers' pit that their own family home was turning into.

Arjuna and Bheema discussed the issue at length as each considered himself the natural protector of the group. 'Brother Yudhishthira worries too much...' Bheema informed his younger brother. 'There is nothing in the three worlds that is as strong as me and I simply cannot be harmed. Duryodhana knows this and that is why he has been trying to take my life. He came close to succeeding by poisoning me and throwing me into the snake-infested river, arranging for poisoned spikes to be placed in the depths for good measure. But not a hair on my head has been harmed and I am a hundred times stronger now than before, thanks to the magic potion of the *Naga*s, which I imbibed when I landed in their netherworld. And I can also protect the four of you and our mother from those abominable cousins of ours. While I am around, no force on earth can touch any of you.'

Arjuna felt a twinge of irritation when he heard his brother's bravado and boasts about his formidable brawn; finally he said with a touch of curtness, 'Yudhishthira was right to worry. It was sheer luck that the snake bites served as an antidote to Duryodhana's poison and that you managed to avoid the spikes. Your strength had little to do with your safe return. We will need much more than just bulging biceps to fight that lot, who are already circling us like predators looking for an exposed spot where they can strike. And I intend to be the shield behind which my loved ones will be safe from all harm.'

Bheema burst out laughing when he heard the lofty speech made by his not-so-hefty brother, who looked even less hefty when standing next to him. But when he saw his brother's face darken with anger and realised that Yudhishthira and Kunti would be very upset if they got into a fight, he hastened to add, 'I am sure that some day in the future you will be a mighty warrior and we will all rely on you to win us a mighty Kingdom and make our beloved cousins look like fools!'

Arjuna noticed Yudhisthira and the twins approaching, so he allowed himself to be mollified, even as he thought to himself, 'Bheema does not realise it, but I will be mightier not only than him but every other man as well. Even the Gods dare not dream of fighting me, for I will never ever allow myself to lose a fight.'

As expected by the brothers and as feared by the elders, a deep chasm developed between the Pandavas and the Kauravas. All attempts to bridge the divide by Bhishma and the other elders, proved futile. All the portents pointed to a bloody conflict at some point in the future as both sides sought to strengthen their positions and warily watched each other.

These early events made a deep impression on Arjuna. He was aware that despite Yudhishthira's claim to the throne through the right of primogeniture, he and his brothers were at a practical disadvantage. The weak Dhritarashtra sat on the throne. Though outwardly caring and affectionate towards the Pandavas, he nursed a secret resentment that they were superior to his own sons in every conceivable way. Prince Duryodhana would do whatever it took to hurt the Pandavas and he had the ear of his father, King Dhritarashtra.

Bhishma, Vidura, and the other elders of the royal household, though fond of the sons of Pandu, owed allegiance to the throne and were bound to serve whoever sat on it. The five brothers, bereft of their father, were on their own, and their position was a precarious one indeed.

Things looked bleak for them and Arjuna swore he would even the odds. It was his fervent desire that he be the rock that sheltered his family from the violent storms that would unleash their fury on them. He would acquire the skills needed to protect his own by sheer dint of hard work and perseverance so that they might all emerge unscathed through the trials and tribulations that lay ahead of them. Thus self-motivated, Arjuna worked hard under the tutelage of the venerable tutor, Kripa, who had been assigned the task of training the Princes in martial arts, but all the while Arjuna looked for the right teacher who could tap his potential to the fullest and make him the finest warrior on earth.

3
Mentor Extraordinaire

Dronacharya came into Arjuna's life at a critical juncture in both their lives. The latter had been looking for a great teacher who would harness his tremendous drive and potential and mould him into an all-conquering knight in shining armour, an invincible one-man army who could realize the cause of his brothers as well as cement his own claim to immortality. Drona, on the other hand, had recently suffered much humiliation and betrayal from a once close friend, and was on the lookout for able disciples who could avenge the insult inflicted on their master. Thus, the coming together of these two was in itself quite propitious. But before the consequences of this alliance are discussed, one needs to step back in time and trace the roots of the enigmatic Brahmin instructor, who gave the world one of its greatest warriors...

The birth of Drona, like much else in his extraordinary life, took place under exceptional circumstances. One day, the great seer Bharadwaja was engaged in his ablutions in the river Ganges, when he caught sight of the beautiful *Apsara* Ghritachi, taking a bath nearby. A sudden gust of wind caused the choppy river to carry away the only garment that draped her body, and the voluptuous sight caused Bharadwaja to ejaculate involuntarily. Aware of the potency of his seed, the seer collected it and preserved it in a vessel. From this, in due course, his son Drona emerged.

Drona grew up in his father's *gurukul*, where he mastered the *Veda*s and martial arts. There he became fast friends with Drupada, heir to the throne of Panchala, who also took his lessons at the same *gurukul*. The two boys were inseparable and promised eternal loyalty to each other. Drupada, in particular, swore to his bosom friend on many occasions, 'We will be friends forever. Everything I own is yours. When I come of age and am placed on the throne, I'll give you an equal share of my kingdom.' Drona always laughed at this and would reply, 'Your friendship alone is more than enough for me.'

Soon the halcyon days of their childhood came to an end and life drew them along their predestined paths.

Drupada became the King of Panchala and Drona entered the second stage of life as a householder. He married the chaste Kripi, twin sister of Kripacharya; they had a son, Ashwatthama, who was the apple of his father's eye. Drona busied himself with his studies and paid little attention to material gains. His wife never complained, although there were stray moments when she wished they could provide more comforts for their son. Presently Drona heard that the great warrior Parashurama, destroyer of Kshatriyas and the incarnation of the Lord Vishnu, was giving away all his possessions to worthy Brahmins, as his time on earth was drawing to an end. Therefore, Drona repaired post haste to the abode of the great sage. But he was too late. Parashurama had already given away all his worldly possessions.

Unwilling to send Drona back empty-handed, Parashurama gave him two options: 'I do not wish you to leave here with nothing. You must choose from the only two things left to me in this world – my body or my weapons and the esoteric secrets of their application and withdrawal that will enable you to use them effectively'. Drona chose the latter and acquired the great warrior's weapons and the deep secrets of their usage. He was well pleased with his acquisitions and returned home; but all his happiness evaporated at the sight that awaited him there.

Ashwatthama, his beloved son, was crying for milk, which he had never tasted and with typically juvenile insensitivity, the local boys were milking the occasion for all its worth. They mixed some white powder with water and proffered it to the innocent child, who drank down the contents and leaped up and down with joy screaming, 'I have tasted milk today and it is delicious'. Drona stood transfixed by sheer visceral pathos, shamed beyond measure at his failure to provide basic sustenance to his only son. At that moment, the hitherto contented Brahmin craved wealth, power and prestige for the sake of his innocent offspring, so that the latter would never know deprivation ever again.

Anxious to remedy his poverty-stricken state, he took his family to Panchala and sought an audience with his childhood friend, King Drupada, who had once promised to give him half his kingdom. However, he was in for a rude shock. Drupada refused to even recognise him, claiming, 'Friendship can exist only among equals; it is presumptuous of a beggar to aspire to friendship with a King, based on some long-forgotten childhood acquaintance. How dare you claim to be a friend of mine? You are nothing but a worthless braggart who does not know his place.'

Having vented his spleen, King Drupada then spoke more calmly, 'I see you have travelled a long way and can do with some food and drink. Never let it be said that Drupada turns away the needy.

Guards! See to it that this man is provided with food and a change of clothes! Then send him on his way.'

Drona was incensed at the cruel insult. Scornfully declining Drupada's offer of hospitality, he departed, resolving to teach the arrogant monarch an appropriate lesson at the earliest moment.

In search of a calling suited to his exceptional abilities, Drona next made his way to Hastinapura, where his brother-in-law, Kripacharya, lived. Kripa and Kripi were the progeny of the great sage, Sharadwan. The sage was renowned for the control he had achieved over his senses and the austerities he was capable of performing which even the mightiest of *rishis* balked at. Lord Indra became worried about the great mastery of *dhanurveda* (skill with weaponry), that Sharadwan was gaining and so sent the nymph, Jaanapadi, to distract him with her beauty. Sharadwan's mind was perhaps a little more under his control than his body, because he ejaculated at the sight of her. It was a momentary lapse which did not even register in his mind. But from this discharge that became divided in two after falling on a reed, the twins Kripa and Kripi, came into being.

King Shantanu found the babies and took them back with him to Hastinapura and raised them in the palace. Later, through yogic clairvoyance, Sharadwan realized what had happened and he claimed the twins as his own. The sage took over his son's education and also trained him in the advanced skills of the warlike arts before sending him back to Hastinapura. Kripa personally made the match between his sister Kripi and Drona.

Both the Brahmins had an affinity for weapons and martial arts that set them apart from the rest of their race and drew them close together.

And so, when Drona made the decision to move to Hastinapura, Kripa could not have been happier. As the inheritor of Parashurama's weapons, Drona had become one of the greatest warriors and even many among the Kshatriyas knew that they were not a match for the Brahmin warrior. Kripa knew that Drona was special and he was more than happy to include the family of three into his lonely household.

Kripa welcomed his sister's husband warmly and attended to all his needs. The hospitality lavished on him cheered Drona considerably. Kripa doted on his sister and he loved Ashwatthama as though he were his own son. His kindness brought tears to Drona's eyes and went a long way to alleviate the pain of Drupada's betrayal. Under that hospitable roof, Drona made his future plans. His eyes alighted on the young Princes of the Kuru clan and he instinctively knew that he had found the mighty disciples he needed to exact his revenge on the arrogant Drupada. He bided his time and waited for the right moment to announce his presence.

One day, the young Princes were playing with a wooden ball and having a good time. But the game came to an abrupt halt when the ball fell into a well and none of them were able to retrieve it. As the boys crowded around the well trying to figure out what to do, a dark-skinned and grey-haired Brahmin appeared on the scene and commented with honeyed sarcasm, 'It is a shame that the progeny of the Bharata clan are not up to the simple task of extricating a ball from the well. I could do it easily in exchange for a meal.'

The brash youngsters were quick to retort, 'Who are you to criticise us in this manner? Since you talk so much, let us see what you can do.'

'If you are as good as your words, we will give you the best meal you have ever had!' Yudhishthira added with a smile.

Drona smiled at the precocious youths and said, 'Not only can I retrieve your ball, but I can do the same with my ring as well, which I am going to throw in after your ball. Now lend me a bow and some arrows.'

As the boys watched with bated breath, he picked up a blade of stiff grass, chanted a *mantra* to infuse it with power and using it like a projectile, he hurled it into the well. The blade attached itself to the ball firmly. Drona repeated this process, hurling blades of grass into the well in rapid succession until a chain was formed, using which, he gently drew out the ball. Then he shot a lone arrow into the well with such force that it went clean into the ring. He repeated the earlier process with several arrows to retrieve the ring from the well.

The young Princes were astounded at this masterly display and crowded around him in admiration. 'Who are you? Where did you learn to shoot like that?' they demanded in unison.

'Go to your Grandsire Bhishma, and report what happened just now. He will tell you the rest,' Drona replied.

The Princes ran to do his bidding. Bhishma heard the account of the boys and knew the truth at once. He rushed out to meet the great master. 'O Acharya! You have done us a great honour by coming to Hastinapura. I have been searching for a preceptor to train the Kuru Princes in the advanced levels of martial arts and your coming is most fortuitous. It would please me greatly if you agree to take up their training.'

Drona accepted happily. The fame of his *gurukul* spread rapidly and Princes from far and wide came to him, begging to be his pupils. Drona was delighted with his pupils but one distinguished himself from the outset and became his favourite. He was none other than the immensely gifted Arjuna.

4
The Honour Student

Before commencing lessons, Drona sent for his pupils and had them assemble before him. He looked at them all in turn with his keen eyes and addressed them with solemn gravity: 'I have taken up the task of training you to excel in the art of war and I will not rest till I have successfully made great warriors out of all of you. In return I expect a special Gurudakshina. Who among you will pledge to give me whatever I ask for at the end of his training?' For a split second there was silence as the princes were hesitant to make a solemn commitment to their Guru without knowing what it was they would be committing to. Then a lone figure stepped forward, majestic purpose writ large on his youthful features, 'I am Arjuna, the Pandava. I swear to you that at the end of my training, I will fulfil whatever it is you desire.' Drona looked into those intent eyes and was pleased with what he saw. Placing his hands on his pupil's shoulders he drew him close and weeping with joy said, 'I will make you the greatest warrior on Earth. There will be none to equal you.'

Drona's instruction of his pupils began in earnest. Bheema and Duryodhana showed an aptitude for handling the mace. Ashwatthama was skilled in the esoteric arts and the arcane lore associated with such skills. Yudhishthira was a proficient charioteer. Nakula showed talent in the equestrian arts and Sahadeva was a brilliant swordsman. But Arjuna was by far the best student as he excelled in every aspect of the science of arms. The sheer passion and dedication he brought to his lessons was unequalled. He absorbed every word Dronacharya uttered and his appetite for knowledge was unceasing. And so it was that Arjuna soon emerged as Drona's star pupil.

Drona was the best of Gurus but there were times when Drona, the father took precedence over Drona, the teacher. He could not help showing a little partiality to his son, Ashwatthama. The boys would be given mugs to bring water and Ashwatthama alone would be given a larger vessel that would enable him to return earlier with the required quantity of water, and Drona would use the extra time to slip him precious nuggets of information that was designed to give him an edge over the others. Arjuna became wise to this scheme at once, and with the help of a special missile of Varuna, the god of waters, he made sure that he returned with his due quota of water at the same time as Ashwatthama so that he would not miss out on anything.

Drona, despite being outmanoeuvred, was amused with his pupil's tactics to ensure that he became the best and was genuinely proud of Arjuna's dedication. But he could not help noticing that Duryodhana had befriended his son and it became increasingly evident that the latter was devoted to the Kaurava prince. This meant that Ashwatthama and Arjuna would be in opposing camps for the rest of their lives and at some point might even have to pit their skills against each other. Therefore, Drona watched the rapid strides made by his pupil with a mixture of pleasure and some unease.

Paternal concern prompted Drona to call the servants aside and give them some precise orders, 'Make sure that Arjuna never eats in the dark. A lamp must always remain lighted for him when he takes his evening meal.' Bemused, the servants obeyed his instructions and made sure the lamps were lit before serving the prince his repast. One day, while Arjuna was dining, a particularly strong gust of wind put out the flames in the lamps and the place was shrouded in darkness. Arjuna continued eating in the dark without interruption as his practised fingers expertly scooped up the food and raised it to his lips automatically out of habit. And then in a moment of insight he realised that with similar practice his skills as an archer could be improved a hundred fold and he would not have to rely on his eyes to find his mark. 'What an advantage it will give me over my opponents!' he thought gleefully.

Excited with his new theory, Arjuna decided to test it at once. He began a rigorous routine that would be performed every single day with his bow and arrow after darkness fell. And sure enough his already formidable skill as an archer was considerably enhanced. On one such night, Drona heard the twang of the bowstring and rushed out to investigate. When he saw Arjuna, his heart filled with immense pride. Brushing his concerns about the future aside, he blessed the sterling warrior who stood in front of him and left. He felt at once humbled and vindicated by the brilliant display of talent he had witnessed and was thankful that he had been given the opportunity to nurture it.

Drona noticed that his charges had gained sufficient proficiency in the science of arms and decided it was time to test them. He had a clay pigeon installed in the uppermost branch of a tree and summoned the princes. When they had all assembled in front of him, he gave them the following instructions, 'Your task today is to sever the head of the bird on my command. As I call out your name you will pick up your bow, select an arrow, take your position and await my command'.

Yudhishthira, as the eldest was called first. As he took his stance, Drona addressed him thus: 'Tell me exactly what you see.'

'I see you, my brothers, my cousins, the tree, and the bird', replied the prince.

'Step back. You will not hit the target', snapped Drona in a voice of steel.

The other princes were summoned one by one and Drona asked them all the same question, received similar answers, and ordered them to step back.

Finally, it was Arjuna's turn. He took his position, pulled back the bowstring and waited. When Drona asked him to tell what he saw, the prince replied, 'I see the head of the bird and nothing else.' His teacher's face lit up on hearing this answer and on his command, Arjuna's arrow whizzed through the air, straight and true, and buried itself in the head of the bird, bringing it down with a heavy thud. Drona embraced his pupil and applauded his superior skill. His four brothers cheered him lustily. As expected, Duryodhana gritted his teeth and stormed off, accompanied by his brothers muttering under his breath about the supposed inanity of Drona's test.

On another occasion, Drona accompanied the princes as they frolicked in the river Ganga. Suddenly, a massive crocodile fastened its serrated teeth on his leg. The great man could have freed himself in an instant but he pretended to be helpless and called out to the princes to rescue him. The youngsters watched the spectacle in mute terror and stood rooted to the spot. Arjuna alone rose to the occasion. Moving like greased lightning, he unloosed five arrows that flew with deadly precision and lodged themselves in the crocodile's jaws prying it open, releasing Drona, and killing the reptile instantly. Drona emerged from the water and spoke to the princes in scathing tones, 'The skills I have taught you will be useless if you don't keep your wits about you. Arjuna is the only one who has prodigious skill as well as a quick wit. And still you wonder why I praise him all the time!'

Drona then drew Arjuna aside and told him, 'I will teach you how to release and withdraw the powerful *Brahmashira* missile. It has terrible power and can burn the entire world to cinders. As such it should not be used against humans although it may be used against Asuras and others of their ilk. The wielder must possess great physical as well as mental control. You have displayed your mastery in archery today and proved your mental strength as well. I believe you are worthy of learning the secret of this supremely destructive *astra* and I trust you to use it wisely.' Thus Arjuna added the first of many celestial weapons to what was destined to become the most formidable arsenal in the world.

Arjuna's single-minded determination to master the warlike arts has been seen on many occasions. But in his pursuit of excellence he could also display a ruthlessness that was dangerous as it spurred him to destroy any obstacle that stood in his way, even if it was made of flesh, blood, and had feelings.

Ekalavya was the son of Hiranyadhanush, chief of the Nishada tribe. Archery was his great passion in life, and he aspired to reach great heights in this discipline. When he heard of Drona's *Gurukul*, he was delighted and decided to ask the great Brahmin warrior to accept him as a pupil. When he arrived at the academy, the other princes were in the midst of a training session led by Drona. He watched with fascination and waited patiently for an opportune moment to make his request. When Drona ended his lessons and the princes had left, Ekalavya walked up to the preceptor and addressed him respectfully, 'I am Ekalavya, of the Nishada tribe. Chief Hiranyadhanush is my father. Would you please accept me as your pupil?'

Drona's refusal was polite but firm, 'I instruct only those of royal birth, therefore I cannot accept you.'

Ekalavya pleaded with him but to no avail. As he made his way back with a heavy heart, his initial bitter disappointment turned to steely resolve.

Ekalavya made a clay statue of Drona, and every day he would seek the blessing of the statue before commencing his archery practice. He would imagine Drona guiding him through the motions, correcting his mistakes, and urging him on to achieve perfection. Gradually, he became an expert archer, whom few could hope to defeat in single combat.

It was around this time that the Kuru princes chose to go hunting. They released the dogs and gave themselves over to the chase. They heard a dog barking frantically and spurred their horses in that direction. Suddenly the barking stopped abruptly and the princes reined in their horses in surprise. The dog came into the clearing, its mouth filled with seven well placed arrows but unhurt in any other way. The princes were taken aback at this sight and wondered aloud about the identity of the mystery archer who seemed to be in a league of his own when it came to skill with the bow and arrow.

The princes made their way to the clearing where Ekalavya was at practice. When questioned about his identity, the Nishada warrior replied, 'I am Ekalavya, the son of chief Hiranyadhanush. My preceptor is none other than the great Dronacharya himself.' On hearing these words, Arjuna turned and left at once, his heart blazing with blind jealousy and resentment.

He went straight to his Guru and complained, 'You promised to make me the best archer in the world! Today I met someone in the woods who seems to be a better archer. Imagine my surprise when he declared that you were his Guru. How could you betray me like this?' Drona was perplexed and he asked Arjuna to take him to see the mystery archer.

On reaching the clearing, Drona understood what had happened. Ekalavya was delighted to see his Guru and approached him with great reverence. He fell at his feet and sought his blessings. Drona was deeply touched despite himself. But Arjuna was almost as dear to him as his own son. Besides, he was the secret weapon he planned to unleash on King Drupada. Therefore he must be appeased at all costs.

With a heavy heart he addressed the noble young man who stood before him eyes glittering with fervent devotion, 'Are you willing to pay me my Gurudakshina?'

'Everything I have is yours to claim, Guruji!' the noble youth replied.

Stamping out the stirrings of pity that rose unbidden, Drona said, 'I want you to give me your right thumb as my Gurudakshina.' Without a word, the righteous woodsman cheerfully severed his right thumb and handed it to Drona. Staunching the bleeding with a rag he went back to his practice, conscientious as ever. But alas, his fingers could no longer perform with their former brilliance. He would always be competent at his chosen discipline but he would no longer have the potential to achieve greatness. Satisfied, Arjuna and Drona left the maimed warrior, having deprived him of any chance for future glory.

Despite, Drona's less than honourable conduct in the matter, in Ekalavya's eyes he remained noble and beyond reproach. However, the youth took a less charitable view of the role played by Arjuna in depriving him of his thumb. Hatred wormed its way into his hitherto kindly soul together with an ardent desire for revenge. Someday, he thought, he would prove to Drona that unlike Ekalavya himself, Arjuna was an unworthy pupil and then with Drona's blessing he would kill him.

5
The Tournament

Drona instructed the Kuru Princes in the science of arms and made mighty warriors of them all. When their education was complete, Drona went to the elders of the royal household. Having paid his respects, he said, 'Great Lords, I have performed my duty to the best of my ability. The charges entrusted to me are now warriors in the truest sense of the term and at this moment they await your command to display all they have learned under my tutelage.'

King Dhritarashtra, Bhishma, Vidura, Kripa and the other elders of the household, were pleased at Drona's words. Dhritarashtra replied, 'O Acharya, our debt to you is indeed great. Your words have made me very happy. My only regret is that I will not be able to watch this magnificent exhibition with my own eyes. I grant my permission to begin preparations for the tournament this very instant.' Consequently, under Vidura's expert supervision, a suitable location was selected and readied for the tournament.

On the appointed day, people arrived in droves to witness the marvellous spectacle. Every member of the royal household had turned up. The excitement was palpable and spirits ran high. Drona, clad entirely in white, entered the arena, followed by his son, Ashwatthama. After he had performed the inauguration, the tournament began in earnest. The Princes trooped into the arena, delighting the audience with their displays on horses and chariots, their swordsmanship, and their proficiency in archery. The crowds roared their approval and screamed for more. They were treated to a contest between Bheema and Duryodhana with their maces. Spurred by their mutual hatred, the two rivals fought with an intensity that made the exhibition bout look like a no-holds-barred battle. The audience started rooting for their favourites and howled for blood. For a moment it appeared that the Princes would be more than happy to oblige. But Drona sent Ashwatthama to intervene before they succeeded in killing each other. Bheema and Duryodhana left the arena glaring at each other, knowing well that this grudge-match would never end while they both lived.

Drona then called for silence and announced that Arjuna, the son of Pandu, would appear before them next. The masses were thrilled as they loved the valiant, young hero as their own and stories about his immense skill were already the stuff of legend. Arjuna did not disappoint them as he held them spellbound. Ever the showman, he put up a display designed to fire up the crowd and showcase his skills in conventional archery as well as with an array of celestial weapons. The applause was thunderous and Kunti's eyes filled with tears as the special place Arjuna held in the hearts of the people became increasingly evident.

Duryodhana watched in jealous rage, hoping against hope that the ground would open up and swallow Arjuna, keeping him interred in its fathomless depths forever.

Just as the tournament was drawing to a close, everyone's attention was drawn to the sound of mighty hands being clapped against each other in challenge. A magnificent youth stepped into the arena, clad in the celestial armour and ear-rings he had been born with. In scornful tones, he spoke to Arjuna, 'You may think that you are the best but I am here to correct that mistaken premise of yours. I, Karna, can not only perform everything you just have but outperform you as well.'

Drona reluctantly gave his permission to proceed. He had not reckoned with some stranger upstaging his star pupil. Karna was as good as his word and performed every feat Arjuna had before him. Duryodhana was elated and cheered wholeheartedly. His glee infuriated the Pandavas and they watched the newcomer with baleful eyes. Arjuna was furious that an unknown warrior had stolen his thunder and smarted under the humiliation.

But Duryodhana went up to Karna and hugging him to his bosom said, 'Peerless warrior! You have earned my esteem and affection. It is truly fortunate that you have come into my life. I place myself and my kingdom entirely at your disposal.'

Karna was heartened by this warm approbation, as it was the first time in his life he had received such treatment from the highborn. He replied, 'Dear Prince, I seek but two things: your eternal friendship and single combat with Arjuna'. Duryodhana was only too pleased to indicate his assent to these demands.

Arjuna watched the proceedings with supreme distaste and told his opponent, 'It will give me great pleasure to destroy an upstart and braggart such as you and consign you to the doom you seem to be craving for.'

Karna remained unperturbed by this harsh outburst and merely remarked with a careless air, 'Your words, barbed as they are, can do me little damage. I hope for your sake that you have deadlier weapons than a pathetically ineffectual tongue at your disposal. Perhaps it would be wiser to let your arrows do the talking.'

By this time, Arjuna's rage had reached a murderous pitch. Without further ado and being scrupulously correct in his conduct, he prostrated himself at the feet of his *guru*, embraced his brothers, and then stood poised to fight. The arena became deathly still as the two antagonists stood ready to duel. There were flashes of lightning and thunder, and the skies darkened with storm clouds. Arjuna's divine father, Indra, had arrived to show his support. Meanwhile, on Karna's side, the clouds were split apart by Surya, the Sun God, and Karna stood bathed in golden rays. At that point, none other than Kunti was aware that Karna was the son of Surya and Kunti had conceived him while she was still unwed. But Kunti could not bear the cruel fate of first being compelled to part with her first-born and then witnessing the unfortunate young man become the sworn enemy of his own brother. She collapsed in a dead swoon.

As the arch rivals took their positions, the venerable Kripa, acting as referee, stepped forward. He said to Karna, 'Young man, you have just challenged Arjuna, the son of Pandu, a scion of the Kuru race. Before commencing the duel, it behoves you to enlighten us about your origins; then Arjuna may or may not choose to fight you as a Prince may deem it beneath him to duel with strangers or commoners.' At these words, Karna's face darkened; he lowered his head in shame as it seemed that no matter what he did or achieved, his lowly birth would forever be held against him.

Seeing his new friend's discomfiture, Duryodhana rushed to his rescue. 'If the only thing that prevents him from engaging Arjuna in single combat is the lack of a kingdom, then it is easily remedied. I crown him as King of Anga.' And, having obtained the permissions of Bhishma and King Dhritarashtra, Duryodhana placed his own crown on Karna's brow before ceremoniously scattering rice grains and sprinkling water on his head.

The entire crowd was up on its feet, praising the impetuous Prince for his magnanimity and kindness. Karna was overwhelmed and looked at his benefactor with profound gratitude. 'I shall be in your debt forever as the kindness you have done me today can never be repaid in a million lifetimes.'

Duryodhana shushed him with a benign smile and said, 'I ask for nothing but your friendship in return.' And in this manner, Duryodhana won himself a loyal friend and a powerful weapon against the Pandavas.

At that moment, an old man hobbled into the arena. He was a charioteer named Adhiratha, a *suta* by caste and he seemed to be in the grip of some powerful emotion. When Karna saw him, he dropped his weapons and bowed before him. Adhiratha hugged his foster son in a tight embrace and shed tears of filial pride.

Watching this poignant spectacle, Bheema, who had been feeling extremely ill-disposed to the person who had dared to upstage his beloved younger brother, roared with laughter and said spitefully, 'So you are the son of a mere charioteer! A *sutaputra*! I am not in the least surprised. Lowly curs like you are not worthy of death at my brother's hands or ruling a kingdom for that matter. Go pick up the reins in keeping with your station in life and particular talents!'

Stung by these words, Karna trembled in abject shame and threw a despairing glance heavenward. Duryodhana sprang to his feet and retorted, 'Bheema! This is exactly the sort of senseless prattle

I'd expect from someone of your inferior intellect. It appears to me that there is some mystery surrounding his birth. His celestial armour and ear-rings mark him out as someone special. Be that as it may, there is little point in nitpicking about the origins of great men. Why even the birth of Kripacharya may be traced to a clump of reeds and Dronacharya's to a household vessel. Questions may be asked about the births of our own fathers. And as for the Pandavas, everyone knows that the story of your births will hardly bear close scrutiny. I think Karna deserves to rule not only Anga but all the three worlds! And if anyone dares to cast slurs against him on account of his birth, he will have to answer to me and I will be pleased to give a fitting reply with my mace.' So saying, Duryodhana placed his arm on Karna's shoulder and led him away. The sun set on these tumultuous events and the crowds made their way home chattering about the marvellous things they had seen.

It was a black day for the Pandavas. Duryodhana had managed to win over the masses on that particular day and made the five brothers look petty by comparison. Moreover, they had come to rely on Arjuna's incredible skills to get them through rough spots and today they had run up against his equal. If this was not bad enough, the charismatic warrior had allied himself with their long-time enemies, the Kauravas.

Yudhishthira was distraught. Arjuna said nothing to his troubled brothers but his initial fury had been replaced with a steely resolve and cold determination that had seen him overcome obstacles in the past. He promised himself that he would continue relentlessly in his quest for excellence and supremacy as a warrior and would keep his eyes open for the means to further hone his skills. He kept thinking dark thoughts about Karna, knowing intuitively that theirs was an enmity that would live until one of them had been destroyed by the other. Smiling grimly to himself, Arjuna envisioned the day he would crush his enemy. Little did he know then that he was thinking of taking the life of his own brother. He would find out one day, but only after he had translated his thought into action.

6
Sworn Rival

Karna would prove a worthy adversary to Arjuna and was a persistent thorn in his side. Their's was an epic struggle for supremacy and despite being evenly matched, only one could ultimately emerge the victor. The odds were stacked heavily against Karna from the start. One could be forgiven for assuming that lady luck was in a conspiracy against him. Arjuna, on the other hand, was fortune's favourite child. Karna's struggles against the trials and tribulations that fate presented, began from his birth, when he came into the world as the unwanted result of a young girl's whimsical folly.

Kunti had received the son-bearing *mantra* from Durvasa, and driven by the impulse of carefree youth, she felt tempted to try out her occult power immediately. The young girl looked out of her window and saw the sun shining gloriously down on her. In a moment of unthinking impetuosity, she decided to summon Surya to see if the *mantra* worked. To her consequent dismay, the Sun God did indeed appear before her, resplendent in his divine armour and ear-rings. The refulgent divinity, under the magic spell of Durvasa's infallible hymn, looked at the beautiful young virgin before him and his eyes sparkled with desire.

Terrified at the sight, Kunti pleaded with him, 'Great Lord, please have mercy on a wretched, silly girl. I only used the *mantra* to see if it would work. As an unmarried maiden, it would be wrong for me to bear your son. The world will denigrate me as a woman of loose morals and no self-respecting man will marry me. I beg of you, please go back to your celestial abode and spare me the terrible fate of an unwed mother.'

Surya was moved by her touching plea but there was little he could do as he was bound by the power of the *mantra*. Seeing that there was no escape, Kunti burst into fresh tears and wailed in despair. The Sun God felt sorry for her and said, 'I have no choice but to place my seed in your womb but I can do one thing for you...your virginity shall remain intact after you deliver our son'.

Kunti saw a ray of hope and bowed before Surya in gratitude. Her mind worked frantically to think of ways to save herself from the predicament she had got herself into. With due deference, she said to Surya, 'O Lord, I thank you for the patience and kindness you have shown me and humbly request you to grant me a boon. Let our son be born with the celestial armour and ear-rings unique to his father, so that I will always be able to recognise him as mine.'

Surya acceded to her request and Kunti fainted away, worn out by terror and relief. When she came to, the Sun God had left, leaving his son behind in her womb.

Kunti kept to her chambers during the course of her pregnancy. When she started to show, the baby bump was cleverly hidden under layers of clothing. Her secret remained undiscovered as it was the general consensus that the Princess was behaving strangely and keeping to herself because of some illness. In due course she delivered a beautiful baby boy wearing the accoutrements of his heavenly father. Kunti wept over her first born and shrank away from the terrible task she had set herself.

Finally, she steeled herself to do what had to be done. She lined a basket with the finest cloth and placed her infant son in it. In the dark of night, she set it afloat on the river, praying to the Gods to watch over him. The abandoned baby was discovered by the charioteer Adhiratha, who took him home to his childless wife, Radha. The couple thanked the Gods for the lovely child they had been given and lavished their love and affection on him. The high-born child, wrapped in the cocoon of his humble foster parents' love, had no idea that lady luck had just played the meanest trick to bedevil his future.

Karna, not surprisingly, showed a marked aptitude for what was considered to be the pursuits of a Kshatriya. He did not wish to follow professionally in his foster father's footsteps and longed to become an outstanding archer. He went to several noted *gurukul*s of the day but was turned away at each one because of his perceived lowly birth. Increasingly dejected, he decided to try a new tack. Parashurama, the formidable sage-warrior, believed to be an incarnation of Vishnu, was known for his intense hatred of the Kshatriyas. Karna went to him in the guise of a Brahmin and was accepted as a pupil.

The days in the *gurukul* were wonderful ones for Karna. His skills burgeoned under the watchful eye of Parashurama and the crusty, battle-hardened Brahmin veteran came to love the talented youth as his own son. Karna was taught the use of divine weapons like the *Brahmastra,* becauseof his proficiency in the field and the great appreciation his Guru had for him.

Then, one fateful day, Parashurama was weary and decided to sleep away his fatigue. Karna affectionately placed his Guru's head on his own lap as he slept under the shade of a tree. At that moment, Indra, being Arjuna's father-benefactor, took the form of a venomous insect and stung Karna in the thigh. The pain was excruciating but Karna endured it manfully, not wanting to disturb his master. The wound started to bleed and Parashurama woke up when he felt the sticky blood. For a moment he stared in silence at his disciple and then the truth dawned on him. Parashurama addressed Karna coldly, 'Who are you? You are no Brahmin, for only a true Kshatriya can bear such agony with such fortitude.'

Thus directly challenged by his Guru, Karna replied, 'I am the son of the charioteer, Adhiratha. My intention was not to deceive you; my insatiable thirst for knowledge drove me to you in this guise. Pray have mercy on me.'

But the damage had been done. Parashurama was furious that he had been duped and unleashed his terrible wrath on the errant lad saying: 'There can be no forgiveness for the likes of you. Deception was used by you to get what you wanted from me, but little good will your ill-gotten knowledge do you in the long run. Pay heed, O Karna of duplicitous nature, the *Brahmastra* will be ineffectual when you need it the most, for you will forget how to use it. Now get out of my sight.'

Karna was traumatised by these venomous words coming from the lips of his revered master. The terrible curse his Guru had pronounced hung over his head and cast a dark shadow over his future. And that future was made bleaker by yet another curse. Once, while practising his skill with arms near a Brahmin's cottage, he caused the death of the Brahmin's sanctified cow through an inadvertently released arrow. The Brahmin was outraged and rejecting Karna's earnest appeals for forgiveness and permission to pay compensation and replace the slain cow with many others, he pronounced a fateful curse: 'You killed a poor, defenceless creature today and you shall meet the same fate. Death will come to you when you are at your most vulnerable, with your chariot wheel stuck in a crevice on the battlefield.'

Thus, due to circumstances beyond his control, Karna's fate was sealed. Nevertheless, being a deep believer in manly effort, he persisted in his single-minded drive to achieve excellence in the art of warfare – sustained only by the unconditional love of his doting foster-parents.

Duryodhana's offer of friendship acted as a magic salve that rejuvenated his wounded spirit and he remained fiercely loyal to his friend till the end of his days. Duryodhana's friends were his friends and his enemies became Karna's as well. Karna came to nurse the heartiest loathing for the Pandavas in general and for Arjuna in particular. Even when he came to know the truth about his birth and parentage, he could not find it in his loyal heart to switch sides, and though his attitude to his other brothers softened, he remained steadfast in his desire to crush Arjuna.

7
Arjuna Wins A Bride

A few days after the tournament, Drona decided the time had come for him to have his long-desired revenge. He sent for his pupils and commanded them to capture Drupada, the King of Panchala, and bring him to the *gurukul*. Anxious to carry out his orders, the Kuru Princes set forth, bedecked in warlike regalia and armed to the teeth.

Duryodhana, his brothers, and Karna, rushed headlong into the attack. Seeing this, Arjuna held his brothers back and said, 'Duryodhana and his cronies can never hope to capture the valiant Drupada with such an imprudent and blustering mode of attack. Let us wait for a strategic moment before jumping into the fray'. And so the brothers held themselves in check while Drupada pummelled Duryodhana's forces into shameful retreat.

At the precise moment when the battle seemed to have gone Drupada's way, Arjuna gave his orders. He recommended that Yudhishthira stay behind. Nakula and Sahadeva would form the rearguard and protect his own chariot, while Bheema would ride at his side. In this formation, the brothers charged into battle. Bheema tore through the ranks of the Panchala warriors, wreaking havoc with his mace. Arjuna made his way towards Drupada with relentless purpose, his sharp arrows thwarting those who sought to impede his progress. When he caught sight of the King, he wasted no time in letting fly his arrows with such precision that Drupada's bow was shattered, his flagstaff severed in half and his charioteer and horses incapacitated. All this happened in the blink of an eye, and even as Drupada reached for another bow, Arjuna had leapt on to his chariot, holding his sword to the beleaguered monarch's throat. Letting out a roar of triumph, Arjuna called out to his brothers.

Arjuna took his royal captive to Drona and humbly presented his *gurudakshina*. Drona took in the sight of Drupada standing before him, a prisoner of war, and noticed that the man who stood before him was a far cry from the haughty monarch of yore. He said to him, 'Everything you own, including your life, belongs to me now. I wonder if you need a friend at this dire moment?' Smiling ever so slightly, he continued, 'You may remember a grievous injury you did to a certain good friend in the past and are perhaps repenting for your misdeed. But I am pleased to tell you that we Brahmins are not known to hold grudges. Willingly shall I return half of what was your Kingdom. You once told me that friendship is possible only between equals and I strive to repair the inequality that you perceived so that we may renew our old friendship. Go in peace to your half of the Kingdom and if you are willing, we can forget the past and begin our relationship afresh.'

Drupada, under his passive demeanour, was seething in impotent rage. With a beatific smile that concealed the intensity of his hatred, he replied, 'You have treated a fallen enemy with magnanimity and kindness. I am not surprised, for you are famed for your nobility as well as your valour. It will be my honour to be your friend. I accept your offer of friendship.'

Drona was pleased with the turn of events and released Drupada, presenting him with half the Kingdom. But Drupada was now a man with a mission. His sole aim in life was to bring Drona to his knees and snuff the life out of him. Brooding over the humiliation that had been handed him by the Brahmin he had once despised, he spent many days mulling over how best to get his own back. He was aware that Drona wielded much greater power than he did. So he decided to beget a valorous son who would vanquish his enemy in battle, and a beautiful daughter who would marry Arjuna, the world's greatest warrior and Drona's star pupil. With this idea firmly etched in his mind, he pondered over a course of action that would bring his plans to fruition.

Leaving his Kingdom, Drupada searched far and wide for renowned Brahmins who were skilled in the esoteric art of consecrating wish-fulfilling, sacred rites. Finally, he found the ascetic brothers, Yaja and Upayaja, who were meditating in their *ashram* on the banks of the great river Ganga. Drupada sensed that he was close to fulfilling his most fervent desire. He approached Yaja, who had the reputation (or rather, notoriety) of not being finicky about purity of action in return for the right price, and narrated his story. Drona, in an act of petty vengeance, had taken half his Kingdom and his prestige and would have to pay for what he had done. The monarch, smarting with fresh humiliation as he remembered his defeat, added: 'It will not be easy to vanquish that wily Brahmin. He is a master of the *Veda*s and has Parashurama's weapons at his disposal. The man is invincible. I wish for a mighty son who can take on the task of killing Drona, and a beautiful daughter who will enable me to make powerful alliances and bring about the destruction of my enemies. If you help me I will reward you beyond your wildest expectations.' Yaja was swayed by the offer and consented to perform the needed rites.

With the help of his brother Upayaja (who was of purer habit), Yaja gathered the materials he required and fixed on an auspicious day. Having completed the rites, he called for Drupada's Queen to receive the sacrificial oblation that would enable her to bear twin children. The Queen requested him to wait while she performed her ablutions. Incensed by her dithering at such a profound moment, Yaja declared, 'I have no need for you; this offering, consecreted by the combined efforts of Yaja and Upayaja, will achieve its purpose.' So saying, he poured the oblation into the sacred fire. The flames soared up high and from their midst emerged a god-like youth with strong features and adorned in splendid raiment. Drupada was thrilled with his warlike bearing and even as he admired his son, a divine voice called out, 'This noble Prince will be the pride of the Panchalas as he is born to destroy their enemy Drona in battle'. Cheers rang out as the entire gathering was on its feet loudly expressing their gratitude to the Gods.

The sacrificial flames then leapt up a second time, and a dark maiden of exquisite beauty stepped out from the blazing core. Even the brilliance of the flames seemed to pale in comparison to her divine features. Her hair was long, black and lustrous. Her eyes were dark and flashing. Her form was perfect. She was without doubt the most beautiful creation to have walked the earth. Her brother helped her out and even as he did so, the divine voice rang out again, 'This jewel among women is an instrument of the Gods. She will bring about the destruction of many Kshatriyas and most of the Kuru clan.'

The twins were named Dhrishtadyumna and Draupadi. Drupada was elated at the successful accomplishment of his mission. He showered the Brahmin brothers with rich gifts and expressed his heartfelt gratitude. News of the birth of the twins spread like wildfire and eventually reached the ears of Dronacharya himself. Resigning himself to the irrevocable working of destiny, he personally brought Dhrishtadyumna to his abode and coached him in the science of arms.

In the great battle of Kurukshetra, Dhrishtadyumna was appointed as Commander-in-Chief of the Pandava forces; and Drona, following the defeat of Bhishma by Arjuna (shielded by Shikandin), took up the generalship of the Kaurava army. The Acharya, who had always followed an unconventional lifestyle for a Brahmin, gave himself over completely to the dark allure of violence, goaded by the taunts of Duryodhana, who accused him of being partial to the Pandavas. He fought with fiendish ferocity. But his decision to use divine weapons against common soldiers led to his conduct being derided and deprecated by all who saw him in action.

An old blood feud heated up when Drona claimed the lives of Drupada's three grandsons, cutting off their heads with his deadly arrows. The bereaved grandfather, accompanied by Virata, the grand old monarch of Matsya, who had lost all his sons, charged towards the offending Brahmin, their entire beings seething with hatred and anger. The battle that followed was intense in the extreme but the mighty Brahmin warrior prevailed and despatched his former friend-turned-bitter-foe – Drupada, as well as Virata, on their final journey.

On seeing the lifeless bodies of his valiant father and sons, Dhrishtadyumna howled in black rage. Overpowering grief threatened to split him asunder and he said with intense feeling, 'Alas! I was born to save Mother Earth from the odious burden of that evil Brahmin, who is a disgrace to his race. If only I could have killed him sooner, the precious blood of my father and sons would not have been spilt in this accursed place! I live now only for revenge and it shall be mine for I am truly my father's son.'

Krishna, who was related to the Pandavas and had consented to be Arjuna's charioteer in the great war, was disgusted with Drona's unethical tactics and decided that his death must be hastened. He knew that Arjuna alone had what it took to defeat and kill the indefatigable Brahmin, but Arjuna the pupil could never bring himself to fight against his respected master, whom he honoured like a father. Making up his mind about what had to be done, Krishna went to Yudhishthira and said, 'O King! Dronacharya is slaughtering your army and will not rest till he has slain the last man. He is like a maddened beast that is so dangerous that it has to be put down. Something has to be done.'

'But what can we do to stop him? He taught us all we know and we are helpless in the face of his might. How can we hope to overpower him?' replied a dejected Yudhishthira.

'Do you remember what he told you when you asked for his advice at the onset of the battle?' the omniscient Krishna asked, gently nudging Yudhishthira down the dark path they would need to traverse in order to kill Drona.

'Yes, I remember! He said that he could be defeated only if he was made to drop his arms. And he would do so only if someone he trusted gave him terrible tidings.'

'What needs to be done is clear. He will drop his arms only if he is informed of the untimely death of his son, Ashwatthama. He trusts only you, so it is necessary for you to convey that false message in order to save those who have placed their trust in you,' spoke Krishna.

On hearing these words Yudhishthira and Arjuna were equally dismayed. Seeing their mutinous expressions, Bheema stepped in to do the needful. 'There is no need for the two of you to look so horrified. This is a battlefield and sometimes you have to dirty your hands in order to survive. Look at the corpses around you... Feast your eyes on the artistry of your teacher. Nobody forced him to fight for the evil Duryodhana. The choice was entirely his to make. He needs to be killed and if there is only one way to accomplish it, then so be it!'

'I cannot bring myself to commit such a foul deed!' said Yudhishthira, anguish writ large on his handsome face.

'It will bring perpetual infamy on our clan if we do this...' reiterated Arjuna.

'Then out of respect for your fine sensibilities, I shall make it easier for you. Indravarma, the Malava King, has an elephant named after that brutish oaf, Ashwatthama. The beast has been causing a lot of damage. Today, Ashwatthama the elephant shall meet his end at my hands,' said Bheema.

So saying, Bheema took up his mace and went out and killed the elephant named Ashwatthama. Without further ado, he called out to Drona in his stentorian voice, 'Ashwatthama is dead!'

Drona's blood turned icy cold in his veins. But he could not trust Bheema the way he trusted his righteous elder brother. So he continued to fight mechanically, launching one celestial missile after another, mowing through the Pandava army like a ravaging predator, until his eyes alighted on Yudhishthira. 'Is it true? Does my son lie dead in this accursed place?' he asked pathetically.

'Ashwatthama is dead!' said Yudhishthira, his voice trembling with the deep self-loathing he felt. Softly he added, knowing he would not be heard, 'The elephant'.

When these words were uttered, Yudhishthira's chariot, which would levitate four fingers above the ground, became surface-bound. His strict adherence to the path of *dharma* had earned him this exalted position above his fellows. But the one corrupting half-truth made Yudhishthira's fall from impeccable virtue, visible to the whole world.

Drona was too distraught to notice, however. The world and its concerns held no meaning for him once the ever-truthful Yudhishthira confirmed his son's passing. He threw down his weapons and sat down in yogic absorption – his soul leaving his body for the abode of *Brahma* (the seventh heaven).

At this juncture, Dhrishtadyumna, who was past caring about honour where his sworn enemy was concerned, rushed at him with a sword, and ignoring the cries of censure from those around him, severed Drona's head from his already lifeless body. Holding aloft the Acharya's head, Dhrishtadyumna whooped like an animal, delighted with himself for achieving what he was born to do and for having avenged his dead family members.

But violence only begets more violence. Dhrishtadyumna himself would meet his gory nocturnal end, when Drona's vengeful son would sneak into the enemy's camp and destroy without mercy, all those who reposed within, exhausted after their exertions on the battlefield. In a weird play of poetic justice, Dhrishtadyumna would pay for his abominable violence on the disarmed yoga-absorbed body of his Guru by himself being denied the right to fight like a warrior and would breathe his last by being kicked and crushed under the cruel and unforgiving feet of Ashwatthama, Drona's son. Thus would end the tragic tale of animus between Drona, Arjuna's teacher and Drupada, his father-in-law.

But all these events of battle would take place much later in the saga. In the meantime, the Pandavas found themselves besieged by Duryodhana's unceasing hatred and jealousy. Giving in to popular demand, Dhritarashtra crowned Yudhishthira as the heir apparent to the Kuru throne. The Prince endeared himself to the masses with his fairness, generosity, and innate kindness. Arjuna armed himself and like his father Pandu had done before, set out to subdue the rebellious factions of the Kingdom and annexe new territories. He tamed hitherto indomitable warriors like the Yavana King, Vipula, and Sumitra, and brought them all under the Kuru yoke. Invaders were repelled by the might of his bow and the boundaries of the Kuru Kingdom were made secure. Arjuna amassed a massive fortune and returned with it to Hastinapura, the Kuru capital, where the citizens gathered to applaud the conquering hero. Once again he was the cynosure of all eyes and the masses worshipped the ground he walked on.

Duryodhana could not bear to see the tremendous achievements of the Pandavas and their increasing popularity. The citizens felt that Yudhishthira should be crowned at once and the eldest Kaurava worried that if this came to pass, he and his brothers would be relegated to the status of poor relatives forever. The thought was so unpalatable that he went back to plotting against the Pandavas with a vengeance. Finally, he hit upon the perfect plan to destroy them. He called Purochana, a henchman of his, and commanded him to construct a wax palace made entirely of inflammable materials, at Varanavata. On its completion, he wheedled his father to command the Pandavas and their mother, Kunti, to go to Varanavata for some much-needed relaxation. Duryodhana then ordered Purochana to set fire to the wax palace at a suitable time and so hoped to send the Pandavas to a horrible death. But sagacious Vidura discovered the evil plot and he not only warned the Pandavas in time but helped them escape.

After this nerve-wracking ordeal, Yudhishthira said to his brothers, 'We were lucky to escape but it is only a matter of time before Duryodhana succeeds in dispatching us to Yama's abode. We must be prudent now. Our uncle, Vidura, has suggested that we lie low for a period till the tide turns in our favour. I am inclined to agree with him. Let us remain hidden and wait out this period of grave adversity in our lives.' As always, his brothers deferred to his wisdom and decided to disguise themselves as poor Brahmins.

While the Pandavas were hiding at Ekachakra in a poor Brahmin's house, they heard about the magnificent *swayamvara* King Drupada had arranged for his daughter. An itinerant Brahmin filled them in on the details surrounding the birth of the twins. The Pandavas listened spellbound as the Brahmin described Draupadi's famed beauty to them. Strange longings rose unbidden in their hearts and they all spent a restless night dreaming about the lovely lady, who would soon be linked irrevocably to their destiny. In the morning, Kunti smiled knowingly and casually suggested that they make their way to the *swayamvara*. The Pandavas responded with alacrity and were soon on their way to the Kingdom of Panchala, where the grand event was to take place.

En route to the Kingdom of Drupada, the Pandavas noticed that the blistering heat was taking its toll on their mother. They decided to rest in the shade and proceed by night, when it would be cooler.

They commenced their journey after the sun had set and found themselves on the banks of the river Ganga, where the King of the Gandharvas was frolicking with his wives. He took umbrage at the brothers for disturbing his privacy and interrupting the revelry, saying, 'The twilight hours belong to the Gandharvas, Yakshas, and Rakshasas. Mere mortals who go about their business under cover of darkness do so at their peril. Therefore be warned.'

'Your words are arrogant as well as presumptuous and unbecoming of a demigod. Mother Ganga offers refuge to all in need, irrespective of the time of day. No one can claim exclusive rights to any of Brahma's creations – be it light or darkness or the oceans or seas. To do so is foolhardy in the extreme!' Arjuna responded at once to the challenge and veiled threat.

'I am Angaraparna and this is my realm. While you are on my land, you are obliged to accept my word as law. Do not be a fool and incur my wrath. Leave my land at once before I decide to teach you a lesson in manners!'

The Pandavas, led by Arjuna, would not be put off by mere threats and stood their ground. Angaraparna was amazed that mere mortals had dared to defy him, whom even the *rakshasas* treated with fear and respect. He could not forgive this slight and so readied his weapons. Arjuna responded in kind. The fight which followed was brief. Arjuna used his celestial weapons to inflict a crushing defeat on the Gandharva King. Grabbing him by his hair, he dragged him and threw him at Yudhishthira's feet.

Angaraparna's wife, Kumbheenasi, approached Yudhishthira with folded hands and begged him to spare the life of her husband. The eldest Pandava, compassionate as always, ordered Arjuna to release his fallen opponent. The humbled King got to his feet and said, 'It takes a great man to show mercy to one he has defeated in battle. I am honoured to make your acquaintance, O Arjuna, wielder of celestial weapons. As a token of my esteem, I shall impart to you the secret science of the Gandharvas, known as *Chakshushi,* which will enable you to perceive all that you wish to see in the three worlds and elevate you to the rank of a celestial entity. In addition, I will give you and your brothers a hundred of our special steeds. They appear at the will of the owner, can change their hues, know no fatigue, and are of unequalled speed.'

Arjuna was touched at the generosity of the Gandharva but he could not help thinking that his deed did not merit such bounty. He gently turned down the gifts saying that as a mortal he was unworthy of them. But Angaraparna was determined to do him a good turn. Offering to receive the *Agneya* missile in return, he persuaded Arjuna to accept the horses. The Pandava and the King embraced one another and swore eternal friendship. Before leaving, the King advised the Pandavas to secure the services of a sage who would bless their ventures and protect their acquisitions. Sage Dhoumya was recommended for the job. The Pandavas thanked their new friend for his sound advice before proceeding on their way.

The five brothers, accompanied by their mother, reached the outskirts of Drupada's Kingdom and sought hospitality in the humble abode of a potter *(kumbhakara)*. It seemed that every high-born Kshatriya had turned up as the place was teeming with warriors and dignitaries from many Kingdoms, all of them dreamed of winning the hand of the incomparable Draupadi. Sages and Brahmins had also arrived in large numbers as the royals would be anxious to appear in the best light and would be munificent in distributing alms and gifts. The Pandavas walked into the huge, decorated area where the *swayamvara* was to be held and were lost in the teeming masses. They settled themselves as inconspicuously as possible in a corner with the Brahmins. Krishna, cousin of the Pandavas and incarnation of Lord Vishnu, alone noticed them and drew his brother Balarama's attention to them.

Drupada had always wanted to marry off Draupadi to Arjuna. He had been devastated when he heard of the death of the Pandavas at Varanavata. But later, persistent rumours had surfaced suggesting they had escaped. The King took heart from these rumours and deliberately designed a test for the suitors with Arjuna in mind, hoping to draw out the elusive Pandava.

On the sixteenth day, Draupadi made her appearance, clothed in the finest apparel, bedecked with jewellery and holding a garland in her hands. The vast assemblage gazed at her in speechless wonder and adoration. Many were so smitten with desire for her that they were willing to do anything to possess her. Dhrishtadyumna led his sister to the stage and announced, 'This is my sister, the Princess Draupadi. My father, King Drupada, will give her hand in marriage to the man who is noble by birth, distinguished in looks, blessed with innumerable skills, and who succeeds in passing the test specially designed for this purpose.'

The Prince proceeded to give the details of the feat the suitors had to perform: 'The target is a golden fish that hangs from yonder pole. Beneath it, there is a revolving mechanism with a hole in the centre. And at the bottom of the pole there is a vessel containing water. Contestants for my sister's hand will have to string the special bow on the dais, and looking into the reflection of the fish in the water, shoot five arrows in rapid succession through the hole in the revolving mechanism and hit the eye of the fish. My sister will be given in marriage to the man who can perform this feat and to none other.' So saying, he and Draupadi stepped back. The clash of symbols signalled the beginning of the contest.

It was a daunting task and the assembled Princes shook their heads despondently. But the Princess looked so enchanting they hardened their resolve and prepared to try their hardest to achieve the seemingly impossible task. The greatest warriors went up to the dais one by one but none succeeded in even lifting the great bow. Duryodhana, Shisupula, Yuyutsu, Jayadratha, and Shalya, all tried their hand at the task but failed miserably and returned to their seats in shame.

When it was Karna's turn, the audience went still as he was a famed archer trained by the great Parashurama himself. He picked up the bow, strung it with careless ease and took his aim. At that moment the clear, dulcet voice of the Princess called out, 'I will never give myself to a *suta*'. A gasp rippled around the arena. Karna cast a withering glance at the sun, flung down the bow and walked away with his head held high.

After that phenomenal archer returned to his seat, there were others who tried their luck but nobody even came close to him. The assembled warriors were disgruntled with their pathetic display and began complaining that the task was impossible. 'At this rate the Princess will remain unmarried and a virgin for the rest of her life!' they muttered in mutinous tones.

At this juncture, a noble Brahmin rose and walked up to Dhrishtadyumna and asked: 'Can a Brahmin try his hand at winning the Princess?' Dhrishtadyumna replied, 'It will be as I declared at the outset. My sister will wed the man who distinguished by birth, looks, and skill, succeeds in accomplishing the given task.'

The congregation watched in amazement as an audacious Brahmin, stepped into the arena to try and beat the Kshatriyas at their own game. The disguised Arjuna picked up the bow, strung it, and proceeded to shoot five arrows straight into the eye of the fish. Thunderous applause broke out and even the celestial deities made their approbation known by showering flowers from above on the hero. Draupadi walked up to Arjuna and shyly placed the garland on his shoulders.

The other suitors were stunned at the turn of events. Their thwarted desire turned to anger. They made their displeasure clear in strident tones, saying, 'How dare Drupada give away his daughter to a Brahmin and a nobody at that? Only Kshatriyas are allowed to participate in such events. We must not allow this travesty to happen.' Assenting cries greeted these words. Others piped in with, 'We cannot kill the upstart of a Brahmin, but let us slay the King and his son and cast Draupadi into the flames.' As things started to heat up, Yudhishthira, Nakula and Sahadeva slipped out. Arjuna took up his bow and stood defiantly in challenge, shielding Draupadi from the impending attack. Bheema uprooted a tree and stood next to his brother, brandishing the tree as if it were a toy and glaring menacingly at the warriors in front of him.

The attack commenced and the brothers had no trouble keeping the raging Kings and Princes at bay. Seeing the spirited defence put up by the Brahmins, the Kshatriyas fought to kill, deciding that it was no sin to kill a Brahmin who willingly stepped into battle. Karna took on Arjuna while Bheema fought the others. The arrows flew thick and fast as the warring antagonists strove to conquer one another. Karna was amazed at the skill of the unknown archer and said, 'Who are you? Your skill is extraordinary. None but Arjuna can withstand me in battle.'

'I am merely a Brahmin who happens to be as good a warrior as Arjuna and infinitely superior to any braggart like yourself!' Arjuna responded with a smirk.

Krishna and Balarama intervened at this point, trying to restore order. In the ensuing confusion, Arjuna and Bheema slipped away with Draupadi to join their brothers before they could be unmasked. Unknown to them, Dhrishtadyumna followed quietly at a distance.

The Pandavas, accompanied by Draupadi, went to the potter's hut where Kunti awaited them. Anxious to convey their happy tidings to her, they called out excitedly, 'Mother! Come see what we have brought today!' Kunti replied absentmindedly from within: 'Whatever it is, share it equally amongst yourselves.' The brothers were appalled at her words and could not bring themselves to look at each other. Kunti stepped out of the house and upon seeing Draupadi, was horrified at her careless utterance.

Once inside the hut, Kunti said, 'I was under the impression that you had returned with alms. We must be careful not to bring infamy upon the Princess just to obey my unwitting remark. At the same time we should see that no harm befalls us by making my words false. With that in mind, do whatever you think best.'

'You won her fair and square. Marry her and make her yours,' Yudhishthira told Arjuna.

'Brother, what you suggest is improper and against Aryan norms. How can I marry when I have two elder brothers who are unmarried? Moreover, we can't just ignore our mother's words,' Arjuna replied.

Yudhishthira reflected briefly on the right thing to do. He noticed the covert glances his brothers threw Draupadi's way and realized that if they were completely honest with themselves, they all wanted her and would go on wanting her. Her beauty was such that no man could remain impervious to it. If they were not careful, they would one day come to blows over her and any possibility of a rift between his beloved brothers had to be averted at all costs. He reached his decision and said calmly, 'Draupadi will be the wife of the Pandavas'.

The brothers and their mother were overjoyed with this decision and felt it was the best thing to do given the circumstances. Just then, Krishna walked in accompanied by Balarama. The Yadava heroes paid their respects to Kunti and enjoyed a happy reunion with their cousins. Krishna derided the Kuru elders for allowing Duryodhana to get away with his evil machinations and expressed his happiness that the Pandava brothers were safe. Wishing them the best for the future, Krishna and Balarama left hurriedly lest they be discovered.

Dhrishtadyumna observed these events from his hiding place and returned to the palace to report to his father. 'They are the Pandavas alright', he said without preamble. 'There are five of them and I saw a venerable old woman whom they addressed as Mother. She is Kunti without doubt. They don't talk or behave like poor Brahmins. I could see royalty stamped over their features and conduct and they have the scarred shoulders and arms of true warriors. And there is one more thing... Krishna and Balarama went to visit them.'

Drupada was ecstatic. 'So my daughter will be the wife of Arjuna! Now my desires are fulfilled. Everything has gone according to plan.'

'Let the wedding be solemnised first...' Dhrishtadyumna said, his forehead creased with some unknown apprehension. And with that loaded statement, he left to make preparations for the feast which was to be held in honour of Draupadi's chosen groom. Drupada, however, was too busy contemplating his revenge and ignored his son's last statement.

The next day saw Dhrishtadyumna going to the potter's hut to personally escort the Pandavas and their mother to the palace. A sumptuous repast had been prepared for them and everyone enjoyed the feast. Drupada watched them and noticed the majestic elegance with which they carried themselves and how they tended to converse about weapons and other topics favoured by the Kshatriyas. The old King became increasingly certain that they were indeed the Pandavas.

After the feast, he addressed Yudhishthira saying, 'Shall we now go ahead with arrangements for the wedding of your brother and my daughter in keeping with the Brahminical tradition?'

'We are Kshatriyas. I am Yudhishthira, the son of Pandu. And yonder are my brothers Bheema, Arjuna, Nakula and Sahadeva,' the eldest Pandava said with a smile.

Drupada was delighted to have his suspicions confirmed and embraced them, promising to treat them as his own sons. He was infuriated with the Kauravas for the shoddy treatment that had been meted out to the Pandavas and assured them that the days of their enemies were numbered. Excitedly he began making plans for the future. 'Once the wedding between Arjuna and Draupadi takes place, Dhrishtadyumna and I will waste no time in winning back your kingdom for you and sending those Godless Kauravas to the abode of Yama.'

Yudhishthira coughed delicately and said, 'We have decided that Draupadi shall be wife to all the Pandavas in keeping with the wishes of my mother.'

At first Drupada did not comprehend the words. But when he did, his face contorted in sheer consternation. 'What you are suggesting goes against the scriptures, customs and rules of nature. If my daughter were to marry five men, she would be abhorred by all as a woman of easy virtue. I will never consent to this. It is a sin against the Gods and they will smite us down for even contemplating it.'

Yudhishthira, however, refused to budge from his stand and Drupada became increasingly bellicose at what he firmly believed was a moral transgression and an anathema. Things would have become ugly but for the timely appearance of Veda Vyasa. With his yogic vision he had seen all that had happened and arrived to resolve the impending conflict. Drupada spoke first, 'O wisest of men! Make Yudhishthira see reason. How can one woman cohabit with five men without sullying her honour beyond redemption?'

'Calm down, O King! The practice of a woman taking more than one husband has become uncommon, though it is by no means without precedent. This, however, is a unique case because it has been preordained. In a former life, the virtuous Draupadi could not get a husband because of her *karma*. She prayed to Shiva for a boon and the three-eyed Lord appeared before her to grant her wish. In her eagerness she repeated her desire for a husband five times and Shiva acquiesced, promising her that she would have five husbands. As you can see, his words have come true,' the great sage said soothingly.

'If this is the result of Shiva's words, then no blame will attach to my daughter or me. Let destiny run its course. I shall give orders for the wedding preparations to commence immediately,' responded Drupada, throwing up his hands in resignation.

In this manner the Pandavas came to acquire a common wife. The wedding of Draupadi to the Pandavas was celebrated with much pomp and splendour. Drupada presented each of the grooms with a hundred chariots, horses, elephants, and maids. In addition, he gave them robes made of the finest cloth, diamonds the size of Ostrich eggs, gold by the bushel, and more precious stones than they could count. But perhaps most valuable of all the gains for the Pandavas was the powerful political dimension of their matrimonial alliance, as Drupada and Dhrishtadyumna were mighty warriors and were a force to be reckoned with.

The Pandavas were happy with their common wife. But could one say that Draupadi was happy with her five husbands? In time she she did come to love them well and did her best to be a good wife to them all. It is to her credit that she was largely successful, as there was never any dissent among the brothers on her account. The virtuous Draupadi bore each of the brothers strong sons, dutifully accompanied them to the forest during their exile and endured the subsequent hardships as best as she could. But in the deepest recesses of her heart, she would always nourish a special attachment to the handsome hero clad in deerskin who won her hand after performing a seemingly impossible feat at the *swayamvara*. She kept these feelings hidden within her, as neither she nor her beloved belonged exclusively to the other. Yet, till her dying breath, Draupadi secretly loved Arjuna more than his brothers.

8
Serpent Princess

When the news of Draupadi's marriage to the Pandavas reached Hastinapura, Duryodhana and his followers were filled with resentment as the most beautiful woman of the age had given herself to their arch enemies. They trooped in to see the blind King and poured out their grievances before him. Fresh schemes were suggested and the best way to rid themselves of their cousins were discussed and discarded as hopeless. For once Dhritarashtra ignored the psychotic ravings of his firstborn and chose to listen instead to the wise council of Bhishma, Drona and Vidura, overcoming his own latent partiality for his sons. He ordered Vidura to go to Panchala and bring the sons of Pandu back with suitable ceremony. Half the Kingdom would be given to them on their return, in the hope of avoiding conflict in future.

The Pandavas were wary but returned to Hastinapura, accompanied by Krishna. The citizens rejoiced on their return and thanked the Gods for keeping them safe. Having paid their respects to the Kuru elders and having presented their wife to them, they headed for Khandavaprastha, which was their allotted share of the Kingdom. It was a bleak, desolate landscape adjoining a large forest and nothing grew on that barren land as far as the eye could see. But the Pandavas remained undaunted as they had grown accustomed to worse injustices at the hands of the Kauravas. Besides, the place, bad as it was, had some merits when compared to Varanavata, which had been built with the express purpose of consigning them to a fiery hell. Seeking the guidance of Veda Vyasa and Sage Dhoumya, the Pandavas selected a piece of land and had it consecrated before proceeding to build a magnificent city. Indra, at the behest of Krishna, sent the chief architect of the *Devas,* Vishwakarma, to help the Pandavas. Soon, thanks to Vishwakarma's endeavours, the wretched piece of land was transformed into a city fit for the Gods and came to be called Indraprastha. People flocked to this new place hoping for a slice of the prosperity it promised. Consequently, the city grew and flourished. Krishna stayed till the Pandavas had settled down and then bid them farewell.

One day, the Sage Narada came to visit the Pandavas, who warmly welcomed him to their abode. The Sage first blessed them all and then revealed the purpose of his visit. He had come to give them a piece of advice concerning their new wife. He told them of the *asura* brothers, Sunda and Upasunda, the sons of Nikumbha, a descendent of Hiranyakasipu, the dreaded *rakhshasa,* who was the father of Prahlad and met his end at the hands of Lord Vishnu in his Narasimha *avatar*. The brothers loved each other dearly and did everything together. Their thoughts, hopes and dreams were entwined and they could easily have been mistaken for a single being that resided in different bodies.

Having decided to acquire enough power to become the Lords of the Universe, Sunda and Upasunda moved to the Vindhyas and began performing the harshest penances and austerities. Legend has it that the mountains began to spout smoke in thick clouds, unable to withstand the heat of their austere efforts. Alarmed, the Gods did everything to sway the duo from their chosen path. But the brothers proved themselves above temptation. Finally, Brahma the Creator appeared before them with the promise of a boon. Snatching at this

God-given opportunity, they replied in unison, 'We seek supreme power that will make us adept in the use of magic and the arcane arts, skilled in the use of any form of weaponry, strong of body with the ability to change our forms at will and the gift of immortality'.

Sensing the darkness in their souls and abhorring their greed, Brahma said, 'It shall be as you ask, except for one thing. The boon of immortality I am unable to grant. But you shall be invulnerable to all but each other'. The brothers were happy with this boon as they felt it was as good as immortality since neither could conceive harming even a hair on the other's person.

Drunk with their newfound power, the demons returned to their fellow *daityas*. Together they embarked on a campaign to bring the world under their yoke. The earth was razed to the ground as all living creatures were subdued with an iron fist. The birds in the sky, the fish in the sea, and even the animals that roamed the earth, were butchered by the brothers. The Brahmins were specially targeted as they had the spiritual merits required to perform sacrifices and promote prosperity. They were deemed a threat and that non-violent class was almost annihilated by the duo who seemed to have lost all sense of reason and had succumbed to bloodlust and the acquisition of power. Kingdom after kingdom was captured and sacked with rapacious abandon. The established religion was abandoned as the *asura* brothers could not abide the *Veda*s. Suffering from the unpleasant attentions of the demon brothers, Mother Earth oozed blood and became a wretched land fit only for carrion.

Furious with the depravity and debauchery of the terrible brothers, Brahma summoned Vishwakarma, the architect of the Gods, and asked him to create a beautiful being that would prove to be the undoing of the abominable duo. Taking the task to heart, Vishwakarma went to every corner of the three worlds, painstakingly gathering every iota of the best and beautiful things and gems, which ran into billions. Having completed this arduous task, he created a wondrous damsel made entirely of these incomparable things. When completed, there was not even a tiny part of her that was not perfectly formed or that failed to captivate all who had the fortune to behold her ethereal beauty. She was given the name Tilottama, after the iotas or bits (*tila*s), from which she had been crafted. Having received her assignment, she circumambulated the Gods and none save Shiva could resist looking at her in wonderment. Brahma himself sprouted four heads and Indra developed a thousand eyes (to replace the thousand vulvas that had sprang up on his person, after he was cursed by Sage Gautama for seducing his wife, Ahalya), when they resisted the urge to gaze upon her exquisite beauty. Shiva, by virtue of his stoical immobility, acquired the appellation *Sthanu*.

The titillating temptress sauntered over to Kurukshetra, where Sunda and Upasunda had gone after laying waste to the world. Having accomplished their goals and finding themselves the masters of all they surveyed, the brothers were revelling in sensual pleasures, surrounded with the choicest of food, finest wines, and beautiful women who were experts in the fine arts of music, dance and love. In this domain of pleasure, Tilottama made her entrance, pretending to pick flowers even as she displayed her voluptuous charms before the hungry eyes of the brothers, impaling them on the spear of her incomparable beauty.

Driven mad with desire for her, Sunda and Upasunda forgot their great sibling love and fought a duel to the death with their clubs and beat the life out of each other. As the two fell, the earth and all her creatures fell silent, saddened despite everything that had transpired, to see such a beautiful bond of brotherhood broken over a bewitching woman.

The Pandavas listened to this tragic tale in spellbound silence, all too aware of the lesson being imparted to them by the great Sage. Narada, having made his point clear, proceeded to caution the Pandavas: 'Wise men always learn from the lessons history has to offer. It would be prudent to have some ground rules where Draupadi is concerned so that you can avoid quarrelling with each other over her.'

The five brothers were deeply disturbed by the tragic tale of the inseparable brothers who were driven to fratricide because of their love for the same woman. They decided to pay heed to the words of Narada and immediately laid down the rules. It was decided that they would take it in turns to be with Draupadi and when she was with one brother, the others would not disturb their privacy or witness their intimacy. Any brother who broke this rule would go into exile for twelve years and take a vow of celibacy. Pleased that his mission had been accomplished successfully, Narada made his departure.

The Pandavas adhered to the rules and lived in blissful harmony. But one day, a Brahmin came to Arjuna in great agitation and begged for his help. Some thieves had stolen his precious cows and he requested Arjuna to retrieve them for him. Arjuna was in a dilemma as his weapons were in Yudhishthira's chamber and Draupadi was with him. He hesitated only briefly as he knew where his duty lay. As a Kshatriya he was obliged to help any distressed man who sought his help. Without further ado, he sped into Yudhishthira's room, snatched up his weapons and made a hasty retreat. After chasing down the thieves and restoring the Brahmin's property, he returned to the palace. Once there, he made hasty preparations for his departure as dictated by the rules framed by the Pandavas, although the brothers were deeply saddened by his going.

Yudhishthira tried to dissuade his younger brother from leaving saying, 'Arjuna, you were merely doing your duty when you broke the pledge. You deserve to be excused this time. I am not at all angered by your actions. Moreover, a younger brother is allowed to take liberties where the elder is concerned. It is an indulgence allowed to younger ones. Your actions were justified. Please stay with us.'

But Arjuna replied, 'Brother, it is unlike you to twist *dharma* to suit personal convenience. We made those rules for a good reason and we should stick to them. I shall retire to the forest for twelve years as punishment for my lapse. Please don't attempt to make me change my mind. Wish me luck instead and give me your blessings.'

Arjuna remained adamant and refused to listen to his brothers' entreaties to remain. With heavy hearts they finally bade him farewell. Divesting himself of his fine clothes and ornaments, Arjuna set off, accompanied by a group of ascetics, scholars and musicians. They journeyed far and wide, visiting many pilgrim sites and offered their prayers to the resident deities. In this manner, they reached Gangadwar (Haridwar). It was a beautiful place and Arjuna spent many days at that peaceful spot in prayer and meditation. One day he stepped into the river to cleanse himself before performing the sacrificial rites. Suddenly he was dragged to the bottom of the river by an irresistible force. He was bewildered to find himself in a luxuriant, underwater palace. A sacrificial fire was blazing in one of the rooms and Arjuna, setting his confusion aside, completed his prayers to Agni.

When he opened his eyes, he saw a ravishing maiden standing demurely to one side, her eyes fastened in adoration on him. Arjuna smiled and admonished her gently saying, 'That was a reckless thing you did, pretty one. Who are you and why did you bring me here?'

'I am Uloopi, the daughter of King Kauravya. You are in the abode of the Nagas. We are known as the serpent people who dwell in the watery depths. When I first laid my eyes on you, I fell victim to Kama's darts of love and have longed for you ever since. There can be no life for me without you. Make me yours and the Gods will bless you for your kindness. If you refuse, I will perish!' the maiden replied.

Arjuna spoke gently but with unwavering conviction. 'O Princess, I cannot fulfil your wishes. I have vowed to spend twelve years practising celibacy and cannot go back on my word.'

The lovely Pricess replied, 'I am familiar with the circumstances of your exile. The rule of celibacy in your case applies only where Draupadi is concerned. Therefore you can give yourself to me without qualms. Moreover, my life will be forfeit if you leave me in this state and it is your duty as a Kshatriya to rescue me from such a fate.'

Arjuna gave in to the wishes of the charming Princess with the eloquent tongue and made her his wife by walking around the sacred fire. Thus, with Agni as witness, their union was consecrated and consummated.

The next day, a grateful Uloopi led Arjuna back to the banks of the Ganga. Her heart was breaking but she knew she had to let him go as he had shown absolutely no intention of staying with her of his own accord. It was evident to her that he had acceded to her wishes out of kindness and did not reciprocate her love. It was a bitter pill to swallow, but Uloopi accepted it with grace and it did not diminish her own love for the Pandava. Before her departure she blessed him saying, 'You shall be undefeated in water. All sea creatures will obey you and spare you from harm. Farewell, my beloved, I will care for you always'.

Arjuna felt as though he were waking from a pleasurable dream that was turning hazy and already fading from his memory. He resumed his travels northwards, accompanied by the Brahmins who had set out with him from Indraprastha. Guided by his companions he visited various holy places in the Himalayan region, made famous by ancient sages, and imbibed the deeply spiritual essence of his surroundings.

During these wanderings, Arjuna stumbled upon a holy spot on the bank of a river. He was informed that this particular place was avoided by all as a monstrous crocodile had made its home in the waters and dragged down everyone who attempted to cleanse themselves or offer prayers at the hallowed spot.

Arjuna was undaunted and said with a confident smile, 'It would take more than a gluttonous crocodile to stop me'. He then stepped into the river to begin his ablutions. The monster had been lying in wait and pounced at once. Latching onto Arjuna's feet with its lethal jaws, it attempted to drag him into the water. But Arjuna freed himself and throwing a powerful arm around the writhing creature, he dragged it to the shore. As soon as the crocodile touched land, it became transformed into a beautiful maiden. Arjuna gazed at this apparition in wonder. The maiden bowed gracefully and touched his feet in gratitude. She then proceeded to tell her story. 'I am an *apsara*. My four companions and I attempted to distract a great sage while he was performing his austerities. Angered by our shallow antics, he cursed us and we were doomed to live as crocodiles for a hundred years till a great man released us from the spell. Thank you for the favour you have done me. I beg you to come with me to the places where my companions reside and do them the same service.' Realizing the significance of Uloopi's blessing, Arjuna accompanied the celestial maiden and freed the others.

Having stopped at all the prescribed places for spiritual worship, Arjuna decided to part company with the holy men and visit Manipur, of which he had heard much. He was received with considerable hospitality by the ruler of the land and no effort was spared to ensure his comfort. While relaxing in the palace, Arjuna saw a beautiful maiden. She was none other than Princess Chitrangada, the daughter of the King. Filled with desire for her, Arjuna wasted no time in pressing his suit with her father.

The Manipuri King was pleased that his daughter's hand had been requested by such a redoubtable warrior and he said to Arjuna, 'Mighty warrior, my daughter is truly fortunate. This match is agreeable to me but I have a stipulation to make first. I have no sons and it is my hope that the sons begotten by Chitrangada will perpetuate my line and take over the reins of kingship from me some day. You may marry her but as the bride-price, you must be willing to hand over any son born to her, so that he will always belong to this land.' Arjuna acquiesced and the marriage between him and Chitrangada took place amidst joyous revelry.

Arjuna spent three years with his new bride and they were blissful ones indeed. Chitrangada gave birth to a healthy baby boy who was christened Babhruvahana. Ever true to his word, Arjuna handed over his son to the King in a formal ceremony before making his departure. It would be many years before he saw his son again.

It was time for Arjuna to complete the remaining years of his exile and he headed southwards. Uloopi, the Serpent Princess who had loved and lost him, was pining for him. She had borne a son by Arjuna and named him Iravan. He grew up as a Naga Prince and became a magnificent warrior. He met his father in the abode of Indra and the usually fearless youngster trembled with apprehension as he revealed to Arjuna the nature of their relationship. The Pandava was pleased to see the young warrior and warmly embraced him. Father and son spent many happy hours together. When the time came for them to part, Arjuna sought the help of Iravan and his Nagas in the epic struggle that lay ahead and Iravan promised to fight beside his father.

True to his word, Iravan fought at Kurukshetra and dazzled all with his display of valour. Skilled in the art of illusion and transmogrification peculiar to the Nagas, Iravan wrought havoc on Duryodhana's army, claiming the lives of five of their uncle Shakuni's brothers. Finally, Iravan was killed by the *rakshasha* Alambusha, who cut off his head with a sword.

Long before these events came to pass, Uloopi, who was miserable living without Arjuna but unwilling to chase after him, heard about Chitrangada and Babhruvahana. She decided to go to them. She felt that in this way, though she could not be with the man she loved, she could be close to those who had the fortune to be loved by him. The love-struck Princess introduced herself to Chitrangada, who welcomed her warmly. Soon Uloopi became like the sister Chitrangada had never had. Babhruvahana became a favourite of Uloopi's and she personally took charge of his education and instruction in the martial arts. She galvanised him with tales of his father's tremendous prowess whenever his motivation or discipline flagged and moulded him in Arjuna's image. Soon the cub was transformed into a lion among men.

Chitrangada and Babhruvahana followed the adventures of their beloved Arjuna from distant Manipur and waited impatiently for any news brought by Uloopi. They wept when he went through hard times and rejoiced when he triumphed over his adversaries. The tales of Arjuna's matchless bravery, legendary valour and accounts of the manner in which he vanquished the greatest warriors of the day, narrated by Uloopi, enlivened their days. Chitrangada and Babhruvahana listened eagerly and nearly burst with pride. In this manner, they were always with Arjuna in spirit. When the great war at Kurukshetra was fought, Babhruvahana arrived with his Manipuri warriors to fight on the Pandava side before returning to his Kingdom.

When Yudhishthira was crowned King after the epic battle, he decided to perform the *Ashwamedha* (horse sacrifice). A special horse was released and given its head to roam as it pleased. An army led by Arjuna followed the horse, and in every Kingdom where the horse chose to stop, the ruler was obliged to acknowledge the supremacy of Yudhishthira or fight Arjuna and his forces. It was the general consensus that taking on Arjuna was tantamount to killing oneself, so the Kings dared do nothing but accept Yudhishthira as their overlord. These Kings, though demonstrating varying degrees of grace in surrender, all provided Arjuna with valuable treasures as a mark of their respect. The horse cantered unchecked, adding new territories to the Pandava empire and filling their coffers to overflowing.

In this manner the horse proceeded to Manipur. Babhruvahana was overjoyed to see his father and rushed out with arms outstretched. But Arjuna was far from pleased with this affectionate display given the circumstances and spoke with acerbity, 'No son of mine would walk away from a fight by embracing the challenger and not the challenge. If my blood truly runs in your veins, greet me like a warrior.'

Stung by these harsh words, Babhruvahana sprang into action. He ordered his soldiers to capture the horse and called his men to arms. And then the father and son faced off, ready to duel.

Arjuna was pleased with the leonine features and valour of his son. But when the two met in a terrible clash of arms, the very earth trembled. They fought long and hard and even the Gods watched the contest to see who would prevail. Chitrangada and Uloopi also watched the epic struggle, the former with tears in her eyes and a nameless dread in her heart; the latter with a strange stillness that was alien to her. It seemed that the two warriors would fight to eternity. But it was all over in a heartbeat. An arrow from Babruvahana's bow pierced his father's heart and Arjuna fell to the ground, dead.

The tragedy of it all silenced the viewers for long moments. And then the wailing and ululating began. Appalled by what he had done, Babhruvahana fainted. Chitrangada ran to her fallen husband and beat her chest and tore her hair in grief. Deciding that life was meaningless now she decided to starve herself to death right there on that spot. When Babhruvahana came to, he also decided to give up his life.

On seeing Uloopi standing dry-eyed and still as if in a trance, Babhruvahana spoke to her saying, 'Is this why you tried so hard to make me a great warrior? So that I would have the blood of my father on my hands? You have got your vengeance on the man who left you. I hope you are happy with what I have done. How could I have thought of you as my mother? You are a demon!'

Uloopi listened without expression or emotion and then said softly, 'I have a story to tell you. Do me the courtesy of listening to what I have to say and then you may judge my actions as you please.' She then began her remarkable tale which had a direct bearing on the man they all loved and who lay dead before them.

During the battle of Kurukshetra, Bhishma the Grandsire of both the Pandavas and Kauravas, was making life extremely hard for the five brothers. The old warrior was an unstoppable force on the battlefield and he was making mincemeat of the Pandava armies. Tens of thousands of soldiers met their doom, unable to withstand Bhishma's unrelenting arrows. Finally, in desperation and before their army could be destroyed to the last man, the brothers decided to engage in a bit of skulduggery. They had heard from Bhishma's own lips that he would never fight a woman, an unarmed man, or a man belonging to a lowly caste. Therein lay the key to neutralising him on the battlefield. On numerous occasions he had refused to fight Shikandin, repeatedly ignoring that warrior's challenges, saying he had once been a woman.

The lad in question had indeed been a woman named Amba. Along with her sisters, Ambika and Ambalika, she had been carried away forcibly by Bhishma during their *swayamvara,* to be given in marriage to Vichitravirya, grandfather of both the Pandavas and Kauravas. Amba was unhappy as she had already chosen another man, Shalva, as her groom. When Bhishma was informed of her feelings, he allowed her to go back to her chosen one with due respect.

Shalva, however, had been thrashed by the famed warrior in battle when he had chased after the Princesses when Bhisma had carried them away, and he rejected Amba. He told her in no uncertain terms, 'Go back to the man who carried you away by force and inflicted a crushing defeat upon me. He spared my life only at your request. Between the two of you, I was made both a beggar who was given his life as alms and a clown who is the butt of ridicule among the Kshatriyas. I will be the laughing stock of the world if I accept you under these less than honourable circumstances. Be gone, for the sight of your face only reminds me of the disgrace I have suffered on your account.'

Hurt and bewildered, Amba returned to Hastinapura. But Vichitravirya refused to accept her too, since she had given her heart to another man. Alone and unwanted, Amba's thwarted love turned to hatred and she turned the full force of her hatred upon Bhishma. Amba prayed to Lord Subramanya, seeking a divine solution to the seemingly insurmountable task of destroying Bhishma. She was given a garland of celestial flowers by the God, who told her, 'The man who wears this garland will be the destroyer of Bhishma.' Amba tried to find someone who would consent to wear the garland and kill Bhishma. She was refused everywhere she went as nobody wanted to incur the wrath of Bhishma and hasten their own departure to the abode of Yama. Driven by her all-consuming hatred, the Princess went to Drupada's Kingdom, where he too, refused her request unceremoniously. Fed up with them all, Amba hung the now offending garland at the entrance of Panchala and departed.

Some wandering ascetics advised her to seek the help of Parashurama, the incarnation of Lord Vishnu. Parashurama felt sorry for Amba and tried to persuade his former student, Bhisma, to marry her. But Bhishma could not oblige his mentor because of the vow he had taken for the sake of his father, to remain celibate. The fiery Brahmin then challenged Bhisma to a duel but neither could prevail over the other. Disgusted, Amba retired to the forest where she performed severe penance for many years to please Lord Shiva. Shiva appeared before her and granted her a boon: 'In your next life, you will bring about the death of Bhishma.' Anxious to begin her next life, Amba immolated herself in the sacrificial flames.

In her next life, Amba was born as Drupada's daughter. One day she saw the garland of celestial flowers given by Lord Subramanya. The wondrous flowers had remained fresh and beautiful over the years. She picked it up and placed it around her own neck. Drupada was angered with the recklessness of his daughter and had her removed to a distant place to avoid any trouble with the Kuru elder. During her exile, the girl performed further penance and transformed herself into the male warrior who came to be known as Shikandin.

It was for this reason that Bhishma refused to fight Shikandin. Although it grieved him deeply to do so, Arjuna turned this to his advantage during the battle. Using Shikandin as a shield, he showered Bhishma with his arrows. Bhishma had been given a boon by his father that he would die only when he wished to. Giving in to fate and wearied by his long life on earth, Bhishma chose to fall, saying in deep contentment, 'It is Arjuna's arrows which succeed in piercing this tough skin of mine, not Shikandin's. What an honour it is to die at the hands of the greatest warrior this world has known!' And thus Bhisma was brought down, resting on a bed of Arjuna's arrows.

Now Bhishma might have been resigned to his fate and even rejoiced at it but his brothers, the seven Vasus, were watching from their heavenly abode and they were incensed. They could not accept that their brother, whom even Parashurama could not overcome in single combat, now lay supine, felled by Arjuna's arrows, and they said to each other, 'That arrogant Pandava's actions are worthy of a weasel or a cunning fox. It is disgusting that he had to resort to such wicked wiles to destroy a noble soul who once sat him on his knee. When his term on earth ends, Arjuna will go directly to hell. The blazing flames of hell will be the most suitable place for him and others of his ilk.'

Bhishma was the youngest Vasu brother, known as Prabhasa. They were demi-gods and lived happily among the celestials. One day, Prabhasa's wife caught sight of Sage Vashishtha's cow, Nandini – the cow of plenty. She requested her husband to steal it so that she could present it to a friend who was a mortal. Prabhasa decided to indulge his wife. Accompanied by his brothers, he stole the cow. Vashishtha discovered what had happened with his yogic vision and was deeply angered. He pronounced a curse saying, 'Let the Vasus be born among men and know the suffering that is prevalent on earth'.

The Vasus were chagrined when they heard about the curse. They returned the cow to the ascetic and begged him to undo the curse. The sage had mellowed by then and said, 'I cannot undo the curse but I will soften it. You will all be born on earth but seven of you will be released immediately. Prabhasa alone will live for a long time. However, his life will be a glorious one and he will be remembered for eternity in the world of men'.

In due course, the Vasus were born to King Shantanu, the father of Vichitravirya and the Goddess Ganga. As promised, Ganga freed seven of her children by casting them into the waters of the river, thereby releasing them from a life on earth with its attendant hardships and sorrows. The eighth child was Bhishma.

The Vasus had missed their brother terribly and they were heartbroken to see the hardships he weathered during his time on earth. Arjuna's destruction of him was the last straw and they vented their rage and sorrow on him. Uloopi had heard about all this from her father, Kauravya, who was related to the Vasus.

The Serpent Princess was aggrieved and decided she should do something to rescue her love from his grim destiny. She spoke eloquently to her father saying, 'Terrible crimes have been committed in the battle of Kurukshetra and the perpetrators have got off lightly. My husband is a virtuous man who has always lived as prescribed by *dharma*. If he is thus condemned, I swear I'll follow him to the farthest reaches of hell. Talk to the Vasus and intercede with them on Arjuna's behalf.'

King Kauravya appealed to the Vasus, who were somewhat mollified as they knew that Bhishma himself loved Arjuna and thought highly of him. They said, 'Arjuna will escape the horrors of hell if he is killed in battle by his own flesh and blood'. Uloopi heard these words and made her plans.

Uloopi's fascinating tale drew to a close. Babhruvahana was shamefaced and regretted the harsh words he had hurled at this noble woman who was the epitome of selfless love. However, Chitrangada and Babhruvahana could still not reconcile themselves to Arjuna's passing and were steadfast in their resolve to kill themselves. Uloopi seemed to have slipped into a trance again. Her eyes were shut and she was completely oblivious to her surroundings.

Suddenly, as the bereaved wife and son watched in amazement, a brilliant green gemstone flew through the air and settled itself on Uloopi's outstretched palm. The gemstone was the most precious possession of the Snake people as it had the power to revive the dead. Uloopi walked towards the fallen hero and placed the gem on his chest. Miraculously, the wound closed itself and Arjuna awakened as if from a deep slumber. Jubilant cries rang out and everyone rejoiced. Chitrangada and Babhruvahana threw themselves at Uloopi's feet and worshipped her like they would a Goddess.

Arjuna listened in silent wonder as he was told all that had transpired. He turned his gaze upon the Serpent Princess and said, 'It was a blessed day when you dragged me to the abode of the Nagas. I owe my existence both in this world as well as the next to you.'

As she looked into the brilliant depths of those captivating eyes, Uloopi knew that she had won her beloved Arjuna's heart at last.

9
THE ABDUCTION THAT SAVED THE LINEAGE

After his delightful sojourn in Manipur, which would prove so important for him in future, Arjuna journeyed on southwards till he reached the holy city of Rameshwaram. While there, he made a point of visiting the spot where Rama, believed to be Vishnu incarnate, and his army of monkeys, had built a bridge to allow them access to Lanka and the Demon-King Ravana, who had kidnapped Rama's beloved wife, Sita, and held her hostage.

Arjuna looked at the historic spot and felt underwhelmed. He had always taken umbrage when people spoke of Rama being the best wielder of the bow the world had ever seen, feeling privately that such an accolade belonged solely to himself. He voiced his thoughts aloud saying, 'Why did Lord Rama make the monkeys haul stone from all over the place to build a bridge? Surely he could have used arrows for the purpose... after all, he was an expert archer. I myself would have done so and saved everyone a lot of trouble.'

An old monkey who was actually Hanuman, Rama's most loyal devotee, responded from the shadow of a tree under which he was resting, 'It seems to me that you have a mighty fine opinion of yourself. Do you actually think that you could have done better than Lord Rama? He was twice the archer you are but he had none of your arrogance. And he was also blessed with common sense, unlike you. He knew that a bridge of arrows could never withstand the weight of the mighty army of monkeys led by the noble King Sugreeva.'

Arjuna was angered that a mere monkey would dare to speak to him in this manner. He answered in anger, 'What would a foolish ape like you know about warfare? I stand by what I have said. If I were to build a bridge of arrows, an entire army, no matter whether it consisted of monkeys or donkeys, could have easily crossed over to Lanka.'

Hanuman smiled coldly to himself and decided that the mortal who thought himself superior to Rama was in desperate need of a lesson. 'Enough of useless talk! Why don't you build a bridge of arrows and then we will see if it can bear my puny self, let alone the weight of an entire army. If you succeed, I'll be your slave but since that will never come to be, what will I win if you lose our little wager?'

'I shall end my life on this very spot if the bridge collapses...' Arjuna said, confident that his bridge made entirely of arrows from his trusty bow would bear the weight of the entire population of the world.

Taking a deep breath, Arjuna drew back the bowstring and sent forth a cluster of arrows that rained down upon the blue waters in a steady stream before aligning themselves perfectly to form a causeway. Within moments a gargantuan construction lay glistening under the sun as the arrows reflected back the beams of light the Sun God tossed their way.

Hanuman looked at the creation with scant respect before playing out an elaborate charade of an aged monkey shuffling across to the causeway, while Arjuna looked on with barely concealed disdain. But no sooner had the monkey laid a toe on the bridge than the entire thing collapsed and disappeared into the sea.

Arjuna was aghast and unable to believe his own eyes. His magnificent construction had been shattered by a mere monkey's toe? Unbearable humiliation pounded his chest in a tidal wave of crushing despair. He could not bear to face anyone in the world knowing that he may not be as good an archer as he had thought.

Without a word, he built a pyre and prepared to consign his body to the flames. Hanuman looked on without pity, thinking that a person possessed of such arrogance deserved nothing better. But as he watched, a noble youth arrived on the scene. The young man stopped Arjuna as he was about to step into the pyre and insisted that he be told Arjuna's reason for his desire to end his own life. Arjuna explained everything to the stranger and thanked him for trying to save his life but added that there was nothing anybody could do as he had lost the wager and his life was forfeit.

The newcomer said, 'A wager made without witnesses is not considered valid and therefore, I cannot let you die. Why don't you build another bridge and the monkey can test its strength, while I act as judge?'

Since Arjuna and Hanuman were both amenable to his suggestion, the challenge was taken up again. This time, Arjuna prayed to Krishna and with the Lord's name on his lips, he began his task. When, as before, the arrow-bridge was completed, Hanuman stepped on it, but this time it held firm. The monkey walked further and even jumped on the bridge but it bore his might stolidly. In desperation, Hanuman assumed the gigantic form he had taken when he had made the leap across the ocean to reach Lanka. Before Arjuna's amazed eyes, he tried yet again to destroy the bridge. And for the final time, he failed.

At that moment, Arjuna and Hanuman realized that they were in the presence of divinity and the events unfolding before them were through the grace of Lord Vishnu. They both fell at the feet of the youth and before their eyes, he became Lord Vishnu in all his magnificence. He blessed them both for realizing the truth and addressed them saying, 'It seems to me that two of my most loyal devotees suffer from the same affliction of arrogance. Arjuna has learnt his lesson thanks to Hanuman, who led him to the brink of death. But now it is Hanuman's turn to make good on the conditions of the bet and repent for his excess pride in his great physical strength. Since you swore to be Arjuna's slave, Hanuman, you will perch on his standard when he rides into battle and use your voice to keep the morale of the troops high and terrify Arjuna's enemies with your war cry. In this way you will fulfil the conditions of the bet. The story of your challenge will serve as a lesson to mankind regarding the folly of pride.'

Arjuna and Hanuman smiled sheepishly at each other after Vishnu had vanished. Arjuna was the first to speak. 'I apologise for doubting Rama's prowess. It is hard for me to accept that anyone can be a better archer than me. In fact, Bheema and I often argue about which of us is better equipped to protect the family. And since you are both the sons of Vayu, it is not surprising that I had a similar falling out with you. But like Bheema, you are also my brother and it is wonderful that we met, despite the circumstances.'

Hanuman was charmed and decided that Arjuna was quite likeable despite his vanity and was undeserving of the initial aversion he had felt for him. 'You don't have to apologise to me. Vishnu himself said that we are both guilty of the same sin. And you say that Bheema is also inordinately proud of his strength, so perhaps I'll meet him one day too and give him the same scare I gave you...' And with eyes twinkling with mischief, the two conspirators bade each other farewell before going in different directions.

By this time, the term of Arjuna's exile was drawing to an end. Little did he realise that a most providential union with a special woman awaited him at this juncture. He continued his pilgrimage and reached Prabhasa, where he was met by Krishna. The two friends were happy to be reunited and Krishna convinced Arjuna to complete his exile in Dwaraka, the capital of the Yadavas. The two then proceeded to Dwaraka on Krishna's chariot and Arjuna regaled his friend with a colourful account of his adventures during his exile. The citizens of Dwaraka had assembled on the streets to welcome the famous hero and there was much celebration in the city to mark the Arjuna's arrival.

Arjuna had made the acquaintance of a number of Vrishni Princes in Drona's *gurukul* and one among them, Gada, was a particularly close friend of his. Gada had told him much about Subhadra, Vasudeva's daughter and Krishna's sister. She was a special young lady and the pride of the Yadava clan as her beauty was matched only by her innate goodness. Arjuna had been captivated by the description and scanned the crowds eagerly hoping for a glimpse of the fabled beauty.

After making sure that Arjuna had settled down comfortably and refreshed himself, Krishna took him for a stroll and pointed out some of the attractions the city offered. He discoursed at length on their unique features despite being well aware that his friend's thoughts lay elsewhere. Suddenly, Arjuna spotted Subhadra, talking and laughing with her companions. Kama, who had been a bosom companion of Arjuna's during his exile, struck again with his dart of love and the smitten hero knew that he would know no peace till he had made the ravishing Subhadra his own.

While Arjuna struggled to compose his thoughts, Krishna remarked with smiling nonchalance, 'Subhadra is a great favourite of my father's. And I suspect she harbours similar thoughts towards you. Gada has not been miserly in lavishing praise upon you; especially as he has always found her to be particularly receptive on the subject.'

Arjuna flushed slightly, knowing that to Krishna he would always be an open book. 'Tell me how I can make her mine. I will do whatever it takes,' he told his friend with the single-minded determination that was so typical of him.

Krishna reflected for a minute and said thoughtfully, 'The *swayamvara* is usually favoured by Kshatriyas but there is a lot of uncertainty involved in that method, as you know and as Karna found to his deep chagrin. Remember how Draupadi turned him down? I love and respect women but they tend to be flighty and it is hard to discern their thoughts. A valiant man should therefore take matters into his own hands and abduct the object of his desire instead of putting his faith on a woman's whims.'

Arjuna was pleased with this answer as the course of action prescribed by Krishna suited him exactly. 'Sounds like a good plan to me...and though I am sure she will choose me in a *swayamvara,* I think I will do the magnanimous thing and spare all of you the trouble and expense of organising one,' he said, eyes sparkling with anticipation and barely concealed mischief.

Aided by his co-conspirator, Arjuna waited at the shrine in Raivataka, where he was informed Subhadra would be present to offer her prayers. Mounted on Krishna's personal chariot and armed to the teeth, he stood in a fever of impatience. Yudhishthira had given his approval for the match and everything was going according to plan. Having completed her worship, which consisted mainly of entreaties to make Arjuna her husband, Subhadra stepped out of the shrine. Quick as a flash of lightning, Arjuna grabbed her by the waist and placed her firmly by his side in the chariot, and spurred the horses towards Indraprastha, noting with satisfaction that Subhadra had put up absolutely no resistance and had simply melted into his arms with a shy, adoring smile.

When the chief of the guards heard what had happened from Subhadra's hysterical companions and personal bodyguard, he rushed to Balarama. The news of Subhadra's abduction spread like wildfire and the Yadavas were furious. Led by Krishna's hot-tempered brother, Balarama, they prepared to follow Arjuna and crush the life out of him. Balarama thundered, 'Let us give him a taste of the Yadava might and show him what happens to those who are imprudent enough to snatch what rightfully belongs to their host and transgress the rules of hospitality!' The Yadavas noisily sounded their assent and made ready to give chase.

As emotions became increasingly volatile, Balarama noticed that Krishna was singularly calm and did not seem in the least concerned. He addressed his brother with some asperity, 'Krishna, how can you be so unconcerned, when that scoundrel has carried your beloved sister away? Is that how friends treat each other? Why do your hands not itch to strangle his impudent neck?'

'Brother Balarama, when you let that famous temper of yours get the better of you, your thinking is impaired. He is our cousin and a great man. We will not find a better match in all the three worlds for Subhadra. A heroic Kshatriya will not wait for his bride to be handed over to him like a dole of alms, nor will he place his faith in the uncertain outcome of a *swayamvara*. He will do what Arjuna has just done, to sustain his honour. Besides, you talk of defeating him in battle! Personally I think that is laughable since only Shiva is his equal in battle. I suggest you do the sensible thing and bring him back in peace,' his brother said consolingly.

Balarama was pacified by Krishna's words of common sense, and he sent courtiers to escort the adventurous Pandava Prince to the capital. Arjuna and Subhadra were welcomed and given a grand wedding to sanctify their union. There was much rejoicing on the streets as Arjuna became a son-in-law of the illustrious Yadava clan and the people were anxious to claim him as their own.

When the term of his exile ended, Arjuna went to Indraprastha with his new bride. His brothers and Kunti were delighted to see the pair. They were much taken with the Yadava Princess, who was beautiful, charming and virtuous. Draupadi alone was less than thrilled with the arrival of her exquisite rival. She sulked moodily in her quarters and refused to come out. Arjuna went to visit her and was greeted coldly with the words, 'Why have you come here? Go back to that Yadava filly. She will be waiting with her arms wide open. The flame of first love does not burn as brightly when a second makes its appearance. It loses its lustre and is eventually snuffed out. I wish you every happiness with your new wife, while I myself shall make a gracious exit, since my love for you has now become redundant.'

Arjuna was sorry to see her so miserable and tried to alleviate her pain, but Draupadi would not relent and continued to wallow in self-pity. In a bid to appease Draupadi, Arjuna ordered Subhadra to remove her fine clothes and dress in the homely apparel of a maid. Although the ordinary garments did little to disguise her beauty, she was told to present herself to Draupadi in this way. Subhadra walked tentatively into Draupadi's inner apartments and fell at her feet, trembling with fear and said, 'Sister, please accept me as your handmaid!'

This pathetic plea was enough to melt Draupadi's heart. Besides, she could not stay angry with Arjuna or the ones he loved for long. She embraced Subhadra and blessed her saying, 'May your husband be without a rival.'

Soon Subhadra gave birth to a beautiful baby boy. He was named Abhimanyu. The little boy had inherited the best of his father and uncles and was everybody's favourite. Blessed with a bright and cheery disposition as well as extraordinary good looks and talent, he spread happiness wherever he went. Abhimanyu would go on to bring much fame and honour to the family name, besides siring the lone successor to the Kuru throne. But in those halycon days, nobody knew that he would be snatched from their lives far too soon to enter the warrior's heaven.

10
Feeding Agni

Agni, the God of Fire, woke one day feeling lackadaisical and somewhat diminished in lustre. He could not understand why he felt this way since it was his nature to be vigorous and fiery. The Fire God approached Brahma, the Creator, to ask if there was anything he could do to regain his former state of well-being. Addressing his concerns, Brahma said, 'The innumerable sacrifices made to you on a daily basis over the years, especially the twelve-year-long sacrifice performed by King Swetaki and presided over by Durvasa and the generous servings of *ghee* employed for the purpose, have slackened your digestive system, which in turn has sapped your vitality. In order to regain your lustre and strength, you must line your stomach with enough animal fat by consuming the whole forest of Khandava.'

Thanking the Creator for his counsel, Agni made his way purposefully towards Khandava. He fell on the forest like a ravenous beast, blazing forth with all his might. The inexorable flames consumed all in their path. But suddenly, dark rain-bearing clouds amassed in the skies above and let fall their watery burden on the forest below. To Agni's dismay, the torrential sheets of water did not let up till the flames had been completely doused. Indra, Lord of the Heavens and wielder of the thunderbolt, had decided to intervene as his friend, Takshaka, King of the Serpents, dwelt in Khandava. Time and again, Agni was thwarted in his attempts to consume the forest and he became increasingly vexed. It was at this juncture that he was told by Brahma that Krishna and Arjuna had been espied relaxing on the banks of the Yamuna and he would do well to seek their help.

And so it came to be that Krishna and Arjuna were accosted by a fiery Brahmin who seemed to radiate heat from the very core of his being, while they were leisurely reminiscing about their adventures on the verdant banks of the Yamuna river. The two friends arose at once and paid obeisance to the Brahmin, offering their services to him.

The stranger said, 'I am ravenously hungy. Will you promise to assuage the pangs that are gnawing my insides?'

'You have my word. Tell me what kind of food you wish to eat and I shall procure it for you immediately,' Arjuna replied.

'I am Agni, the God of Fire, and I do not partake of the food of mortals. It is my desire to burn down the Khandava forest and devour its denizens. It is essential I do this for my well-being, but Indra is bent on preventing me from achieving my purpose as his friend Takshaka lives there with his family. I need the two of you to fight off the thousand-eyed God and his watery missiles while I go about my business, and also to prevent the creatures of the forest from escaping,' said Agni.

'We will be honoured to serve you, Lord of the flames,' responded Arjuna, pleased as always at the prospect of a new adventure. 'But we will need your help as our adversaries are celestial beings. I have many divine missiles at my disposal but my bow is not strong enough to withstand their power and neither is my chariot.

Therefore, I request you to provide me with a suitable bow, chariot, and an inexhaustible quiver of arrows. Krishna will also need a weapon that can match his supreme prowess. We have what it takes to carry out the arduous task you have assigned us but we need to be outfitted with the proper equipment in order to withstand the mighty Lord of the heavens and his fellow celestials.'

Agni closed his eyes and meditated on Varuna, the God of Water and a guardian of the universe. When the deity appeared before him, he gave him some instructions: 'Hurry to your abode and fetch me the Gandeeva bow, the two inexhaustible quivers, and the chariot drawn by swift steeds which has been emblazoned with the emblem of the ape. I know King Soma has given them to you but Arjuna is destined to have them as he will achieve mighty deeds with them. Fetch the celestial discus for Krishna as he is its rightful owner and it will serve him best.'

Varuna hastened to do Agni's bidding and soon Arjuna became the proud owner of the Gandeeva bow, the most coveted of all weapons, covered with the finest gold, and truly a thing of great beauty. It had been wrought by Brahma in days of yore for the sole purpose of ridding Mother Earth from the burden of evil she was forced to carry periodically and only a truly great man could own and use it for the purpose for which it was created. The Creator had wielded it for a thousand years before handing it over to Prajapati. Others who had the honour of wielding the divine bow were Indra (Shakra), King Soma, and Varuna. This fabled bow had rare powers and blessed was the man who had the good fortune to wield it. Arjuna loved it like a wife and was seldom seen without it.

Once, Yudhishthira was defeated soundly by Karna on the battlefield and driven all the way back to his quarters in the army camp. Arjuna came to check on his brother and Yudhishthira, thinking Karna had been killed, smiled with pleasure. But on discovering that Karna still lived, he lost his temper and berated Arjuna saying he was not worthy of the Gandeeva. The wielder of the Gandeeva was furious at the insult and whipped out his sword to decapitate his brother in order to fulfil a vow he had taken to kill any man who called him unworthy of his great bow. Krishna had to step between the feuding brothers to prevent his bosom friend from carrying out this threat. Such was the love Arjuna had for the Gandeeva. He carried it all his life and performed great deeds with it. And it was only towards the very end of his life that he returned it to Varuna at the behest of Agni, on the banks of the river Brahmaputra.

In addition to the Gandeeva, Arjuna was also given the inexhaustible quivers and a fully equipped chariot to which were yoked the fleetest steeds in the universe. Agni presented Krishna with the formidable Sudarshana *chakra* and Kaumodaki mace. The two heroes were thus equipped and rendered invincible in battle.

Arjuna climbed into his chariot and twanged his great bow. The dreadful sound that emanated from it chilled with fear the hearts of all who heard. Krishna held up the wonder discus on his finger. The two warriors were ready to do battle and they charged off in opposing directions. Arjuna would take on Indra while Krishna would prevent the inhabitants of the forest from escaping Agni's hunger.

Assured of protection, Agni conjured up raging flames that licked the edges of the forest. The fiery tendrils became fiercer as they made their foray inwards. Soon the entire forest was consumed by towering walls of thick flame. The heat that emanated from Khandava was so overpowering that it threatened to scorch the very heavens. Water bodies in the forest boiled over, killing the creatures that lived within, while those near Khandava evaporated completely. This awesome spectacle was reported to the Lord of Heaven and Indra was annoyed. He made ready to foil Agni's efforts yet again.

Massive clouds covered the sky and heavy rain lashed down on Khandava. But it was not enough to stop Agni, and the water dried in mid-air. Undaunted, Indra sent forth more clouds which had drawn their moisture from the great oceans and Khandava was buffeted on all sides by torrential sheets of water. Thick black smoke rose up and hung over the forest like a pall. Arjuna sprang into action. Arrows flowed ceaselessly from his great bow and formed a sheet against the downpour. This protective shield prevented a single drop of water from reaching the burning forest and also sealed off all escape routes for its creatures.

As it happened, Takshaka was not in the forest that day, but his wife and son Ashwasena, were there. Indra whipped up a ferocious storm in the vicinity of Arjuna's chariot, which the hero had to contend with; and simultaneously, Ashwasena's mother swallowed her son and made an abortive attempt to escape. But Arjuna saw her and pierced her head with a well placed arrow, killing her instantly. Furious, Indra conjured up a gale to throw Arjuna off balance. It was at this moment that Ashwasena made good his escape from his refuge within his dead mother. Arjuna was furious that the wily serpent had used his mother's love to escape and pronounced a curse, 'O Ashwasena! Coward that you are, nobody will ever speak well of you.' Krishna and Agni also made their displeasure towards Ashwasena clear.

After this incident, Ashwasena bore an abiding hatred for Arjuna and waited in patience to avenge his mother's death. When the battle of Kurukshetra had been in progress for many days, Arjuna and Karna met in fierce combat. Sensing an opportunity, the wily Naga assumed the shape of an arrow and snuck into Karna's quiver. Unaware of its presence, Karna aimed that terrible arrow at Arjuna. The deadly missile flew towards its target unerringly, poisoned with the venomous malice of the serpent. Krishna, sensing its presence, pressed down hard on the chariot so that it would sink into the earth. The thwarted arrow barely missed its mark, piercing the golden diadem that had been given to Arjuna by his heavenly father instead. So potent was the poison that it scorched the diadem before sending it plummeting to the earth.

The disgruntled Naga then returned to Karna and said, 'I would have slain our mutual foe if you had only aimed straight! Make haste and use me again and this time we shall not fail!'

'Who are you?' a bemused Karna queried.

'I am King Takshaka's son, Ashwasena. My mother was murdered by that brute of a man who stands yonder, and I am determined to avenge her death. So make haste and make sure that your aim is true this time.'

But Karna spoke with lofty disdain saying, 'Karna does not depend on others to win his battles for him. Go from here for I have no need of your services. I am more than capable of destroying Arjuna unaided.'

Inflamed by Karna's rejection, Ashwasena reverted to his own shape and loomed large over Arjuna's chariot, determined to kill him before Karna did. Krishna warned Arjuna of the origins of the loathsome creature that stood before them. Remembering the coward from Khandava, Arjuna sent six sharp arrows zooming into the sky in rapid succession and cut the great serpent to pieces.

But these events were obscured by the mists of time and in the meantime, Arjuna, engrossed in the task entrusted him by Agni, rued the manner in which Ashwasena had escaped. He vented his feelings by turning his wrath on Indra. Unloosing the *Vayavya* missile, he effectively scattered the clouds, allowing the sun to beam down on the forest and complement the efforts of Agni. Krishna had also been busy – his discus ruthlessly mowing down all who sought to escape the fiery appetite of Agni. Indra looked down and was pleased with the valour exhibited by his son but even as he marvelled at Arjuna's prodigious skill, he made plans to take the fight to Arjuna.

Accompanied by the celestials, Indra decided to confront Arjuna and Krishna in direct battle. A deadly encounter followed with Arjuna and Krishna holding their ground and repulsing the celestial onslaught time and again. Indra and his Gods were soon wearied as they had never encountered warriors of this calibre before. Suddenly a divine voice rang out, 'Khandava is fated to be destroyed in this manner. Know that Krishna and Arjuna cannot be defeated in battle. Retreat gracefully.' On hearing this, the celestials returned to their abodes and Krishna and Arjuna blew on their conches triumphantly. Agni was jubilant and blazed on for an entire fortnight, thriving in the furnace of his own making as he felt his lost vigour returning to him in full measure.

Khandava and its denizens were consumed almost completely when Krishna and Arjuna spotted an *asura* running for his life, closely pursued by Agni. Seeing the discus raised with deadly purpose by Krishna, the *asura,* known as Maya, threw himself at Arjuna's feet and begged for sanctuary, which was mercifully granted. Thus, apart from Maya, Ashwasena, and the Saranga birds, which were the offspring of the sage Mandapala, Khandava and its fauna were completely destroyed to sate Agni's hunger.

The Fire God was pleased with the two heroes and blessed them for the successful manner in which they had carried out the task assigned to them. As a tribute to the marvellous feat achieved by Krishna and Arjuna, the celestials rained down flowers upon their heads, accompanied by loud cries of approbation.

Indra, accompanied by his retinue, came down to earth in order to felicitate the warriors and he granted Arjuna a boon. Ever devoted to his quest for excellence as a warrior, Arjuna requested his divine father to give him various missiles and deadly weapons. To this, Indra replied: 'You will have your heart's desire when the time is right. In the near future, when you come to acquire the grace of the three-eyed Lord, the weapons you seek will be yours. May the Goddess of Fortune ever smile upon you.' So saying, Indra departed, his heart filled with pride over the deeds accomplished by his mighty offspring.

Flushed with their success, Arjuna and Krishna, accompanied by Maya, walked towards the banks of the Yamuna. At that quiet spot, Maya voiced his gratitude. 'Arjuna, I owe you my life. Caught between the terrible flames of Agni and Krishna's discus, I would have travelled to Yama's abode if you had not granted me refuge. It behoves me to return the favour in any way I can. So I beg you to command me.'

Arjuna smiled indulgently saying, 'Your generous offer alone is payment enough and I only ask that you always remain as well disposed to us as you are now.'

Maya would not be thwarted however. 'I am an accomplished architect, the Vishwakarma of the *asura*s. My talent, I am sure, will be of some use to you. Allow me to serve you in some manner'.

'You feel indebted to me for saving your life and therefore I cannot bring myself to command you. However, I do not wish to disappoint you. Do Krishna's bidding and I will consider that as service to me,' replied Arjuna gently.

Maya then turned to Krishna, who ordered him to build a grand palace and royal court (*sabha*) for Yudhishthira. The *asura* was delighted and promised to do his utmost. 'The palace I will build for Yudhishthira will be my crowning achievement and will be unequalled in the three worlds. It will serve as a monument to the tremendous feat achieved by Arjuna today and the compassion he showed towards another being. People will talk about it long after we have departed this world and sing Arjuna's praise.'

In this manner, Yudhishthira came to acquire the magnificent *sabha* that was the pride of his kingdom. True to his word, Maya made it something very special and he successfully completed it in fourteen months. The construction occupied an area of five thousand square cubits. There were columns of pure gold that were encrusted with rare and precious stones that twinkled merrily and dazzled the eye of the beholder. Maya created artificial ponds with marble steps leading into them and placed lotuses made of rubies and emeralds. He also made bejewelled fish, birds and tortoises. Entire floors were paved with crystal that resembled the clear surface of water. The splendour of the *sabha* was unrivalled in the known world.

Unfortunately, it also stoked the flames of Duryodhana's greed and envy to new heights and prompted him to deprive the Pandavas of their kingdom and send them into exile for fourteen long years.

11
Arjuna's Quest for Celestial Weapons

Yudhishthira, in keeping with the wishes of his ancestors and in consultation with Krishna, performed the *Rajasuya* sacrifice at Indraprastha, after bringing all the kingdoms of the ancient domain under his suzerainty. This sacrifice would put him on equal footing with Indra, the King of the *Devas* and entitled him to share the former's throne at Indralokha. In this quest, he was ably aided by his brothers. Arjuna, Bhima, Sahadeva and Nakula, rode out to the north, east, south and west respectively, using their individual talents to subjugate mighty rulers. The success of the sacrifice, the prosperity of Indraprastha, and the collective achievements of the Pandavas, which won them the respect and love of all who encountered them, infuriated the eldest Kaurava. Jealousy threatened to consume him entirely and he withdrew into a shell of bitterness and toxic rage.

In order to lift him from his depression, Duryodhona's uncle, Shakuni, hatched a typically artful scheme to deprive the Pandavas of their kingdom and their possessions. Yudhishthira's fondness for dice was well known, even though he was not a skilful payer. At the insistence of Duryodhana and against the wishes of the Kuru elders, Dhritarashtra sent Vidura to invite the Pandavas to a game of dice. Shakuni, playing on behalf of Duryodhana and using foul methods, cheated the guileless but gambling-addicted Yudhishthira into staking and losing his kingdom, his brothers, himself, and finally, his wife Draupadi.

As if the Pandavas had not been humiliated enough, Duhshasana, Duryodhana's brother and co-conspirator, dragged Draupadi by the hair and brought her before the gathering of men, to be displayed as their slave. He cruelly ignored her pleas that she was not fit to be seen in assembly as she was menstruating and was wearing only a single cloth. The assembled gathering was horrified at the debased act being perpetrated before their eyes. But Karna laughed at the Princess and told her, 'You are now a slave of the Kauravas and can no longer afford your haughty airs. Perhaps you should throw yourself at the feet of your masters and beg one of them to accept you as his wife. Pray that this time you will be considered worthy enough not to be gambled away.' With these petty words, Karna paid the Princess back for her humiliating rejection of him at her *swayamvara*.

Seeing Draupadi stand trembling with shame and blanching from the intensity of Karna's hatred for her, Bheema lost his temper. Throwing a look filled with menace at Karna and quaking with fury, he berated Yudhishthira in the harshest terms for reducing them to this state. 'How could you do this to Draupadi? Even a hardened gambler has the decency not to stake the whore who shares his bed. Sahadeva! Bring me a flaming torch! I will burn the hands that were depraved enough to commit the foul act of gambling away a beloved wife. They would have done well to have strangled their owner rather than to have performed this wretched deed.'

Yudhishthira lowered his head in shame. Arjuna urgently addressed his raging brother, who was like a maddened elephant about to run amok. 'Bheema! Get a hold of your temper! See how those hyenas are laughing at this display of dissent amongst us. Our unity is our biggest strength and you should not do anything to jeopardise that. Be patient, let them have their day. Our time will come and we will have our revenge.'

Bheema calmed down a little on hearing these judicious words, although he continued to glower at the Kauravas, his eyes dark with the promise of a day of reckoning in the future.

Goaded by Karna, Duhshasana proceeded to pull off Draupadi's garment. It stands to the eternal shame of the Kurus that none went to her rescue, despite her heartrending cries for help. Duryodhana went a step further by slapping his thighs lewdly and inviting her to come and sit on his lap. Draupadi closed her eyes in shame and called to Krishna, the manifestation of the universal protector, to preserve her honour. Krishna responded at once and a miracle took place that would live in the hearts and minds of men and women forever.

Duhshasana's efforts to rip off Draupadi's garment proved futile. To his frustration, every time he tugged at the single garment, a new one took its place. The discarded garments formed a massive pile on the floor but he remained unsuccessful in disrobing the wife of the Pandavas. Finally he gave in to sheer fatigue and collapsed wearily.

Bhima's temper flared again and he pronounced a terrible oath: 'May I rot in hell for all eternity if I do not destroy the evil Duhshasana in battle and drink his blood. And Duryodhana, your days are numbered, for I shall smash your thighs in battle with my mace!'

'Mark my words, Karna, I swear you will meet your end at my hands for the countless wrongs you have done us!' Arjuna vowed.

'Vile Shakuni! Sahadeva will put an end to your cheating days when he claims your worthless life! And I will personally dispatch Uluka, your son, to the nether regions!' Nakula promised, his handsome face rendered savage by the force of his passion.

Realizing that divine intervention had saved Draupadi and his sons were sliding recklessly towards a great precipice that would bring about their fall, Dhritarashtra finally acted. He returned their lost Kingdom to the Pandavas and requested them with almost inane insensitivity, to forgive and forget the terrible wrongs they had suffered at the hands of his sons. Sick at heart, the Pandavas trudged homewards.

Duryodhana was furious with his father for returning his ill-gotten gains. He alternately badgered and emotionally blackmailed his father into finally ordering the Pandavas to a rematch and another game of dice. The loser would have to go into exile for twelve years and spend the thirteenth year in hiding. If discovered, they would have to go into exile again for the same duration. Yudhishthira agreed to these terms, choosing to adhere to the laws of *dharma* and the Kshatriya tradition of not refusing a challenge, rather than following the laws of common sense. Shakuni cast his loaded dice again, and won again. The Pandavas lost their Kingdom once again and were exiled for thirteen years.

Dressed in nothing more than bark, the Pandavas, accompanied by Draupadi, left their Kingdom, having entrusted their elderly mother, Kunti, to the care of Vidura. The citizens followed them to the dge of the forest, beating their breasts, tearing their hair and sobbing wildly. They cursed Dhritarashtra and Duryodhana for their treatment of the righteous Pandavas.

Utterly dejected, the Pandavas headed to Dwaitavana, where it had been decided they would begin the term of exile. Their surroundings were beautiful and restful but did little to soothe the injured spirits of the Pandavas. They all felt tormented and grief-stricken. Draupadi was particularly unhappy, her lovely tresses hanging limply beside her wan face. She had vowed not to tie up her hair again till Duhshasana had received his comeuppance at the hands of Bheema.

The brothers discussed their situation and found there was little comfort to be had. Duryodhana would certainly not be idle during their exile. While they were languishing in the forest, he would use the time and money from the Pandavas' treasury to consolidate his position and make powerful alliances. The three most formidable warriors of the age – Bhishma, Drona, and Karna, would fight on the Kaurava side. They were all disciples of the great Parashurama and had celestial weapons to call upon. Things looked dark indeed for the Pandavas.

While they were brooding thus in Dwaitavana, Veda Vyasa came to visit them. He spoke words of comfort to the brothers and helped lighten the burden of anxiety they had been carrying around. Drawing Yudhishthira aside, he spoke thus: 'Do not fear the Kauravas. Their ill-gotten gains will prove to be their undoing in the long run. They will wallow in luxury and waste their time in self-indulgence. In the meantime, you will have to use the years of exile constructively to gain advantages over your enemies.'

'Your words fill me with hope and purpose and my heart is filled with gratitude,' answered Yudhishthira.

'I shall shed some light on the path that you must follow. Listen carefully, for I am about to bequeath the secret knowledge of *Pratismriti* to you. Teach it to Arjuna, for he will achieve great things through its use. Tell him to perform penances to win the favour of Shiva and Indra in order to procure weapons that will enable him to wipe out his enemies and reinstate you on the throne. In the meantime, the rest of you should leave this place and go elsewhere to cleanse your hearts and please the Gods.'

'Yours words have pierced the darkness that has held us in thrall for so many days. We will do exactly as you say. I humbly beg of you to bless us and remember us in your prayers,' said Yudhishthira, standing before the sage with folded hands.

'So be it. Take heart, for justice is on your side and everything you have lost will be returned to you,' spoke Vyasa gently.

After the great sage had departed, Yudhishthira wasted little time in calling Arjuna and outlining the plan of action, as advised by Vyasa. He imparted his recently acquired knowledge to his younger brother, summoned the rest of his family, and then told Arjuna, 'Take the secret knowledge I have given you and use it to please Shiva and Indra, so that you may acquire the weapons needed to annihilate our enemies. The hopes of your family are invested in you. Go with our blessings... Your destiny awaits you!'

Arjuna was embraced by each of his brothers, who were too overwrought to say anything to him. Draupadi's magnificent eyes were wet with tears when she addressed Arjuna saying,: 'The path before you is difficult and filled with obstacles but if anyone can overcome them, it is you. We all have the utmost confidence in you. Every moment we spend away from you will feel like an eon and you will be in our thoughts constantly. I pray to all the Gods to keep you safe and help you achieve our collective goal.'

With a heavy heart, Arjuna said his farewells and left on his mission to propitiate the Gods and acquire celestial weapons. The yogic science of *Pratismriti* gave Arjuna the ability to journey with the rapidity of thought and he soon reached the Himalayas. This remote and mountainous region was believed to be frequented by the Gods and was the haven of devotion and spirituality.

Equipped with his beloved Gandeeva, Arjuna negotiated his way across the rough terrain. At Indrakila, he was stopped by a venerable sage who had been meditating under a tree. The ancient being seemed to emanate an aura of goodness and vitality. He asked, 'Who are you? And why have you brought weapons to a place that does not harbour violence of any kind?'

'I am a man on a mission,' replied Arjuna.

'Be that as it may, there is no need for you to carry your weapons here. You will find there is little use for them. Why don't you discard them and proceed freely from here?'

Arjuna declined politely but firmly and made ready to move on. The stranger was pleased with the strength of his purpose and unflinching resolve and so revealed his true identity. It was none other than the Lord Indra, who had come to bless his son as he embarked on this great endeavour, and to encourage his efforts. Indra said: 'I am pleased with you Arjuna, my son. Ask me for a boon. Anything you desire shall be yours.'

Arjuna folded his hands reverentially and replied, 'I seek divine weapons and missiles, as well as the knowledge pertaining to their use.'

'Why don't you ask for something more pleasant?' his father asked to tease him. 'It is unfortunate that fate has dictated that you will face inordinate toil and suffering in this world. But you have a choice – you can abandon this life and come with me to heaven, where a life of ease and luxury awaits. Just say the word, and I will take you to paradise, where you will be elevated to the ranks of divinity.'

'Divine Father, your concern for my welfare warms my heart. However, heaven will be worse than hell without my brothers at my side. It is true that we have endured much and lost even more. Our enemies have the upper hand and I will never forgive myself if I abandon my brothers at this time of dire need. Yudhishthira has placed his trust in me and has sent me on a quest to find the means to crush our opponents. I will not let him or the others down. Our fates are linked for better or worse and I would not have it any other way.'

'Your selflessness is a lesson for all mortals. I am proud to be your father. You will be granted your boon after you have seen Shiva with your own eyes. Strive to that end and success will be yours.' So saying, Indra returned to heaven.

Arjuna began performing *tapas* in earnest. Dressed in nothing but bark and deerskins and subsisting on next to nothing, he focused his entire being on the three-eyed God. His penances increased in severity as the months rolled by. He stopped eating and not even water touched his lips. Air and utter devotion were his only sustenance. Impervious to heat or cold, light or darkness, and every bodily need, he channelled every ounce of his being towards winning Shiva's favour. The intensity of his austerities was such that even his surroundings became affected. Streams dried up and vegetation died away, unable to withstand the heat of his penance. The sages in the vicinity were disturbed and they rushed to Shiva for help. On hearing their worries, Shiva reassured them: 'Do not worry! His intentions are pure and worthy. I shall give him what he desires.'

Shiva and his consort, Parvati, disguised themselves as hunters and set off to meet Arjuna. They were accompanied by their retinue, similarly garbed. As they drew near, Shiva spotted an *asura* in the form of a boar, charging towards Arjuna, with the clear intent of killing him. Both the Lord and his devotee dispatched their arrows at the same instant, killing the loathsome creature instantly.

Arjuna was not happy to see the hunter and said, 'It was boorish of you to shoot, knowing that it was my quarry. I saw it first and shot it. Give up your foolish claim or I shall make you do so.'

'It is you who are claiming credit though you don't deserve it. Vainglorious people such as you deserve death at my hands,' resplied the hunter.

At the end of this exchange, a fierce duel broke out between the two. Arjuna was astonished by the prowess of his antagonist. His own infallible arrows missed their mark and inexplicably became absorbed by the hunter's body. Worse, he himself sustained countless injuries and his body became bruised and bleeding, while his opponent remained unmarked. Suddenly, the inexhaustible quiver of arrows given to him by Agni became empty. Shocked, Arjuna wondered if he were fighting a God or a demon. Deciding that none but Shiva could stop him in combat, he increased the ferocity of his attack.

Arjuna lunged at the hunter, trying to trap him with his bowstring but his bow was snatched away effortlessly. Picking up the empty quivers, Arjuna attempted to smash his tormentor's skull but the quivers themselves broke into smithereens. The two opponents began an intense bout of wrestling with the Pandava getting the worst of it. Pummelled to within an inch of his life, Arjuna fashioned a *lingam* with his bleeding hands, placed a garland of flowers around it and began praying to Shiva for help.

To Arjuna's surprise, the garland sailed through the air and landed on the hunter's broad shoulders. The truth dawned on him and he flung himself at Shiva's feet, begging forgiveness. But Shiva raised him up and embraced him. As he received the Lord's healing touch, Arjuna's myriad wounds disappeared and he felt revitalised. Shiva spoke, 'Your courage and fortitude are unmatched. I am pleased with you. In acknowledgement, I grant you divine vision. Henceforth, you will be unconquerable in battle as none, be it man, *Deva*, or *asura*, will be able to withstand your might."

Shiva and Parvati then resumed their divine forms and stood before Arjuna, who worshipped before them on bended knees. Pleased, Shiva offered him another boon. Arjuna requested the *Paashupata* weapon, which was Shiva's favourite. It could produce innumerable spears, maces, and arrows that could annihilate whole armies. Even the Gods were not proficient in its use. Shiva assented and said: 'It is my favourite weapon, although it is extremely dangerous. When used unwisely, it can destroy the entire universe. However, you have proved you are worthy of this weapon and I shall give it to you along with instructions on how to release and withdraw it.'

In this manner, Arjuna obtained the *Paashupata* from Shiva. In his magnanimity, the Lord returned his Gandeeva bow as well and restored the inexhaustible quivers. He then instructed Arjuna to go to heaven, where he would obtain more celestial weapons.

Shiva and Parvati then disappeared. Arjuna stood rooted to the spot for long moments, unable to believe his good fortune. He went over the scene of his encounter with Shiva over and over again in his mind. Surely, he was the most blessed among men for not only had he seen Shiva, but he had been touched by him, spoken to him, and received the Lord's favourite weapon from his own hands. Flushed with elation, Arjuna thought pityingly of his enemies. They would pay heavily for their sins. He would make sure of it.

While he mused thus, the guardians of the universe appeared before him, one at a time. Varuna, the presiding deity of the Water Bodies; Kubera, the God of Wealth; Yama, the God of Death; and Indra, the Overlord of Heaven, appeared before him. These were the *Lokapalas,* the guardians of the universe and overlords of their respective domains. They had come to gift him with divine *astras* that would help rid *Bhoomi Devi* (Mother Earth), of the burden of evil she carried, or at the very least, lighten it considerably.

On account of his penances and recent encounter with Shiva, Arjuna was bathed in a radiant glow. Yama gave Arjuna his *Danda* and instructed him how to best use it to his advantage. Varuna, in turn, presented the mighty Pandava with his most powerful weapon, the *Varunapasha,* which had stood him in good stead in many memorable battles against the evil *asura*s. Kubera presented him with the *Antardhana,* which could vanquish enemies with ease. Finally, Indra addressed his son: 'On the strength of your remarkable achievements, you have been elevated to the status of a celestial. It is time for you to visit *Swargalokha*. The *Devas* require your assistance in certain pressing matters. Prepare yourself, for I will send for you soon.'

Arjuna worshipped the *Lokapalas* with fruits and flowers, thus further endearing himself to them. They blessed him in unison and assured him of success in the terrible battle that loomed ahead. Then the divine beings returned to their respective abodes, leaving Arjuna with his heart filled to the brim.

In due course, Matali, Indra's charioteer, made his appearance, guiding the wondrous flying steeds through the clouds. On landing, he requested Arjuna to step into the chariot as his father Indra, awaited him in Amaravati. Anxious to carry out his divine father's wishes, the ever-dutiful son purified himself quickly in the Ganga and accompanied Matali to heaven.

Marvellous sights bemused Arjuna's senses as he soared through the skies. He saw a multitude of heavenly beings stationed at various points in the sky and they dazzled the eye of the beholder with the brilliant light that emanated from them. Matali informed him that these were the souls of those who had been the most virtuous and earned the most merit during their tenure on earth. When viewed from the world of men, they appeared as stars. Arjuna was charmed with this stellar information.

The captivating journey through the skies ended all too soon and Arjuna laid eyes on Amaravati – the famed city of the *Devas*. The beauty of this slice of heaven took his breath away. He felt doubly honoured as Indraprastha, his own capital city, built by the Pandavas, had often earned favourable comparison to Amaravati.

The denizens of the city thronged to pay their respects to their beloved King's son.

Arjuna was led directly to Indra's palace, where his father greeted him with much pomp and ceremony. Embracing him warmly, Indra bade the Pandava sit beside him on the throne. All the *Devas* in attendance conveyed their felicitations. After this reception, Arjuna was taken to rooms that had been specially prepared for him; and his every need was catered to. A bevy of beautiful attendants bathed him in a large tub filled with perfumed water and dressed him in the finest apparel. The choicest delicacies were prepared for him and the best entertainers in the realm performed their art for him.

However, even in the midst of all this luxury, Arjuna indulged himself sparingly and that too, out of respect for Indra. His thoughts were seldom far removed from his brothers. Thinking of them and Draupadi made him sorrowful as he fully understood the hardships and privations they were enduring.

Bearing this in mind, Arjuna worked hard under the watchful eye of his father. He was given information about the divine *astra*s he had in his possession, and others he received during his sojourn in heaven. Indra presented him with his personal weapon, the *Vajra,* which would enable him to marshal the forces of thunder and lightning for warlike purposes. But in addition, Indra wished Arjuna to learn music and dance from Chitrasena, as he foresaw these skills would prove useful in Arjuna's thirteenth year of exile.

One day, the great *rishi* Lomasha, arrived in Amaravati in the course of his wanderings in the three worlds. He bowed his head to the overlord of heaven but was surprised to see Arjuna sharing the celestial throne. It was extremely unusual for mortals to be shown such favour and the *rishi* wondered if it was merited. Reading his thoughts, Indra proceeded to enlighten the venerable saint on the subject. 'Arjuna is not a mere mortal, although he was born as one to the peerless Kunti. The third of the noble Pandava brothers, he has already distinguished himself, and had the good fortune to meet the three-eyed God. He is in Amaravati to obtain celestial weapons to eliminate the evil Kauravas.'

Pleased with the increasing respect he saw in Lomasha's eyes, Indra continued, 'Arjuna and Krishna are none other than Nara and Narayana, reborn on earth. They lived in Badari, at the mouth of the Ganga, and performed many feats of glory. They consented to live among men to fulfil my personal request. Evil has gained the upper hand on earth as various *asura*s and men, by dint of their penances, have won boons that have made them reckless, arrogant and wicked. Arjuna and Krishna were born to fight the forces of darkness and restore light.'

On hearing this, Lomasha went over what he knew about the famed duo in his mind. The ancient *rishi*s, Nara and Narayana, commanded a great deal of respect in all three worlds. They were the sons of Dharma and Ahimsa, the upholders of righteousness and non-violence respectively. The austerities they performed frightened the Gods as they suspected the duo had nefarious designs in thus seeking to accumulate ascetic merit. So they sent the most talented *apsara*s and musicians from among the *Gandharva*s to tempt the holy men and thwart them in their purpose. Amused with this transparent ploy and choosing to refrain from pronouncing a well-deserved curse on the frivolous *Gandharva*s, Narayana produced from his thigh a damsel whose beauty made the *apsara*s seem plain by comparison. Thoroughly abashed, the *Gandharva*s obtained permission to make Urvashi, as the damsel was named (having emerged from the *uru* or thigh of Narayana), one of their own. Seeking the blessings of the two *rishi*s, they returned to their abode.

Another story that bore testament to the *rishis'* greatness, was the tale of King Dambhodbhava. This monarch ruled over the earth and was extremely arrogant. Taking umbrage at his treatment of them as inferiors, the Brahmins, with incredible shrewdness, suggested to him that Nara and Narayana were in fact, the most superior beings in creation. Incensed, the King took the bait and hastened to the hermitage of the two *rishi*s. He challenged the ascetics and provoked them beyond measure. Nara took on the mighty monarch and his huge army single-handedly and having decimated them, brought King Dambhodbhava to his knees.

Legend also had it that while churning the ocean of milk in order to procure the nectar of immortality or *amrita,* Narayana requested the help of Nara to prevent the *asura*s from getting their hands on it. Nara was only too happy to oblige his old friend, and using his infallible arrows to sever rocks from the mountains, he blocked the route to heaven, where the blessed nectar was safely ensconced, forcing the *asura*s to retreat to their proper place in the bowels of the earth and the fathomless depths of the ocean.

As he came to the end of his recollection, Lomasha felt privileged to have met Arjuna and bowed his head in respect and admiration. Indra then requested the *rishi* to visit the Pandavas, who were pining for their beloved sibling and give them the joyous tidings of Arjuna's successful accomplishment of his goals. He also instructed Lomasha to take the Pandavas on a *Teerthayatra* and visit various sacred places so that their sins could be purged and their souls purified. The saint assented to all of this and carrying Arjuna's message of love to his brothers, he departed.

When Arjuna's term of instruction under Chitrasena drew to an end, Indra summoned him, for it was time for the formidable warrior to perform some tasks for the *Devas* in return for the favour they had shown him. Indra then said to Arjuna: 'The *Danava*s or *Nivatakavacha*s, are sworn enemies of the *Devas*. They make their home in the middle of the ocean. There are thirty million of them and they are terrifying foes as their power and skill is tremendous. As your preceptor, I ask for their destruction.'

'Consider it done, revered father!' replied Arjuna instantly.

Matali arrived to serve as Arjuna's charioteer. Donning the armour of impenetrable mail and picking up *Devadatta,* a conch shell – both gifts from the celestials, the gallant warrior made ready to leave. His trusty Gandeeva, the inexhaustible quivers, and the newly acquired divine *astra*s, completed his arsenal.

Matali drove the chariot into the depths of the ocean, past the multitudes of rainbow-hued fishes, gargantuan tortoises, and other sea creatures. When they arrived at the city of the *Danava*s, the denizens fled in terror and barred the gates, thinking that the *Devas,* led by Indra, were mounting another attack. Arjuna blew his conch in challenge, and the sound sent vibrations rippling across the world. Seeing but a lone warrior, the evil hordes armed themselves and mounted a massive attack. They attacked Arjuna in droves, like waves crashing on a single rock. But they were rebuffed time and again as the wielder of the Gandeeva ploughed through their defences like an avenging fury.

Realizing that brute force and strength of numbers would not be sufficient to hold the mysterious warrior in check, the *Danava*s resorted to illusory tactics. Suddenly, Arjuna found himself besieged by huge rocks that rained on him from above; torrential sheets of water that pounded him; and fierce flames that erupted around him. Using the *Madhava* missile given him by Indra, Arjuna pulverised the rocks. The weapon known as *Vishoshana,* took care of the torrential rain and dried it in mid-air. He took care of the flames by dousing them with yet another divine *astra*.

No sooner had Arjuna tackled these threats than the battleground was engulfed in inky darkness. Matali, who had been in many fierce battles and never turned a hair, was completely shaken as his senses failed him in the blackness that surrounded them. He cried out in fear and an infuriated Arjuna destroyed the illusion of darkness. The *Danava* hordes then became invisible to a man and succeeded in perplexing the Pandava, who was beginning to tire from the relentless onslaught on his senses. Sensing his distress, Matali encouraged and spurred him on. Arjuna grabbed Indra's favourite weapon, the *Vajra,* and hurled it at the offending *Danava*s. The powerful weapon pierced through the spell that caused the illusion and destroyed it. Stripping them of their disguise and deception, the *Vajra* brought about the complete destruction of the *Danava*s. Matali was impressed and told Arjuna his valour and prowess were unmatched.

While returning to Amaravati, Arjuna noticed a city that seemed to be encased in a strange bubble. Matali informed him that it was another stronghold of the *Danava*s. The city was known as Hiranyapuri, which was under the control of a woman called Puloma. Her sons, the *Kalakeya*s, resided there and within its protective boundaries, spun their webs of evil. They had obtained a boon from Brahma which did not allow the celestials to touch them. It was their foolhardy assumption that if the Gods themselves could not bring about their death, then surely no mere mortal could do so. This was about to cost them a heavy price. Arjuna released the *Paashupata* missile and immediately scores of weird beings emerged. Their faces appeared savage and they were armed with deadly weapons. They fell on the *Danava* forces like a ravenous pack of wolves and exterminated them, leaving not a single *Danava* standing.

Having successfully accomplished his mission, Arjuna returned to Amaravati, where he was hailed with the respect due a conquering hero. Indra and the other *Devas* sang his praises and told him he was invincible. The Kaurava warriors like Bhishma, Drona, Kripa, Karna, and Ashwatthama, they said, were nothing more than ants who would be crushed under his feet. In a show of approbation, Indra presented Arjuna with impenetrable armour, that had been made especially for him. He placed a golden diadem on Arjuna's head, which thereafter earned him the moniker, *Kiriti* or 'The Diademed One'. Silks and precious jewels were also presented to him.

Arjuna's quest for celestial weapons had been a resounding success and his sojourn in heaven was now at an end. It was time for him to return to his brothers. The Pandavas and Draupadi had completed their *Teerthayatra* and were awaiting the return of Arjuna at Badari. One day, they saw a bright light in the sky which seemed to come closer and closer to them. They realized it was a chariot that shone with the brilliance of a billion suns. And to their immense joy, Arjuna was standing in the chariot, decked in fine clothes and bedecked with exquisite ornaments.

Arjuna leaped down from the chariot and rushed to his brothers. He paid his respects to Yudhishthira first, before embracing each one in turn. Draupadi shed tears of happiness when Arjuna approached her. Taking off the jewellery which had been made to perfection in the land of the *Devas,* Arjuna handed them to her. Responding to the eager questions of his brothers, Arjuna narrated his adventures from the moment of their parting. They were thrilled to see the weapons he had acquired and begged him to give them a demonstration. Never one to desist from showing off, Arjuna proceeded to release the missiles and call them back. The earth rumbled in protest as the powerful weapons did untold damage to the surroundings. The *Devas,* the sages, the *Lokapalas*, and even Shiva, descended *en masse* to dissuade Arjuna from using the weapons without just cause, as they had the potential to reduce the three worlds to ashes. An embarassed Arjuna acceded to their request and put away his weapons. The relieved celestials returned to their homes, pleased to have averted a major catastrophe. Before leaving, Indra approached Yudhishthira. He blessed him saying that he would one day rule the world.

The Pandavas were ecstatic to be reunited, and mightily proud of Arjuna's accomplishments. Now that they were together again, no force on earth could touch them. They sat around chattering like excited schoolboys and laughed uproariously imagining the looks on the faces of Duryodhana and his brothers when Arjuna unleashed his potent weapons on them. The trauma, anxieties, fears, and sufferings of the past few years fell away like dead skin from the back of a snake, and they felt rejuvenated. They had spent a long time feeling depressed, but that was all in the past. From their new position on top of the world, the view was much rosier and they were prepared to take on any challenge that life had in store for them. It was a glorious day and the brothers held the memory of it in their hearts for the rest of their lives.

12
Brihannala, the Eunuch

During Arjuna's sojourn at Amaravati, Indra ordered a grand celebration to mark his visit. All the prominent *devas* and revered sages were invited and accepted with glad hearts. On the big day, the assembly hall was filled to overflowing with illustrious guests. Arjuna was given the place of honour and was the proud occupant of half of Indra's throne. At the King's signal, the *gandharvas*, famed for their mastery of the performing arts, began playing enchanting music as the *apsaras* began to dance.

As the delightful music wafted through the air and the dancers gyrated in perfect harmony with it, the audience found their hearts soaring with exhilaration. Arjuna was enthralled since he had never seen anything like it before. His eyes fastened on the most beautiful *apsara* – Urvashi, of famed beauty. Given the role she had played in his illustrious family tree, the hero found her particularly fascinating and as he ran over the details of their association in his mind's eye, he felt privileged to see her perform.

The Kuru line could be traced all the way back to Manu, who was the grandson of Aditi, the mother of the *devas*. Pururavas was born to this noble King's daughter, Ila. Ayus was his heir and Nahusha was the next in line. Nahusha was a great and virtuous King, who was offered Indra's throne when the latter incurred the sin of killing a Brahmin. But the hitherto kindly and just monarch then became a conceited tyrant. He lusted after Indra's wife, Sachi, and the lady brought about his downfall with the help of Brihaspati, Indra's preceptor. She told Nahusha to visit her in a palanquin drawn by the *saptarishis*. Anxious to make it to the rendezvous as quickly as possible, the King hastened his doom by kicking Agastya, hoping to spur him into moving faster. The great *rishi* cursed him to become a serpent. It was Yudhishthira who eventually released him from the curse. Yayati was Nahusha's son. The Yadavas and the Kurus were descended from his sons Yadu and Puru respectively. Dushyanta and his son Bharata, after whom this great country is named, were born several generations later in the Puru line. Urvashi had been Pururavas' lover and borne him his son, Ayus.

This illustrious ancestor of Arjuna's had a rather unconventional origin. Manu's son, Ila, was out hunting with his brothers when he chanced upon Shiva and Parvati engaged in passionate lovemaking. The three-eyed God was not pleased with the intrusion upon his privacy and cursed Ila, turning him into a woman. Ila begged both Shiva and Parvati to have pity upon him. Shiva relented somewhat and allowed Parvati to decide his fate. The Goddess decreed that Ila would spend six months as a man and for the remainder of the year he would be a woman. While Ila was a woman, she attracted the attention of Buda, the son of Soma, and Pururavas was born of this unusual coupling.

Urvashi's creation also took place under unorthodox circumstances as she had emerged from the thigh of Narayana. Pururavas was famed for his valour and on occasion, even Indra requested his help in the good fight against the forces of evil. While returning from one such battle, he met an *apsara* who was wailing in distress as her companion, Urvashi, had been carried away by the demon, Keshin. Pururavas immediately took off in pursuit, tracked down the villain, vanquished him in combat, and rescued Urvashi. After this thrilling episode, the two fell passionately in love

It was not surprising that Pururavas was attracted to the *apsara* as her beauty was such that no man could remain impervious to it. Urvashi, on the other hand, being a veteran in the art of love and a celestial, was above the tender emotions that are both the blessing and bane of the human condition. The whole purpose of her existence was to give and receive pleasure. And yet, despite being a creature of transient feelings, for a spell she did experience love and the intense emotions that characterise it. But as was often the case, the path of true love was beset with seemingly insurmountable obstacles. Urvashi was a *gandharva* and their code forbade union with mortals. The lovers had no choice but to refrain from declaring their mutual love and go their separate ways for the time being at least.

It was about this time that Urvashi wandered into the hermitage of Varuna and Mitra. These ascetics were performing a rigorous sacrificial ritual that required them to practice severe austerities and strict celibacy. While the duo was thus engaged, Urvashi walked in aimlessly, lost in thoughts of Pururavas, completely unaware of how devastatingly beautiful she looked flushed with love. Varuna and Mitra could not remain immune to her charms and they spilt their seminal fluids. It was from this discharge that the great sages Agasthya and Vashistha emerged. Their fathers, were deeply ashamed of their lack of control and cursed the object of their untimely desire. The nymph, they pronounced, would have to descend to the world of man and cohabit with one of its inhabitants. Urvashi could not believe her ears! This was a blessing in disguise to say the least, as her fondest desire was about to be fulfilled.

In due course, Urvashi and Pururavas were united in the bonds of matrimony. But before consummating their love, Urvashi imposed three conditions on her husband: he had to make love to her thrice a day; but never when she did not desire it; and he was not to appear in the nude before her. Pururavas agreed to these exotic terms and the two proceeded to enjoy conjugal bliss.

The *gandharva*s were unhappy with the way things had turned out, as Urvashi was the fairest of them all and supremely talented. They hatched a plot to get her back, as she did not tire of her mortal lover and return to them as they had expected. The nymph had two lambs as pets and she adored them. She kept them by her side always, even at night, when she would tie them to the side of her bed. On a fateful night, the *gandharva*s sneaked in and removed one of her lambs. The little creature bleated piteously. Urvashi heard its cries and called out for help, crying even more desperately than the stolen lambs. Pururavas went after the lamb at once, forgetting that he was naked. As he raced after the offenders, a brilliant flash of lightning, produced strategically by the wily *gandharva*s, exposed his nudity to his wife.

True to her word, Urvashi went back to the jubilant *gandharva*s, as Pururavas had failed to adhere to her conditions. Her lover was nearly prostrate with grief and wandered about like one demented, calling her name. He searched high and low for Urvashi, determined to win her back. For a long time his efforts were fruitless and all that remained to him were the bittersweet memories of their time together.

Finally, he found her in a lotus-lake near Kurukshetra, frolicking in the guise of a swan, with her close companions. Urvashi had gone back to being the blithe spirit she had been before her meeting with

Pururavas. The love she had borne him had faded and now she spurned his advances. Finally, wearied by his tiresome persistence, she agreed to spend the last night of the year with him and give him a son. She kept her word but Pururavas was not satisfied. Legend has it that he worshipped the *gandharva*s fervently and with great devotion, till they appeared before him. Pleased with his worship, they offered him a boon. He seized this opportunity and asked them to make him a *gandharva,* so that he could be with Urvashi. His wish was granted and the lovers were reunited once more.

Arjuna smiled to himself as he watched the woman who had been his ancestor's fate, wondering where fact parted ways with legend. Not taking his eyes off her, he wished he could summon the courage to ask her all about Pururavas. While he mused thus, Indra caught the admiring glances he threw Urvashi's way. 'I shall arrange a special treat for my son tonight,' he thought. 'He has mastered the use of the divine *astras* and Chitrasena has taught him music and dance. Urvashi shall teach him the art of love... It should be a pleasurable experience for him.'

When the performance ended, Indra sent for Chitrasena and made his wish known to him. The latter called Urvashi and passed on the instructions of their overlord.

Urvashi was immeasurably pleased with the assignation that had been given to her. Arjuna was a handsome and valiant man. His accomplishments made him stand tall even among the celestials. She had caught him staring at her during the performance and been pleased. Dressed in her most alluring garments, with flowers in her lovely locks and bedecked in dazzling jewellery, she walked towards Arjuna's apartments. The *devas* who had the fortune to see her that night, envied Arjuna within their hearts.

Arjuna was relaxing in his chambers when an attendant brought word that Urvashi wished to meet him. Surprised at the hour she had chosen to visit him, he hastened to meet her. Bowing his head and lowering his eyes in a reverential attitude, he said: 'Mother, you do me great honour! What is it you seek from me? I shall treat your every wish as a command!'

Urvashi bristled at being addressed in this manner and said haughtily, 'Do I look like anybody's mother? Lord Indra wishes me to spend the night with you. It gives me great pleasure to carry out his orders as I have been struck by Kama's darts of love and am possessed by the most ardent desire for you.'

'But how can this be?' Arjuna asked aghast. 'Pururavas and Ayus are my revered ancestors! I respect you like my own mother!'

'What a filthy hypocrite you are! You spent the evening ogling me and now you deny harbouring amorous thoughts towards me!' raged Urvashi.

'I looked at you with eyes of worship as it was truly remarkable that the wife of my great ancestor stood before me. My thoughts were not improper as I was merely thinking that it was the good fortune of the Kurus to be associated with a lady of your standing,' explained Arjuna.

But the historic significance was lost on Urvashi at that moment and in her spectacular rage she looked lovelier than ever. 'Stop treating me like some ancient being! I am an *apsara*; your petty mortal laws have no hold over us. We are allowed to do what your self-righteous, so-called civilisation, forbids. Many scions of the Kuru race, who made the ascent to heaven on the strength of their noble deeds, have been accepted by me as lovers and none of them had any ridiculous moral scruples. So there is no reason for you to have any qualms about the services I am about to perform.'

'I beg you to be reasonable, for what you ask I am unable to do. In my eyes it would be tantamount to the gravest sin. Command me as a mother would her son and I will gladly oblige,' Arjuna pleaded with her, still unable to look her in the eye.

'How dare you spurn me!' said Urvashi, her voice quivering with anger. 'No self-respecting man turns away a woman who gives herself to him out of love. You are not a man and your manhood is merely a vestigial organ that serves but ornamental purposes. I condemn you to spend the rest of your life shorn of your manhood. You will live in the inner apartments of women and they will laugh at you for being a eunuch!' With these words, Urvashi stormed out of Arjuna's apartments, seething with rage and humiliation.

Arjuna stood trembling with mortification and wished he could go back in time and prevent this unfortunate incident from ever taking place. He repaired to Indra's palace post haste and told him all that had passed, concluding with Urvashi's deadly curse. To his surprise, Indra laughed aloud and said, 'I am not surprised. There is nothing in the three worlds to match the rage of a woman scorned. But I am impressed! Your forbearance is extraordinary. Even the most rigid *maharishis* forget their vows of celibacy when they set eyes on Urvashi and become quivering masses of lustful desire. You on the contrary, rejected her even though she offered herself to you.'

'I cannot be amused father. The loss of my manhood is no laughing matter,' said his son sadly.

'You should have more faith, my son. Would I allow such a thing to happen? This curse is actually a blessing in disguise,' Indra said. He laughed at the look of extreme disbelief on Arjuna's face and went on: 'The curse will come into effect only in the thirteenth year of your exile, which you are supposed to spend incognito. Nobody will suspect the great Arjuna is a eunuch!'

'And I will regain my manhood at the end of that year?' Arjuna asked doubtfully.

'Certainly! I will send for that impudent nymph who dared to curse my son and make sure of it. Although I can't say I blame her – she is not used to such treatment. Usually she has to beat men off with a stick to keep them away! And did you actually address her as mother? Great-great-great-grandmother would have been closer!' And Indra burst into such riotous laughter which his relieved son privately thought was most unbecoming in one who was the King of Heaven.

Thus, in the thirteenth year of the Pandavas' exile, Arjuna had the perfect disguise at hand. His brothers were less fortunate, and Yudhishthira spent many sleepless nights wondering how best they might conceal themselves during the final year, when they were supposed to live incognito.

Towards the end of the twelfth year, the brothers were dwelling in a dense forest when they were approached by a Brahmin who seemed to be greatly agitated. His precious *arani* (flintwood) stick, which was used to start sacrificial fires, had got entangled in the antlers of a curious deer and the animal had made off with it. He begged the Pandavas to retrieve the same for him.

The brothers responded at once and took off after the thieving deer. However, they could not catch up with it though they followed the spoor expertly. Drained by their efforts, the five of them sat under a tree feeling exhausted and miserable. Giving in to the dejection they had been fighting with mixed results since they had been exiled, the Pandavas complained bitterly about the turn their lives had taken. They wondered why it was that they were being tormented in this manner when they had tried their utmost to lead blameless lives.

Bheema thought that he should have given in to his baser instincts and killed all the Kauravas when they had tried to cheat them out of their Kingdom. Arjuna agreed with his brother and said he wished he had given Karna a taste of the Gandeeva when he dared to abuse his brothers and Draupadi. Sensing that this conversation would be detrimental to their rapidly dwindling spirits, Yudhishthira ordered his brothers to stop the pointless discussion and decide on a fresh course of action.

Nakula was asked to scale a tree to locate a lake or pond where they might quench their thirst. And when the elder twin spotted a lake, Yudhishthira handed him a couple of quivers and told him to fetch some water. Nakula hastened to do so. But as he approached the lake, his thirst increased a hundred-fold and he was nearly delirious with the craving for a sip of the precious water that beckoned invitingly to him. He ran towards the lake, cupped his palms, scooped up some water and raised it to his lips. At that moment, an authoritative voice rang out: 'Stop! I am a guardian crane and this lake belongs to me. You have to answer my questions satisfactorily before drinking the water. Disobey me at your peril!' Nakula decided that a mere crane was no match for a Pandava, and drank the water. Immediately he fell to the ground and was dead to the world.

The remaining Pandavas waited impatiently for Nakula to return with the water. When he did not, Yudhishthira became uneasy and sent Sahadeva after him. The youngest Pandava met with the same fate as Nakula, and he was soon joined by Arjuna and Bheema. Finally, Yudhishthira found the seemingly dead bodies of his brothers and was shocked. He wondered why his heart continued to beat after seeing such a dreadful sight. Like the others before him, he decided to drink some water before dealing with the situation.

As Yudhishthira knelt to drink the water, the crane spoke to him. Realising that the crane was not what it seemed to be, he asked it to reveal its true identity. When he looked up, a *yaksha* was perched on the branches of the tree. It told him what had happened to his brothers and warned him that he would pay the same price if he did not answer the questions posed to him. Yudhishthira agreed to the terms. The *yaksha* then peppered him with a barrage of complex philosophical questions. Yudhishthira's replies were worthy of Dharma, his revered father, as they sparkled with eloquence and a profound understanding of universal truths.

The *yaksha* was pleased and told him that he would spare the life of one of his brothers. Yudhishthira chose Nakula, much to the surprise of his interrogator. When asked why he had chosen his step-brother's life over that of his own brothers, Yudhishthira replied that since his father had two wives, it was only fitting that each had a son left alive. The *yaksha* then transformed into Lord Yama (also known as Dharma), Yudhishthira's heavenly father. Yama hugged his son and told him that he had passed the final test and had done him proud.

Bheema, Arjuna, Nakula and Sahadeva were restored to life. Yama revealed that it was he who had stolen the Brahmin's flint-stick in the guise of a deer and now handed it back to them. He also granted Yudhishthira a boon, wherein he and the others would escape detection in the thirteenth year of exile. He blessed them all and returned to his domain.

The Pandavas discussed recent events excitedly and were more upbeat about the challenge ahead of them. Brimming with newfound confidence, the Pandavas and Draupadi sat down to talk about where and how to spend the thirteenth year. Yudhishthira turned to Arjuna first. 'You have had the opportunity to travel across the length and breadth of this land. None of us know it as intimately as you do. Where do you recommend we spend the final year of our exile?'

'There are many beautiful places that will serve our purpose admirably. But the kingdom of Matsya, ruled by King Virata, is best suited to our needs. He is a kindly old man and is sure to treat us well if we go in disguise,' replied Arjuna.

'It sounds perfect!' Sahadeva enthused. His approval was important to the others as he was regarded as the intelligent one.

'It is just as well that Arjuna took the time to scout suitable locations even as he romanced a bevy of beautiful maidens during his exotic travels!' Bheema said cheekily. Draupadi looked petulant on hearing this and Arjuna shot his rambunctious brother a dirty look. Yudhishthira brought the discussion back on track with his usual tact. 'I am glad that is settled. Now we have to decide how best to conceal our true identities while we are there.'

'Yudhishthira, you were born to rule the whole world! The cleverest disguise will be inadequate to hide your regal bearing and nobility!' Arjuna said with great feeling.

'Don't worry! I intend to play up my strength or weakness, depending on how you view it,' Yudhishthira said cheerfully. "I will go as a Brahmin named Kanka, and offer my services to the King. I'll tell him I was employed by Yudhishthira to play dice with him and to keep him entertained with discourses on politics, philosophy and *dharma*. Sage Brihadashwa taught me the art of *akshahridaya*, playing dice expertly, during our *teerthayatra* – so there is no danger of my losing anything of value this time.'

'That is a great idea! Such a role will not be very different from your own personality and will allow you to play it convincingly,' said Sahadeva.

'So Yudhishthira is going as a Brahmin skilled in dice. Perhaps I'll go as a cook...' said Bheema.

'I did not know you could cook, brother! I somehow thought that eating was your special talent,' said Nakula teasingly. Arjuna and Sahadeva erupted in gales of laughter while Yudhishthira looked on indulgently.

'I'll have you know that no matter what many ignorant people think, I am a gourmet not a glutton. It is about time my expertise in all matters culinary is put to good use. King Virata shall feast on my choice preparations and I will also wrestle with any challengers, to entertain the King. And in my spare time, perhaps I could train the youngsters in his kingdom to wrestle and help them develop a good physique,' said Bheema.

'Good food and plenty of fighting! It is sure to keep you happy, given the circumstances...' Arjuna said to his brother, with a smile tugging at the corners of his mouth.

'Try to keep the extent of your physical prowess under wraps, otherwise people will talk and the resultant publicity could help our enemies discover us,' cautioned Yudhishthira.

'Don't worry, I'll be gentler than Draupadi here,' said Bheema, ignoring the snorts of disbelief that accompanied this assertion. Instead, he asked, 'What about Arjuna?'

'Urvashi's curse will come into effect in the thirteenth year. So I will go as the eunuch Brihannala and teach music and dancing – which I learnt from Chitrasena – to the young Princess, Uttara,' said Arjuna. Something in his tone made his brothers refrain from uttering any witticisms.

'I have decided to call myself Granthika, and offer my services in the royal stables,' Nakula said. 'King Virata will soon have some well-trained horses.'

'The handsomest trainer in his Kingdom no doubt!' said Bheema jovially, slapping his younger brother on the shoulder. 'I hope the women in his land are less fervent in their admiration than the women in ours!'

'Not to worry brother, women admire the hired help a lot less than they do royalty!' said Sahadeva. 'The cattle herds are an immense source of wealth in Matsya. Since I have a knack for making cows yield more milk, I shall seek employment in the royal cowsheds under the name Tantipala.'

Yudhishthira looked sorrowful when he heard this. 'You are mother Kunti's favourite and the family baby. How our mothers would weep to see you employed as a cowherd!'

'Do not feel unhappy on my account brother! Even Lord Krishna was a cowherd. If the protector of the universe can do it, why can't I?' replied Sahadeva with his usual cool logic.

'I wish all of did not have to suffer in this manner,' said Yudhishthira broodingly. 'And what about Draupadi? How can we hide our shining star in all its brilliance at Matsya?'

'It will not be too much trouble. I have been thinking about it and have decided to work for the Queen as a *sairandhri*, since I can braid hair beautifully, make garlands, and help her enhance her looks by the skilful application of cosmetics,' said Draupadi.

The brothers looked at the Princess of Panchala and then down in shame as they remembered what she had suffered on their account. They sat in silence for a few moments and then Bheema said bracingly, 'We have Dharma's boon and that will allow us to escape detection in Virata's Kingdom. It is only for a year and when it ends, our enemies will have to answer for all their heinous sins against us with their blood.'

'If they do not return what is rightfully ours, I will destroy them. Yudhishthira will then sit on the Kuru throne with Draupadi at his side and prosperity will once again be ours!' vowed Arjuna.

Having made their plans, the Pandavas made ready for their departure. Sage Dhaumya offered prayers to propitiate the Gods to watch over their endeavours and protect them from harm. He instructed the brothers on how to avoid detection while at Matsya. The Pandavas were grateful for his advice and thanked him with heartfelt gratitude. Yudhishthira then turned and requested his small band of followers to travel on to Panchala, where they would be safe. Thanking them for the good wishes and companionship they had provided, the Pandavas bid them farewell before turning towards Matsya.

After a long and uneventful journey, the Pandavas and Draupadi approached Matsya. The Kingdom was skirted by a dense forest which they traversed under cover of darkness. Arjuna had thought of a clever ruse to hide their weapons. He knew of an ancient cremation ground in the forest, which had not been used in a long time. There was a huge *Shamee* tree there, which would be the ideal hiding place for their tell-tale weapons. The brothers quickly repaired to this location and divested themselves of their weapons, which they then wrapped in white cloth to give the appearance of a corpse. Nakula scaled the tree and tied the 'corpse' to one of the uppermost branches. As a further precaution, they tied a foul-smelling carcass to one of the branches to ward off nosy travellers. Having performed this task, the brothers proceeded towards Matsya.

Before entering the city, the Pandava brothers and Draupadi sought the blessings of Goddess Durga. Pleased with their collective devotion, she appeared before them and promised them her protection. She assured them that the bad times were drawing to an end and with her blessings, their enemies would be crushed. The Goddess also assured them that she would guard the boundaries of the Kingdom and repel the spies who would be scouring the world for them. The Pandavas fell at her feet and thanked her for the blessings they had received.

After this divine reassurance, the Pandavas hugged each other before taking it in turns to present themselves to King Virata and offering their services in the capacities they had discussed. The old King thus hired a Brahmin skilled in dice, a cook who doubled as a professional wrestler, a eunuch with expertise in dance and music, a trainer for his horses and a keeper for his cows.

Not surprisingly, the Pandavas excelled in the services they had undertaken and Virata was pleased with them. In particular, he took to Yudhishthira, and came to rely heavily on him for advice on matters concerning the governance of his Kingdom. The King insisted his courtiers treat the Brahmin with the same respect they accorded him. Bheema, as Ballava the cook, catered admirably to the King's hearty appetite for rich food and wrestling bouts, winning his affection in the process. Princess Uttara and her companions delighted Virata, Queen Sudheshna, and the courtiers, with their charming dance performances and musical shows choreographed to perfection by Brihannala. Regular inspections of the royal stables proved that the horses were superbly trained and Granthika was suitably rewarded. Tantipala's contribution was invaluable as the cattle were in fact the source of wealth in Matsya. Their yield had never been better.

In this manner, the Pandavas settled down comfortably in Virata's Kingdom. Draupadi, however, had a tougher time of it. Queen Sudheshna had been reluctant to hire her as she felt threatened by her impeccable beauty. Draupadi had reassured the Queen, telling her there was no need to worry as she already had five jealous husbands among the *gandharvas*. They were on an important mission and could not take her with them. If the Queen offered her protection, her husbands would be grateful and return the favour many times over. Sudheshna was persuaded on hearing her entreaties and accepted Draupadi as a *sairandhri,* albeit with a touch of misgiving, as there was something about the beautiful young woman that spelt trouble.

Sure enough, Draupadi was soon in distress as Keechaka, the commander of Virata's forces and Queen Sudheshna's brother, became attracted to her. He pursued her relentlessly, ignoring her protests that she was a married woman. Keechaka wielded a lot of power and influence in the Matsya kingdom and was unused to women fleeing from him and his ardent proclamations of love and offers of rich presents. Draupadi's refusal goaded him beyond endurance and he begged his sister to help him out.

Remembering her initial nervousness on hearing about the *sairandhri*'s powerful *gandharva* husbands, with their penchant for violence, Sudheshna tried to dissuade her brother. But he refused to listen. Insisting that he was more of a man than the five husbands put together, he continued pestering both Draupadi and his sister. The Queen yielded first and promised her assistance.

Draupadi was ordered to fetch some wine for the Queen from Keechaka's palace. Tremulously, the unhappy Panchala Princess requested that someone else be sent as the Commander was making improper advances towards her. Her protests were brushed aside and she found herself making her way unwillingly to the man who was making her life so unpleasant. True to form, Keechaka resumed his overzealous and unwelcome courting as soon as he got Draupadi to himself. Her steadfast refusal yet again, pushed him over the edge and he made a grab for her.

Struggling free from Keechaka's embrace, Draupadi fled. She ran to the King, knowing that Yudhishthira would be with him. Keechaka caught up with her as she ran and kicked her, sending her sprawling across the floor. Her desperate pleas for help went unheeded as Virata dithered, refusing to pull up his powerful Commander, and Yudhishthira signalled that she should not make a scene and blow their cover.

An infuriated Draupadi decided that she had had enough of being molested by men while her supposedly great husbands did nothing to protect her. She turned her feminine charm and artful ways on Bheema, who could never resist her. Angered by her tears, the mighty Pandava decided to punish Keechaka. On Draupadi's suggestion, it was decided that it was time to rid the world of Keechaka.

As per the plan, Draupadi pretended to be willing at last to surrender to Keechaka and arranged a liaison with him at a secluded spot. When the lusty Commander turned up for the rendezvous, his heady anticipation clouding his better judgement, Bheema was waiting. Like a maddened tiger, he fell on Keechaka and mauled him to death, leaving his mangled carcass to rot.

The messy death of Keechaka stunned everyone and there was a deadly backlash that almost caused the undoing of the Pandavas. Draupadi was found at the scene of the crime when Keechaka's desperate relatives came looking for him. Their horror was replaced by fury when Draupadi proudly informed the onlookers that her husbands were responsible for what had happened and anyone who dared to misbehave with her would receive similar treatment. Her dumbstruck audience decided she was a witch and carried her away forcibly to be burnt on Keechaka's funeral pyre. Bheema rescued her from this hideous fate but their position remained delicate.

The King and Queen were shaken by the loss of a stalwart of the Matsya Kingdom and tended to look upon Draupadi with ill favour. The Queen suggested that Draupadi leave as her presence was noxious and had brought calamity in its wake. However, as Draupadi pleaded with her and assured Sudheshna that it was only for a little bit longer, she relented and agreed.

Eventually the news of Keechaka's death reached the Kauravas. The Commander of Matsya was a man famed for his iron physique and fighting skills. Crushing such a man to death in a deathly embrace and leaving nothing but grisly pulp behind, was no mean feat. Duryodhana felt that Bheema alone was capable of such brutality, guessing correctly that Draupadi would have been the cause of the upheaval at Matsya.

At that juncture, King Susharma of Trigarta, suggested that the time was right to invade Virata's Kingdom as their formidable Commander lay dead. Duryodhana agreed enthusiastically, saying that it would give them a chance to sniff out the Pandavas while helping themselves to the prodigious wealth of Matsya. Battle plans were drawn up and it was decided that Susharma would attack the Kingdom and lead the cattle away, drawing the main army, while the Kauravas would then swoop down on the unprotected Kingdom and move in for the kill.

While the battle plan of Duryodhana was being put into effect, King Virata was blissfully unaware of the impending menace. After the death of Keechaka, he found himself leaning on the capable shoulders of Yudhishthira for support. The latter was pleased to help their benefactor in any way he could. So when the cowherds brought news of Susharma's attack, Virata, accompanied by his sons, readied his forces, giving positions of great responsibility to the Pandava brothers, with the exception of Arjuna. It was a wise decision. They vanquished Susharma's army after a tough fight and forced the aggressor into admitting defeat.

Meanwhile, the Kauravas attacked from the north and took possession of the cattle that were the pride of the Kingdom. Panicky messengers appealed to Uttara, King Virata's son, begging him to intervene. The old King loved to brag about the great valour of his son even though the young Prince had led a cosseted life and was better with words than weapons.

The young Prince, sitting with his sister and her companions, was flattered to have all the attention focused on him. As the King's youngest son, he tended to be overlooked more often than not. Pleased that everyone was looking to him for protection and rather puffed up with self-importance, he said, 'It is unfortunate that such a thing has happened. I would like nothing better than to ride out after those thieves and give them a taste of my sword. But unfortunately, I do not have a skilled charioteer to guide my horses, so my hands are tied. It is too bad, as otherwise those scoundrels would be writhing under my victorious feet and begging for their cowardly lives. I would have been the very epitome of destruction and my enemies would have taken me for Arjuna, the greatest warrior of the age. He is my hero, although I could teach even him a thing or two about warfare!'

'You should not let a small thing like the absence of a charioteer stand in the way of personal glory,' Draupadi told the Prince, barely able to repress her laughter. 'Brihannala was the charioteer of the great man you mentioned and has even been coached by him in archery. Therefore, Brihannala's skill with the bow is considerable. You will be able to do battle with the Kauravas with this warrior by your side.'

'Brihannala? It takes more than grace, a perfect sense of rhythm, and an extraordinary ability to wiggle the hips, to drive a chariot and wield a bow,' the Prince said, looking doubtfully at the eunuch who was cowering in a rather exaggerated manner in a remote corner.

'I speak the truth when I say Brihannala has driven Arjuna's chariot and that matchless warrior never had any cause for complaint. If he were here he would confirm it himself,' Draupadi persisted, turning away to hide a smile.

'O brother, do borrow Brihannala to be your charioteer today,' Princess Uttara said enthusiastically. 'Thrash our enemies in battle and bring back their colourful garments as tokens of your stupendous victory. I will dress my dolls with their clothes.'

Caught up in the moment, Prince Uttara rose to the occasion magnificently. He ordered his weapons and armour be brought to him and a chariot readied. He even helped Brihannala put on the armour, when the task seemed too much for the eunuch. After making a pretty speech on his own formidable heart and might, while his sister and her companions cheered him on, he ordered the eunuch to drive him into battle.

As the fleet steeds closed the gap between him and the Kauravas under the expert hands of the charioteer, Uttara found his courage draining as he realized this was no longer a game. His stomach began to churn when he saw the hardened Kaurava veterans like Bhishma, Drona, Kripa, and Karna, all of whom Brihannala helpfully pointed out to him with a stirring monologue on their achievements, and the Prince almost threw up in sheer terror. Hurriedly swallowing the foul effluence that rose thickly in his throat, he said shrilly, 'Brihannala, I want you to turn back at once. I am too young to die a painful death at the hands of these mighty warriors. Let us get out of here while we still can.'

'I hope you speak in jest Prince! You are a scion of a mighty race and you cannot possibly be considering flight,' said Brihannala.

'Of course, I am deadly serious. Take a look at the battle-hardened warriors before you! I will be crushed like an insect under their feet. For pity's sake! Turn back immediately!' yelled Uttara.

'You mean you are going to flee in terror like a woman and go back to the ladies you were boasting to not so long ago? They will laugh at you!' said Brihannala in utter disbelief.

'I don't care!' shouted the terrified Prince. 'The laughter of women cannot inflict grievous injury on my person. How can anybody expect me to fight this formidable army all by myself and unaided by my valiant father and brothers? I order you to turn back!'

But Brihannala was implacable. 'I will do no such thing. If you flee from the foes who are threatening you and your own, great infamy will be your lot. You will be laughed at, reviled and despised universally. Your family will be shamed and rue the day you were born. Fighting bravely against great odds and dying while trying to protect those who depend on you, is infinitely preferable to running like a coward. Now be a man and fight!'

'This is madness! I don't have to listen to a eunuch. You can stay here and do as you please. I will not stay a moment longer!' So saying, Uttara jumped down from the chariot and ran away as fast as his puny legs and unbearable terror would allow. Brihannala brought the chariot to a halt and ran in pursuit of the Prince in flight. The gathered Kaurava forces watched in amazement as a lone warrior made a hasty exit from the battlefield while a strange creature dressed in flowing skirts and armour chased him, hair billowing wildly. Then they burst into raucous laughter, pointing at the absurd spectacle and roaring with uncontrollable mirth.

Brihannala caught up with the errant Prince and grabbed him by the shoulder. Uttara tried to free himself from the iron grip of the eunuch but met with little success. Trying a different tack, he said desperately, 'Let me go Brihannala, I will give you more wealth than you dared dream of!'

'My honour means more to me than all the wealth in the world,' replied the eunuch. 'Take heart Prince! The *sairandhri* did not exaggerate when she praised me to high heaven. Take the reins of the chariot. I shall fight and win back the stolen cows. However, the weapons you have brought are inadequate for the task at hand. But I know just how to get my hands on what we need. I happen to know where the Pandavas have hidden their weapons.'

'This is against my better judgement, but for some strange reason I am drawn to you and feel compelled to do as you say,' said Uttara, as bewildered as he was terrified.

The Prince, guided by Brihannala, reached the *Shamee* tree where the Pandavas had stashed their weapons for safekeeping. Initially, Uttara was unwilling to scale the tree and retrieve the weapons as he believed he would be damned for all eternity if he polluted his person by touching a corpse. But soon he was persuaded to do as asked. As he undid the shroud, an impressive heap of battle paraphernalia lay before his amazed eyes. He looked up at the enigmatic person before him and asked, 'Who are you? How could you possibly know about these weapons? It is obvious that the Pandavas went to great lengths to keep them hidden. Aren't they in exile? What do you know of them?'

'I am Arjuna, the Pandava. We chose your father's Kingdom for the final year of our exile. Kanka is Yudhishthira, Ballava the cook is Bheema, Nakula and Sahadeva are Granthika and Tantipala. And the Queen's *sairandhri* is Draupadi, our wife.'

'That is impossible! Arjuna is my hero and I have dreamed of meeting him since I was a boy. How could I not recognise him? What you say befuddles the mind and confounds the senses. I will believe your tale only after you tell me the ten names of Arjuna and narrate the manner in which he earned them,' challenged the Prince.

'So be it. Listen carefully; I am called *Arjuna* because of my unblemished countenance; *Partha,* after my mother Pritha; *Phalguna,* as Phalguni is the star under which I was born; *Kiriti,* because Indra presented me with a golden diadem to commemorate my conquests against the enemies of the Gods; *Swetavahana,* since I rode a heavenly chariot, driven by white steeds, presented to me by Agni, when I helped him consume Khandava; *Jishnu,* because when provoked, my rage is dreadful to behold and I become the scourge of the three worlds. I have sworn to kill the man who injures my brother Yudhishthira and spills his blood, and it is on account of this oath that I was given this name. *Bibhatsu* was the name given to me because of my strict adherence to fairness and ethical conduct in battle; *Vijaya,* because I have not and never will, lose a battle; *Savyasachi,* because I am ambidextrous and can use my right and left hands with equal skill while wielding weapons.

And finally, *Dhananjaya*, because I bring prosperity wherever I go. It was given to me when I singlehandedly filled our treasury to overflowing by my conquests, before Yudhishthira performed the *Rajasuya* sacrifice.'

'I believe you!' whispered the awed young Prince. 'It is an honour to share space with you. I beg your forgiveness if you and your brothers have been slighted in any way during your stay.'

'There is no need to apologise. We have been treated with nothing but kindness and respect,' replied Arjuna gently.

'Knowing who you are has instilled courage in me. It makes me ashamed of my abject display of cowardice earlier. I would give anything in the world to go back in time and behave like a man if only to earn the respect of the hero I have admired since boyhood,' lamented Uttara.

'Do not be too hard on yourself Prince. It is your first time in battle and braver men have faltered in similar situations. I know you to have the heart of a warrior. Have more faith in your ability – as I do. Now let us make haste. We have a battle to win!'

Encouraged by Arjuna's words, Uttara rode into battle, proud to be the charioteer of the world's greatest warrior. Later, he would redeem himself in the great battle of Kurukshetra, where fighting with lion-hearted courage, he would go on to bring great honour to his family before attaining a warrior's heaven, slain by Shalya.

In the meantime, Drona had been pondering over the appearance of the Prince's charioteer. Despite the strange apparel, the creature was the spitting image of Arjuna. He gazed worriedly at the sky above and the dire omens he saw convinced him that there was a bloodbath to be expected in the battle ahead.

At that precise moment, the Prince and his charioteer were making their way back to the battlefield; only, now their roles were reversed. Drona's suspicions were confirmed. Turning to Bhishma, he said, 'I am convinced that it is Arjuna we are confronting. No one else would dare to fight us single-handedly.'

'That is great news! It means we have smoked the Pandavas out of their hiding before their exile has ended! That means they will have to go back into exile!' said an exultant Duryodhana, who had overheard Drona's words.

'Not quite...' replied Bhishma quietly. 'Their exile ended five months and twelve days ago.'

'How can that be? If that were true, why are they still hiding? Why have they not crawled back to beg me for a share of my Kingdom?' asked Duryodhana, his face flushed with scorn.

'I think that for some strange reason, they are unwilling to take a chance where you are concerned,' his Grandsire replied dryly. 'According to the lunar calendar, their exile ended a few months ago. But they waited in case you chose to follow the solar calendar. And before you get excited, let me tell you that even by that reckoning, their exile ended six days ago. Arjuna is no fool. He knows this, which is why he has chosen to reveal himself. I suggest you take this opportunity to make your peace with him, let us avoid the bloodshed which is otherwise inevitable.'

'I will do no such thing!' exclaimed Duryodhana angrily. 'We shall fight him today when he is alone and unaccompanied by the rest of that brood, especially that brute, Bheema. He shall be killed today and his brothers can weep for him and themselves when I send them packing, yet again.'

'It is impossible to defeat Arjuna in battle. His skill is extraordinary. This world has never seen a warrior like him and never will again,' cautioned Drona.

'Why is it that Drona, Bhishma, and Kripa, insist on singing Arjuna's praises in this biased manner?' burst out Karna, incensed as always to hear words of praise spoken about his rival. 'You are all scared of him! Flee, if you wish. I will destroy him for Duryodhana!'

'Karna! This is neither the time nor the place for your senseless swaggering! Only a fool would think he can fight and win against Arjuna all by himself. All the forces of the three worlds combined would be insufficient to destroy him in combat!' said Kripa, with great feeling.

'I suppose this is the perfect time and place to wax eloquent about Arjuna's greatly exaggerated skill? Our troops need the encouragement after all! You Brahmins should content yourselves with chanting *mantras* and leave the fighting to true warriors,' Karna replied, scorn and sarcasm dripping from every word he uttered.

'How dare you!' Drona's son Ashwatthama, snarled at him, angered by the blatant disrespect Karna had shown his revered uncle and beloved father. 'Do you realize that you have achieved nothing that gives you the right to have such an inflated opinion of yourself? As I recall, you had to flee from the *gandharva* Chitrasena, when he attacked us in the forest. It was Arjuna who rescued the lot of you. Where was your vaunted valour then? And you talk about defeating the mighty warrior coming towards us without the help of my father, uncle, and the Grandsire!'

'Silence!' Bhishma bellowed. 'This is not the time for petty squabbles. When Arjuna drives into battle, Yama's presence can be felt in the opposing camp. I can sense the dark Lord even as I speak. Arjuna will try to capture Duryodhana; therefore the King must be protected at all cost. I suggest he take half the army and head towards Hastinapura. In the meantime, the rest of us will hold Arjuna in check.'

The Kurus did exactly as Bhishma suggested. In terms of experience, wisdom, and strategic planning, there was none to equal him. With the great man at the helm to guide them, they braced themselves for the storm that threatened to burst over their heads in the form of Arjuna.

Meanwhile, the lone warrior approached the Kuru forces. One look at the soldiers arrayed in battle formation convinced him that it was Bhishma who had devised the strategy to repel him. He saluted the Kuru elders in true warrior style, sending two arrows each to the feet of Bhishma, Drona, and Kripa, to pay homage. Then he turned and gave his instructions to Uttara. 'The Grandsire hopes to engage me while Duryodhana makes off with the cows and his cowardly self. Turn the chariot towards Hastinapura, and I shall teach him what happens to thieves and scoundrels.'

Uttara obediently guided the horses while Arjuna mowed down the Kuru defence. Freeing the cattle, he sent them in the direction of Matsya. Duryodhana fled towards the main body of the army.

Bhishma, Karna, Drona, Kripa, and the others, intervened to save their King and launched a savage attack against Arjuna. But Arjuna was invincible; he unleashed wave upon wave of arrows, repulsing the Kurus time and again. Bhishma, Drona, and Karna were forced to retreat on more than one occasion. As they regrouped en masse and attempted another attack, Arjuna released the *Sammohana* (hypnotising) missile, and they all fell to the ground, curled in the foetal position, asleep as if in their mothers' womb.

Uttara screamed with excitement and high spirits, delighted that he had actually been a part of the pulverising attack that had crippled the mighty Kurus. Arjuna, basking in the glow of the young Pince's adulation, smiled indulgently and said, 'We must not forget our promise to the Princess. Collect the garments of the slumbering warriors. Make haste, we do not wish to delay your triumphant return to Matsya.'

'You are being kind, but I cannot take credit for your victory,' said Uttara humbly.

'I ask it as a favour of you as we'd like to keep our identity a secret for a little bit longer,' said Arjuna to the young Prince.

Uttara finally acquiesced and proceeded to relieve the defeated warriors of their cumbersome upper garments and heavy jewellery. Working to the discordant rhythm of thousands of rumbling snores, he completed his task and loaded the booty onto his chariot. Arjuna, as Brihannala again, took up the reins of the chariot and pausing only to return the weapons to their place on the *Shamee* tree, the incongruous duo quickly made their way back to Matsya.

While the young Prince was thus making the transition to manhood, King Virata had returned to the Kingdom in buoyant spirits. However, on hearing that Prince Uttara had rushed away to do battle with the Kauravas, with none but a eunuch for company, his happiness vanished in a trice, to be replaced by a gnawing anxiety for his youngest son. Sensing his worry, Yudhishthira hastened to reassure him. 'Set your mind at rest, my King! The Prince will be safe if Brihannala is with him.'

At that moment, a messenger rushed in, bearing glad tidings about the Prince's triumph over the foes of Matsya. The old King was overcome with filial pride and relief. He gave orders that Uttara and his charioteer be welcomed with all the pomp and splendour due to conquering heroes. Barely able to sit still while he waited for his son to return, the King ordered a game of dice be set up, despite Yudhishthira's weak protests that gambling in such an emotionally turbulent state could lead to nothing but trouble.

With the game underway, Virata began praising the valour of his young son profusely. He continued while Yudhishthira reiterated that he had foreseen just such an outcome, since Brihannala had ridden out with the Prince. The old King bristled with anger on hearing that the approbation in the Brahmin's voice was for the lowly eunuch and not for his heroic son. Enraged, he flung the dice at the offender so hard that he drew blood. Draupadi, who had been watching quietly, rushed forward with a golden dish and collected the blood before it could touch the ground. Having done this, she retreated as quickly as she had come.

Virata was bemused at this display, but some inner instinct for survival warned him to let the matter rest. On hearing the heralds announce the arrival of Prince Uttara, he sprang to his feet. His son entered the room, his face alight with the warm welcome and praise the citizens of Matsya had showered on him. But seeing the wound inflicted on Yudhishthira, he froze in his tracks. Great agitation stole over his features as his eyes swept the scene, taking in the telltale evidence of his father's temper and foolhardiness. In a voice shaking with terror, he demanded to know why the Brahmin had been hurt. On hearing his father's account, Uttara was inconsolable. 'Father! You know not what you have done! You must beg Kanka for forgiveness. Do as I say without asking any questions. Otherwise a great calamity will befall us all!'

The King was flummoxed, but sensing the urgency in his son's voice, he acquiesced, albeit grudgingly. Yudhishthira, gracious as ever, told the King that he had already been forgiven and there were no hard feelings.

Brihannala came in at that moment and paid obeisance to the King. Yudhishthira's brow had stopped bleeding, so Arjuna did not notice anything amiss. Uttara let out his breath slowly, glad that a disaster had been averted. To his father's many queries about the details of his victory, he said only that the son of a God had saved him and Matsya, and that he was not at liberty to divulge his name but that all would be clear soon. Virata was bursting with curiosity, but he decided to let the matter rest since, under the circumstances, everything had gone smoothly and his Kingdom and his sons were safe from harm.

A couple of days later, the aged monarch stepped into his courtroom. To his surprise and indignation, he found Kanka comfortably ensconced in the seat meant for visiting Kings!

'How dare you sit on that seat, which is meant for royalty? I will have you whipped for your insolence!' shouted the stunned King.

'Your Majesty! He deserves to occupy the throne of Indra, for he is none other than the greatest ruler this world has seen – my brother, King Yudhishthira, the mighty Pandava!' Arjuna intervened gently.

'But that can't be! If what you say is true, where are his other valiant brothers, and where is Draupadi?' asked the stupefied monarch.

Arjuna introduced the remaining Pandavas and their wife to the King, stripping away the disguises they had adopted. The old King was overcome with emotion, and filled with remorse for his treatment of Yudhishthira. Prince Uttara stepped forward and said, indicating Arjuna, 'This is the deity who rescued me from the Kurus. I owe my life to him.'

'The Gods have been kind to me and to this Kingdom. We must have done something wonderful in our former lives to deserve this honour. I must repay the favour somehow! And I know what to do...my daughter, Princess Uttara, the jewel of Matsya, shall be given to Arjuna in marriage.'

'Your benevolence is boundless, your Majesty, but since I have been your daughter's teacher for a year, it will go against the creed of *dharma* if I were to take her as my wife. I shall accept her for my son Abhimanyu, instead,' replied Arjuna.

'So be it!' said Virata, his eyes filling with tears of joy.

The Pandavas took up residence in the town of Upaplavya in Matsya, and sent word to their kinsmen, while King Virata began preparations for a grand wedding. The Pandavas were thankful that their arduous exile was finally over. Arjuna was doubly thankful as his manhood had been restored, just as Indra had predicted. The irrepressible Bheema patted him on his shoulder and said, 'Brihannala was talented no doubt, but I am glad Arjuna is back. I was afraid we would be forced to make you dance for Duryodhana on the battlefield and hope he laughs himself to death.'

'It would be simpler to have an eating competition between the two of you. Everybody knows that when it comes to gluttony, you are unbeatable,' Arjuna retorted.

Nakula and Sahadeva laughed with gay abandon at the japery of their elder brothers, while Yudhishthira watched them all fondly, even as his heart grew heavy contemplating the battle ahead and the suffering they still had to endure.

Abhimanyu, Krishna, Dhrishtadyumna, and many others, arrived to show their support, glad that the Pandavas had not only survived their terrible ordeal but emerged stronger than before. And so, gathering their allies close to them, the brothers waited, hoping against hope that Duryodhana would come to his senses and avert the pointless violence and destruction that lay ahead.

13
Arjuna's Charioteer

The years in exile had made the Pandavas all too familiar with great suffering and privation. They had lost their father at a young age and endured countless hardships – they had fought to stay alive; roamed the land as poverty-stricken Brahmins; lost their hard-earned kingdom to Duryodhana; and been exiled for thirteen years. The brothers therefore decided that it would be in the best interests of all to sue for peace as war would bring in its wake death, destruction, and misery for both the victor and the vanquished.

Yudhishthira and his brothers did all in their power to bring about a peaceful resolution to the problems between the cousins. They were even willing to give up Indraprastha, which was their's by right, and settle for five villages instead. Peace envoys attested to the same when they spoke on behalf of the Pandavas, at the court of Hastinapura. Sanjaya, Bhishma, Drona, Kripa and Gandhari, did their utmost to make Duryodhana do the right thing by his cousins. But the Kuru Prince, encouraged by cronies like Karna, Shakuni and Duhshasana, remained as obstinate as ever and refused to part with even an iota of his ill-gotten gains.

As a last resort, Krishna went to speak to the Kauravas, though he knew the great battle was preordained and fate would run its irrevocable course. And sure enough, his mission was unsuccessful, as Duryodhana famously declared he would not surrender to his cousins even as much land as could be covered by the tip of a needle.

The Pandavas had no alternative but to reclaim their Kingdom by force. Preparations for war had been going on covertly on both sides since the Pandavas had come out of hiding but now these assumed battle urgency as both sides attempted to strengthen their positions before the conflict that had been brewing for so long and which had finally come to boil. The warring factions attempted to bring over prospective allies to their respective sides. Krishna was by far the most sought after.

It was a blessed era and those who lived in those times were fortunate, as Lord Vishnu had taken the form of an *avatar* and graced the earth as Krishna. He was without doubt, the most redoubtable being in existence. Even as a mere lad, he had performed miracles – killing demons like Putana, Keshin, the evil Kamsa, and the wrestler Chanura. He had lifted Mount Govardhana with his little finger, in order to protect his people; and tamed the great serpent Kaliya, and made the waters of the river Yamuna fit to drink again. With great nobility for one so young, he had turned down the throne of Mathura and restored it to the aged Ugrasena.

As an adult, he continued to perform marvellous feats. The demon Narakasura, was slain by him and the beautiful women the demon had enslaved, were rescued and taken under his wing. Krishna also went to Draupadi's aid when the odious Duhshasana attempted to disrobe her after the dice games. He protected his people from the powerful king of Magadha, Jarasandha, and had them removed miraculously to Dwaraka, to keep them safe from his savagery.

Given his remarkable feats over the years, it was hardly surprising that both the Pandavas and Kauravas desired to have him fighting on their side, for it was well known that where Krishna went, victory was sure to follow. Arjuna and Duryodhana personally travelled to Dwaraka to enlist Krishna's help. They both reached his chambers at the same time. Krishna was fast asleep. Without a word, Duryodhana seated himself on a richly wrought seat placed at the head of Krishna's bed. Arjuna took up his position at the foot of the bed and stood there respectfully. Positioned thus, the cousins did a thorough job of pretending the other did not exist.

When Krishna woke, Duryodhana spoke up first. 'Krishna! War is inevitable between us and our cousins. I have come to seek your help. And let me inform you that I was here first. You are related to us both and it behoves you not to show any prejudice or partiality in this matter. Therefore, knowing your greatness and unblemished conduct, I ask that you grant my request first.'

Krishna spoke softly. 'Duryodhana, while it may be that you came first, the fact remains that I saw Arjuna first. Secondly, custom dictates that the youngest speak first, so I will have to allow him first choice. But you were correct in saying that I have to treat you both equally, so this is what I have decided. One of you can have the mighty Yadava army, while I offer only myself to the other. And I must inform you that I shall not pick up a weapon or take part in the actual fighting, as I refuse to fight those who are related to me by blood. Now the time has come for you to choose. Arjuna, you have the first choice.'

'I choose you, Krishna,' Arjuna said without the slightest hesitation.

Duryodhana's face, which had been distorted with molten rage, turned gleeful. 'And I choose your army!' he said quickly.

Having received Krishna's consent, he went to Balarama, his *guru*, to convey the happy tidings, convinced that he had got the better part of the bargain. Balarama was not so pleased with the turn of events and informed Duryodhana that he himself would not take sides in the battle and had decided to go on a pilgrimage instead. The eldest Kaurava shrugged, listened to the well meaning advice he was given with half an ear, and returned to his Kingdom in high spirits, contemplating his good fortune that Arjuna, for all his brilliance in warfare, was not blessed with a brain the way he himself was. Meanwhile, the object of his scornful thoughts was equally convinced that Duryodhana was a blundering fool for not realizing that the mightiest armies in all the three worlds would not be equal to even a tenth of Krishna.

Krishna himself wondered aloud if Arjuna had done the wise thing in choosing him over his army. 'Are you absolutely sure that you made the right choice Arjuna?'

'Without a doubt!' came the sanguine reply. 'With you on our side, there is no way we can lose. Duryodhana is a fool not to realize that. And since you will not be taking part in the actual fighting, will you consent to be my charioteer? It has long been a fond hope of mine.'

'So be it! It will be as you wish.' Replied Krishna, knowing that it was destined to be so.

'The battle is already won! I can feel it in my bones!' exclaimed Arjuna.

Krishna only smiled at his friend's childlike exuberance, and was secretly sorry that he could not spare him the anguish that was to follow, as the price of victory.

But Arjuna was right about one thing. Krishna would have a pivotal role to play in the outcome of the battle of Kurukshetra, and it was he who controlled the ebb and flow of the war. Long before the battle commenced, Krishna began to set in motion events that were intended to influence the outcome of the battle in favour of the Pandavas. *Bhoomi Devi* had complained about the burden of sin she was carrying, and Lord Vishnu had agreed to take on the form of an *avatar* and walk on earth in order to offer her surcease from suffering. Thus, it was Krishna's task to root out the evil that had become almost invincible, and thus ensure victory for the Pandavas, who represented all that was noble in this epic clash between good and evil.

Jarasandha, Shishupala, Ekalavya, and Ghatotkacha (the son of Bheema), among others, were those killed through the direct intervention of Krishna, or as a result of his stratagem, with someone else actually striking the killing blow. These men had to be killed as they would have otherwise fought on the side of the Kauravas under Duryodhana, and tilted the scale precariously in favour of the evil Kauravas; and they would have tormented the innocent if left alive.

King Jarasandha, the mighty Emperor of Magadha, was a force to be reckoned with in those days. His valour and courage were extraordinary and his achievements legendary. He had given his beloved daughters, Asti and Prapti, in marriage to Kamsa, Krishna's maternal uncle, who was notorious for his cruelty and tyranny. He was furious with Krishna for widowing his daughters and never forgave him or his people. To his dying breath, he sought to destroy them.

The Emperor attacked Mathura seventeen times and each time he was repulsed by Krishna, who destroyed his vast armies to a man on each occasion, sparing only his life. When he returned for the eighteenth time, Krishna also had to contend with a threat from a deadly warrior named Kalayavana. He knew that while he was engaged with the fearsome warrior and his soldiers, Jarasandha would swoop down on his people like a hawk upon fledglings, and kill them without mercy.

In order to protect the citizens of Mathura, Krishna conjured up an impenetrable fortress, said to have been ninety-six miles long, from the bottom of the sea. Within, nestled like a pearl within the protective confines of an oyster, lay a delightful Kingdom that had been crafted to perfection, with beautifully wrought homes for the populace and marvellous buildings. Pillars of sheer gold dazzled the eye as they caught the rays of the sun and outshone it in magnificence. Precious gems adorned the various edifices in the Kingdom, lending considerable allure to the surroundings. Gorgeous flowers and tall trees bloomed everywhere, making the place appear radiant and green. The treasury was filled to overflowing, thanks to the munificence of the great Lord. The whole place embodied prosperity and blessed were the people who had been chosen to live within its hallowed walls.

When the fortress was ready for human inhabitation, Krishna transferred the citizens of Mathura with their belongings and cattle, to the newly founded Kingdom of Dwaraka on the sea, with his yogic powers. Ensuring his people were safely ensconced within, Krishna and Balarama went to take care of Kalayavana. The former led his antagonist to a cave where Muchukunda reposed in deep slumber, having won a boon from the *deva*s for his services. Kalayavana, thinking he was Krishna, kicked the saintly man savagely and woke him. When Muchukunda opened his eyes to see who had thus disturned his sleep so rudely, Kalayavana was burnt to ashes.

Having thus disposed of one threat, Krishna and Balarama turned their attention to Jarasandha. They tricked the King into believing they were fleeing; scaled a mountain, and returned to Dwaraka. In so doing, they freed themselves and their people from Jarasandha's grasp forever. Later, Krishna engineered a wrestling bout between Bheema and Jarasandha and helped the valiant Pandava to emerge victorious.

Krishna himself narrated the story of Jarasandha's miraculous birth to Yudhishthira and his brothers, while they were contemplating the performance of the *Rajasuya yajna*. 'The terrible King of Magadha, who is famed for his strength, believed to be equivalent to a thousand elephants, was born to King Vrihadratha and his twin wives. Vrihadratha had promised to treat his wives equally and always endeavoured to do so. Preoccupied with the duties of governing a Kingdom and carrying out religious rites and rituals that demanded abstinence and fasting, the King allowed many years to elapse without producing an heir. Anxious for a son, he consulted wise men everywhere and tried everything they recommended in order to impregnate his wives, but met with no success.

Finally, he went to the sage Chandakaushika and begged for his help. Moved by his plight, the sage meditated briefly and lo! A perfectly formed mango appeared out of nowhere onto his lap. He gifted it to the King and told him to give it to his wife immediately to eat. The King hastened back to his palace filled with hope, and gave the mango to his two wives.

The sisters cut the mango in half and consumed it. Soon, they conceived and delivered their babies at exactly the same time. However, both delivered half a baby. They were horrified. Filled with revulsion and superstitious dread, they ordered the midwives to discard the malformed pieces of flesh.

As the two halves lay alone and unwanted, by the providence of fate, a *rakshasi* by the name of Jara, happened to find them. Delighted with the choice morsels of human flesh that would no doubt prove to be a most satisfactory repast, she greedily scooped up the two pieces and without further ado proceeded to join them in order to make it a less cumbersome load.

As soon as she had done so, the monstrous pieces of flesh became a baby boy that was flawless in all respects. Angered at the disrespectful handling of his person, the infant began squalling and the sound shook the mountains. His parents came rushing out on hearing the noise and saw the boy made whole. Jara graciously decided to forego her meal and instead, revealed all that had happened and presented the baby boy to his proud parents. And so he came to be called Jarasandha in her honour.'

As Krishna concluded his story, Yudhishthira broke the hush that had fallen over the little group. 'Despite the wondrous events surrounding his birth, I find it hard to believe that he has dared to make an enemy of you, continues to defy you, and still has breath left in his body!'

'His death will not be by my hand. But that is not to say that I will have no part in it...' Krishna replied and smiled rather enigmatically before continuing. 'It will be impossible to perform the sacrifice with him alive as he will never submit to you. But there is no cause for worry, as we can defeat him easily using clever strategy. I need your permission to take Arjuna and Bheema with me to Magadha, where we will defeat him using a plan that has been formulated by me. If you have faith in me, send your brothers along on this mission, and you will have helped rid the world of a heartless despot.'

'You don't need to ask my permission. I would trust you with my life. By all means take them along and if it is not asking too much, please keep Bheema from getting into one of his infamous brawls.'

'Don't worry Yudhishthira, I am sure Krishna will ensure Bheema's fighting instincts are channelised in the right direction,' said Arjuna, his eyes twinkling.

'And for my part, I'll try to protect Krishna and Arjuna from the love-struck women who are always luring them into romantic escapades and keep them focused solely on the task at hand,' said Bheema affably, cheered immeasurably by the prospect of a fresh, violent conflict.

The trio set off for Magadha, disguised as Brahmins. Jarasandha welcomed them warmly although their attire, somewhat at odds with their warlike demeanour, aroused his suspicions. Also, they refused to enter through the city gate, choosing instead to make a more ominous entrance by obliterating the mountain peak, Chaityaka, one of the natural fortifications of Magadha, nor would they partake of food that contained salt.

Having catered to their unusual demands, Jarasandha began questioning them. Krishna then revealed their identities and the purpose of their visit.

'So you are not just a lowly cowherd but a despicable coward as well! Why am I not surprised Krishna? I suppose it is because this is precisely the kind of dishonourable behaviour I can expect from someone of your lowly standing!' Jarasandha bellowed at Krishna, galled by the sheer audacity of the trio.

'I don't see how you are qualified to talk about honour, given the many atrocities you have committed, oh King of Magadha. Innocent people have been senselessly slaughtered because of your arrogance, and what of the Kings you have captured and imprisoned, who are to be sacrificed to Lord Shiva?' Krishna replied in a low voice that was as even in its tone as it was deadly.

'I suppose you would be less aggrieved if I were to sacrifice those Kings to Vishnu instead?' came the snide rejoinder from Jarasandha, to the accusations that were being hurled thick and fast at him.

'Neither Shiva nor Vishnu would condone such inhuman practices, oh King! And the time for discussing the ethics behind your actions is long past. Today, you shall answer for your sins!' answered Krishna, as implacable as a stone pillar.

'We will see about that Krishna... what is it be? Do I have to fight the three of you single-handedly, or do I have to face your armies? It hardly matters to me, as I will make mincemeat out of whatever or whomever you throw my way!' said Jarasandha, his voice like a trumpet call.

A moment of utter silence followed his words, then Krishna spoke with cool detachment: 'We challenge you to single combat with any one of us. The choice is yours!'

'So be it! I will not even consider fighting with a cowherd who has the bad taste to appear uninvited before those who are his superiors. Such an act would be beneath me. And Jarasandha, famed for possessing the strength of a thousand elephants, does not fight little boys, even if they are considered fine warriors by those who do not know better. I choose Bheema, because he alone can match my physical strength.'

Hasty preparations were made for combat, which was to be a fight to the finish. The two behemoths faced each other in the arena erected specially for them, and lunged at each other with an almighty roar. The contest raged for fourteen days, with neither fighter pausing for even a bite of food. Both fought with the grim intent to kill and employed every trick they had ever learned to gain the upper hand. They fought with gigantic maces, and when those deadly weapons were smashed to smithereens ,unable to withstand the repeated blows against their agate-like bodies, the two fought with their bare fists, which were far deadlier. They wrestled with the implacable ferocity of wild beasts and the ground shook under their feet. A huge crowd had gathered to watch and they exhorted the participants to further exertions, revelling in the terrible violence that was unfolding before their bloodthirsty eyes.

Sweat ran in rivulets down the straining bodies of the two combatants and their eyes were red with fury. The fight went on and on...with neither combatant gaining the upper hand, though it was not for want of trying. On the fourteenth day, Jarasandha began to tire but he fought harder than ever, knowing that his life would be forfeit if he slowed down. Sensing the end was near one way or the other, Bheema shot a glance at Krishna, hoping for some guidance; and the latter, prepared for this precise moment, held up a twig and split it in two before throwing it aside. Bheema understood at once what he needed to do.

Lifting up the gigantic body of Jarasandha, Bheema spun him around before hurling him to the ground. Grabbing hold of his ankles, he tore the prostate body in two and hurled the pieces away in opposite directions, thereby emerging the victor in the deadliest fight he had ever been in. The crowd around him looked on in fearful silence. Bheema was a frightening apparition indeed, covered in the dead man's blood and bone fragments.

Having accomplished what they had set out to do, Krishna, Arjuna and Bheema, acted quickly. They dragged Jarasandha's body to the entrance of the Kingdom ,to serve as a warning to the citizens, in case anyone had the foolishness to think of putting up a fight. The imprisoned Kings were released next and they were only too pleased to promise fealty to King Yudhishthira, before returning thankfully to their domains. Finally, having crowned Jarasandha's son, the noble Sahadeva, as King, the trio departed.

Arjuna looked at his brother admiringly, marvelling at his great strength and feeling extremely proud of him. Seeing the look on his face, Bheema said, 'It was a good fight. Despite his many flaws, that man was no coward and he fought most heroically.'

'He had to die Bheema. There was no other way...' Krishna said, looking ahead as though he could see something in the perpetually shifting haze of the future, which the others could not.

'I am relieved he is no longer around. Somehow it makes me feel easier in my mind. Did he hurt you badly Bheema?' Arjuna asked.

'Now there is no need to be insulting Arjuna! Of course I am none the worse for wear. However, I would have been happier if Jara had done the sensible thing and gobbled up those two pieces of flesh instead of joining them up and inflicting Jarasandha on a hapless world!' answered Bheema with his usual insousience.

With Jarasandha out of the way, preparations for the *Rajasuya Yajna* began. The Pandavas worked hard to ensure that everything went smoothly. Invitations were sent to rulers and wise men all over the world and every single one of them attended, to honour Yudhishthira. The great sacrifice commenced with Veda Vyasa himself taking on the duties of head priest. The *yajna* was carried out without a hitch and declared a tremendous success. When it was time to distribute the sacrificial libations to the honoured guests, Yudhishthira asked Grandsire Bhisma to choose the person, the foremost of the gathering, who deserved to be honoured first. Without hesitation, Bhishma declared Krishna as the one most deserving to receive the sanctified offering first. Immeasurably pleased with the Grandsire's words, Yudhishthira agreed that Krishna was indeed the best of them all. Sahadeva, as the youngest, carried the ritual offering to Krishna, who accepted it with his inherent grace.

The entire gathering broke into spontaneous applause in approbation of Bhishma's choice; but there was one in the prestigious crowd who was far from happy. It was Shishupala, the famed King of the Chedis. He voiced his disapproval in strident tones. 'Yudhishthira! Have you taken leave of your senses?' he said, shaking with fury. 'You are still young in years so your gross error in judgment is understandable. But Bhishma should know better, given his famed knowledge and wisdom. I realize now that his reputation is ill-deserved. And as for Krishna, it is disgraceful that he accepted the first offering knowing well that there were others in this assembly far more deserving of the honour. King Ugrasena is seated here along with his father Vasudeva, and the cowherd deems himself more worthy than his elders? Drupada, Drona, Kripa and Bhishma himself, should have been considered. Yudhishthira! I came here not because I fear you but from respect. However, it would appear that I overestimated your judgment and integrity.'

Having made his feelings clear, Shishupala stormed out of the assembly in high dudgeon, closely followed by his supporters. Yudhishthira was dismayed as this virulent outburst had cast a pall over the auspicious occasion. He ran after the King of Chedi, wishing to pacify him. 'Wait! O King of Chedi, it is not for us to question the judgment of the Grandsire, for he is truly the wisest of us all. Besides, his decision has the approval of all present. Perhaps you are allowing your passions to cloud your vision. You will be doing me a great favour by reconsidering your position.'

Bhishma, displeased with this disruption, intervened. 'Reason is wasted on one who is oblivious to the glory of Krishna, so don't waste your breath on the Chedi King,' he told Yudhishthira. 'If he is unhappy with what has been decided by older and wiser heads, then it is his prerogative to leave. Don't stop him,' Bhishma said with majestic disdain.

Sahadeva also chimed in. 'I say this to all among you who are unhappy with the worship I offered to the noblest soul in this gathering – only the truly unworthy would question the worth of Krishna, and it would give me great pleasure to crush such heads beneath my feet.' The celestials rained flowers upon his head and cries of, 'Well said!' rent the air. However, some of the Kings present flushed with anger. Bhishma, on his part, smiled at Sahadeva conveying his approbation to the youngest Pandava.

At this, Shishupala, who had paused hearing Yudhishthira's plea, took instant umbrage and turning on Bhishma like a rabid dog, said, 'Bhishma! Your mind grows feeble with old age; that is why you chose to honour a cowherd over other eminent personages. There is nothing at all remarkable about Krishna and every so-called miraculous act he has supposedly performed since birth, can be traced to charlatanism – of which he is no doubt a master. And since you cannot see through his chicanery, I can only assume that you have forgotten your learning in your dotage, and as a result of the long years of celibacy you had no choice but to practice on account of your own impotency!'

'Are you not aware that it is only through the mercy of Krishna that you are still alive?' Bhishma snarled at him. 'No man would dare to talk to me like that and draw another breath. Krishna is destined to be your slayer, but he has given his word that he will forgive you a hundred faults. Your life has been given to you in the same way a beggar receives alms. At the time of your birth, you had an extra pair of arms and a third eye. A number of ill-omens marked your coming, and you looked so hideous that all the wise men advised your parents to get rid of you immediately and they were inclined to do so. But divine intervention saved your life. A heavenly voice declared that you were destined to meet your end at the hands of the noblest being to walk this earth, and that this person would be revealed to all because your deformities would vanish on being placed on his lap. Your mother then handed you over to every person who came to visit and in this manner discovered that Krishna would be your slayer. Anxious to keep you safe, she begged him to forgive you a hundred times over and with typical magnanimity, Krishna agreed. You are tempting fate when you carry on in this manner."

'Say what you wish old man, but I will not fear the cowherd. In fact, I challenge him to a fight. Then you will see what happens to those who dare to provoke the Bull of Chedi!' Shishupala shouted, hastening his doom with every foul word he uttered.

Krishna had remained silent during this heated exchange; only his lips moved, although the movement was almost imperceptible. Now he broke his silence. 'Shishupala owes his life to a mother's love. I have never harmed him and neither have my people. But he has never missed a chance to do us a wrong turn. Once, when the men were away, he sneaked into Dwaraka and set it on fire. He cruelly raped one of our young women and slaughtered many innocent citizens. All this and more have I forgiven but today he has gone too far.'

With a quick movement, Krishna sent the *Sudarshana Chakra,* which had appeared miraculously on his finger, blazing towards the King of Chedi. In a split second, his decapitated head rolled across the floor and came to a standstill before the horrified gathering. Yudhishthira ordered his brothers to give a fitting funeral to the fallen King, worthy of a brave if brash warrior. He was deeply disturbed by the inauspicious turn the *yajna* had taken. The atmosphere had turned muggy with menace, resentment, envy and anger. He shuddered at the thought of what this meant for their future.

At this point, however, all that mattered was that two invincible warriors of the day had been hastened to their deaths by Krishna.

Another purer and more unfortunate soul, also met his end before the battle of Kurukshetra. It was the blameless son of the Nishada King, Ekalavya.

On the eve of the battle of Kurukshetra, Ekalavya, the Nishada Prince, decided to offer his services to Duryodhana. Krishna tried to dissuade him, for maimed or not, he was still a dangerous foe and posed a threat to his beloved Arjuna. He said to Ekalvya: 'This is not your war. Your place is in the forest with its creatures, over whom you hold sway. It is unwise of you to join in this conflict that does not concern you and fight on the side where evil reigns supreme.'

'I agree with your words, Krishna. But true evil reigns in the heart of the man who will shamelessly raise his bow and let loose deadly arrows in the direction of the *guru* who taught him all he knows! That is precisely why I have chosen the opposing camp,' calmly answered the Prince.

'Arjuna does what he does because necessity dictates his actions. Do not allow your hatred for him to cloud your better judgment!' urged Krishna, knowing the nobility of Eklavya's soul.

'I do not care about the son of Kunti! My *guruji* must be protected at all costs, and I will guard him with my life. Anyone who dares to threaten him will fall prey to my marauding arrows! This I swear with all my heart!'

Sensing that Ekalavya's mind was made up, Krishna lured him into a protracted discussion on the ethics of the matter, knowing well that the Nishada Prince felt strongly about the subject and would lose himself in the argument. While Ekalavya ranted on and on, Krishna plunged a dagger into his back. Having struck the mortal blow, he revealed his divine identity to the unfortunate soul who lay at his feet, bleeding to death. The agonised expression on Ekalavya's face changed to one of ecstasy and he said, 'I am truly blessed to have the honour of dying at your hands!'

'You are a good man and a truly noble soul. Future generations will listen to your story and draw inspiration, courage, and fortitude from it. Your name will become synonymous with those qualities,' said Krishna, feeling deep sorrow welling within his heart like a wellspring.

Eklavya then spoke once more. 'I can ask for nothing more but I beg one last favour of you. My mother should not know a moment's grief on my account.'

'So be it!' Krishna assured the dying Prince.

Relieved and having achieved complete peace of mind, Ekalavya breathed his last and departed from a world which had been cruel to him, but which had not managed to dim his ardour for life or broken his spirit. Krishna blessed the fallen hero. To keep his word to the dead man, he went to his mother and claimed her life as well, to spare her the misery and grief of losing her noble son.

In his role as Arjuna's charioteer, Krishna guided the Pandavas successfully through the labyrinthine paths they had to traverse in order to achieve victory over their cousins. By bringing about the deaths of Jarasandha, Ekalavya, and Shishupala, before the battle, he removed three major obstacles that would have obstructed the path to triumph.

On the eve of the battle, Arjuna was surveying the battle formation of the enemy ahead of him when he saw the beloved faces of his Grandsire, teacher, relatives, and former friends. He crumpled within and lost heart. His limbs felt leaden and he shivered as if suffering from ague. Sweat moistened his brow and all the fight went out of him. At that moment, a mere greenhorn would have been a fiercer antagonist on the battlefield.

Krishna watched the sea change in Arjuna, who only a few moments ago had been raring to have a go at his persecutors and redress the wrongs done him and his own. He was mightily displeased and sternly reprimanded Arjuna for his unmanly hesitation. But Arjuna declared that he would rather beg for alms than turn his bow against the Grandsire or his *guru*, or any of the beloved faces he saw on the opposite side.

It was a starkly critical moment; time was running out and the outcome of the battle which had been preordained, hung by the most fragile of threads. Krishna sighed and drawing in a deep breath, began to speak. He talked about a man's *karma* or duty and how its performance with a complete lack of attachment absolved him from any wrongdoing incurred in the process. He explained to Arjuna that desire was the root cause of evil in the world and one should perform what one was born to do in accordance with one's station in life, without becoming entangled in a web of emotion. Addressing Arjuna's reluctance to kill his relatives, Krishna told him that the physical body may be destroyed and reduced to ashes, but the soul itself, which is housed within, would always remain untouched as it was eternal and would merely pass on to another body. He reminded the sorrowing Arjuna that awareness of these truths was the first step towards the acquisition of true knowledge which, when tempered with faith and devotion, takes the embodied soul towards enlightenment and salvation.

Arjuna listened to this discourse, but his doubts continued to plague him. He said as much to Krishna. The Lord then chided him gently and said that it was his arrogance which was blinding him to the truth; that he was being presumptuous in thinking that he had any control over what had been decreed by divine will; that he was simply an instrument to carry out what was pre-destined, and so he should discharge his duty without any doubt or vacillation. To drive his point home, Krishna revealed his Cosmic Form or*Vishwaroopam,* to his beloved friend and devotee. The two great armies stood poised for battle and were observing with avid interest Arjuna's moment of hesitation. But none had the good fortune to see the Lord in his divine form, for Arjuna alone had been granted divine vision, being as he was that rarest of individuals, who had been singled out from the time of his birth to carry out the will of the Blessed Lord.

Following this miracle, Arjuna felt fresh courage flow through his veins. Renewed purpose once again made his resolve razor sharp. The precious knowledge imparted solely to him, covered him like an impenetrable suit of armour and he felt invincible. The weak indecisive individual who had been ready to throw down his arms and allow his enemies to tear him to pieces, vanished like a transient image in a dream and in its place stood Arjuna, the greatest warrior on earth, the scourge of his enemies and destiny's chosen one. He was finally ready to do what he had been born to do.

When the battle commenced, it was Krishna who urged the Pandavas to implement clever strategies that would claim the lives of Bhishma and Drona. At Krishna's behest, Shikandin would drape feminine apparel over his battle gear in a parody of womanhood, knowing well that the gallant Grandsire would not fight a woman. The ploy, for all its perceived lack of ethics, worked like magic. Bhishma, that peerless ancient with his unshakable values, embraced his own death by allowing Arjuna to use Shikandin as a shield from behind which he fired the mortal arrows that felled the formidable warrior. It was Krishna again who was the real mover behind the deceitful half-truth that his son was dead, which Yudhishthira uttered and so caused Drona to drop his arms and sit on the ground in yogic meditation, making him a ripe target for the murderous blow that Dhrishtadyumna struck him. Krishna made his presence felt at every turn and influenced the course of the battle to ensure victory for the Pandavas.

On more than one occasion, when death cast its shadow over Arjuna, Krishna intervened to keep the dark Lord at bay. During the battle of Kurukshetra, Bhagadatta, the ruler of the ancient Kingdom of Pragjyotishapura, was mowing down the Pandava forces mounted on his deadly elephant, Supratika. It was the twelfth day of the battle and Bhishma had fallen the previous day. Rushing in to fill the void left by Bhishma, Bhagadatta fell on the hapless soldiers like a marauding predator feasting on its kill and cut a bloody swathe across the Pandava forces. The old warrior was the son of the *asura,* Naraka, whom Krishna had killed, mounted on Garuda, with his wife Satyabhama by his side. And Arjuna had approached this mountainous Kingdom of black crystal, when Yudhishthira expressed the desire to perform the *Rajasuya Yajna,* determined to bring all the northern regions under his sway.

Leading his army over the treacherous terrain, Arjuna had found Bhagadatta waiting for him. The two heroes had fought for eight days, at the end of which, Arjuna bested the ageing monarch.

Bhagadatta had been gracious in defeat. 'Your father was a good friend of mine, Arjuna but he would never have prevailed over me in battle, mighty warrior though he was. Today you have proved yourself greater than Pandu, and I know he would have been proud.'

Arjuna paid due respect to the great man and requested him to honour them by attending the *Rajasuya Yajna* they were going to perform. Bhagadatta promised to come and sent Arjuna away with rare and exceedingly valuable presents accumulated by Naraka himself in a bygone era. But the memory of his defeat to a mere youth rankled, and when the battle of Kurukshetra commenced, Bhagadatta allied himself with Duryodhana, hoping to avenge his humiliation.

The valiant old man, whose fatal flaw was his mean-spirited pettiness, was borne into battle by the elephant, Supratika. Together they resembled the formidable mountains from whence they came, and they slaughtered their enemies with deathly efficiency, despatching thousands to the nether world. Bheema and Yudhishthira tried to halt the advances of the duo, but failed miserably.

Arjuna heard the cries of his men and rushed to their aid, but he was stopped *en route* by the *Samsaptakas*, mercenaries who had sworn to conquer or be killed in battle. An entire *akshauhini* of these warriors had belonged to Krishna and Duryodhana had received them along with the rest of Krishna's army. An *akshauhini* consisted of 109,350 infantry, 65, 610 cavalry, 21,870 chariots and 21,870 elephants. This formidable group of men challenged Arjuna to a fight, and Arjuna had no choice but to respond, leaving the rest of his army to the mercy of Bhagadatta.

Arjuna fought and vanquished the *Samsaptaka*s before turning his attention back to Bhagadatta, who was proving to be increasingly irksome to him and his brothers. The veteran welcomed Arjuna's advance and replied in kind. An epic battle then took place between the two heroes. Bhagadatta on his mountainous mount launched a furious attack against Arjuna, who was in his chariot with Krishna at the helm. From his vantage position, reminiscent of Indra who used to wage war against the *asura*s from amongst the clouds, Bhagadatta showered arrows on Krishna and Arjuna, tormenting them. Krishna, with unparalleled skill, manoeuvred the chariot to the blind side of the elephant, leaving Bhagadatta vulnerable to Arjuna's *Gandeeva*. But Arjuna scorned this manner of killing a worthy opponent or his mount.

Supratika, however, continued to trample men and fellow beasts or mauled them by imprisoning them between its fearsome tusks and dashing them to the ground and savaging them to bloody pulp if they still had breath left. Arjuna became infuriated with the great beast and turning his great bow towards Supratika, he let fly winged darts that smashed its armour like eggshells. More shafts buried themselves in the thick hide and blood flowed like a red river. Arjuna then focused on Bhagadatta, cutting off his flagstaff and standard. Before the son of Naraka could recover, he found ten arrows lodged in various points of his body. His counterattack was rebuffed with insulting ease and infuriatingly, Arjuna was smiling carelessly even as he drove Bhagadatta closer to death with every passing second.

Incensed with the younger man's audacity in the face of such a dangerous opponent as himself, Bhagadatta hurled his lance at Arjuna and displaced his golden diadem. Replacing it on his head with infinite calm, the Pandava broke the bow Bhagadatta had snatched up, along with the quiver containing the arrows. Holding his goad like a spear and chanting a divine *mantra*, Bhagadatta converted it into the invincible *Vaishnava* missile and released it. The goad, infused with the power of the *mantra*, flew with unerring accuracy towards Arjuna's bosom. Quicker than thought, Arjuna released missile after missile to tear it apart but it still came towards him without slowing. Just when it seemed that the goad would find its mark, Krishna stood up with a smile and received it on his chest. Arjuna watched, mute with horror, but the missile transformed into a garland of flowers and reposed gently on Krishna's chest.

Rapidly recovering his equanimity, Arjuna said, 'O Krishna! Why did you do that? That missile was intended for me! You swore you would not participate in this accursed war!'

'I did not promise to stand aside and watch you die. Besides, the charioteer's job is to steer his master to safety if his life is ever threatened, and do all in his power to keep him safe. You may not realize it, but for a moment there, you were as helpless as a newborn babe. Moreover, I was just recovering my property...' Krishna replied.

'What do you mean by that Krishna?' Arjuna asked, all at sea.

'It is an old story. Lord Vishnu, to better carry out his role as the protector of the Universe, has four diverse forms. One form remains in a state of constant vigilance, monitoring the good and evil acts that take place in the world. Another takes the form of an *avatar* and descends to the world of mortals to actively uphold good and root out evil. A third form is engaged in the performance of severe austerities for the benefit of mankind, and the fourth form slumbers for a span of a thousand years. On awakening from this life-giving sleep, the Lord grants boons to the deserving. *Bhoomi Devi* once approached the Protector at this precise moment of awakening and begged that He give her son his personal weapon in order to make him invincible, and her wish was granted. Naraka thus acquired the *Vaishnava Astra* and with it in his possession, he was emboldened to become one of the worst villains this world has seen. I had to kill him to save the world from his wrongdoings. Bhagadatta, his son, then became the proud owner of the *Vaishnava*. And he, failing to learn from the mistakes of his father, once again sided with evil, thereby compelling me to intervene. The *Vaishnava* is unstoppable and even Shiva and Indra are powerless against it. Without it, Bhagadatta should be easy enough to slay. Hurry Arjuna, his end draws near!"

Without further argument, Arjuna first killed Supratika with a well placed arrow. Bhagadatta leaped off the dying beast before it hit the ground. Arjuna then severed the piece of cloth that kept the old man's drooping eyelids held up. When he was thus blinded, Arjuna struck the fatal blow which claimed the life of the valiant son of Naraka.

This was not the only time Krishna saved Arjuna from certain death. He warned Arjuna when Ashwasena concealed himself in Karna's arrow, hoping to avenge his mother's death. Knowing that Karna had obtained a special weapon from Indra with the intention of using it on Arjuna, Krishna made sure that the weapon was used on another. When Abhimanyu died a hero's death, Krishna mourned with his best friend, stood by his side, and helped him achieve the seemingly impossible task of revenge he set for himself, swearing to forfeit his life if he failed.

Arjuna considered himself the most fortunate man in the universe as he was the proud recipient of Krishna's friendship. And he was right in thinking so, for the world has never known a more loving friend, a more courageous comrade-in-arms, or a wiser mentor.

14
Death Of A Hero

Abhimanyu, the son of Arjuna and Subhadra, was believed to be an incarnation of the Moon God, Soma. The lad had inherited the best characteristics of the Pandavas and his maternal uncle Krishna, and was everybody's favourite. Everyone, including step-mother Draupadi, adored him for his exemplary qualities. He was a devoted adherent of *dharma* like Yudhishthira, robust like Bheema, gallant and skilful like his father, handsome, gentle, smart, and witty like Nakula and Sahadeva, and as cheerful and savvy as Krishna.

Although the noble youth lived for only sixteen years, his heroic feats and tragic death made him immortal. He was like a shooting star that blazed across the heavens, bathing all in its brilliance, and then fading all too soon. In the battle of Kurukshetra, he proved his mettle and showed the world that he was truly his great father's son.

When the Pandavas were sent into exile following Yudhishthira's humiliating loss in the game of dice engineered by Shakuni, Krishna took Subhadra and Abhimanyu away with him. Though he was well looked after by his mother and uncle, the little boy missed his father deeply. Subhadra told him the ugly story and instilled in him a steely determination to win back for his father everything he had lost to the greed and guile of wicked men. He would confide in his uncle Krishna and promise in his childlike lisp that he would win back the Kingdom for his father and uncles. Krishna would smile and encourage him, knowing well what was written in his destiny.

The young Prince was a precocious child and quickly mastered the Vedas and martial arts – to the pride of his father and uncles. He grew up proud and strong and everyone agreed that he equalled his legendary father in terms of martial prowess. Arjuna arranged his marriage to Princess Uttara, daughter of King Virata, shortly before the great war. Their posthumous son, Parikshit, would be the perpetuator of the noble lineage.

Abhimanyu joined his father on the battlefield of Kurukshetra and distinguished himself from day one. He was but a mere stripling but he put hardened veterans to shame with his dazzling fighting skills. Few people could withstand his might and Bhishma's eyes were laden with tears when he witnessed the young hero fight as if he were Arjuna himself. The Pandavas came to depend heavily on him and Abhimanyu rose to the challenge. He proved equal to every daunting task they threw his way, until a particularly heavy burden proved too much even for someone as valiant as he.

When Bhishma fell, Drona was given command over the Kaurava forces. Pleased with Duryodhana for the faith he had in him, the Acharya granted him a boon, and Duryodhana asked him to capture Yudhishthira alive in order to finish the war. Drona mistakenly thought that the Kuru Prince had finally come to his senses and wished to spare the life of his noble cousin, but was immeasurably saddened to discover that Duryodhana merely intended to challenge his rival for the throne through another game of dice and so send him back into exile. Sick with distaste, the Archarya agreed to the boon he had promised but stipulated: 'I will do all in my power to capture Yudhishthira alive, but I must warn you that it will be a futile attempt if Arjuna is there to protect his brother. As his teacher, I have always known that there is none to equal him in straight combat. Therefore, if I am to carry out this task, something must be done to remove him from Yudhishthira's side.'

Duryodhana summoned his cohorts and they hatched a plan to separate the brothers. Susharma, King of the Trigartas, offered his services. Arjuna had crushed them when they had refused to submit to Yudhishthira prior to the *Rajasuya Yajna* and had forced the mutinous men to pay tribute. The defeat at Matsya, suffered at the hands of the Pandavas, when the Trigartas aided by the Kurus had sought to capture King Virata, had been yet another blow. Susharma and his brothers hated the Pandavas in general and Arjuna in particular, with a passion that bordered on lunacy. Seating themselves around the sacred fire and with Agni as their witness, they took the *Samsaptaka* oath, swearing to kill Arjuna in battle or be killed themselves. Thus, a formidable suicide squad bent on the destruction of Arjuna, came into being.

Duryodhana was jubilant with the vow made by the Trigarta brothers, as it could potentially turn the tide in their favour. In addition, the *akshauhini* of the Samsaptakas he had acquired from Krishna would keep Arjuna's hands full, leaving the Acharya free to capture Yudhishthira. Delighted with his diabolic plan, Duryodhana sat back and wallowed in pleasurable anticipation of a heady victory on the morrow.

When the Pandavas heard from their spies about the plot to capture Yudhishthira, they were deeply distressed. Yudhishthira was the first to speak: 'If the Acharya captures me alive, all is lost!'

'Don't worry, King Yudhishthira! While there is breath left in my body, Drona will not be able to lay a finger on you,' said Arjuna confidently, though he had mixed feelings. He was annoyed and angered that his *guru* had decided to go after the noble Yudhishthira, but baulked at the prospect of harming the man who was his revered mentor.

An enraged Bheema spoke up with characteristic brusquerie.

'I never understood why you are so fond of him, Arjuna. You keep saying that it was your fortune to have such a great teacher even when he was clearly partial to that lout he sired, Ashwatthama. And it is my belief that you would still be the best warrior of all time even if he had not taught you. It is about time we did something about him. How could he agree to such a craven request?'

'They all give in to Duryodhana eventually out of some twisted sense of morality. Let us not worry about those things. Our job from this point onwards is to keep Yudhishthira safe from our teacher,' Arjuna said, determined to avoid a quarrel with his belligerent brother on a subject they had argued about many times before.

'But it is said that the Acharya is one of the best warriors of all time! And with Parashurama's weapons, he is well nigh invincible. I tremble to think of the future now that he has me in his sights,' Yudhishthira said in tones of despair.

'Do not let that man worry you, my dear brother,' Bheema said stoically. 'Arjuna can trounce him on any given day of the week, his fine scruples notwithstanding. And we have Dhrishtadyumna on our side, and you know that he was born to slay the Acharya. It is only a matter of time before he pays the price for following his fool of a son and going over to Duryodhana's side!'

Despite Bheema's rousing words, a cloud of unease settled over the Pandava camp. It was as though Drona had cast a noose around their collective necks and was drawing it tighter and tighter to choke the life out of them. Determined to keep his promise to Duryodhana, Drona made several attempts to capture Yudhishthira. But he simply could not make it happen. Every time he neared the eldest Pandava, Arjuna would materialise at his side, as if telepathically sensing his elder brother's need; and, eyes blazing with wrath, Arjuna would go on to repel his teacher with furious vigour. The *Samsaptakas* descended on Arjuna like a swarm of pestilential bees, but even their frenzied fury could not match the prowess of the third Pandava brother. It was as if he had sprouted wings and could magically divine where he was needed most, and transport himself to that exact spot faster than the mind could conceive.

The allies of the Pandavas also threw themselves into the fray as they knew what was at stake and selflessly sacrificed their lives to keep Yudhishthira safe. Every time the Kauravas made inroads into the Pandava army, they were driven back by sheer force of will, even though the Pandavas were often hopelessly outnumbered. And Arjuna seemed to be everywhere at once. Drona was frustrated time and again in his attempts to capture Yudhishthira and it seemed there was little he could do to salvage the situation.

Duryodhana was being driven to despair by the repeated failures and thwarted desires. 'Why is it proving so hard to annihilate those scoundrels Karna? This battle should have been over long ago. Surely our superior eleven *akshauhini*s should have been sufficient to quell their measly seven? Why is victory proving to be so damn elusive?'

'We knew it wouldn't be easy Duryodhana...' Karna said solemnly. 'They fight to avenge the countless insults and wrongs done them. They fight with the fury of their biting humiliation and a deep-rooted desire for revenge. I think they got through the hard years of exile by fantasizing about how best to kill us. That she-devil, the enchantress Draupadi, has kept the flames of their wrath blazing with her constant reminders of what we did to her and them. It will not be easy to break them.'

'Am I going to lose everything Karna? I would rather die than let those usurpers prevail over me!' said Duryodhana, looking every inch the spoilt child he had always been, but still managing to endear himself to his best friend.

'Don't be depressed, Duryodhana! There is no need. I will destroy your enemies for you. Unlike your other allies, I am more than a match for the Pandava brothers. Bhishma and Drona are too soft. They fight on our side despite loving the Pandavas more. That is why Bhishma allowed himself to be rushed to his deathbed and Drona dithers over capturing Yudhishthira!'

'I knew it! Those two old men have been thorns in my side for a long time! I shall shame the Acharya into giving me what I want!' So saying, Duryodhana rushed off to harangue his *guru*.

Drona was already smarting over his failure to capture Yudhishthira. He knew that the men were sniggering behind his back and making snide remarks about his great age while questioning his suitability for the Kshatriya art of war. When Duryodhana came storming into his tent, demanding to know why he had not made good on his promise and accusing him of base treachery, he snapped: 'I have done all in my power to serve your interests. You forced this war on us despite our repeated warning that Arjuna cannot be withstood in battle even when he is fighting all by himself. With Krishna as his charioteer, even Lord Shiva will be hard pressed to defeat them. But I swear to you that by sundown tomorrow, the Pandavas will lose one of their mightiest warriors. And believe me, they will feel his loss to their own dying days!"

On the next day, Arjuna was challenged by the *Samsaptaka*s yet again, and he went to battle determined to finish them off once and for all. Drona arranged his army in the *chakravyuha* formation. This was a complex wheel-shaped formation that was virtually impossible to penetrate. Only four men alive knew how to break into it – Krishna, his son Pradyamuna, Arjuna, and Abhimanyu.

Drona used his deadly formation to slaughter the Pandava forces, all the while drawing closer to Yudhishthira. With Arjuna away, lured by the *Samsaptakas* to a remote corner of the battlefield, they were helpless. In desperation, Yudhishthira turned to young Abhimanyu, who had made himself indispensable to the Pandavas. 'My child, I am afraid we have a heavy burden to place on your shoulders. This accursed formation of Drona's is destroying us and I believe you know how to penetrate it. We need you to deliver us from this great evil. It shames me greatly to ask you to put your life at risk, but there is no other way.'

'O King! You do me great honour by assigning a task of such magnitude. It is true that I know how to break the *chakravyuha*. When I was still in my mother's womb, my father told her about this particular formation and the means to break into it. However, my mother fell asleep just when he started to explain how to escape from it, and I heard no more. It is too bad that my mother's attention span about matters pertaining to warfare is so limited!'

'Don't worry, Abhimanyu! Once you have breached the *chakravyuha*, we will follow at your heels and together we will shatter it from within!' Yudhishthira assured him.

'I will also back you up, and so will Dhrishtadyumna and the Panchalas. We will tear apart the Acharya's formation and when we are done, he will dare not show his face on the battlefield again!' Bheema said, reiterating Yudhishthira's assurance.

'Give me your blessings, my uncles! Today I will perform feats the likes of which this world has never seen before. I will make my father and uncle Krishna proud of me!' Abhimanyu cried out, and then commanded his charioteer to proceed.

'Tread with caution Abhimanyu and make sure we are close behind. You are the best among us and we cannot afford to lose you!' Yudhishthira entreated the retreating figure, tears filling his eyes. At that point he loathed himself and begged the Gods to keep the boy he loved more than his own sons, safe from harm. But on that day the Gods were not listening.

'This is an awesome burden that you have been asked to carry. It poses a terrible risk to your life. You don't seem to realise the gravity of the situation because in your youth, the most hazardous tasks seems possible. Perhaps you should think carefully before accepting...' cautioned Sumitra, his charioteer.

'I am my father's son. He has trained me for moments like these. There is no way I'll let him down by denying this request. How do you think he would have acted in the same situation? Would he have feared for his life or put his brother's safety before his own? Men who tremble when it is time to test their mettle, are fit only for suckling at their mothers' breast! Let us proceed without delay and talk no more about caution, which for me is usually synonymous with cowardice. Take me forward! Victory and everlasting glory shall be ours!' So saying, Abhimanyu urged his charioteer forward.

At breakneck speed, Abhimanyu charged at the tremendous forces arrayed against him without batting an eyelid and fought with a ferocity that belied his tender years. Within seconds, he tore through the Kaurava ranks like a battering ram and forced an opening that allowed him to enter the dreaded *chakravyuha*. Without losing momentum, he charged through the ranks, forcing the enemy to give way. The soldiers who threw themselves at him to stop his headlong charge were dead in an instant.

Meanwhile, the Pandavas attempted to follow Abhimanyu, even as the Kaurava forces rushed to stop them. Jayadratha, the King of Sindhu and husband of Duhshala, sister of the Kauravas, fought like a demon and held back the Pandavas while sealing off the breach Abhimanyu had opened up. Led by Bheema, who fought with maniacal desperation, the remaining army fought to find their way to the young Prince who was trapped within, but to no avail.

Jayadratha held firm, and when he saw the Pandavas' eyes fill with dreadful fear as they worried helplessly over their beloved Abhimanyu's fate, he smiled with savage satisfaction and thought to himself, 'I have had my revenge against the Pandavas. It feels even better than the best sensual delight! Such a pity that Draupadi is not around to witness the humiliation of her useless husbands. But she will hear about the role I played today and wish she had given herself to me!'

The King of Sindhu allowed his thoughts to travel back to the day that had ended in abject humiliation for himself. He fought all the harder as he revisited that old wound to his pride and pried it open to feed his fury... One day, during their exile, the Pandavas had gone to hunt for food, leaving Draupadi behind with sage Dhaumya. Jayadratha happened to be passing that way and like many men before him, was captivated by her ravishing beauty. Realizing that she was alone, he decided to carry her away by force. Ignoring her enraged cries of protest and Dhaumya's frantic injunctions to do the right thing, he dragged her to his chariot and drove swiftly away. Her nails tore open deep furrows on his arms but he only laughed at her and urged his horses on, shouting to his men to fight off the Pandavas should they give chase.

When the Pandavas returned, they realised what had happened and went after her captor with lightning speed. Swiftly covering the distance between them, they dispatched the rear guard with ease and closed in on Jayadratha. Fearing for his life, despicable coward that he was, Jayadratha left Draupadi behind and gave the horses their head. Arjuna handed a weeping Draupadi over to Yudhishthira and bade him return while he himself set off in pursuit of the abductor with Bheema by his side. As they set off, Yudhishthira entreated them not to slay the blackguard for the sake of their cousin, Duhshala, who was the sister of the Kauravas and the wife of Jayadratha.

Soon, the duo caught up with Jayadratha. As if sensing the presence of the mighty warriors, his horses bolted. The King of Sindhu leapt off the chariot and took to his heels. In his haste, he lost his balance and fell hard. Bheema caught up with him and grabbing him by the hair, dragged him to his feet. 'You dastardly rogue! How dare you carry away a helpless lady and a married woman at that, by force?

And when confronted by a real man, you run like a frightened little mouse!'

'Did you say she was a lady? She sleeps with five men already so I thought one more would not make much of a difference!' Jayadratha spat out, humiliation and anger unloosening his tongue. Seeing the look of rage that convulsed the faces of the brothers who stood towering over him, he hurriedly shut his mouth and tried to run away.

'You have dared to slight the most virtuous woman that ever lived! For that alone you do not deserve to live! I shall rip out that filthy tongue from your mouth and feed it to the dogs. Then I will crush your skull with my bare hands!' Bheema roared.

'Control yourself, Bheema. Remember what Yudhishthira said. We should spare his life for Duhshala's sake, even if he is the basest creature in existence!' Arjuna said, spearing Jayadratha with a look of extreme repugnance but interposing himself bodily between his enraged brother and their cowering captive.

Bheema snorted in disgust and pushing Arjuna aside, proceeded to shave Jayadratha's head with his sword, all the while muttering imprecations against his elder brother, his repressive ways, and lack of judgment. He was deliberately clumsy and left a crisscross of cuts and bruises across his captive's offending scalp. Then he trussed him up like a chicken and made him declare with the bloody sword at his throat, that he was a slave of the Pandavas, before dumping him unceremoniously into the chariot and speeding back to Yudhishthira and Draupadi.

On their return, Bheema dragged Jayadratha like an animal and threw him at Yudhishthira's feet and kicked him repeatedly for good measure. 'Bheema! Is this any way to treat a defeated foe? Have I taught you nothing about *dharma*? Release him immediately!' Yudhishthira admonished his brother.

'What do you wish, Draupadi? Would you also like to kick the brute who misbehaved with you? Or shall I kick him some more for you? He is our slave! You can order him to do whatever you want,' said Bheema defiantly, ignoring his brother and the reprimands on his conduct, which he had been hearing since he was a little boy. Arjuna looked a little abashed, but the twins, between peals of scornful laughter, were making inappropriate suggestions about tasks for their newly acquired slave.

'Release him at once! This conduct is most unbecoming of a Kshatriya!' Yudhishthira remonstrated with his brother.

'Let him go! The very sight of him is offensive to me. You have punished him by shaving his head. That is enough for me!' said Draupadi, tossing her hair back with magnificent contempt.

Yudhishthira patted Jayadratha awkwardly on his shoulder and said, 'You are free to return to your Kingdom. Erase the unhappy events that transpired today from your memory and start life afresh. Live according to the laws of *dharma* and you will be rewarded. Go with God!' The King of Sindhu limped homeward, suffused with shame and with the jeers of Bheema and the twins ringing in his ears.

The memory of that terrible day gnawed away at him and he found sustenance in rage. Basking in the flames of that anger, he plotted his revenge. Turning his back on his Kingdom, he repaired to the banks of Ganga and began practising severe *tapas* to win the grace of Lord Shiva. The years rolled by and the consuming rage he so ardently nourished within himself, strengthened his resolve and helped him adhere unswervingly to his chosen path. Finally, his deadly perseverance paid off. Lord Shiva appeared before him and granted him a boon.

'Great Lord! I wish to destroy the Pandavas in battle! Nothing would bring me more joy,' Jayadratha said on his knees.

'What you ask of me is impossible, as the Pandavas cannot be defeated in battle. However, you will prevail over them just once! But even then, you will not be able to stop Arjuna,' answerd Shiva.

Jayadratha was disappointed, but even he knew better than to argue with the Destroyer. Promising himself that he would make his one victory over the Pandavas count, he prostrated himself at Shiva's feet. In the years that followed, his disappointment vanished for somewhere in his black heart he sensed that he had acquired the power to do them grievous harm and was well pleased. Holding on to his hate, he bided his time and waited for the day when he would pay the Pandavas and Draupadi back for the humiliation he had suffered on that fateful day.

Thus it came to be that on the thirteenth day of the battle, Jayadratha dealt the Pandavas the deadly blow that would cause them to lose a life that was precious to them all. Blissfully unaware of the converging circumstances that would soon lead to his doom, Abhimanyu rode without fear to meet his death.

No sooner had Abhimanyu broken into the *chakravyuha,* than his escape route was sealed off and he was surrounded by hostile enemy ranks. Undeterred, he slaughtered all in his path and effortlessly dispatching thousands to their deaths, he worked his way deeper, all the way to the heart of the formation. The enemy soldiers were as helpless as hens in a coop with a wolf in their midst. Convinced that Arjuna's son was no mere mortal, but a supernatural being capable of destroying the entire universe if he so chose, the soldiers fled for their lives in blind terror, and the resultant stampede was an ugly sight indeed.

Drona was hugely impressed even as he watched the carnage on all sides and recalled that Bhishma had said on the first day of battle that Abhimanyu was a warrior par excellence. 'Truly that boy is a marvel. His father's son without a doubt!' he told Kripa.

Seeing his mighty army fleeing from a mere slip of a boy and hearing the lavish praise from Drona's lips, Duryodhana was enraged and decided to fight Abhimanyu himelf. Seeing this, Abhimanyu smiled in anticipation and raised his bow in answer. Drona marshalled his troops and ordered them to spare no effort in saving their King. Soon Duryodhana was drawn away from the young Prince by the expert manoeuvring of his men and Abhimanyu was thwarted. Furious at having his prized opponent snatched away, the Prince vented his fury on those closest to him and found solace in the life-blood they spilled on the battlefield.

Karna approached his enemy's son with a casual air, having decided that the lad had been allowed to do enough damage. But he had underestimated Arjuna's son. Abhimanyu shattered Karna's armour in an embarrassingly short time and forced him to retreat. Turning to Shalya, Abhimanyu wounded him severely and would have killed him had not the latter's charioteer rushed him to safety. Asmaka charged at him, furious that a mere slip of a boy was effortlessly putting paid to their dreams of victory. Abhimanyu killed him with a single arrow.

Duhshasana and Karna tried again to kill the infuriating lad but found they could not get close to him as he showered them generously with his deadly arrows. Duhshasana's bow was shattered and he himself rendered unconscious. Karna's brother was killed by Abhimanyu in the blink of an eye and Karna could only watch helplessly as he was fighting for his own life.

Duryodhana's son, Lakshmana, then led the charge against Abhimanyu. The two Princes had been rivals for the hand of Balarama's daughter, Vatsala. The Princess had chosen Abhimanyu but her father arranged her marriage to his favourite pupil's son instead. On the day of the wedding, aided by Ghatotkacha, Abhimanyu had carried away the bride. Lakshmana had to endure the humiliation of having his lovely bride snatched away from under his nose. The two rivals now met in a heated clash, their mutual antagonism adding an extra impetus to the fierce duel that followed. An arrow from Abhimanyu found its mark and Duryodhana's son crumpled to the ground lifeless, having lost to his hated rival yet again.

Seeing the lifeless body of his son, Duryodhana roared, 'I want that devil dead! Now! If there is a man among you, kill that murdering brute!'

Hearing his anguished command, Drona, Karna, Duhshasana and the other warriors, gathered around Abhimanyu again, circling him like a pack of ravenous wolves. Ignoring the code of combat, they launched a combined attack on him. But it did them no good. Drawing on his innermost reserves of strength, Abhimanyu fought like never before. Despite his youthful optimism and refusal to acknowledge death, somewhere at the core of his being he sensed that his time was running out and he wanted to do all in his power to aid his loved ones before leaving them, never to return.

Using the illusory powers Arjuna had learned from the *gandharvas* and taught him, Abhimanyu created the illusion of thousands of Abhimanyus fighting by his side. These deadly killers destroyed wave upon wave of soldiers in a never-ending flow. This unearthly spectacle terrified the Kaurava ranks and they started attacking each other, imagining Abhimanyu to be in front of them. The apparitions around them laughed gleefully, gloating at their mortal fear. The valiant Prince howled in grisly merriment along with his many illusions, as the bodies piled up around him in the thousands.

Karna saw the army falling apart under Abhimanyu's onslaught and he turned to Drona. 'We have to stop him before he ends the war on this very day! Tell us what must be done! He seems to be impervious to my arrows, whereas I am hurting from his deadly darts that have found their mark!'

'I am not surprised. It was I who taught Arjuna the art of strapping on the armour in such a way that makes it impenetrable. Abhimanyu has received the secret from his father. Therefore, it is virtually impossible to find a vulnerable spot on his person,' replied Drona grimly.

'There must be something we can do!' Karna persisted, eager to counter the rampaging lad.

'There is only one way and yet I hesitate to say it out loud... It calls for actions so craven that even to contemplate them is enough to earn us eternal contempt from our fellow human beings,' murmered Drona in a low voice, struggling to contain the conflicting emotions raging within him.

'This is not the time to hesitate! We must do whatever it takes to stop this maniac from killing us all!' Karna and Duryodhana screamed at him in unison. Duhshasana, Shakuni, and the others, added their voices to the plea. So Drona gave in.

'So be it! Future generations will malign our memory, but let whatever will be, be. His charioteer must be killed first, and then the reins of his horses severed. This will compromise his mobility. While he is thus disadvantaged, he must be disarmed. To do that, his bow has to be shattered from behind as Arjuna's son cannot be deprived of his weapon in straight combat. Only then will it be possible to kill him!' Drona's voice shook as though his tongue could not bring itself to articulate the poisonous words that issued from his lips in bilious wisps.

Without pausing to think or allowing his conscience to intervene, lest his resolve weaken, Karna killed Abhimanyu's charioteer and rear attendants and cut off the reins. From behind, he broke Abhimanyu's bow with a well-directed arrow and thus disarmed him. With grudging admiration, he noticed that Abhimanyu was still unafraid and still deadly. The lad was without fear. His entire being was focused on killing as many of the enemy as possible, for it would mean that there would be so many less standing in the way of victory for his loved ones. He grabbed a sword and a shield and leapt to the ground. With these weapons, he fought on foot and continued to kill warriors by the dozen, refusing to yield to the death that was frighteningly close and hell bent on claiming him. Then, an arrow from Drona severed his sword at the hilt and Karna shattered his shield.

Abhimanyu was inching closer into death's deadly embrace but still he would not quit. Picking up a chariot wheel, he charged at Drona.

But a cloud of missiles from the soldiers who rushed at him like beasts of prey moving in for the kill, smashed the chariot wheel to smithereens and he stood unarmed, naked before his deadly foes. He knew death was near but he refused to tremble.

Searching for a weapon, in the briefest moment of respite allowed him by his attackers, he bodily threw those who rushed at him, his eyes finally fixing on one in particular. Picking up a fallen mace, Abhimanyu attacked Ashwatthama and killed his horses and rear guards. Swinging the mace in mighty arcs, he demolished chariots and disabled elephants. Duhshasana's son, Saindhava, also snatched up a mace and charged towards Abhimanyu, determined to put an end to the destruction wrought by him.

The two warriors attacked each other and each dealt fierce blows upon the other. Abhimanyu could barely stand, as even his great reservoir of strength was almost gone. Yet he fought on, with the adrenaline coursing through his veins and his own indomitable spirit urging him on. Reeling from the tremendous impact, the two combatants swooned and fell to the ground. Saindhava was the first to recover. Abhimanyu stirred and struggled to get into a sitting position when Saindhava raised his mace and smashed it onto his skull, crushing it like an eggshell. The greatest young hero Mother Earth had nurtured, fell on the blood-soaked battlefield of Kurukshetra. He would never rise again.

A great cheer went up from the Kaurava forces and the sound was bloodcurdling. The Kaurava soldiers danced around Abhimanyu's lifeless form with gay abandon, baying like hounds. The birds of prey that were forever circling the battlefield, refused to approach the fallen hero as if they themselves abhorred the repellent actions that had brought about this unspeakable tragedy; they maintained a disdainful distance from the ghastly celebrations. Drona too, turned away from the grotesque spectacle to hide his tears and offer a silent prayer for the bereaved father. His heart felt like lead... he had lived too long on this earth.

The Pandava forces heard the awful sounds and were engulfed in a tidal wave of despair, unable to believe that the Gods could condone such a heinous deed. Believing that the once-noble age of *Dvapara* was rapidly drawing to a bloody conclusion, they ran blindly, hoping to hide from they knew not what. Yudhishthira mechanically tried to rally the men but met with no success. He himself was barely holding on to sanity, heartsick and inconsolable as he was. Bheema and Ghatotkacha were weeping on each other's shoulders, clinging to each other like children. The twins Nakul and Sahadv and the five sons of Draupadi, were wailing and ululating like women. They dragged themselves back to the camp, chased by the sounds of raucous laughter and revelry of their enemies.

Back in his tent, Yudhishthira bent his head, unable to bear the twin burdens of guilt and grief. 'What have I done? I sent one who is dearer to me than life itself, to his death! How am I going to face Arjuna? What words of comfort can I offer Subhadra? Think of Uttara and her unborn child! If only I could go back in time and change the course of events...I would gladly give my life in exchange for his! Even if we win this accursed war, it will be but a hollow victory for life without Abhimanyu will have no meaning for any of us!'

While Yudhishthira lamented thus, the others grieved in silence. Veda Vyasa suddenly appeared, as was his wont when the Pandavas needed him the most, to offer comfort and succour. Embracing Yudhishthira, he said with embalming kindness, "As Dharma's embodiment, you should understand the nature of death. You must not allow grief to gain mastery over you.'

'Where is the *dharma* in this? How could death claim blameless Abhimanyu? He was only sixteen years old... I sent him to his death before he could fully experience the joys of marriage or fatherhood. What has he done to deserve this fate?' asked Yudhishthirain utter despair.

'Abhimanyu achieved more in his sixteen years than most men do in a lifetime. He fought valiantly, brought honour to his family, and is a credit to the human race. People will talk about his courage for ages to come. The lad has gone to the warriors' heaven and is in a better place than all of us,' said the sage.

'It makes no sense to me! Why should good people die?' Yudhishthira asked tearfully.

'There are no answers to these questions. To search for them is an exercise in futility. All we can do as human beings is accept what has happened and move on because life waits for nobody,' responded Vyasa. 'Let me tell you a little story. When Brahma created mortals he became worried about their capacity to breed and multiply. He knew the earth would be overrun and all would then be lost. His apprehension soon manifested itself as a roaring fire that threatened to destroy the whole of creation. Rudra appeared before him, calmed the distraught Creator, and urged him to find a more rational solution to his dilemma – one that did not involve the complete annihilation of his fine work. Thus encouraged, Brahma set forth the law of death. All who are born, must die. Death can claim life however it wants – accidents, sickness, war, murder, famine, and other natural disorders. Death is therefore an incontrovertible facet of life itself. There is no escaping it. And the truly wise man refrains from giving in to immoderate grief and finds solace in calm acceptance.'

Seeing that his words had helped the brothers survive the worst of their grief, Veda Vyasa departed. Yudhishthira stiffened his resolve and waited for Arjuna, dreading the task ahead of him. No one dared meet his tormented gaze and immersed themselves in their own overpowering sadness.

15
Arjuna Avenges His Son's Martyrdom

Arjuna and Krishna in the meanwhile, were speeding back to the camp after slaying the *Samsaptakas*. It had been a victorious day for Arjuna as he had finally destroyed the irksome suicide squads down to their last man. But he was feeling far from jubilant. A premonition of disaster stole its way into his consciousness and a nameless fear seized him and held him paralyzed. He addressed Krishna saying, 'Something terrible has happened! I can feel it deep in my bones. A great sense of loss overwhelms me; my mouth has run dry and my throat is parched with an unquenchable thirst. If something has happened to Yudhishthira, I will not be able to bear it! Hurry Krishna! I will know no peace till all my loved ones are accounted for.'

'Don't worry about your brothers. They are not destined to die on the battlefield of Kurukshetra,' Krishna said, even as he urged the tired horses to greater speed. As they sped towards their destination, Arjuna's fear increased and his heartbeats were a rapid staccato of mounting anxiety.

'Do you hear that Krishna? The camp is engulfed in deathly silence. There is no music playing and the soldiers are not chatting with each other as is their wont. They are all avoiding my gaze and staring steadfastly at the ground! I am so worried! Where is Abhimanyu?

He is usually the first to greet me, keen on exchanging notes about the day's happenings. Where is he?'

Krishna was strangely quiet as they entered the camp. Still nobody addressed a word to Arjuna, who grew increasingly agitated. 'This infernal silence is killing me! Where is Abhimanyu? Drona arranged the troops in the *chakravyuha* today. To the best of my knowledge, there is no one in this army save Abhimanyu who has the knowledge and skill required to break it. Surely the child did not pierce it and enter its deadly jaws? It would have been a suicidal mission for he knows not how to escape its confines!'

He looked around at his brothers, who refused to meet his accusing gaze. They all remained seated with their heads down, drowning in a sea of grief, and his worst fears were confirmed. 'Is Abhimanyu dead? Did mighty warriors like my brothers, Dhrishtadyumna, and Satyaki, stand by while our enemies slaughtered him? Was there nothing they could have done? Or am I mistaken in thinking they are men when they are nothing more than disguised eunuchs who belong to a harem? What will I say to Subhadra or his young wife? He was Draupadi's favourite! She always said that Abhimanyu was closest to me in spirit and looks, and for that reason she loved him as much as she loved me! How will I face her, having failed to protect Abhimanyu? Where in all the three worlds will I find comfort to offer them? Surely I am the most unfortunate man alive to outlive my own son!'

Krishna put a protective arm around his friend and said, 'Do not grieve over him. He deserves far more than that. You should be proud of what he achieved on the battlefield today. No man can have a worthier son! Memories of him will abide as long as there is life in this world. I promise you that. Do not stare so accusingly at your brothers. They would rather die than have you blame them for the death of Abhimanyu. You know they would have all willingly given their lives in exchange. But death is a cruel master, and what happened was beyond anyone's control.'

For a few moments there was profound silence. Nobody dared to say a word, for Arjuna was also Jishnu, and his rage was terrifying to behold. Then Arjuna spoke again, 'I want to know exactly what happened. How could Abhimanyu die despite having at his back the Pandavas as well as the Panchalas? It appears I was mistaken in my belief that I was leaving him in safe hands. If I had known that my faith was misplaced, he would not have been out of my sight for even a second. Speak up brave warriors, and tell me exactly how this atrocity transpired.'

Yudhishthira spoke then and his voice was agonised: 'I take full responsibility for what happened. Drona's *chakravyuha* was laying our army to waste and he was drawing closer and closer to me. I became desperate and asked Abhimanyu to break the formation. He did not hesitate and rushed off to do as we asked. The plan was to follow at his heels with our men and force our way into the formation and smash it from within. But Jayadratha put paid to our efforts and successfully sealed the breach Abhimanyu had opened up. We fought long and hard, but to no avail. The lad was isolated from us and hemmed in on all sides. And then those soulless villains slew him.'

'My Abhimanyu was all alone when he died! There is no way on earth he could have been defeated in straight combat so those scoundrels played foul! They would have had to surround him and disarm him before killing him. And he fought to his last breath and died far from all who loved him! My son was slaughtered! I cannot bear it! It is more than I can stand!' And Arjuna fell to the ground in a dead swoon.

When he came to, a great struggle was going on within him. Deep grief and primordial rage were battling for mastery, and miraculously, the two were conjoined and burst out of him in an explosive rush. His voice came out in a towering crescendo as he roared, 'I swear that by sunset tomorrow, Jayadratha, the dastardly villain who was responsible for the death of my son, shall be dead by my hand. All who stand between me and him shall perish. And if I fail to keep my word, this body of mine would have proved worthless and shall be consigned to flames. This oath I swear on everything I hold holy!'

Arjuna twanged his Gandeeva fiercely as he took his fearsome oath, while Krishna stood at his side and blew on the *Panchajanya*. The twang of that mighty bow and the blare of the famed conch wafted its way to the Kaurava camp and brought in its wake the chilly spectre of death. The dissolute celebrations that had been going on in full swing came to an abrupt halt as that blood-curdling sound resonated around the groups of huddled soldiers. The earth under their feet trembled as though *Bhoomi Devi* herself feared the wrath of Arjuna.

Jayadratha heard the ominous sound and he was more frightened than he had ever been. Spies came running in, bearing news about Arjuna's oath, and the King of Sindhu knew with terrifying certainty that death was not far from him. His entire body shook like a leaf as panic sent shockwaves rippling through it. Shiva's words came back to him with alarming clarity. The great Lord had warned him that he would never be able to stop Arjuna. Unwilling to die a horrible death at the hands of that mighty warrior, he decided that discretion was the better part of valour and he should flee to save his life.

Having made up his mind and anxious to put as much distance between him and Arjuna as possible, he repaired post haste to Duryodhana's tent to announce his departure. 'Arjuna has vowed to kill me tomorrow. I have no wish to die at his hands and so it is best that I return to my Kingdom,' he informed Duryodhana.

'You are overwrought, so you do not see that his oath is actually a blessing for all of us!' said Duryodhana, smiling with satisfaction. Seeing his brother-in-law was in a pathetic state and staring uncomprehendingly at him, he continued, 'Arjuna has rashly sworn to enter the sacred fire if he fails to kill you. Now, all we have to do is make sure you are safe, and then we will be rid of that braggart with more brawn than brain. His brothers will lose heart without him and then we can help them out by mercifully dispatching the rest of that accursed lot to the nether regions to keep him company. This whole ugly business will be over by tomorrow!'

'But they say he is the best warrior in the three worlds and there is none who can conquer him! And no one can deny that he has remained undefeated in battle,' said Jayadratha doubtfully, though Duryodhana's confident words had cheered him somewhat.

'That is nonsense!' scoffed Duryodhana. 'Karna can take care of him in a minute. Besides, we have other mighty warriors on our side like Drona, Kripa, Ashwatthama, Duhshasana, Chitrasena, Shalya and Bhurishrava, who will all be entrusted with the responsibility of keeping you safe tomorrow. Moreover, you are a great warrior yourself; did you not stop the supposedly invincible Pandavas today and prevent them from breaking into the *chakravyuha*? You have just won the war for us! If you don't believe me, ask Drona.'

The two men went to Drona's tent, to talk about Arjuna's oath and how they could turn it to their advantage. The Acharya spoke kindly to Jayadratha and told him to be brave even in the face of death, as it was not something that was in the hands of mortals. He then assured the two men that he himself would protect Jayadratha from Arjuna. His confidence restored, Jayadratha shrugged away his despondency and promised he would stay and see things through.

Meanwhile, Krishna was not too happy about his friend's reckless oath. He drew him aside to remonstrate with him. 'You have behaved in a rash and foolhardy manner. It would have been wiser for you to talk things over with me first. Since you have given the Kauravas ample warning, they will go all out to stop you from achieving your objective. Drona plans to arrange the army in yet another complex formation called the *chakra-shakat vyuha* or 'carriage-wheel'. As you know, it is notoriously difficult to penetrate. To make matters worse, he has added a few elaborate enhancements, complicating things a hundredfold. It will resemble a wheel from the front and have an inner sanctum in a lotus sub-formation at its back. The lotus conceals a needle-like *suchi-vyuha* and Jayadratha will be safely ensconced within, protected by every *maharathi* on their side. You have jeopardised your life and risked making us look like fools!'

'It does not matter. Their combined strength will not be enough to stop me. Clever strategy and strength of numbers will do them little good. They killed my son; nay, they slaughtered him, and they will pay a heavy price for it! His passing has left a void that nothing but blood can fill. They can throw every little thing they have in their possession at me! I am Arjuna, the invincible Pandava, the best among the best. All else are like dust when compared to me. With you by my side I will not fail in this task I have undertaken. Tomorrow, I will sever Jayadratha's head, even as Drona and the rest of the warriors watch hamstrung by their impotence. Abhimanyu will be avenged; of that I am certain. As certain as I am about my own noble destiny.'

'I entertain no doubts about what you are capable of doing, Arjuna, but even then it is not wise to tempt providence. Calm yourself and pray to Lord Shiva before you retire for the night. God knows we can use his help on the morrow!'

The two men sat rigidly overcome with emotional strain and tension. Their breathing was laboured and grave thoughts swirled round and round their heads in a dizzying flurry, like the spokes on chariot wheels. Finally, with a great effort, Arjuna calmed down and spoke to Krishna. 'I cannot bring myself to face Subhadra and Uttara. The sight of their suffering will kill me quicker than any missile. Will you please go to them and comfort them?' His friend acceded to this request and went to the bereaved women at once.

Drawing them to his chest like a mother would her wounded children, Krishna soothed them with tender words that lanced the misery from the grave wound inflicted on them and left something closer to acceptance in their bosoms. He then returned to his chambers, but he continued to worry about Arjuna. He marvelled at the supreme power of fate over which even the Gods had little control. Summoning his charioteer, Daruka, to his side, he gave him an order. 'Ready my chariot and have my weapons placed within. If you hear the *hrishabha* (bull) note issuing from my conch tomorrow, you will know that I want you to rush to my side. Be prepared! If

Arjuna decides to end his life, then the world will also come to an end! I will make sure of it.'

Meanwhile, Arjuna, who had cried himself into a disturbed slumber, had a strange dream. He had been brimming over with the recklessness and confidence spawned by ravaging rage during his heated discussion with Krishna, but sleep brought with it a few stray tendrils of anxiety. However, he remembered Krishna's advice and murmured Shiva's name intermittently, begging the great Lord to help him avenge his son.

Transported to the drowsy realm of dreams where anything is possible, Arjuna found himself confessing his innermost fears to Krishna. Just saying the words aloud to a trusted friend made him feel immeasurably relieved. Krishna took his hand gently in his and suddenly they were soaring through the skies. They traversed great distances within seconds and it was as if Lord Vishnu's mount, Garuda, had lent them its wings. Finally, they arrived at Lord Shiva's abode, on the snowy heights of the Himalayas.

The three-eyed Lord sat with his consort Parvati, surrounded by his companions and devotees. The rarified, mountain air reverberated to the sound of their worship. The two friends performed their obeisance before the holy couple. Shiva smiled at the duo and they found their cares leaving them, to be replaced with a sense of abiding peace. Krishna and Arjuna were told to fetch a bow and arrow from a celestial lake close by. These were in the guise of fanged serpents but the two experienced little difficulty in retrieving them. Then Shiva personally gave Arjuna a lesson on the use of his weapon of choice, the famed *Paashupata* missile. Thus armed with the weapon of the Destroyer God himself, and feeling incredibly blessed with the favour shown by the Lord, Krishna and Arjuna returned to camp, finally confident of taking on the onerous task that had to be accomplished by sundown the next day.

The next day dawned to a heavy sense of apprehension in both camps. The Pandava camp was subdued, with everyone going about their business determined not to think of what would happen if Arjuna were to fail. Tension ran high and all eyes were on the third Pandava brother. Arjuna seemed calm, as if this day were no different from any other. With Krishna by his side, he gave crisp orders before departing. He entrusted Satyaki with the task of protecting Yudhishthira from Drona. He embraced his brothers briefly, refusing to acknowledge the fear in their eyes, and urged Krishna to proceed to the battlefield. It was time to act upon his oath and he was ready. Today, he would avenge what had happened to his son.

The Kauravas had also prepared themselves under the expert guidance of the Acharya. Drona, determined not to have anyone accuse him of letting down the Kauravas and favouring the Pandavas, spared no effort towards protecting the King of Sindhu from Arjuna. He positioned himself in the vanguard of his formidable battle formation and stood with his troops like an impenetrable rock between Arjuna, his former pupil, and Jayadratha. Arjuna coolly surveyed the battlefield and his keen eyes immediately caught the weak spot in this death trap. He asked Krishna to drive towards Durmarsana, who stood with an elephant battalion, on Drona's flank.

Arrows flew from the Gandeeva like a veritable torrent and annihilated Durmarsana's men in seconds. Duhshasana saw what had happened and rushed to give aid to his brother. But soon he himself was in grave need of help, and he fled towards Drona for protection. Krishna had been chasing down the hapless Kuru Prince and he reined in the horses when he saw the Acharya. Arjuna, respectful as always, looked at his beloved *guru* and bringing his palms together, he sought his blessings for the successful accomplishment of his oath. Drona smiled at his student and assured Arjuna that though he wished him well, he would have to conquer him, Drona, before killing Jayadratha.

An almighty clash commenced between the two warriors. The conflict raged back and forth with neither gaining the upper hand. 'You know very well that the two of you can keep at this all day, given that neither of you wishes to slay the other. We have wasted enough time already. Let us depart without further delay!' Krishna urged Arjuna impatiently. Finally Arjuna concurred and the two friends made to break away.

As Krishna steered the chariot in another direction, the Acharya called out to Arjuna, 'It is said that Arjuna never leaves without defeating his enemy. How is it that you are retreating today?'

'The answer is simple. You are not my enemy but my teacher! Moreover, you cannot be conquered in battle,' replied Arjuna, impatient to reach his quarry. Watching his retreating form, Drona smiled despite himself.

Anxious to make up for lost time, Arjuna ploughed through the Kaurava ranks, scattering all who had the misguided gumption to stand in his way. Kritavarma, King of the Bhojas, made a valiant attempt to impede his progress and was rewarded for his efforts with an embarrassing defeat in an insultingly short time. Arjuna's chariot weaved its way through the battlefield under the skilful hands of Krishna, leaving in its wake corpses piled as high as mountains. The Kaurava soldiers could not withstand this furious onslaught and fled helter-skelter in all directions.

Srutayudha, King of Kalinga, challenged Arjuna to combat. They fought briefly and the King was a fine opponent and proved that he truly deserved his reputation as a warrior who had never suffered defeat. But on that day, no man could hold his own against Arjuna. Rather than engage in prolonged combat, Arjuna made short work of Srutayudha's horses and instantly gained the upper hand. Srutayudha was stupefied for a second and then outraged. His reputation was on the line and it looked like Arjuna might kill him if he did not give way. Determined not to retreat and deciding to emulate his opponent, he hurled his mace at Krishna. The missile flew faster than thought and Arjuna could only watch in horror as it found its mark on Krishna's sturdy shoulder. Hardly daring to breathe, he looked down to see the extent of damage suffered by his best friend. Krishna met his terrified gaze with a cheeky smile. He was completely unharmed. Not so the man who had flung the mace at him, for it had rebounded and struck the thrower in his chest, killing him instantly. 'I'll explain what happened while driving,' Krishna said to a gaping Arjuna. 'Jayadratha is still too far away for my liking.'

'Srutayudha was the son of Varuna, Lord of the Waters and the gentle River Goddess, Parnasa. On his birth, the Goddess feared for her son as he was to lead a mortal's life on earth. Since she could not bear the thought of her precious offspring coming to harm, she begged Varuna to give him a boon that would make him invincible. The Lord of the Waters agreed to present him with a mace that would render him unconquerable in battle, but warned that there was a caveat. Should the mace be used against an unarmed individual, it would recoil and kill the person who had thrown it.

In the heat of battle, Srutayudha forgot this crucial injunction and paid for it with his life.'

Seeing the miraculous way in which Srutayudha's end had come about, the Kaurava soldiers lost heart. Taking advantage of this, Arjuna forged his way deeper into Drona's *chakra-shakat vyuha,* trying to reach Jayadratha. King Sudakshina fell while bravely trying to salvage the situation for the Kauravas. These fierce battles had taken their toll on Arjuna and he was bleeding from the many wounds he had received. For a brief moment his strength flagged and he leaned against the flagstaff for support. Without turning his head, Krishna spoke to him softly. His words were gentle and encouraging. Listening to that soothing voice, Arjuna's felt his strength returning as if he had imbibed the essence of a dozen elephants. The two of them were ready to do battle again, side by side, the way they always had over the years.

Duryodhana watched with mounting rage as Arjuna cut his army to pieces. The foul scavengers that had descended *en masse* on the battlefield had embarrassingly congregated on the Kaurava side of the army. It was as if the gluttonous feeders on death and destruction were convinced that all they had to do was follow Arjuna's chariot if they hoped to fill their guts to overflowing. He turned on Drona with a vengeance: 'You have let me down yet again. Arjuna has penetrated your formation and is on his way to Jayadratha. The King of Sindhu wished to leave on hearing of the oath, but I stopped him and we decided to place our trust in you. Apparently that was a gross error in judgement! You fight on our side but you harbour traitorous thoughts and that is evident in your actions!'

'I will not hold your harsh words against you. Instead I shall forgive your impertinence in the manner of a father forgiving an errant son. Despite my great age, I fight with every fibre of my being to ensure victory for the Kauravas,' replied Drona with great dignity.

'Forgive me! It is my great anxiety about Jayadratha that makes me forget myself. I do not doubt your intentions. Have I not placed my future in your hands?' said a contrite Duryodhana.

'And I won't let you down while there is breath left in this ageing body of mine. Now that Arjuna is focusing solely on getting to Jayadratha, who is still a long way from him, I will be able to capture Yudhishthira for you. You can keep the King of Sindhu safe in the meantime.'

'But how am I supposed to do that when Arjuna made short work of you, my teacher?' aked Duryodhana, nonplussed by the veteran warrior's words.

'Don't worry, I won't leave you without protection,' said Drona, wincing slightly at the cursory summation of his epic battle with Arjuna. 'I am going to give you golden armour which I shall lace myself. Thanks to a special technique that I will be using, it will be impenetrable and you can confront Arjuna confidently.'

Duryodhana felt much better securely outfitted in his special armour and he went in pursuit of Arjuna with a large force. Drona's words had restored his confidence and he felt upbeat about their chances of preventing the third Pandava brother from fulfilling his oath. He pictured Arjuna being consumed by the deadly flames of Agni, his brothers tearing out their hair in despair, and Krishna completely neutralised by the turn of events. It was a euphoric series of images and Duryodhana was immeasurably cheered.

While Drona was encouraging Duryodhana, Arjuna had tackled many legions of the Kaurava army and was drawing closer to his quarry. Feverish with impatience, he requested Krishna to make the horses go faster. But the horses, despite galloping with great heart, had just about had enough and were on the last leg of their rapidly dwindling strength. Krishna said they would perish if they were not attended to at once.

So Arjuna jumped down from the chariot and proceeded to fight on foot. Krishna unharnessed the horses and began pulling out the arrows that had struck them at various points. He called out to Arjuna that they must be given water. No sooner had he said it than a single arrow pierced the ground near his feet and a fount of clean water erupted from deep within the earth and a little pool formed on the spot. Arjuna then put up a barricade of arrows that shielded his charioteer and the horses from the hostile warriors on all sides. In the safe confines of this enclosure, Krishna tended to the animals, attending to their wounds, sponging their heaving flanks, giving them draughts of the life-giving water Arjuna had miraculously dredged up, and murmuring words of encouragement to the noble beasts who were gallantly sharing the great burden their masters had taken upon themselves.

In the meantime, the soldiers, seeing Arjuna unhorsed, made a concentrated attack, thinking that he was more vulnerable without his mount. But Arjuna on foot was still faster than most men mounted on the swiftest steeds. No man could get close to him as his arrows mercilessly felled all who made the attempt.

The horses had recovered thanks to the loving ministrations of Krishna and were yoked back to the chariot. Arjuna mounted and they continued on their quest. Duryodhana had caught up with the two friends and he called out to Arjuna with typical bravado, 'Well! Well! If it isn't the great Arjuna himself! I have heard so much about your accomplishments on this very battlefield. Truly I am blessed; for today, I will be able to see for myself whether my dear cousin is as accomplished as all that!'

Without pausing for breath, Duryodhana began a savage attack and Arjuna replied in kind. Krishna had assumed that the fight would be over in seconds and hoped that his friend would go for the kill and destroy the man who was the root cause of all the hardships endured by the Pandavas. But to his surprise, Arjuna's arrows, famed for their unerring accuracy, merely bounced off Duryodhana's golden armour.

Seeing Krishna's puzzlement, Arjuna explained, 'Looks like Drona has taken measures not to leave his precious Prince to my mercy. He has put impenetrable armour on him. Little wonder that he did not shrink as he usually does when he sees Bheema or me. But reinforced armour or not, it is laughable that he actually thinks he can defeat me, and I shall trounce him soundly and show him the error of his ways!'

Arjuna then killed Duryodhana's horses, his charioteer, and with a final florish, shattered his chariot. And then he shot precisely aimed arrows into the only vulnerable spots on Duryodhana's person – the tender area under his nails. Duryodhana screamed like a girl as his afflicted nerve-endings sent waves of agonising pain rippling through his body. Ignoring his tormentor's voice, which politely enquired if he had seen enough or would perhaps prefer further demonstration of his abilities, he ran for his life.

While Duryodhana was abandoning any pretensions to dignity, Drona was making a determined effort to fulfil his promise. But Arjuna's bosom friend, Satyaki, who had been entrusted with the task of keeping Yudhishthira safe, fought like a lion and kept Drona from accomplishing his objective. Time and again, Drona was driven away by the ferocity of his attacks.

Yudhishthira, however, was more concerned about how his beloved brother was faring. There was no way of ascertaining if Arjuna was alive or dead. He decided to send Satyaki to enquire about him and also to render aid if necessary. Satyaki's protests that his place was with him were quickly overruled.

Consequently, Arjuna saw Satyaki making his way towards him. He was not happy to see his friend had left his charge. He realized that Yudhishthira must have sent him to his aid and wished Satyaki had stuck to the orders he himself had strictly issued. Now he had two things to worry about – the pursuit of Jayadratha as well as the safety of his brother, who was now vulnerable to capture by the Acharya. Muttering savagely under his breath about his big brother's foolhardiness, he decided he had no choice but to continue after Jayadratha. Krishna's voice cut urgently into his thoughts: 'Arjuna! Satyaki, who is dear to you, needs your assistance! Bhurishrava has him at his mercy and he will die if you do not intervene.'

Satyaki was clearly tired out from his repeated encounters with Drona. Despite that, he fought valiantly, for he was no mean warrior and had been trained by Arjuna himself. However, on this occasion, Bhurishrava overpowered him and as he lay comatose on the ground, kicked him savagely. Grabbing him by the hair, Bhurishrava moved to sever his head.

There was a blood feud between Bhurishrava and Satyaki, and this accounted for the depth of hatred between the two, which caused them both to forget the code of chivalry when it came to a confrontation between warriors. Satyaki was the grandson of Sini, a descendant of Yadu, the son of Yayati, and an ancestor of the Pandavas. Sini and Vasudeva, Krishna's father, were brothers. It was Sini who attended the *swayamvara* of Devaki to win her hand for his brother. Not one to bother with formalities, he abducted her forcibly and carried her away in his chariot, on Vasudeva's behalf.

Somadutta, Bhurishrava's father, had set his heart on marrying the lovely Princess and he refused to yield her to another man and one who had used force. In the bitter duel that followed, Somadutta was bested and he collapsed to the ground in a heap. Sini kicked his fallen opponent and prepared to behead him. However, seeing the terrified expression on the gentle Devaki's face, he softened and released him.

Somadutta then offered prayers to Shiva and obtained a boon from him. He asked for a son who would avenge the insult he had suffered by defeating a descendent of Sini in battle and kicking him. And so it came to be that Satyaki found himself in the ignoble position he was in.

While he lay helpless in the grip of Bhurishrava, Arjuna acted. He could not allow his dear friend to be killed in this fashion and he simply did not have the time to ponder over the rights and wrongs of the situation. A single arrow from his bow lopped off Bhurishrava's arm just when it was on the verge of cutting off Satyaki's head. The warrior watched in disbelief as his arm flopped onto the ground like a fish out of water.

Bhurishrava's eyes met those of Arjuna and he addressed bitter words to him: 'Son of virtuous Kunti. You have committed a foul act. How could you do this to me without warning while I was fighting someone else? Surely your elders have taught you honourable conduct in battle? What you have done has besmirched your fair name and you will come to regret it!'

Arjuna felt a twinge of conscience but replied defensively: 'A man cannot be a mute spectator when great evil is being perpetrated before his eyes. You had vanquished your opponent and rendered him unconscious. But instead of showing mercy to a fallen man, you shamed him by kicking him and attempting to kill him while he lay defenceless as a newborn babe! I could not let that happen to my enemy let alone a dear friend.'

Bhurishrava listened to Arjuna's words in agonised silence. Deciding that he had no wish to live bereft of a limb and with his honour called into question, he gathered a few arrows and spread them clumsily on the ground. Then he sat down in a yogic position and began meditating. It was time for him to quit the world by taking the *Prayavrata* vow, whereby he would abstain from food and drink until his soul departed this mortal world.

All around, warriors watched in awe as Bhurishrava sat thus. Arjuna felt his eyes well with tears as he contemplated the noble warrior he had helped destroy. Through a haze, he saw Satyaki awaken and grab a sword. Divining his intention, Arjuna shouted to him to stop. A chorus of voices joined in, but Satyaki was past caring. With a swift stroke, he beheaded Bhurishrava, who, engaged in *prayopaveshana,* was deep in a state of meditation. As his head rolled onto the ground, many voices were raised in horror and condemnation. To them, Satyaki snarled, 'How dare you talk to me of righteousness, when Abhimanyu was killed by foul means only yesterday? I swore to kill the man who kicked me and abused my person, and I had no choice but to carry it out! He would have done better to renounce the world before and not after shaming me!'

Arjuna decided he had no time to stand and debate the matter as the sun would soon set. So he turned said to Krishna and said, 'Let us make haste, for we have to take care of the execrable vermin who was responsible for Abhimanyu's demise'. And so the two men pressed ahead. Satyaki and Bheema also joined them and helped protect their flanks. Yudhishthira had sent Bheema to help Arjuna and he fought hard to overcome both Drona and Karna, who sought in vain to keep him from his brother.

Jayadratha was within Arjuna's line of vision, but Duryodhana, Karna, Shalya, Kripa, Ashwatthama and Vrishasena, interposed themselves between the two antagonists to present insurmountable obstacles. Arjuna was a whirlwind of destruction as he disposed of scores of men, horses and elephants. But time was his most implacable enemy as the sun made his rapid descent over the horizon, effectively siding with the Kauravas, and Karna, his son. Daylight was fading faster than the speed at which the arrows were killing those who stood in Arjuna's way and Krishna felt the stirrings of anxiety in his heart. Arjuna had come achingly close to Jayadratha and had succeeded in killing his charioteer and knocking over his flagstaff. But the six *maharathi*s had come between them again.

Krishna spoke quickly: 'Arjuna! Listen carefully... you will not be able to kill Jayadratha while he is guarded thus by Duryodhana and his watchdogs. We need to win by strategy. I will use my yogic powers to convey the illusion of sunset, and then Jayadratha will drop his guard. You must strike then and strike swiftly. And there is something important you should know. At the time of Jayadratha's birth, his father – King Vriddhakshatra – heard an oracular prophecy that predicted his only son's death at the hands of a mighty warrior who would decapitate him. Angered by this violent prophecy, the King pronounced a curse on the person who would cause his son's head to drop to the ground, saying that the person would himself die, as his own head would burst into a hundred pieces at the same instant. Arjuna, in order to protect yourself, you must cut off his head and then send it flying through the air to land in his father's lap so that it does not touch the ground. The old King has taken up asceticism after handing over the Kingdom to his son, and is currently meditating in an *ashram* a few miles from here. Get ready and may victory be yours!'

True to his words, Krishna used his powers to obscure the brilliance of the sun and darkness descended all of a sudden on the battlefield. A great roar of triumph went up from the Kaurava ranks as they began celebrating with wild abandon, hardly able to believe that the impossible had happened and Arjuna had been thwarted. Under cover of darkness, Arjuna quickly inched closer to his quarry, stealthily killing the men who still stood around him. Suddenly, Jayadratha, his son's murderer, was within his reach. Pausing only to fix a special arrow, shaped like a thunderbolt, on to his trusted Gandeeva bow, Arjuna released it along with all the rage and pain within him, like deadly venom.

The terrible shaft cleanly severed Jayadratha's head from his body. Arjuna followed up with a rapid succession of missiles to carry the head across the heavens with the speed of a shooting star, propelled by the rage of a bereaved father. The arrow with its grisly load began a downward spiral and with deceptive tenderness, deposited it in the lap of the aged monarch, who was deep in meditation. It was a bizarre spectacle – the old man was initially oblivious to his dead son's head nestling in his lap and continued his prayers. Having concluded his meditation, he opened his eyes and met the dead stare of his only son. His heart almost stopped in horror as he leapt to his feet. When he jumped up thus, Jayadratha's head with its curly black hair and gold ear-rings, fell from his lap and onto the ground. On the instant, Vriddhakshatra's own head burst into a hundred pieces, fulfilling his own dire curse.

Krishna let out a huge roar of triumph and it resonated in every corner of the battlefield. He then removed his illusion of sunset and the sun once again bathed all in a final burst of radiance that lasted for a few glorious moments before it finally retired wearily for the night. Arjuna joined Krishna's jubilant celebration and the two blew long and lustily on their conch shells. Bheema, Satyaki and the few other Pandava supporters in the vicinity, joined in with their own conches. Yudhishthira heard the sounds of triumph and the heavy weight he had been carrying in his heart finally lifted.

The Pandavas and their supporters were elated with Arjuna's success while their opponents were numb with dismay. Passions ran high and the fight continued into the night, as slowly but surely, the age-old rules regarding righteous conduct on the battlefield, agreed upon by all, started being infringed by both sides. The fighting had become dirty and it would get a lot dirtier by the end.

The initial rush of euphoria that Arjuna experienced on avenging his dead son, soon vanished, yielding place to an aching emptiness that nothing could ever fill. Abhimanyu was gone from his life and he was not coming back. He looked at the enemies who converged on him *en masse*, dispassionately at first. And then he gritted his teeth, stiffened his shoulders, breathed air into his chest and stood poised to take them on. Abhimanyu had believed in the Pandava cause so fervently that he had sacrificed his life for it. His death could not be in vain. Arjuna gazed at the first stars that appeared in the firmament and promised himself that he would win the battle for himself and his brothers, but mainly for Abhimanyu.

16
The Possessed and the Pledged

While the Pandavas were in exile, Duryodhana and his cohorts helped themselves liberally to their ill-gotten gains, congratulating themselves on the clever way in which they had managed to achieve their ends. For Karna, whose life had always been beset with sorrow and humiliation solely on account of the mysterious circumstances of his birth and the subsequent lack of definition of his position in the rigidly defined social strata of the age, this was a halcyon period of prosperity. Always at Duryodhana's side, who was dearer to him than life, Karna, for once, was happy.

However, the Kuru elders were not quite so happy with all that had transpired as they felt that they all stood poised at the brink of great calamity and destruction. Dhritarashtra worried endlessly as his advisors, chief among them being Vidura, constantly told him that they were all going to pay a heavy price for the terrible events they had permitted to happen. Dhritarashtra knew he was chiefly to blame as he had allowed disproportionate affection for his firstborn to cloud his better judgment and block his ears to the wise council of his well wishers. The blind old king veered between guilt and apprehension as he obsessively worried over what would happen to his sons. He shuddered to think of what might happen if Bheema snapped the chains of restraint that Yudhishthira had so judiciously placed on him.

Bhishma, Drona and Kripa, among others, were vocal in their condemnation of Duryodhana and they never lost an opportunity to remind him all was not lost and he could still redeem himself if he returned to the Pandavas what was rightfully their's, after the period of exile. The eldest Kuru Prince remained adamant, however, and ignored, sulked or raged – depending on his mood at the given time. On the rare occasions Duryodhana felt despondent, he would turn to Karna to bolster his confidence. His best friend could never bear to see him dispirited and would do all in his power to cheer him up.

Like a spoilt adolescent, Duryodhana fretted and fumed while concocting his ill-conceived schemes to get rid of the Pandavas in general and Bheema in particular. However, when Karna came into his life and their friendship blossomed over a shared hatred, everything changed. The reassuring presence of Karna gave Duryodhana's confidence a potently sharp edge. He had always felt that despite Bheema's superhuman strength, his own superior skill with the mace would allow him to prevail over his hated rival. Arjuna was the one Pandava brother he had secretly feared as he was nothing short of a magician with the bow. But the tournament organised by Drona had been a golden day in Duryodhana's life, if not for others, as Karna had achieved the seemingly impossible feat of surpassing the excellence of the third Pandava brother. And if that had not been enough, Duryodhana's offer of friendship had been welcomed and reciprocated. Karna became the lynchpin on which Duryodhana's evil plans revolved.

The world has seldom seen a friendship as deep as their's in terms of love, loyalty and devotion, yet it was also the backbone of great evil. Karna was completely blind to the many faults of Duryodhana and often encouraged him in his deceitful ways. Gradually, despite being a generous, loyal and kind-hearted person of inherently noble disposition, Karna took on some of the attributes of a villain simply by constantly consorting with those with evil proclivities. He would perform deeds so heinous that they caused irreparable harm to his soul. But his innate nobility was never entirely lost and would manifest itself on many occasions.

With Karna behind him like a veritable tower of strength, Duryodhana's scheming became more intense than ever before and his unceasing hatred of his cousins now bordered on paranoid lunacy. Abandoning all pretence, the Prince worked towards annihilating the Pandavas with fanatical fixity of purpose and Karna aided and abetted him every step of the way. The combined hatred and anger of the friends would eventually come close to wiping out the entire Kshatriya race. The cream of the age would be obliterated, Mother Earth would wear garments drenched with the blood of her finest sons, and a river of tears would be shed.

The Kuru elders foresaw all this and did everything in their power to weaken the unholy bond between the two. Karna's constant bragging, vainglory, and his tendency to egg on Duryodhana in his efforts to crush the Pandavas, earned him the contempt of Bhishma, Vidura, Kripa and Drona. They never missed an opportunity to do a comparative analysis of Karna and Arjuna, and always pointed out that the third Pandava brother was superior in every way. As chance would have it, Karna himself provided the grounds for his detractors to belittle him.

Many Brahmins would come to Dhritarashtra's court, bringing news of the exiled Pandavas. Duryodhana loved to hear of their suffering as it enhanced his enjoyment of the wealth he had stolen from his cousins. However, any reports of their triumphs dulled his spirits and he would grow despondent. Arjuna's acquisition of divine weapons and his meeting with the three-eyed Lord was told and retold with great gusto by every person to visit the court. And if this was not enough, the Kuru elders, not without a hint of malice, took to repeating it every time Duryodhana was within earshot. This caused the tempestuous Prince to fall into a deep depression.

Duryodhana's cronies tried to cheer him up. Karna reminded him of their own prosperity and compared it to the penury of the Pandavas saying, 'You need not fear them anymore Duryodhana; we sent them off into exile in abject disgrace, don't you remember? While we live like the Gods in heaven, they have been brought lower than the meanest beggar. They live in the forest like wild animals, are clothed in bark, and subsist on roots and berries. We live in a palace fit for Kubera, dress in the finest apparel, and eat the choicest delicacies. Their whore of a wife is now their maid whereas our ladies are the envy of Goddess Lakshmi herself! We want for nothing, so you must not sully your happiness by brooding over those miserable creatures.'

Duhshasana chimed in, 'Karna is right, for blessed is the man who lives to see his enemies suffer while he himself prospers. The Pandavas must be emaciated with starvation by now; Draupadi too, has probably aged a thousand years and her beauty is sure to have faded, leaving her looking like a hag and her husbands must hate enduring the sight of her!'

'All you say is true and it gladdens my heart,' said Duryodhana, 'but sometimes I worry that we will lose everything we have gained. What if our enemies come back, reclaim their Kingdom, and become more prosperous than ever before? I will not be able to endure it. Death will claim me before I allow that to happen!'

Karna became upset when he heard his friend ramble on morosely about loss and death. He decided to provide a distraction for Duryodhana, to lift him out of his depression. 'I know exactly the thing to cheer you up. Let us go to Dwaitavana. I hear the Pandavas are residing there. There is also a ranch there and it is the time of the year when stock-taking of the cattle and other livestock is done. If we volunteer to supervise the process, your father will surely let us go.'

Duryodhana became excited at the prospect and decided it would be great fun to go poke fun at the Pandavas and watch Draupadi perform the menial chores of a maid dressed in nothing but bark. Divining their intentions, the Kuru elders warned Dhritarashtra and urged him to forbid them from going. But Duryodhana got his way with his father as usual and left the capital with a large retinue, eager to put up a flagrant show of vulgar prosperity.

However, things did not go in the manner expected by Duryodhana and Karna. Indra saw the procession from his vantage point in the heavens and decided he would not stand by and watch Duryodhana humiliate the Pandavas. He summoned Chitrasena, Arjuna's former teacher and King of the *Gandharva*s, and ordered him to do battle with the Kauravas.

The *Gandharva* King was pleased with the task assigned to him; summoning his followers he rushed to the most picturesque spot in Dwaitavana and set up camp. When the Kauravas arrived, their scouts recommended the same spot, as it was surpassingly beautiful and close to the hermitage where the Pandavas were staying. However, while attempting to prepare the site for their royal master, Duryodhana's men found themselves unceremoniously evicted from the spot.

When the news reached Duryodhana, he reacted with characteristic aggression and arrogance, and fighting broke out between the two camps. Initially, the Kauravas had the upper hand but when the *Gandharva* King joined the fray, the balance tilted the other way. Chitrasena and his *Gandharva*s trounced the Kauravas soundly and sent them scurrying for cover. Karna rushed to meet the audacious usurpers who dared to challenge the might of the royal house, but found he had no answers for the divine weapons Chitrasena possessed. He had no choice but to flee for his life.

Abandoned by his allies, Duryodhana was taken captive. Pleased with the royal booty they had captured, the *Gandharva*s crowed with delight. The scattered forces of the Kauravas were alarmed at this turn of events and a few of them rushed to the hermitage to beg the Pandavas for assistance as the Crown Prince had been taken hostage by the *Gandharvas*.

Bheema roared with laughter when he heard the tale. 'Serves that scoundrel right! Duryodhana must have come here to laugh at us, but I doubt he is laughing much now!'

'Is that how you respond to the misfortune of your relatives, Bheema? It is a despicable way to behave and you know it!' Yudhishthira severely chastised him.

'I only know that at long last Duryodhana is getting his just desserts! Hopefully the *Gandharvas* will hold him captive in an enchanted cage in a distant corner of the world for the rest of his natural life. With him out of the way, the Grandsire will be able to talk some sense to the indulgent fool who is sitting on the throne and we will get our Kingdom back at the end of our exile. It will be the solution to all our problems,' Bheema rhapsodised happily.

'Wouldn't that be wonderful? I wish we could have seen the battle and the humbling of Duryodhana!' Nakula said, infected by Bheema's contagious glee.

'Nakula! I will not tolerate such talk. It is immoral,' said Yudhishthira sternly.

'Was it not immoral when they tried to kill us? Was it the height of virtue when they stole our Kingdom and humiliated our wife? Why should I weep over the misfortune of our worst enemy? To hell with him,' burst out Bheema, his face red with outrage.

'If we rejoice over a fallen foe, how are we different from him whom you condemn so harshly? Did he not come here to do the same to us? As decent human beings, we must strive to do the right thing even by our enemies,' reasoned Yudhishthira.

'Fine! Then you cry over him all you want. I'll stop laughing since you think it is unseemly, but I am not shedding tears for that wretch!' said Bheema.

'We need not lament. But remember that a humiliating defeat has been meted out to members of our family by the *Gandharvas*. It is a shame for the entire clan and that includes us. The family name and honour must be redeemed. I suggest you and Arjuna make haste to rescue the Kuru Prince,' said Yudhishthira.

'Let us go Bheema!" Arjuna urged his mutinous brother. 'Just imagine the moment when Duryodhana looks up happily to see the face of his blessed rescuer and finds you instead!'

'Now that would be a fine moment indeed!' said the second Pandava brother, immeasurably cheered.

'Besides if the *Gandharvas* lock him up in an enchanted cage for the rest of his natural life, you won't be able to break his thighs in battle like you swore. And I will be denied the pleasure of using my hard-earned celestial weapons on that sorry lot, especially on Karna!' Arjuna added.

'You are right, Arjuna. Can we go along with them to see Duryodhana bound up in a *Gandharva's* chariot?' Nakula pleaded with his eldest brother.

'Certainly not! The two of them are adequate for the task. And since their opinions are setting such wonderful examples for their younger brothers, it is preferable you remain here," said Yudhishthira firmly.

Laughing all the while, Arjuna and Bheema prepared themselves for battle while the twins watched wistfully. 'Don't worry! I'll give you every juicy detail of the heroic rescue of our worst enemy when I return. And you can watch when I break his thighs in the near future. That is a promise!' said Bheema.

Yudhishthira shook his head at this cavalier disregard of the moral code he so faithfully adhered to; but his lips twitched nevertheless and he was glad nobody was looking his way.

Arjuna and Bheema gave battle to the *Gandharvas* when they refused to release the Kuru Prince and the other royal captives, including the women. A short conflict took place and Arjuna slew *Gandharvas* by the hundreds. Chitrasena appeared before him, convinced that the brothers had no idea of the evil motives of Duryodhana. Arjuna, recognising his former friend and mentor, lowered his weapons immediately. After a brief discussion, Chitrasena realised that the

Pandavas, despite knowing all, were acting in accord with the purest code of clan *dharma,* and so agreed to hand over his captive to Yudhishthira.

The eldest Pandava thanked Chitrasena for sparing Duryodhana's life. The *Gandharva* King was moved when he saw the manner in which Yudhishthira treated a bitter foe. Feeling humbled, he freed his captives and returned to the celestial abode of the *Gandharvas*.

Yudhishthira turned to Duryodhana and chastised him in the avuncular tones of a well-meaning elder. He advised him not to allow hatred and anger to cloud his judgment and mar his happiness before giving him leave to depart. Duryodhana flushed with barely suppressed rage and humiliation. Through lowered eyes, he thought he saw the Pandava twins shudder with the humongous effort to subdue the laughter that bubbled within them; and Arjuna's calm mien surely belied the contempt he felt for Duryodhana's predicament! He could not bring himself to cast a glance at Bheema, but he could almost feel his gaze boring into his flesh. With a supreme effort of will, he forced his feet to lead him away from the Pandava camp.

Duryodhana trudged along, feeling sick at heart. He camped on the bank of a river and sank deep into the quicksand of anger, hate and despair. Karna found him there. He was so delighted to find him alive that he completely misread the situation. 'Duryodhana, you are alive! It must be on account of some good deed in a former life that I have been spared the grief of separation from you. Chitrasena's accursed illusions forced me to retreat from battle but clearly you were more than a match for him. Truly, it is your destiny to rule all three worlds!'

Unable to bear the praise he did not deserve, Duryodhana burst out, 'Born to rule the three worlds, you say? Alas! I am little more than a beggar. Yudhishthira spared my life and returned it to me as a gift of alms!'

Narrating all that had transpired with the air of a man who derived masochistic pleasure by rubbing salt into his own festering wound, Duryodhana announced that he had made the decision to end his life by foregoing food, since it would be too hard for him to live out a life that was received as largesse from a hated enemy. Moreover, he felt all who knew him would be shamed by association, and he wished to spare them that ordeal.

Duryodhana refused to listen to all the earnest entreaties of his followers. Transferring his responsibilities to Duhshasana, he began his preparations to observe a fast unto death.

Meanwhile, the *Danavas* and *Daityas* who resided in the remote crevices of the earth, were horrified with this development. In a bygone age, when the great clash between good and evil represented by the *Devas* and *Asuras* took place, the *Danavas* and *Daityas* had been defeated along with the others of their ilk. They were then handed over by Dharma, on behalf of the Gods, to Varuna, one of the Guardians of the Universe, in chains. Using his signature weapon, the noose, Varuna bound them further and held them entrapped in the bowels of the sea, in order to keep the world safe from their evil designs.

Banished but not vanquished, the creatures of darkness waited over the eons with the patience of the damned, slowly gathering strength and ever on the lookout for an opportunity to restore the balance in their favour. Sure enough, the tide was starting to ebb, signalling yet another great conflict between the forces of good and evil. The residents of the limbo realm between life and death elected Duryodhana as the champion of their cause, as they sensed in his black heart a soullessness that matched their own.

When reports of Duryodhana's decision to end his life reached them, they were distressed. An occult rite of tremendous power was performed in order to bring the Kuru Prince before them. At the end of the ritual, a female form emerged from the flames. She was a fearsome apparition born of deadly intent and her eyes reflected the terrible purpose she was to serve. Black hair and dark robes bellowed in bilious gusts as the fiend stepped forward to receive the command of her creators. Her name was Kritya.

Ordered to bring Duryodhana before her creators, Kritya did so immediately. In a daze, the Kuru Prince found himself in the midst of an unholy gathering. Mission accomplished, the woman who had ensured that a great calamity which had come close to being averted but which would now proceed on course, stood quietly to one side.

The *Danavas* then addressed Duryodhana: 'Why do you wish to forsake your life? You are a scion of a great dynasty and destined to be the greatest of your illustrious lineage. If you persist in pursuing this ridiculous fast you have undertaken, nothing but ignominy will be yours to claim. On the other hand, if you proceed on your assigned course, great glory will be yours!'

'Ignominy is already my lot and I cannot see how that can be undone. Death, with its cold embrace, is all the comfort I seek, for glory is beyond my reach,' said the wretched Prince, the memory of his disgrace still raw in his mind.

The *Danavas* and *Daityas* sat him down in their midst and spoke reassuring words to him: 'You do yourself a great injustice by conceding defeat and refusing to reach for the glory that awaits you. Ever since the defeat we suffered at the hands of the *Devas* and our consequent imprisonment, we have been performing penances to win a boon from Shiva and you are the fruit of our austerities. Shiva himself created your upper body with indestructible diamonds, to render it immune to weapons; and Parvati, the three -eyed God's other half, devoted her attentions to your lower half and used celestial flowers to make you irresistible to the fairer sex! As a child of this divine couple, you are no ordinary mortal!'

Wonderment suffused Duryodhana's face and he spoke in hushed tones: 'I never knew any of this!' At the time of his birth, a number of evil omens had been seen. The air was rent with the howling of jackals, the braying of donkeys, and the shrill screams of crows. Vultures ventured boldly among the living, and whirlwinds swirled across the region, uprooting trees and conjuring up mighty dust clouds that blocked clear vision. Holy men had prophesised that the child would cause the destruction of the clan and should be killed. But Dhritarashtra could not bring himself to harm his firstborn and had disregarded their advice. Vidura too, had spoken about this during the ill-fated game of dice, much to Duryodhana's anger. His detractors had taken to bandying the story of his birth whenever he was around, much to his secret embarassment.

Now that the *Danavas* had told him the real truth of his origins, the Prince became ecstatic. He had secretly begrudged the Pandavas their divine origins and enjoyed calling them bastards who had a whore for their mother. But with this revelation, he felt sure that since he had been created by Shiva and Parvati, he was truly superior to them and the rightful heir to the throne.

The *Danavas* hastened to press their cause further. 'Since you are the great hope of our people, we are doing everything possible to help you. Many have been assigned the task of taking possession of the souls of the great warriors on your side, like Bhishma, Drona and Kripa. As a result, they will lose the humanity and innate nobility that is often the bane of many a great warrior and succumb to bloodlust. They will fight with the ferocity of beasts of prey and rip the Pandava army to shreds, like a deer in the jaws of a tiger. The soul of Narakasura, who was slain by Krishna, will enter Karna's body and render him terror incarnate on the battlefield. The slain *Asura* longs for vengeance and it will be his when Krishna is forced to watch Arjuna die, powerless to stop Karna's arrows, imbued with the essence of the mighty *Asura*. In addition to this, we have procured the services of the *Samsaptakas* for you. As you know, these warriors are invincible because of the terrible oath they have taken and they will definitely neutralise Arjuna in battle, celestial weapons notwithstanding. Go with courage and cast away your grief. In a short time you will reign over this world. We will continue to perform sacrifices for your victory as you are a beloved ally and the champion of our cause!'

Kritya carried the wonderstruck Prince back to the bank of the river where she had found him. His eyes were closed as if in deep slumber and his body shook with the force of some inner conflict. The woman with the dead eyes then placed her lips on his and siphoned away all his fear and uncertainty. In their place she left a hardened spirit without a conscience, that would clinically obliterate all traces of reason or compassion and rejoice in the misery of others. The fiend, with her vile errand done, licked her lips with deep satisfaction and vanished.

The next morning, Duryodhana awoke with a smile on his face

and a ravenous appetite. Feeling like he had been given a fresh lease of life, he decided to perform the *Rajasuya* sacrifice, which the Pandavas had performed earlier, ensuring that his sacrifice would be by far the superior one in terms of opulence if not reverence and devotion. It had long been a dream of his and Karna was determined to make it come true. He set out to conquer the earth and present it to his friend.

At the head of a mighty army, Karna marched across the length and breadth of the known world, subduing many a mighty monarch. One of the first victims he claimed was Drupada, the father-in-law of his *bête noire,* Arjuna. That grizzly veteran of many battles had his pride deflated by Karna and was forced to accept the overlordship of Duryodhana. Some of the most famed warriors of the day met a similar fate. Bhagadatta, Rukmi, and the son of Shisupala, were all vanquished in single combat and forced to pay tribute. This was the hour of glory for the much-maligned son of a *suta* and his valour was acknowledged even by those who lay choking in the dust of bitter defeat. Having accomplished his mission, Karna returned triumphantly to Hastinapura and for a brief period even his worst detractors were silenced.

Duryodhana was overwhelmed with happiness and bragged about Karna's achievements like a proud father. Their combined success seemed to bear out the prophecy of the *Danava*s and the two men could not have been happier. It was decided that time should not be lost in performing the *Rajasuya* sacrifice. However, the holy men he consulted, told Duryodhana that he could not perform the *Rajasuya* since his father and Yudhishthira were still alive; but suggested he perform the *Vaishnava,* which was equally meritorious and which only Vishnu had performed in days gone by. Duryodhana agreed and in due course, with the gold Karna had forcibly exacted from various vassals, he constructed a golden plough and used it to till the hallowed lands where the sacrifice was to be performed. This, the holy men had assured him, would allow the *Vaishnava* to be performed without hindrance. And so a great sacrifice was performed in the midst of the noblest and most valiant men of the day. In terms of ostentation, everybody agreed it was unrivalled. The Pandavas were also invited but they politely declined.

Despite his recent triumphs, Karna did not enjoy the goodwill of a faction of the court. The defeat suffered at the hands of the *Gandharvas* and the capture of Duryodhana, indicated to all the elders that Karna was unequal to the task of protecting the successor to the throne. They pointed this out to Duryodhana time and again, but he was past listening. Karna himself was as arrogant as ever and brushed off the incident like a speck of dust on his raiment. Born with celestial armour and ear-rings, he was invincible and always dangerous. Karna knew this and remained complacent. Indra knew this too and worried ceaselessly over the safety of his son, Arjuna. Finally, he decided to act.

Surya, Karna's divine father, discovered Indra's dishonourable intentions and hastened to warn his son. He appeared before Karna in a dream. Though deep in slumber, a wondrous portal opened and the son of Radha found himself kneeling before a Brahmin who shone with the lustre of the sun. The Brahmin addressed him: 'I have come to warn you, for your life has come under a great threat. Indra is determined to aid his son Arjuna in the great battle that is in the offing, and he will stop at nothing to ensure victory for the Pandavas. He means to take advantage of your great generosity and kind heart to deprive you of your most valuable possession. Everybody knows that you never turn away anyone who comes to you for alms and refuse nothing that you own. Indra knows this as well, so he will come to you one of these days as a poor Brahmin and demand the divine ear-rings and armour you were born with. Under no circumstances should you part with those. For without them, your life will be endangered.'

Karna's eyes became moist with emotion as few people other than his foster-parents and Duryodhana, cared about his welfare. In a voice choked with emotion, he said, 'May I know the identity of the person who cares so much for my safety?'

The Sun God replied, 'I am Surya of the divine radiance. You are like a son to me and I am moved by the intense devotion you have always shown me. It is in your best interests to heed my words.'

'Alas, I cannot do that for I have sworn to give my very life to one who comes to me in supplication, should he so desire it. If Indra asks for my ear-rings and armour, I cannot refuse him. The world will then know that Karna's generosity and charity know no limits. Mothers and fathers in the ages to come will tell their children my story and hold me up as a shining example of virtue. This will be my legacy to the three worlds and I cannot allow it to be tarnished out of cowardly regard for my personal safety!'

Surya tried again to make Karna change his decision but his son stood fast and refused to budge from his principled stance. Sensing the Sun God's growing agitation, Karna hastened to assure him, 'I am fortunate enough to have earned the affection of the Lord of the Thousand Rays. Who will dare to challenge me when I am bathed in your precious radiance? Besides, despite your concern, Arjuna cannot harm me. The only thing he has in abundance is conceit and vainglory, neither of which can harm me. Karna is the equivalent of a hundred Arjunas!'

Sighing in resignation at such foolish talk, the deity tried a different approach. 'If you insist on giving away the talismans of your invincibility, so be it. But be sure to ask Indra for something in return. He has a weapon, a *Shakti* of limitless power that he used in another age to annihilate the *asuras*. There is nothing in the world that can withstand the boundless power of that *Shakti*. You must somehow obtain it from him in return for your ear-rings and armour.' Karna agreed at once and thanked Surya with an overflowing heart and bathed his divine father's feet with his tears before cruel wakefulness intervened to separate father and son.

Karna was in the habit of beginning his day by offering worship to his guardian deity. Indra appeared before him just as he was finishing his prayers to the Sun God. Rather haughtily, as was the wont of even the lowliest Brahmin in those times, he demanded alms from the man he was helping to destroy. Karna smiled at him in recognition but carried on the charade. 'Ask me anything your heart desires and it is yours. What is it you want? Riches beyond your wildest dreams? Women whose beauty will put the *apsaras* to shame? Cattle to rival the herds of the mightiest monarchs? Food enough to feed an army? A fabulous assortment of precious stones that even Indra, the Lord of the Heavens, does not have the good fortune to own? Perhaps a Kingdom to rival Indraloka? What shall it be?'

'Your reputation for generosity is well-deserved!' Indra said dryly. 'But I desire none of these things. I want you to give me the *Kavacha* and *Kundala* you were born with.'

'What possible use can you have for them? You wander the earth, singing the praises of the Lord and begging for alms. I, on the other hand, am a warrior and the things you demand from me are invaluable to me as they keep Yama from claiming me. Ask me for something else.'

However, the Brahmin was persistent in his one demand and Karna gave up playing the innocent and spoke directly to the father of his mortal enemy. 'I know that you are the Lord of the Heavens. I am fully aware of the purpose of your visit. However, I am willing to part with the divine accoutrements that render me immortal; but in return it behoves you to grant me a boon.'

Despite himself, Indra was filled with admiration for the resolute figure who stood before him, courageous in the face of imminent doom. 'Surya has warned you I see. But no matter, I will grant you a boon in return for the alms I seek. Choose wisely!'

'I would like to be the proud owner of the *Shakti* that you have in your possession, famed for its sheer destructive power!" Karna answered clearly.

'It is yours. But you can use it only once, and then it will return to me,' Indra cautioned him. Then, seeing the jubilation on Karna's face, he felt the tiniest stirring of something close to pity. 'I feel it is only fair to warn you. My *Shakti* will claim the life of a worthy foe but he will not be the one you seek to destroy, for that one is under the protection of someone whose powers are unrivalled in the three worlds. Know this and beware!'

'I will take my chances,' came the nonchalant reply and Karna proceeded to slice off his birthright with a sharp knife. Blood poured down his noble form in a myriad rivulets but the mighty warrior did not flinch from the terrible physical agony. Flowers rained down on his bleeding form as even the normally golden radiance of the sun took on a blood-red hue and the Gods showed their appreciation of his inimitable bravery. Drenched in his own blood, the hero of unparalleled munificence, handed over the sordid gifts demanded by the Brahmin. Indra accepted them and blessed him saying, 'Your body will not be disfigured and you will regain the shining countenance and form that is peculiar to your father, in recognition of the courage and nobility you have displayed today. Hopefully it will also do something to allay the burden of perfidy that is increasingly becoming associated with me.' And with that sardonic remark, Indra departed, well pleased with the task he had accomplished on that day.

When news of the event spread, Arjuna's brothers were overjoyed. Duryodhana's cronies were displeased and Duhshasana politely enquired if Karna had given his brains away as well. Karna was ready with a testy rejoinder when Duryodhana intervened to placate his dear comrade. He remembered what the *Danavas* had told him and placing his arms around his friend's shoulders he said, 'Karna will crush Arjuna with or without divine aid. I have complete confidence in his skills'. His friend beamed and the others fell silent, not daring to disagree but unanimous in their belief that Karna had behaved most injudiciously and it would cost him dear.

The consequences of Karna's generosity were to prove disastrous for the Kauravas. But that would come later. When it seemed that war between the cousins was unavoidable, Krishna went to Hastinapura as a peace envoy. In his infinite wisdom, he was aware that the war would come to be, but he nevertheless wished to do all in his means to secure peace. But his mission was doomed to failure as Duryodhana remained intractable. Not one to give up easily,

Krishna decided that a different tack was called for. Since Karna was the one man Duryodhana relied upon completely, perhaps that hero could be dissuaded from picking up arms. If he could somehow manage to impress upon Karna the blood bond he shared with the men he sought so desperately to kill, then maybe his newfound empathy for the enemy would also force Duryodhana to give up the idea of waging war. It was a desperate move and a hopeless one Krishna knew, but it was something he felt obliged to do.

With this in mind, Krishna decided to pay Karna a visit. Since he himself had elected to stay with Vidura, it was unlikely that the proud son of Surya could be induced to visit him. Krishna went personally to the abode of Karna, with Satyaki driving the chariot, and took him to a secluded spot where they could talk freely, far from prying eyes and eavesdropping ears.

They walked some distance in silence. Krishna seemed lost in thought, as if he were preparing for something excruciatingly delicate and even more painful. Karna sneaked a look at him and his features softened. He knew that he should be wary of Arjuna's best friend, but there was no denying that it was uplifting to walk at the side of a man everyone said was God. Elation filled his soul but a strange presentiment warned him that he was going to suffer and suffer greatly.

Krishna spoke suddenly: 'You are a good man, Karna. I have always known it; there is kindness in you and bravery too. You are generous to a fault and no man can ask for a more loyal friend. Moreover, I am aware that fate has used you as a plaything, but you have prevailed! At the same time, it has also to be admitted that you are something of a braggart..."

'Braggart?' Karna shouted, stung to the core. 'I am a braggart whereas Arjuna has always been the epitome of humility in its purest form?' His prickly tone belied the rush of affection he felt for Krishna despite himself and the thrill he had experienced on hearing the words of praise spoken by the great man himself.

Sensing this, Krishna laughed good-naturedly. 'I have to admit that the two greatest warriors of our time are all too aware of their worth. Don't interrupt me again, Karna. What I have to say is important. You are a truly noble soul with an innate understanding of *dharma*. And it is for this reason that you do not belong with Duryodhana and his cronies. They are all base, self-serving creatures, without a trace of compassion or any of the other fine human attributes for that matter. You are far too intelligent not to be aware of all this. And yet you have cast your lot with that contemptuous gaggle and in doing so, you have chosen death over life. Why should you do something that is so detrimental to the self as well as to *dharma*? In fact, I have always wanted to know why you chose to oppose Arjuna in that fateful tournament. What made you turn towards the evil Kauravas and away from the noble Pandavas?'

Karna heard the genuine concern and chagrin in Krishna's voice and was deeply moved. Not even Duryodhana knew the extent of the suffering he had undergone because of his lowly birth. Loneliness and humiliation had been his consorts for too long and he had forgotten how to unburden his heart. But Krishna was giving him an opportunity to do so and he spoke from a wellspring of deep sorrow and pain. 'I will tell you what you want to know. And I must confess this is rather new to me. People have always been unstinting in their condemnation of me and nobody really cared to understand me or my feelings. But the time has come for me to explain.

You say that Duryodhana is an evil man. And it must be true because you are omniscient, though my heart screams in agony on hearing the withering scorn in your voice for my dearest friend. But to me, he will always be the noblest soul to have walked on Mother Earth. Do you know what it feels like to be known as *sutaputra*; the contempt that is flung your way on account of your birth, through no fault of your own? With the exception of my parents, I have seen nothing but abhorrence in the eyes of all who have looked at me; because none can bear my gumption in not being content to drive a chariot and having chosen instead to pick up a bow; and then having the temerity and audacity to excel in my chosen way of life.

But when Duryodhana looks at me, he makes me forget all of that. He makes me feel I am someone special, whom he considers invaluable. Arjuna is lucky to have so many people who love him and would willingly lay down their lives for him. Why, you are his best friend and beloved cousin! What more can a man ask for? On the other hand, Duryodhana has me... universally scorned and despised. Duryodhana is all I have. And so he will always be more to me than my own life!

You speak of the tournament and my instinctive antagonism towards Arjuna. Let me tell you a story... My father Adhiratha found me floating on the river in a basket. My mother told me that I must have been abandoned by a Princess. I used to dream about the lady who chose her honour and security over me. Surely she must have been a Princess of easy virtue, who went on to sire legitimate sons with some cuckolded monarch and has forgotten all about me. That child, she condemned to a life of unimaginable hardship! You wince but I fear that is the sad truth.

As a mere lad who knew no happiness unless he had a bow in his hand, I travelled across the length and breadth of the land, looking for a great teacher who would accept me into his fold. I was turned away by them all – Drona sent me away, as did Parashurama. Finally, I was forced to employ deception. Disguised as a Brahmin, I got into Parashurama's *ashram*. For a while at least, I basked in the glow of his precious approbation. But even that did not last. I was found out and sent away in disgrace and with a curse pronounced on me that will hang over my head to my last day!

And then I heard about the great tournament that was going to showcase the skills of the Kuru Princes. Like everyone else, I gravitated towards the venue. Once there, I saw Dronacharya, the man who had rejected me (though I had swallowed my pride and pleaded, nay, begged him to accept me), who stood proud and tall with Arjuna by his side. It was clear that the same man who refused to nurture my talent had adopted a lesser one. I admit it, black jealousy stole its way into my heart, and I could not help but think that the arrogant youth who was dazzling the crowd with sub-standard archery skills, complacently secure in the love of his brothers and his teacher, had stolen something that should have been mine by right, for between us, I was by far the better archer. Surely I was more deserving of the things that callow youth had been blessed with...

Witnessing the crowds pour their love and affection on his pampered head, I lost control of my better judgment and challenged him. You know what happened after that. The royal clowns found the need to draw attention to my lowly birth and Bheema was kind enough to announce my status as a *sutaputra* to the masses. There I stood in front of thousands, the weight of humiliation sitting heavy on my shoulders, when Duryodhana saved me from ignominy and crowned me King of Anga! In return he asked for nothing but my friendship. For that alone, I will love him more than anyone else, more than my parents, my wife or sons, even more than the Sun I adore!'

Krishna had been listening and there was compassion in his eyes. But a note of impatience crept into his voice when he said, 'I can see that you feel obliged to Duryodhana, but in truth he has gained more from the relationship than you ever did. Without you, he was like a snake whose fangs were bereft of poison. You have made him potent. He has always been secretly scared of Arjuna, and he needed you to counter that particular threat; so he offered you a crown. What is a crown to someone like him? You do not know your own worth, and you did yourself a great injustice by accepting the Kingdom of Anga. Why, you are fit to rule the whole world!'

On hearing the last averment, Karna laughed bitterly. 'I must have heard you wrong. Surely you did not say that a *sutaputra* can rule the whole world? And I resent your implication that Duryodhana is merely using me. His affection for me is genuine. I am as dear to him as he is to me, and the unbreakable bond of friendship we share is precious to me.

You make it sound as though I am nothing more than a weapon to him, a mere tool to fulfil his deranged fantasies! But that is as far from the truth as it is possible to get. I can prove it to you. Let me tell you an incident that will bear out my point. I once went to visit him in his palace but he was not there. So I sat down to wait. His wife Bhanumati, suggested we play a game of dice to while away the time. It was an engrossing game. I found that I had gained the upper hand and became excited with the thrill of it. Suddenly, Bhanumati interrupted our game. Like the good wife she was, she had heard her husband's footfall and rose at once to serve him. Caught up in the moment and annoyed at her sudden movement, I tugged at her waistband to detain her and the delicate garment, embroidered with pearls, ripped, scattering precious gems all over the floor, just as Duryodhana stepped in.

The two of us froze in a tableau of guilt although we were as innocent as a couple of newborn babies. She was anguished that her husband might suspect her chastity and I was mortified at the stupid impetuosity that had made me forget the rules of good conduct and treat my friend's wife the way I had. My friend took in the scene at a glance and walked towards us. Bending down to the floor, he asked if he should pick up the pearls so that they could be strung together later. I opened my mouth, struggling to find the words to express what my gushing heart was trying to say, and to somehow apologise for my indelicacy; but he pre-empted me and said that those he loved would never do anything to breach the trust which that beautiful emotion engendered, and resumed the task of gathering the pearls with complete nonchalance as though the matter merited no further discussion. Where in the annals of all history would you find a better example of the love and faith one man bore another?'

'It must be admitted that Duryodhana can show winning grace on occasion, to those he holds dear, if not to others, and you do owe him a lot,' Krishna said tactfully, realizing that attacking Duryodhana was not helping his cause. 'But let us forget all that for a moment. Have you ever wondered who your real mother is?' The question was injected into their conversation with great delicacy.

'Wonder about my real mother? Radha is my mother. I will acknowledge none other...' Karna said a little too quickly. Then, seeing the knowing look in Krishna's eyes, he rushed on, 'It is my fondest wish to be able to discard all thoughts of her the way she discarded me with scarcely a thought for my well-being. But I am unable to do so. My dreams are haunted by a beautiful woman whose features are never clear to me. I yearn for the love of this woman, Krishna...

But why did you ask me that? Do you know who she is? Is she... is she alive?' There was so much longing in his voice that Krishna wished fervently that fate had been kinder to this tormented soul.

'I do know her identity. As you guessed, she is a Princess. She had you while she was still a maiden. And despite what you may think, it was not easy for her to make the decision to part with you. Her father was a King. And she was no more than a frightened girl at the time, scared about the consequences of her rashness. The noble lady in question did go on to marry and she has five noble sons. But you are wrong in your assumption that she has forgotten all about you. Not a moment goes by when she does not think about the beautiful baby boy, her firstborn, who she was forced to cast adrift. In fact, the golden ear-rings and armour you were born with were given to you by your father on her request, as she wished to be able to identify you in future and do everything possible to make amends, perhaps even find a way to keep you close to her. But that was not to be.' Krishna paused, debating the merits of telling Karna more.

'My mother is a Princess and the daughter of a King! So the *sutaputra* is actually a Kshatriya by birth! No wonder Parashurama cursed me the way he did. He said that only a true Kshatriya could bear pain the way I did,' Karna said with heavy irony. 'Tell me about my mother, for now I will know no peace until I have learned everything about her. Do not waste another moment – tell me who she is!'

Seeing Krishna hesitate, Karna looked deep into his eyes and saw the terrible truth staring back at him. 'You said she had five sons after me; it cannot be! This is one of your devious plots to further the cause of the Pandavas and separate me from Duryodhana. You are trying to make a fool out of me! I bared the secrets of my heart to you, and now they are being used to my detriment! This cannot be true... Kunti is my mother? It is too much to accept, given all that I have suffered!'

'I wish I could make it easier for you, but there is no escaping the truth. Kunti is your mother and the Pandavas are your brothers,' Krishna said gently.

Karna was trembling violently. It was as if he had been kicked in the groin. 'Who is my father?' he asked in a hushed voice.

'You wake up to him every morning. And he in turn watches over you all day. He is none other than your preferred and favourite deity, Surya.'

Karna sank to his knees. Burying his head in his hands, he wept and wept and wept. Life had been hard on him and he had responded by becoming harder still. It had not been his way to dwell over his many hurts and cry over the unfairness of it all. He had always been bold and resilient, having the courage to stare adversity in the eye without blinking. Through sheer tenacity he had dragged himself from the bogs to the highest echelons of society. He had staunchly weathered all the criticism and invectives that most who knew him had tossed his way – fiercely proud in the belief that no matter what they did, nothing would crush his indomitable spirit or suppress his tremendous talent. His 'lowly birth' had been the root cause of the many evils that had befallen him, and on discovering that he was everything he had been scorned for not being, he wept. He cried for everything he had lost and everything he had gained. He cried for all that was and all that was to be.

When Karna had regained control over his emotions sufficiently to speak, he said, 'I thought that cruel fate had done its worst to me but I was wrong! It appears that there is no limit to the terrible things that I am called upon to endure. Surely there was never a man more hated by destiny than me! Surya is my father, Kunti is my mother, and the Pandavas are my brothers... And yet to the world I always was and always will be, a lowborn orphan who knew not his place! I fear that my sanity is deserting me, for suddenly I have this unbearable urge to laugh!' And laugh he did. The star-crossed hero laughed loud and long and hard. It was a heartbreaking sound.

With great effort, Karna fought for control. An image of Duryodhana floated across his tortured mind and he grabbed at it with the air of a drowning man reaching for a friendly rope that hung within his reach. Hanging on for dear life, he tried to inure himself to the recent revelations that had with their jarringly sudden impact, come frighteningly close to destroying him as well as his iron will. Slowly and with great effort, he reverted to being the casehardened man his trials and tribulations had made him into. He turned to Krishna and said, 'You have always known this. Why tell me now? I was right about you. This sudden revelation of an ugly truth is a ploy to separate me from Duryodhana. But that will never happen. I swear it on the life of my real mother!'

Krishna's eyes had become inscrutable, sensing the change in the man who stood before him. 'I am merely offering you the gift of life. Death is approaching you and it will claim you if you do not reconsider your position. Surely you realize that? Why should you throw away your life when you can rule the world? As Kunti's firstborn, you are the eldest Pandava. If Pandu had been alive, he would have been proud to claim you as his heir apparent. Yudhishthira will gladly hand over the Kingship to you. Bheema will hold the regal umbrella over your head; Arjuna will drive your chariot; Abhimanyu will ever be at your side; and Nakula, Sahadeva, Draupadi's five sons, and all the Panchala heroes, will follow you wherever you go. The world will be at your feet. Moreover, you will become as dear to Draupadi as the other Pandavas.'

At the mention of Draupadi, Karna's expression changed. He was not one to forget insults.'Do not talk to me about that woman. Did you think I would give up my honour for that bit of used goods?'

Krishna's eyes flashed. 'It is disgraceful statements like that which bear testimony to the depths to which you have sunk, Karna, having kept close company with the likes of black-hearted villains like Duryodhana. You are angry with Draupadi for refusing you at the *swayamvara*. But you had your vengeance did you not? It was your abominable suggestion that she be stripped in front of the entire assembly. The Gods cursed you on that day and your mothers, Kunti and Radha, wept with despair because you had stooped to the basest level of conduct. Never has this world seen a more virtuous woman than Draupadi, and you know it. Yet you were party to that most terrible of deeds which was performed against her, simply because your pride had been injured.'

Karna flushed with shame and genuine mortification. 'My behaviour on that day was unforgiveable and I have regretted it ever since. I have always tried to do the right thing, despite what Bhishma, Drona and the others, say about me. It is true that I was greatly attracted by her. And it was unendurably hard for me to accept that the woman I had lost my heart to would refuse to accept it because of my birth. How do you think I felt when she humiliated me in front of that illustrious gathering and when I found out that it was Arjuna who had won her? Hatred and anger sprang forth from thwarted love and made a beast of me. I am not trying to exonerate my sin, but I need you to understand. My sin against Draupadi weighs heavily on my conscience and makes me sick with self-loathing. If there was any way I could make amends for my atrocious behaviour, I would do it immediately.'

'Then come away with me from this den of sinners. Take up the cause of the Pandavas. Duryodhana will not go to war without you. Think of the countless lives that will be saved if only you make the right decision now. Do not hesitate, come with me!' urged Krishna.

'You make it sound like I have an easy decision to make. The truth about my birth does little to change things, as you well know. The meandering course my life has taken will not be altered by it. Hitherto, I have been held in contempt for being a *sutaputra*, but if I were to leave with you, I would be despised as a coward and a traitor as well. Fate will have the last laugh, and that I cannot allow. My legacy to the world must not be tarnished. It must always shine bright, long after I have drawn my last breath. That satisfaction at least I will not allow anyone to take from me.

It is true that death harkens at me. I have heard the footsteps of the dark Lord, and they grow louder by the day. But I welcome death! Life has been cruel to me and I have little fondness for it and even less desire to prolong it. The only person I care about is Duryodhana, and I will happily die for his cause even if it is a doomed one. My courage on the battlefield shall be unmatched and my triumphs will be lauded in the years to come. I know that a hero's death awaits me; I am anxious to embrace it and enter the warriors' heaven. When we meet again, it shall be as enemies, for I am still determined to fight Arjuna to the death, and I know you will have me killed to protect him. But painful as that thought is, I shall endure it, for death holds no fear for me. In fact, I am confident it will treat me more kindly than life has, and give me everything I have longed for but never been fortunate enough to receive.

But there is one thing I must beg you to do for me. Think of it as a desperate attempt to atone for a deadly sin. You must promise me that you will never tell anyone else the terrible secret you told me today, especially the Pandavas. Yudhishthira, with his ridiculously blind adherence to *dharma,* will insist on giving the Kingdom to me. He is perfectly capable of making Bheema and Arjuna comply, even though they may find it hard to do so. And I will hand it over to Duryodhana, make no mistake. If that were to happen, then all will be lost and Mother Earth will be shrouded in darkness, perhaps forever. I do not want to be the harbinger of such monumental disaster. Let fate run its inexorable course. I may be its hapless victim, or even its pitiable instrument, but I refuse to be its traitorous henchman as well!'

Krishna hugged Karna and said, 'So be it, Karna! You make me proud, for despite constant exposure to evil, you have somehow preserved a remnant of purity and goodness. You may go now with my blessings. I wish it were not so, but you are doing the right thing by the code of higher ethics. Your actions today have made you the great hero you always aspired to be. It is unfortunate that you have been despised and scorned so by your contemporaries, but future generations will speak kindly of you and revere you in the same way as the Pandavas. Go in peace!'

Karna looked at Krishna one last time and allowed his approbation to wash over him like a precious panacea. The turmoil in his soul dissipated and left in its wake a blessed acceptance. And then he walked away without looking back.

Having concluded his business in Hastinapura, Krishna decided to leave at once. He reflected that he had done all in his power to explore a peaceful solution to the problems between the cousins. He had failed, of course, but that was part of the grand scheme of things and he decided it would be futile to mull over matters any more than he already had. While on his way out of the city, he made a brief halt to thank his host, Vidura, for his gracious hospitality. Kunti was dwelling at that kindly man's residence and she looked at Krishna anxiously, for she had placed her utmost faith in the Lord and hoped fervently that he would be able to somehow avert war. But Krishna shook his head and she knew that all was lost.

Kunti spent the next few days in agony. She worried ceaselessly over the safety of her sons. With the reality of war staring them in the face, there was little else to think about. Watching the fervent preparations Duryodhana was making for the massacre ahead, made her feel worse. Bhishma, Drona, Kripa and Karna, would be fighting for that accursed son of Gandhari and it made Kunti heartsick to think of what they were capable of doing. But she realized that the veteran warriors loved her sons almost as much as she did and would not harm them. Karna, however, hated them, and his hatred bothered her the most.

The mother of the Pandavas decided that it was time to meet her firstborn and do what she could to save him from the sin of fratricide and her younger sons from mortal peril; and perhaps prevent the war from even taking place. And so it came to be that one morning, having offered up his prayers to the benign Sun God, Karna found his real mother who, after giving birth to him, had wasted little time in sending him out of her life in an ornate basket, as an orphan drifting towards his unknown destiny in the harsh world that lay waiting to recieve him. Mother and son stared at each other, neither daring to speak first. Then Karna said, 'How may I, the son of the charioteer Adhiratha and Radha, be of service to you?'

The barb found its mark and Kunti cried out like a wounded soul. The words poured out of her in a rush: 'Radha is not your mother. I am. You were born to me by the grace of the Sun God. Sage Durvasa taught me the son-bearing *mantra,* and in a moment of playfulness, I used it while still a maiden and became pregnant with you. The thought of disgracing my father and becoming an outcast was more than I could bear. In order to save my honour, I had to let you go! But believe me when I say that this sinner has led a wretched life thereafter. Guilt and sorrow have been my twin companions ever since. I suffered the loss of my husband; have known frightful poverty; I have been forced to live upon the charity of others; and worst of all, I lived to see my daughter-in-law disgraced and my sons exiled.

But none of that compares to what I went through when I forced myself to part from you and later, when you and Arjuna met in that tournament and became mortal enemies. My two sons not knowing they are brothers and determined to kill each other! Fate has been cruel to me. But it is still not too late. Now that you know the truth, you cannot fight your brothers. For then you will be guilty of the sin of fratricide and I will be guilty of causing your damnation in the next life as well. You must promise not to harm your brothers. Leave Duryodhana and take your rightful place at the head of the Pandavas. Karna and Arjuna will be united and nobody and nothing will be able to touch the two of you! Everything you lost because of me will be restored to you and somehow the great wrong I did you will be righted!'

At that point, Surya too, spoke to Karna: 'Kunti speaks the truth, Karna. She is your mother and I am your father. You must listen to her for her advice is sound and entirely for your benefit. A nobler son I could not have asked for and it is with pride that I claim parentage. If you persist on serving Duryodhana, you will be hastening towards your destruction. Do as Kunti says, go join your brothers.'

Karna listened respectfully to the well-meaning words of his father, but he knew that he would be unable to comply as his mind was irrevocably made up. Turning to address the mother who had abandoned him, he felt the anger he had suppressed all along come boiling to the surface. 'How can you call yourself my mother? You chose to abandon me when I was a helpless infant and you still think of yourself as my mother? With a single heartless action, you condemned me to a lifetime of persecution, cruelty, and ill-usage. If it had not been for Radha, I would have even lost the gift of life. Did you know that her breasts which had been fallow for many years, filled with milk when she saw me? She nurtured and loved me unconditionally. That noble woman is my mother, not you.

Even after all this time, you care little for me. You talk about your suffering, but you don't pause to think, for otherwise you would have known that what I was put through, thanks to you, was infinitely worse. I know why you are here after all these years of neglect. I am under no delusion that you have come because you care just a little bit for my personal safety. You come because of the worry you feel over the safety of your sons. After all, I can destroy them in the same time it took you to cast me adrift!

All your talk about my birth, the bonds of brotherhood and fratricide, has been carefully crafted to separate me from my friend and procure the safety of your sons! Why are you so worried about me committing the sin of fratricide? Have you no confidence in your Arjuna? I myself agree with your assessment of the outcome of our contest, but there are many who would say that each of us stands an equal chance of being vanquished by the other. Are you not concerned about him committing the same sin? But it is nothing to you whether I live or die. I know that Arjuna will never hear about this elder brother from you. I don't think you will do it, for you would rather have me die at his hands than have your precious sons realise that you are not the noble lady everybody makes you out to be!'

Unable to bear the harshness of his verbal assault (which was all the more brutal because of the truths it contained), Kunti almost swooned but then softly said, 'It is a pity death has not claimed me, for no mother should hear such words from her son. But I have earned it in full measure. I understand your hatred and anger, but I want you to know that my love for you and Arjuna is the same. Is it too much to ask that I not be forced to choose between my sons as they insist on fighting each other?

I came here hoping to do my bit to avert a terrible tragedy. But there was another reason as well. Just once, I wanted to see my firstborn look at me the way my other sons do – with love and respect. And on hearing my wretched story, extend towards me some of the kindness and generosity you are famed for – perhaps a little understanding and even forgiveness. But I was asking for too much. Your hatred for me is palpable and it has impaled my soul like a cruel spear.' So saying, Kunti dissolved in tears of the deepest misery.

Seeing her thus, Karna felt his anger fade away as quickly as it had come. His own eyes welled with tears and he wondered at his treacherous heart which filled to the brim with love for the woman who sobbed wretchedly in front of him, while simultaneously breaking at the memory of the terrible injury she had done him. He realised that verbally lashing his mother in order to make her hurt the way she had hurt him, would do little to redress the wrongs that she had done him. Nothing was going to change. There was no turning back for either of them.

'Tears cannot do much at this stage. There is no changing the past and there is no altering the future. My path is fixed and I will go wherever it takes me. Do not worry about your five sons. I promise that at the end of this war you will still be the mother of five. Upon my honour, I give you my word that Yudhishthira, Bheema, Nakula and Sahadeva will be spared by me, though killing them is an easy feat for me to accomplish. However, Arjuna and I will do battle unto death and at the end of our epic clash, only one shall remain standing. We will let destiny decide who it is to be. And you should not worry too much about your precious Arjuna, for we both know who destiny's favourite child is, don't we?'

Having uttered those sardonic words, Karna turned away from the woman who had turned him away from her life and almost destroyed him in the process. He decided that he would not think of the events of the past few days, as they would only demoralise him and sap his resolve and strength, which he would need in the days to come. For the time had come to fight – for honour, glory and immortality.

17
Kurukshetra

Shortly after this episode in Karna's life, the great armies gathered by Duryodhana and Yudhishthira rode to battle. Duryodhana handed the command of his army over to Bhishma. Before accepting, the Grandsire placed two conditions before the Prince. He said that he loved the Pandavas and Kauravas equally and therefore would not be able to bring himself to harm the five brothers. Instead, he would kill ten thousand soldiers every day. The second condition was that Duryodhana would have to choose between himself and Karna, as he refused to share the battlefield with a base, despicable character like Karna.

On hearing this, Karna sprang to his feet, quivering with rage. 'You don't have to make the choice, Duryodhana. I refuse to serve under this old man who does nothing but undermine me, not realizing that he does not help our cause by demoralising me thus. Let him go ahead and fight to the best of his flagging abilities. Shikandin will finish him off in a trice as he, or I should perhaps say 'she', was born to do, and then I will return to the battlefield to achieve what he most certainly cannot!' And with those heated words, Karna stormed off.

And on the tenth day of battle, Bhishma fell to the arrows of Arjun. When news of the Grandsire's fall came to Karna, he felt a wave of sadness wash over him. Now he would never win the grand old man's approval and prove himself worthy of his approbation. He had secretly wanted Bhishma to think of him as a hero, but it appeared that it was too late to dazzle the great warrior with his feats of valour. While he brooded thus, Karna felt compelled to visit the Grandsire.

He waited patiently for all the visitors to leave the warrior lying on his bed of arrows, before going to pay his last respects. Expecting to be received with scorn and contempt, Karna was surprised when Bhishma smiled at him and waving the guards away, beckoned him closer. He knelt down next to the aged warrior and asked, 'What have I done to make you hate me thus? Why do you despise me so? Is it my lowly birth? Or do you perceive me to be an evil man?'

Bhishma sighed wearily and replied slowly, 'I do not hate or despise you, Karna. It is true that I have been harsh with you, but I had specific reasons for treating you the way I did. The secret of your birth is known to me. It pained me deeply to see Kunti's firstborn pick his brother as his mortal enemy and then egg Duryodhana on in his designs to destroy the rest of your brothers. You have always been the driving force behind his villainy and together, the two of you have brought this calamity upon us all. I foresaw it and that is why I tried to demoralise you. I wished to take the edge off your potential for destruction and stop you from encouraging Duryodhana to annihilate his own kith and kin.'

Karna spoke hesitantly, 'If you know about my birth, then do you think of me also as your grandson? Am I blessed enough to have that good fortune?'

'Yes child, you are dear to me and as much my grandson as the others. But an extremely headstrong and wayward one! That is the reason why I had to be harder on you than the rest.' Bhishma smiled fondly at the radiantly handsome warrior at his side before continuing, 'I suppose, it would be futile to ask you to take your rightful place by the side of your brothers?'

Karna nodded. 'No force on earth will induce me to leave Duryodhana now. With you gone, we are like babes deprived of their mother, and the Pandavas will have an easy task of finishing us off. Death is close at hand, and we can all smell it in the very air we breathe. Duryodhana will need me all the more now and I shall be there for him and stay true to him even if it means having to forfeit my worthless life.'

'It is as I expected. But remember that we are fortunate to live in an age where Lord Vishnu has chosen to take form as an *avatar* and honour us with his presence amongst us. It is a golden era and will be much talked about in the ages to come. Therefore, we should all strive to conduct ourselves with the utmost propriety, so that we may serve as examples for future generations. Your extreme hatred and jealousy of Arjuna clouds your reason and makes you go against the grain of your nature and do shameful things. Be prudent and conduct yourself with temperance.'

Karna bristled a little but realizing that the Grandsire was merely trying to counsel him on *dharma* for his own good, he held his temper in check and replied, 'I know that my flaws are many but despite what you think, I have always striven to do the right thing and keep my legacy free from blemish. And Krishna himself assured me that people will hold my memory in high esteem and regard me as a hero long after I have departed from this world. In fact, I can say with confidence that I will be more beloved than Arjuna. History will judge me to be the true hero, my shortcomings notwithstanding; for unlike him, I have not had the Goddess of Fortune pandering to my every whim. Perhaps it is just as well that Mother Kunti cast me away, otherwise I would have been forced to live in the shadow of her three sons and deprived of any chance for glory, the way the Pandava twins have been. And that would have been unendurable for me.'

Bhishma shook his head sadly. 'This is exactly what I warned you about. You let your baser emotions overpower you and lose sight of the path of good conduct and righteousness. The sons of Madri have never had cause for complaint as they are blessed to be a part of the Pandava fold, and they know it. Their three elder brothers dote on them, as does Kunti.

Though Sahadeva is not from her womb, he is her favourite. And how have they been deprived of the chance of glory? The Pandavas would not be the Pandavas without them. Did you know that Yudhishthira, Bheema and Arjuna, do nothing without consulting Sahadeva first? His refined intellect is highly valued by his brothers and he is the brain of that group. And if he is the brain behind the Pandavas, then Nakula is the life and spirit. His perennial good cheer keeps them all going when the road is rocky and full of peril. And most importantly, the twins have never envied the more famous twosome, Arjuna and Bheema, or their eldest brother Yudhishthira, who was born to rule the world, but rather, they take pride in their achievements as if they were their own. Sometimes we have to learn our lessons from those of tender years and this is such an instance. Cast your envy aside, Karna, and allow yourself to be the noble man you are.'

'It is ironic that, despite the fact that I disagree with almost everything you say, I am still happy that you have said these things to me. For

I have often longed for the day when you would stop looking at me as if I were a particularly loathsome insect and counsel me like a grandfather. That day has come and I am glad to know that you harbour no ill-will towards me. I will try to get rid of my lowly passions and be the hero you would like me to be. But I cannot and will not leave Duryodhana the way you wish me to. It is my destiny to fight, and fight I will, with the aim to win. If that is not possible, then I will die with honour and go to the warriors' heaven!'

'You make me proud, for a truer friend would be hard to find. But you don't have much time left. Go now and fight for honour and glory! My blessings will follow you and give you heart as you take the path destiny has allotted for you!' And the grand old man placed his hand on Karna's forehead and blessed him.

On returning to camp, Karna was besieged on all sides by his cronies, who were thrilled that he would be fighting for them instead of languishing in his tent, unable to settle his differences with the Grandsire. Duryodhana was particularly happy and he roared to all within hearing: 'My friend fights on the morrow! And it will be the day the Goddess of Victory joins forces with the Kauravas! With Karna on our side, we need fear nothing!'

The eleventh day of battle saw Karna pick up his weapons and ride into battle in a blaze of glory. His men were jubilant and cheered vigorously as he rode to take his position on the battlefield. He filled the gaping void left by Bhishma's absence so effectively that he soon emerged as the champion of the Kaurava forces and the scourge of the Pandavas.

Initially, remembering the words of Bhishma, Karna was careful not to let his violent emotions get in the way of good conduct and focused solely on the task of winning the war for Duryodhana and enhancing his own legacy for posterity. He also remembered his promise to Kunti. On four different occasions he had– Nakula, Sahadeva, Bheema, and Yudhishthira at his mercy but he spared their lives, contenting himself with merely jabbing them with a few viciously aimed barbs where he pointed out the ignominy of receiving one's life as alms from a hated adversary, together with the helpful suggestion that they ought to leave the fighting to the real men and seek safety in the lap of their mother like children. Seeing the hatred on the faces of his brothers, Karna was saddened despite himself. Surely a time would come when the truth would be revealed to them, and they would think more kindly of him for sparing them. While Karna mused thus, the vanquished foursome could do little about their humiliation. But they all lost no time in lodging bitter complaints with Arjuna about how obnoxious their tormentor-in-chief was, and urging him to hasten the demise of their sworn enemy.

As the battle raged on with heavy losses being sustained on both sides and victory nowhere in sight, passions ran high and soon the demons that were caged within the breast of every man on the battlefield, fought to find release. And when the fragile bonds of civilized conduct snapped, those demons burst forth to befoul the hallowed grounds of Kurukshetra.

Karna, caught up in the heat and blood of battle, found himself fighting hard to maintain his equilibrium. His newfound self-control vanished when Arjuna's son, Abhimanyu, penetrated Drona's deadly *chakravyuha* and began laying waste to the Kaurava army. When he saw the lad, who was the spitting image of his father in spirit and flesh and heard the paeans of exaggerated praise Drona heaped on him, Karna felt the senseless hatred and malice he bore the father turn towards the son. Abhimanyu, like Arjuna, had the air of someone who was used to being loved. The adoration of all who knew him surrounded him like a shield and gave off a shimmering aura that was singularly repellent to Karna.

Perhaps Karna sensed that he would never realise his dream of killing Arjuna while Krishna stood at the latter's side. The loss of his divine armour and ear-rings to Indra; the warning that the deadliest weapon in his possession was not meant for Arjuna; the constant reminders by those who were supposedly on Duryodhana's side, about his rival's superiority; the ramifications of the curses placed on him by Parashurama and the old Brahmin – were all insurmountable obstacles in his quest to take the life of his mortal enemy. He felt the hand of fate that day and chafed at its injustice. Perhaps this was the only chance he would have of doing his worst enemy irreparable harm and he seized the opportunity.

Maddened by a venomous impulse beyond his control, Karna wrung out from Drona the means of killing Arjuna's son, and led the pack of human wolves that shamelessly surrounded, disarmed, and slaughtered the mere lad who was nevertheless one of the greatest warriors the world had seen. And with that single heinous act, Karna blackened his soul and tarnished his image for all time.

On the following day, Arjuna aided by Krishna, fulfilled his oath to send Jayadratha to the abode of Yama, despite the best efforts of Karna and the rest of the Kauravas to shield him. When Jayadratha's head was summarily despatched from the battlefield by a cluster of arrows from Arjuna's inexhaustible quiver, Duryodhana was beside himself with grief and fury. He chided both Karna and Drona saying, 'You have both proved your extreme uselessness to me today. The Acharya has failed to take Yudhishthira captive like he swore to do; and to compound his ineptitude, he has let Arjuna snatch Jayadratha away from under his nose and allowed thousands of my men to perish. As for you Karna, despite having four of the Pandavas within your grasp, you chose to let them escape; thereby proving you have an unrivalled capacity for utter stupidity.

When I berated you for your foolish lapse in judgment, you assured me that these four brothers were beneath you and that you would kill Arjuna and bring this battle to a swift conclusion. But to the best of my knowledge that has not happened, for Arjuna is very much alive and seems hellbent on destroying my army to the last man. If I had known that the two of you were fit only for talking and not for fighting, I would have left you behind with the women. And there is no need to look so affronted! I speak the truth and if you wish to prove me wrong, I encourage you both to pick up your idling weapons and fight like the valiant men you claim to be!'

Given the sharp edge of Duryodhana's acerbic tongue, Drona and Karna seethed with rage. Like maddened elephants they charged into the fray despite the fact that at the onset of the battle, it had been agreed that the fighting would be suspended after sunset. They tore the Pandava attack apart with their combined fury. Unable to withstand this onslaught, the Pandava forces fled in abject terror. Karna chased after them, picking them off like ripe fruit so that men lay piled up around him, high as mountains, as far as the eye could see.

Yudhishthira was alarmed and begged Arjuna to confront Karna. The third Pandava assented, eager to fight his arch rival. He asked Krishna to take him towards the rampaging warrior. But his charioteer appeared not to have heard him, for he drove towards Bheema's son Ghatotkacha instead, and addressed him: 'Ghatotkacha! Your father and his loved ones need you. Karna appears to be consumed by fearsome bloodlust and he is claiming hundreds of lives even as we speak. Our men are fleeing in all directions. It is also time for you to avenge the death of your beloved cousin and friend, Abhimanyu. It was accursed Karna who spearheaded the attack against him and had him slaughtered. You and Arjuna alone are capable of fighting Karna, but I am sending you forth on this vital mission as it is the twilight hour and the powers of the *Rakshasas* are considerably enhanced at this time. So I suggest you make haste and show that scoundrel what happens to cowards who disarm their opponents from behind without warning!'

Ghatotkacha's eyes turned red with fury when he was reminded of the treacherous manner in which Abhimanyu had been slain. 'I am privileged to be able to serve my kin. But it is useless to fight villains like Karna using the honourable code of conduct prescribed by the Kshatriyas. Tonight, I will fight like a *Rakshasa,* using all the powers at my disposal. All who oppose me shall perish without mercy. Abhimanyu will be avenged and I will have had the fortune to perform the ultimate service for my father and loved ones!' Ghatotkacha bowed to Krishna and Arjuna, and charged off in the direction of Karna.

Krishna, watching him go, was satisfied. His friend looked at him in puzzlement and wondered what exactly he was up to. But before he could question him, his charioteer took him to another part of the battlefield where the fighting was heavy and Arjuna found himself engaged in the task of keeping his men and their hopes of victory alive; and he forgot about the questions that had remained unasked on his lips.

Ghatotkacha, with his *Rakshasa* hordes, descended on the Kaurava forces like a swarm of deadly hornets. He used the powers which were unique to his kind to create terrifying illusions that infested the minds of the common soldiers and filled them with a sense of profound horror. They felt their spines and hearts crumble to pieces and began to question their own sanity. They fled in droves, caught up in paroxysms of horror. Karna, however, was unperturbed and proceeded to counter Ghatotkacha's every move expertly. While the mighty antagonists were engaged thus, the *Rakshasa* Alayudha approached Duryodhana and asked permission to engage the Pandava forces in combat with his followers. He had a personal score to settle with them as Bheema had slaughtered many of his allies. Duryodhana was glad to receive this timely offer of assistance and quickly gave his permission for the *Rakshasa* to attack.

Alayudha and his followers attacked the Pandava forces with vigour, and the besieged troops were helpless as they had no response to the supernatural powers of the *Rakshasas*, particularly at night, when their powers were increased manifold. The evil Alayudha challenged Bheema to combat and the latter was hard-pressed to fend off his relentless harassment. Krishna sensed that Bheema was struggling, so he interrupted Ghatotkacha, who was doing battle with Karna, and sent him to render aid to his father.

Ghatotkacha and Alayudha clashed in an almighty struggle of *Rakshasa* strength as they were evenly matched. They raged and cursed each other, bleeding profusely from the wounds inflicted by the powerful weapons they used. Alayudha was the first to give ground, and even as he was rallying to resume the fight, Ghatotkacha severed his head and hurled it at Duryodhana, howling all the while with fiendish glee.

Caught in the spell of unstoppable bloodlust, Ghatotkacha attacked the Kaurava soldiers indiscriminately, sparing none, even those who threw down their weapons in supplication and begged for mercy. Blood spurted in all directions like grotesque geysers and the son of Bheema gloried in the destruction and havoc he was wreaking among his enemies. Veteran warriors found their courage had abandoned them as they watched Ghatotkacha tear their comrades to pieces, using his teeth to rend the flesh off fallen soldiers and to rip off their limbs with his own massive hands and throw them asunder. They fled the battlefield like frightened mice, keening and ululating like female mourners.

The fleeing soldiers ran to Karna and begged him to help them by putting an end to the terrible *Rakshasa,* who was surely the worst adversary any of them had ever seen. Even Arjuna was preferable to Ghatotkacha, as the third Pandava had a sense of fair play and could never bring himself to slaughter defenceless men in such a manner. Heeding their pleas, Karna tried to stop Ghatotkacha.

The *Rakshasa,* however, was a relentless force of nature that night. Trying to stop him was like pouring a small bucket of water over a raging fire and hoping that it will be sufficient to douse it. Karna succeeded in neutralising some of the *astras* released by Ghatotkacha, but he was unable to find a weak spot in his defences, that would allow him to move in for the kill. In the meantime, Bheema's son carried on his killing spree. Without warning, he attacked Karna and destroyed his chariot, leaving him standing on foot.

Duryodhana, already reeling from the death of Jayadratha, despite the formidable measures that had been taken to keep out Arjuna, panicked on finding that his army was being annihilated. Terrified at the prospect of defeat and ruin, he turned to Karna and begged him to use the special *Shakti* that Indra had given him, to get rid of Ghatotkacha. He spoke in a voice of distraught frenzy, his eyes glazed as though not entirely in control of his senses.

The plea was taken up by the frightened troops as well, and a million voices urged Karna to use his special weapon to kill Ghatotkacha. Karna hesitated, for he knew that with the weapon gone, his chances of killing Arjuna would be almost non-existent. But the exhortations of Duryodhana and his men rose to a crescendo and slowly but surely they drowned out his misgivings. His mind became sluggish as an eerie impulse got hold of it, snuffing out all resistance and directing him to use the *Shakti* given to him by Indra.

Mechanically, Karna reached for the weapon and directed it at the monstrous *Rakshasa,* who was still in the throes of bloodlust. With inexorable purpose that gave added impetus to his limbs, he released the *Shakti,* and it surged towards Ghatotkacha. When Bheema's son saw death hurtling towards him, the all-consuming rage that had taken possession of him and caused him to kill without compunction, vanished, leaving only a clear sense of purpose and duty. In the few seconds of life left to him, Ghatotkacha engorged his already massive body to gargantuan proportions, and was growing as if to touch the sky, when Karna's missile hit him in the heart with unerring accuracy. Death was instantaneous and he fell heavily to the ground, crushing an entire *akshauhini* of the Kaurava army under his bulk. Bheema's mighty son, who had always helped the Pandavas when they needed him most, lay dead, having given them everything he had to give, including his own life.

On his demise, the jubilation in the Kaurava army was matched only by the sorrow in the Pandava camp. But two men in both the armies showed emotions that were markedly different from those around them. Karna felt a wave of bitter defeat wash over him even as his men danced around him in ecstasy, as he sensed that his own death was imminent. Before his emotions could get the better of him and deprive him of his courage, he reassured himself with the thought that one way or the other, it would be best to get this sordid business over and done with, and put an end to his miserable existence in a world that had been so consistently cruel to him right from the moment of his birth.

Krishna also reacted somewhat inappropriately to the grievous occasion and whooped with delight while prancing around like a frolicking deer. Arjuna looked askance at this jocose display and asked his friend why he was celebrating the death of a Pandava's son. Krishna smiled before replying: 'His death ensures your safety and that is the reason for my happiness. Indra had given him his invincible *Shakti* and Karna was planning to use it against you. Now that it has claimed its victim, it will return to its original owner and Karna from now on, is well and truly at your mercy.'

Arjuna was somewhat disturbed on hearing this and said: 'Was it necessary to sacrifice Bheema's son for me? The boy was dear to all of us, particularly to Yudhishthira, for he was always there to help us during trying times. Abhimanyu also loved him. It grieves me sorely to hear that he had to die for me to live.'

'I never do anything without just cause, Arjuna. It is my duty to ensure that only the truly righteous emerge triumphant in this apocalyptic conflict. I had to make Karna use the *Shakti* on someone other than you, for without you there can be no victory for your brothers. Ghatotkacha was the ideal choice. It will be painful for you to hear this, but the truth is Bheema's son was a *Rakshasa* with a proclivity towards evil. And while it is true that his own kith and kin brought out the best in his ferocious nature, others were not so lucky. Like most of his ilk, he had scant respect for divinity and went about disrupting sacrifices, killing holy men, and generally harassing the god-fearing. If Karna had not taken his life, then I would have had to do it myself, and I was reluctant to do so out of sensitivity for the love all of you had for him. His demise is for the best. Ghatotkacha went from this world like a hero rather than a villain hunted and killed by myself; and his father and uncles can draw comfort from that and take pride in his achievements. By forcing Karna to use the *Shakti* he had reserved for you, Ghatotkacha has done the Pandavas and the rest of the world a great service. Karna is now like a deadly serpent without its poisonous fangs, or a lion without its mighty claws!'

'I am sorry to have questioned your judgment, Krishna,' said Arjuna. 'But there is one thing I do not understand. If Karna had such a weapon in his possession, why did he not track me down on the battlefield and use it immediately? Surely that makes more sense... I would have done just that had our roles been reversed.'

'Karna would have gladly used his weapon on you at the earliest had I allowed him to. He has been trying to engineer an encounter with you from the moment he picked up his weapons and set foot on this battlefield. I, however, made sure that never happened and kept him occupied with other opponents. And on the rare occasions when your paths crossed, I confounded his senses ever so slightly and made him a little befuddled and uncharacteristically slow.'

Arjuna shook his head in mock disapproval before embracing his friend. 'What a deadly adversary you make! I am the luckiest man in the universe to have you for a friend and cousin. Otherwise, surely all my powers notwithstanding, my life would have been worth nothing on this battlefield!'

Having eliminated yet another threat that could have potentially altered the outcome of the battle, Krishna set his sights on Drona. The Acharya, embittered by the constant questions being raised about his loyalties as well as his capacity for warfare, had started using divine weapons on ordinary soldiers. This was forbidden by the codes of warfare, and Krishna decided it was time to get rid of the Brahmin warrior for good. So it came to be that the Acharya, deceived by Yudhishthira at the urging of Krishna, came to believe that his son Ashwatthama had passed away. This was the one blow the mighty Drona could not withstand, as he loved his son above all else. He dropped his weapons and decided to end his life. His soul had just departed his body when Dhrishtadyumna snuck up on him and severed his head, ignoring Arjuna's entreaties to hold his hand; as well as the other warriors deprecating such an unworthy act. But Drupada's son was past reason and he held up Drona's head, well pleased that he had fulfilled his destiny.

The Kauravas had been struck a grievous blow as they had lost their Supreme Commander. In a daze, Duryodhana turned to Karna, and placed the mantle of command on his shoulders. Surya's son stood with his head held high and promised his best friend to do all in his power to end the war. The men stood around their new champion and screamed his name aloud, showering Karna with their love and respect. As he stood in the midst of that boisterous gathering, Karna saw in his mind's eye, death waiting for him just across the battle lines, and he knew that his time was drawing nigh. Yet his heart filled with gladness and he was confident that the straight path of destiny he had chosen for himself was indeed the right one.

Having accepted his fate, Karna felt strangely calm. He was determined not to let his friend down while he lived. That night Duryodhana and Karna found themselves alone and they drank and talked as they had often done. Sensing that all was not well with Karna, Duryodhana questioned him and asked if there was anything he could do. To that Karna replied: 'Tomorrow, I will make you a present of Arjuna's head. But in order to do that, I need a small favour from you. In every respect, Arjuna and I are evenly matched but he has an advantage. I am not talking about his Gandeeva or the inexhaustible quivers which Agni gave him; or the unworldly *Gandharva* steeds that draw his chariot; or his banner which Hanuman imbues with his presence; or the innumerable celestial weapons in his possession. My main concern is the dark-hued Lord at his side. You know as well as I that he does a lot more than hold the reins, guide the horses, and shovel horse excreta. He controls the ebb and flow of the battle with his fingertips. It is only thanks to his sagacity that Arjuna escapes death at the hands of his betters. My own charioteer is no match for Krishna. But that can be remedied if Shalya, the King of Madra, could be persuaded to drive my chariot, for his expertise as a charioteer is legendary.'

Shalya was the maternal uncle of the Pandava twins, Nakula and Sahadeva. When he heard that war had been declared between the cousins, he collected a large army and set out to do his duty by his sister's sons. When Duryodhana heard about this from his spies, he decided it would be prudent to employ a bit of trickery to get the King of Madra to fight for the Kauravas instead. He had rest houses readied along Shalya's route and ordered his men to spare no expense in pandering to the famously degenerate tastes of the lusty old man. Sure enough, the King of Madra was flattered, thinking that Yudhishthira had done him great honour by taking care of him in this manner. He asked the attendants to take him to their master, as he wished to convey his gratitude in person. To his surprise, Duryodhana emerged and fell at his feet. Shalya blessed him and asked the Prince how he could be of service. In reply, Duryodhana begged him to employ his might for the Kaurava cause and Shalya had no choice but to agree.

Having promised Duryodhana he would fight for him, he nevertheless said that he would have to meet Yudhishthira and explain in person. The Pandavas were bitterly disappointed when they heard how Duryodhana had outmanoeuvred them, for they had been counting on the King's support. Shalya hugged his sister's sons and soothed them. He assured them that his blessings, for what they were worth, would be with them. And the Pandavas had to be content with that.

Yudhishthira was unwilling to let Duryodhana get away with his thievery and wondered how best the situation could be turned to their advantage. Inspiration hit him suddenly and he addressed Shalya: 'Karna will try to get you as his charioteer to counter the advantage Arjuna has in Krishna. Duryodhana will persuade you to take on this role. While you are being utilised thus, I would like you to demoralise Karna to the best of your ability and chip away at him mentally, so that he becomes more vulnerable. If you have any regard for us, you must do as I ask.' Shalya consented and took his leave.

And so, when Duryodhana requested him to drive Karna's chariot, the old King was prepared. He put up a tremendous show of belligerence, calling Karna every awful name he could think of. But gradually he allowed himself to be persuaded after inserting his own condition that at no time would he be deferential to Karna and would say what he pleased to him. Having no other choice, Karna agreed, wondering if he wasn't better off with his own humble yet well-disposed charioteer.

Both sides had consulted their astrologers and an appropriate hour was settled upon for doing battle. Karna bowed respectfully to Shalya and ascended into his chariot only after the King of Madra had taken his place in the charioteer's seat. Duryodhana ran out to him and said: 'I know in my heart that you will win this war for me Karna, and not fail me the way the Grandsire and the Acharya did. The world will remember this day for the tremendous victory its greatest warrior achieved!'

Karna did not trust himself to speak, but he smiled bravely at the man who might never know the tremendous sacrifice he was making for him. 'Karna has, since the day he had the fortune to meet you, always done his best for you and he will do the same today. While there is breath in my body, I will strive to serve you to the utmost of my ability.' And with those words, Karna went on the way to his death.

Briskly, he asked Shalya to take him to Arjuna. His charioteer acquiesced but remembering his promise to Yudhishthira, he decided to dishearten Karna, and began by keeping up a steady diatribe of verbal barbs and cruel jibes ranging from his opinion of Karna's lowly birth, to soliloquies on Arjuna's brilliance, and prophesies about the bloody end of the man whose chariot he drove. Initially Karna was composed, as this was exactly what he had expected from his charioteer. It was no secret that his heart was with the twins and that he had no great liking for the man he thought was a *sutaputra*.

Ignoring Shalya's sharp tongue to the best of his ability, Karna focused his attention on arraying his troops in a brilliant formation of battle. Arjuna rose to the challenge and led the attack against Karna. There was heavy fighting in all quarters and Karna distinguished himself that day as a warrior second to none. Krishna saw him fight and was saddened that before Surya set for the day, he would witness his son's life-blood spilled on the battlefield of Kurukshetra.

In the meantime, Bheema and Duhshasana were fighting each other. The hundred sons of Dhritarashtra had been mown down by Bheema, and only two remained. While the two antagonists fought each other, their mutual hatred engulfed them like a storm cloud and showered the spectators with blood. Bheema was delighted to finally have in his grasp the villain who had dared to drag his wife to the assembly by her hair, and then attempt to disrobe her with his filthy, lecherous paws. Maddened with fury by that awful memory, which after all this time could still inflame his rage to feverish pitch, he sprang out of his chariot like a beast of prey and was on Duhshasana in seconds.

Bheema hurled him to the ground, smashing his spine to pieces, so great was the force of the blow, nourished as it was with his furious anger. 'Here at last I have got the hand that had the temerity to touch my wife, it deserves to be punished as does its owner!' Saying thus, Bheema ripped out the limb that had sullied a woman's honour, staring all the while at the dying man who writhed at his feet. Choking on his hatred as the life left Duhshasana's body through the gaping hole which was all that was left of his arm, Bheema knelt and ripping open his victim's chest, cupped his hands together and gulped down the blood that pouring out in copious streams.

Bheema licked his lips and said with relish, 'That was by far the tastiest thing to pass my lips!'

Even as the warriors around the dead man and his wild nemesis watched mute with horror, Bheema danced about the corpse like a raving mad man, whooping with devilish glee. 'Draupadi has been avenged! I have fulfilled the oath I took. The fool who dared to incur my wrath lies dead at my feet. Now all that remains for me to do is to break open the thighs of the other vile creature born to Dhritarashtra, and that too, I shall achieve at the earliest!' He addressed these last words to Duryodhana, who was sobbing and shuddering with the vehemence of his grief over the brutal death of his last surviving brother. Men fainted with terror, or ran from that accursed place, while others wept openly to see what war had done to the scions of the noble Kuru line.

Duryodhana mastered his sorrow, and bellowing with rage, he ordered his troops to massacre the Pandavas and spare no one. The soldiers turned on each other, determined to finish the conflict once and for all. Karna made towards Arjuna even as his brother rushed out to meet him. The Gods gathered in heaven to watch the contest between the two. Duryodhana and Yudhishthira, seeing their champion fighters charging towards each other with grim purpose, ordered their men to gather around to show their support.

As the penultimate moment drew closer, Karna addressed Shalya: 'I am going to fight for my life and should I fail, what do you propose to do?' To his surprise, his charioteer for once refrained from heaping scorn on him. 'I have watched you fight with great heart in the face of an impending doom that would have destroyed lesser men. Your courage is a lesson for all and you are indeed the greatest warrior of all time. It is a privilege to watch you fight. Victory will be yours and my prayers go with you, but if the unthinkable were to happen, I will personally avenge you!'

Karna was gladdened beyond measure to hear the words of approbation from one who had hated him. King Shalya's sincere wish to see him win, despite the fact that his blood relatives fought on the other side, heartened Karna and renewed his sense of purpose.

Strangely, Arjuna had asked the same question of his charioteer, who replied, 'Such a thing can never happen but if it does, I will tear apart Karna and Shalya with my bare hands and the earth will be scorched to the ground, unable to withstand the heat of my anger!' Arjun was touched with his friend's response and said, 'I don't know why I asked such a question...with you by my side, victory is always certain!'

The fight between the brothers commenced. The combatants fought with ordinary weapons, feeling each other out, probing for weaknesses and openings. So great was their skill and so fluid their movements, that to the spectators it seemed they were watching a dance, albeit one of death. Arjuna was impressed with the display put up by his mortal foe. But even when he caught himself admiring Karna, that admiration was tinged with frustration. He realised, to the detriment of his pride, that despite the machinations of his divine father and friend, which had resulted in Karna losing many of his natural advantages, they were still evenly matched, and he had to draw on every ounce of his strength and fortitude to triumph over him.

With a roar of fury, Arjun unleashed a divine weapon called the *Agniastra*. Flames shot out of the missile and engulfed Karna's chariot. His opponent responded in kind with the *Varunastra,* which doused the flames. Thick smoke rose from the embers and wafted towards Arjuna, stinging his eyes and clogging his throat, making him cough. He had to use the *Vayavyastra* to draw up a fragrant breeze and chase the smoke away.

Summoning a more powerful weapon, called the *Aindrastra,* Arjuna released it. This missile conjured up thousands of arrows, that attacked Karna as well as the watching army, killing soldiers in droves. Surya's son felt his anger boil and he thought bitterly that Arjuna's reputation for nobility and fair play was ill-deserved. It galled him that it was himself who was considered the feckless one, when in fact, Arjuna was the one who was employing such devilish tactics. Spurred by his anger, he released the *Bhargavastra,* which had been the weapon of his Guru. It was a truly superior missile, which countered Arjuna's *astra* with embarrassing ease and then proceeded to wrap the third Pandava in an energy-sapping haze even as it wreaked havoc among the Pandava forces.

Bheema's strident words penetrated the deathly haze and rang in Arjuna's ears: 'Can you hear the Kaurava curs laughing at you Arjuna? Are the lowborn too much for you to handle? Admit defeat and I will kill him myself and win back the honour that is fast slipping from us while you dawdle thus!'

But even those insulting words could not induce him to throw off the torpor that held him prisoner. A strange inertia had Arjuna in its grip and he found himself unwilling to fight Karna with the best of his formidable arsenal. Something stayed his hand. It could have been that his blood recognised its own even when his head could not.

Krishna sensed what was happening and spoke to him: 'What is wrong with you? Where did this unmanly hesitation spring from? Remember who you are and the purpose for which you walk this earth. That man who stands against you embodies the spirits of the demons from another era. They are implacable foes whose hatred will chase you from this life to the next and the ones after that if you do not put an end to it. Wake up and do what you were born to do!'

Arjuna broke free from the chains that had held down his spirit and called forth the *Brahmastra*. It tore apart the effects of the *Bhargavastra* –but only with a supreme effort from Arjuna. Overcoming his reluctance, the third Pandava fought with renewed passion. He and his mighty bow merged into one entity and arrows issued in a fluid and effortless stream, almost in telepathic response to his thoughts and needs.

Karna was fighting for his life. It was an awesome sight to watch as he surpassed all else in the Apollonian splendour of his beauty, power and grace. Picking up the deadliest weapon in his depleted arsenal, he hurled the *nagastra* at his younger brother. Death latched itself onto that missile of deadly power and time stood still as it raced to claim Arjuna for its own. The hero saw it come but was powerless to stop it. His brothers felt the blood drain from their faces and a horrible fear seized and held them in thrall. Krishna alone responded as everyone else stood paralyzed. Just as the weapon hastened towards its mark, Krishna urged his *Gaandharva* steeds to their knees, with the result that the arrow buried itself in Arjuna's diadem and burnt it to a crisp. In that instant, Arjuna was born again.

The Pandavas and their supporters screamed their relief while their opponents wailed in despair. Karna was in agony. He knew that if it had not been for Krishna, he would have triumphed despite the great odds against him. As it was, he had come heartbreakingly close to victory. Despite knowing all along that where Krishna went, victory followed, he found it difficult to accept and he clenched his teeth in thwarted fury.

The fight raged on between the valiant brothers. Karna had no weapons left in his possession that were powerful enough to carry the day. He felt a terrible chill rise from his limbs to gradually settle in his heart. Death was close and stood ready to take him. 'Not just yet!' he thought, furiously fighting on with demonic determination. He thought about Duryodhana, and decided that he had to try and perform one last service for him. If he could not kill the accursed Pandava, he could certainly destroy his army. With this in mind, he summoned the *Brahmastra*. But at that crucial moment, he could not for the life of him remember the *mantra* to invoke it. Parashurama's curse had taken hold.

Even as Karna struggled to recall the words, one of the wheels of his chariot sank into the ground. The old man's curse had also come true, as if to prove the adage that misfortune never comes alone. Karna tried in vain to dislodge the stubborn wheel, but it only sank deeper and deeper into the mire. Shalya prayed fervently to the Gods who had seen fit to hamper the *purushakara* of this great hero with more than his fair share of adversity. But Arjuna was already moving in for the kill.

Seeing him draw near, Karna called out to his brother: 'Arjuna! If you are a Kshatriya who knows the code of conduct, restrain your hand till I free this accursed wheel!' Arjuna hesitated on hearing these words, as it went against his grain to attack an opponent in such a palpably unfair fashion.

But Krishna's voice broke through his indecision: 'You are a fine one to talk about conduct, Karna! Was it good conduct when you and Duryodhana decided to use foul means to try and kill the Pandavas or rob them of what was theirs? Was it the epitome of noble ethics when you suggested that Draupadi ought to be disrobed as she was your slave? Was it fair play when you disarmed the boy Abhimanyu by breaking his bow from behind? How is it that you have suddenly become such an adherent of *dharma* that you dare to preach its laws to Arjuna?'

The words of the Lord-charioteer battered away at the last dregs of Karna's resistance. Karna felt sick with remorse as he finally realized that though he could not have controlled the events of his birth and life which had contributed to his misery, he could and should have controlled his actions and striven for a higher standard of nobility. Hanging his head in shame, he went on with his efforts to free the wheel.

Arjuna's thoughts were on Abhimanyu and he invoked a divine weapon called the *Anjalika*. In a clear voice he uttered: 'If I have been a good man who always stuck to the path of *dharma,* let this weapon find its mark and put an end to Karna's existence on Mother Earth.'

Karna abandoned the wheel and determinedly, if futilely, attacked Arjuna by shooting ordinary arrows, as he no longer had the strength to summon divine weapons. He refused, as he had all through his life, to submit tamely to cruel fate. Arjuna's missile flew towards his neck and severed his head cleanly. As Karna fell to the ground, a bright light escaped from his chest and flew towards the sun, which had turned red, as if in mourning. The Gods showered flowers on the fallen hero, even as the whole earth fell silent, mourning the loss of a beloved son who had been brave, noble, generous to a fault, and loyal unto death.

18
Duel Unto Death

After the death of Karna on the seventeenth day of battle, a cloud of doom descended on the tattered remains of what had once been a mighty army. Duryodhana was terribly distraught. He had lost the Grandsire, Drona, his beloved friend Karna, his brothers, and even his son, Lakshmana. Yudhishthira on the other hand still had all his brothers. The Prince tried to rally his troops, but nobody was in the mood to fight. The sight of Shalya driving an empty chariot broke his will and he wept disconsolately as he was led away from the battlefield.

Kripacharya tried to comfort him as best he could, but Duryodhana felt that life had lost all meaning for him with Karna gone. Even the death of his brothers and son had not affected him as deeply. While he mourned thus, Kripa advised him to end the suffering at once and call for a truce. But the Prince shook his head sadly and said, 'I realised a long time ago that this war with the Pandavas was going to end badly for us, but we have all crossed the point of no return. The idea of suing for peace now is repellent to me and I refuse to even contemplate it. After having the entire world at my feet, to do with as I pleased, it would be impossible for me to embrace a life where I will be alone and at the mercy of my cousins. Death is close to me and I will leave this world fighting to the very end, the way a Kshatriya should. I have lost everything that is dear to me, only my honour remains and I will not let go of it at this fell hour.'

Duryodhana's decision was applauded by all. Shalya was appointed Commander of the Kaurava forces, on the recommendation of Ashwatthama, Drona' son. Remembering his promise to Karna, to avenge him or die trying, Shalya rode out to battle, to be confronted by the faces of his sister's sons and their brothers. The dear faces were set in grim lines and the King of Madra knew that his own countenance was far from friendly. Today they would all fight to kill.

Krishna had told Yudhishthira that he alone was capable of neutralising the threat Shalya posed. And so the eldest Pandava prepared his battle plans. He decided to attack the Commander of the Kaurava forces with his brothers, Shikandin and Dhrishtadyumna, protecting and supporting him.

Shalya fought heroically and more than lived up to his reputation as a warrior par excellence. Forgetting the ties of blood that bound him to the twins, he fought with only the aim to destroy. The Pandava army was almost tottering under the savage attack and Yudhishthira was furious with the man responsible for the carnage. The serenity that characterised the eldest Pandava, vanished on that day and left in its wake a killing fury. He challenged Shalya to a duel and the two men were soon engaged in deadly combat. There was little to choose between them as they matched blow for blow. Yudhishthira shattered his opponent's armour and Shalya responded by breaking the Pandava's bow. Having gained the upper hand, Shalya pressed his advantage and tore open Yudhishthira's armour with precise arrows and also killed his horses. Kripa and Ashwatthama rushed forward to help Shalya and together the trio harassed the eldest Pandava mightily.

Seeing him in duress, the other four Pandavas charged in to counter the attack. Like a pack of converging lions, they closed in on the

King of Madra. Driving away his supporters, they gathered around the lone figure. Bheema disarmed Shalya and killed his charioteer as well. Shalya's horses were out of control and he jumped out of his chariot with sword and shield in hand. But Bheema smashed both. Yudhishthira seized the moment and hurled a spear at the King of Madra. The weapon found its mark in Shalya's chest and felled him to the ground.

The Kaurava soldiers, on seeing their Commander dead, took to their heels, knowing that the fall of Shalya marked the end of the war. Duryodhana rallied his men by ordering his remaining troops to shoot at the deserters. When some sense of order was restored, he led the charge against the Pandavas himself. Galvanised by the actions of the Kuru Prince, the soldiers fought with renewed vigour and spirit.

Seeing the Kaurava Prince in the thick of the fighting, his uncle Shakuni went to extricate him with the help of his son, Uluka. The Pandava twins, who had been hankering for the blood of the man who was the root cause of their troubles, went after him. Nakula made short work of Uluka while his brother fought Shakuni. Hard-pressed to keep his end up, Shakuni turned tail and fled, only to be pursued by Sahadeva, who was determined not to let the evil man escape. 'I knew it all along! You are nothing but a coward who excels at cheating and nothing else. At least prove that you are a man possessed of some virility by standing and fighting like one!' he shouted after his fleeing uncle. But disregarding his taunts, Shakuni continued to run till a sharp javelin thrown by Sahadeva separated his cowardly head from the rest of his body. The twins were euphoric when they saw the much hated head roll in the mud, with the once-scheming brains spilling out, jarred loose by the impact of hitting the hard ground. They cheered jubilantly and their cheers were taken up by all the others on their side.

In the meantime, Arjuna was systematically destroying the rest of the army with his Gandeeva, determined to finish the battle on that cataclysmic day. Arrows streamed from the great bow in an endless flow and slew thousands of soldiers. He had just about finished off the remnants of the Kaurava army with Dhrishtadyumna circling around, picking off the troops trying to flee. Duryodhana realised that he had been thoroughly and utterly defeated. Not a single soldier remained of the formidable army he had raised. For a moment he stood silently staring at the mangled remains of his men with disbelieving eyes. Then with the air of one who knew not whether he was asleep or awake, he withdrew slowly and unobtrusively from the battlefield with only his trusty mace for company. Kripa, Ashwatthama, and Kritavarma, the three remaining stalwarts from the Kauava army, who had managed to stay alive, also withdrew discreetly.

With the sound of the boisterous cheering of the Pandava army ringing in his ears, Duryodhana fled, craving nothing but blissful oblivion. There was great revelry on the Pandava side and everyone was thrilled that the bloody conflict had finally ended. They were all glutted with blood and could take no more. Dhrishtadyumna, Shikandin, Satyaki, and the other proud warriors who had fought in the greatest war of all time and lived though it, pranced around, giddy with excitement, their usual pomp and dignity having deserted them.

The Pandavas themselves were feeling far from sanguine. They knew that the war was not officially over while Duryodhana still lived. Five pairs of eyes searched the blood-soaked battlefield of Kurukshetra, looking in vain for their cousin. Krishna suggested that Yudhishthira send out scouts and offer a reward to anyone who could shed light on the whereabouts of the eldest Kaurava.

While the brothers waited for news about him, Duryodhana had come to a decision. His body and soul were wearied to a point beyond human endurance. He simply could not bring himself to fulfil his responsibilities or even think of them. The defeated warrior looked around for a place to conceal himself so that his spirit could begin to revive. He saw a lake and an idea struck him like a bright shaft of sunlight.

The Prince knew the secret of making water stand still and could breathe underwater for as long as he wished. Duryodhana decided to enter that watery haven and make a fresh start. The fatigue and sorrow that had him in its deathly grip, began to loosen its hold once he was safely ensconced within the lake, gently held there like a foetus within the soothing fluids of the womb. Duryodhana felt that he had been born again. While he mused thus, a strange thought took hold of him. He remembered that the preceptor of the *Asuras*, Shukracharya, possessed knowledge of the secret craft of *Sanjivani*, which could bring the dead back to life. Kacha, the son of Brihaspathi, Guru of the *Devas*, had finagled it out of him. Duryodhana decided that if he could somehow acquire knowledge of that esoteric craft, he would be able to revive everyone he had loved and lost.

Excitedly, the Prince decided to perform *tapas* to achieve his goal. While he was readying himself for this venture, Ashwatthama, Kripa and Kritavarma, approached him. Duryodhana told them that he would be ready to fight soon and to leave him alone in the meantime. All was not lost and they could still triumph over his cousins. Heartened by his optimism, the trio left him and returned to their camp.

But, their conversation was overheard by a group of hunters; and rightly judging that this information was of great value, the men went in search of Yudhishthira, dreaming of the riches they were about to acquire. Overwhelmed with excitement, they rushed headlong into the Pandava camp, even as the guards attempted to detain them. Bheema came out to ascertain the cause of the disturbance and the hunters poured out their story to him. The second Pandava was delighted and hugged them to his chest. He thanked them heartily before lavishing wealth upon them, beyond their wildest expectations.

Bheema wasted no time in relaying the information to Yudhishthira. The brothers, accompanied by Krishna, Dhrishtadyumna, Shikandin and Satyaki, called for their chariots and raced towards Lake Dwaipayana. When Yudhishthira espied the still lake that provided Duryodhana with his last sanctuary, he felt the rage he had long suppressed in his heart burst forth. In a voice hoarse with anger, he called out, 'Come out and fight like a man, you scoundrel! What do you mean by hiding like a rat after bringing about the destruction of an entire race? So much death and destruction has been our lot only because you have a black heart without the capacity for kindness. You started this war and you will end it by forfeiting your life! Come out and stop behaving like a coward!'

To these acid words, Duryodhana replied with infuriating serenity, 'I am not hiding because I am scared of you. It has been an exhausting ordeal for both of us and I feel that both sides need to rest awhile before we commence fighting on the morrow.'

'This is a fine time for resting. There will be plenty of time for you to relax in comfort after we have despatched you to the abode of Yama, where you can join the accursed souls of your brothers!' yelled Yudhishthira in fury.

'I have no desire to fight. As you have kindly informed me, I have lost all my loved ones and I care not for the Kingdom and you are welcome to take it. It is yours to do with as you please. For my part, I shall wander these forests and pursue asceticism.' Duryodhana's tone was infuriatingly calm and reasonable, as though he were talking to a particularly obdurate child.

'The crushing defeat we have inflicted on you seems to have left your arrogance unaffected! How dare you presume to give me something I have already won, as if I am a beggar seeking alms! Stop your incessant prattle and come out! Steeped in ignominy as you are, I am surprised you are not utilising this chance to redeem what is left of your honour,' said Yudhishthira with withering scorn.

'How can I fight when I have nothing left to fight with? My loved ones are gone, my armies have been vanquished, and I don't even have a proper set of weapons to defend myself with. Knowing all this, if you still wish me to fight, let it be so. But the world will finally know that for all his talk of *dharma,* Yudhishthira is no better than the rest of us inferior mortals.'

Hearing Duryodhana lecture him on virtue and morality, Yudhishthira finally lost the self-control he was famous for and walked right into the trap laid for him by his mortal foe of admittedly inferior morality but far superior cunning. Goaded thus, Yudhishthira said with uncharacteristic sarcasm, 'I am so happy to have you in my life, if only to advise me on how to conduct myself according to the code of *dharma*. You can stop your whining about being alone and unarmed. Pick any weapon you prefer and choose one of us as your opponent. And if you succeed in defeating your chosen man, we will place the crown on your head and relinquish our claim to the Kingdom.'

When he heard these words, Duryodhana came out from the water with a triumphant roar, his mace resting menacingly on his shoulder. Eyes smouldering with hatred, he advanced on the brothers. 'I thank you for your magnanimity, Yudhishthira. People have often mistaken your nobility for sheer stupidity, but those of us who know and love you so well, know the truth.' Pausing meaningfully, he looked at each of the Pandavas in turn, taunting them with his piercing eyes. 'Today one of you will fall victim to my mighty mace. Of that there can be no room for doubt, as nobody, and I mean nobody, can wield a mace better than me. Who may that be, I wonder?' And with a carefully careless smile, he turned towards the attendant who had brought him a helmet and a suit of armour, and busied himself with preparations for the upcoming battle, not deigning to even look at the suddenly anxious group who waited in miserable suspense.

Krishna rounded on Yudhishthira and took him to one side. Yudhishthira had seldom seen such furious anger directed towards himself by the Lord who walked among men, and he quailed in the face of it. When the Dark Lord spoke, his words sounded like a whiplash and stung Yudhishthira with their impact. 'Duryodhana is right about you! Your unfathomable lack of practical sense is what masquerades as a passion for *dharma*! So many men have fought and died to see you installed on the throne, and you cast away their sacrifice with your infernal propensity to gamble! Balarama has told me often that Duryodhana is his most accomplished pupil and will never be defeated while he holds a mace in his hand. By letting him choose his weapon, you have doomed us. And if that were not enough, you let him choose his opponent! Bheema alone has the strength to prevail against him, and even that may not be enough.

While the lot of you were languishing in the jungle as a direct result of your insatiable love for dice, Duryodhana spent every single day practising with his mace. He used an iron statue of Bheema to motivate him and to prepare him for an encounter with his sworn enemy. His skill has been supplemented with long years of practice and he is now unbeatable. Bheema will never win in a fair fight. And if your brother is defeated, you will have only yourself to blame.'

Yudhishthira was crushed and looked so miserable that his brothers could not bear it and rushed to his side. Bheema spoke: 'Don't worry Krishna, we have all learned to work our way around Big Brother's well-intentioned blunders. I will not let that scoundrel defeat me. The anger which I have nursed against him all these years for every injury we have endured at his hands, will sustain and help me to overwhelm him, despite his supposedly superior skill with the mace."

Krishna smiled and spoke words of encouragement to him. Then Bheema turned to the man he hated more than any other. 'Coward and swaggering bully that you are, I suppose you will pick one of the twins to fight with and overpower them with your mace or your odious trickery, that are both equally potent? Everybody knows that you develop cold feet whenever you see Arjuna, so it must be your intention to prove the world wrong and triumph over him with a weapon that does not play to his strengths. Surely, you don't intend to fight Yudhishthira for the throne? He will be so repelled by your evil nature that it will be hard for him to even get close to you. It is a colossal pity that you do not have the courage to fight me, for I will prove once and for all that I am your better in every conceivable way!'

Duryodhana smiled maliciously before replying, 'Don't exert your brain too much, Bheema. The Creator failed to give you much of that asset and your limited resources will not be able to take the strain. I can see through your pathetic little ploy. Of course, I intend to fight you. It was my design all along, for the others are beneath me. And I shall defeat you, make no mistake!'

Bheema and Duryodhana would have rushed each other then and there, but for the timely intervention of Balarama, their *Guru*. He had gone on a pilgrimage, having disdained to take part in a war that would have pitted him against his blood relatives or Krishna. Having completed his religious tour, he arrived on the scene, anxious to see for himself what had transpired in the war. On being informed by Krishna that his foremost disciples would decide the outcome of the great battle, he gave his approval and suggested the great match take place at nearby Samantapanchaka, the most hallowed of grounds. In a bygone era, when the great Parashurama had gone forth on a bloody mission to rid the world of Kshatriyas, his divine anger obliterated his compassion and rendered him terrible. At the place called Samantapanchaka, he created five lakes, with the blood of the men he slew and offered them to the souls of his ancestors, whom he revered above all else. It was at this consecrated spot that Richika, one of his forefathers, appeared before him. Having commended him for his valour in avenging the death of his father, *rishi* Jamadagni, he granted him a boon. Parashurama asked to be cleansed of the sin of killing, and his wish was granted and the lakes were sanctified. Richika then ordered him to desist from his self-appointed task of ridding the world of Kshatriyas and the fiery warrior assented.

And so it was that Samantapanchaka came to receive yet another oblation of blood. Having adjourned to that legendary spot and with Balarama presiding, the epic clash between the cousins, Duryodhana and Bheema, commenced. The small group of men who witnessed this grand spectacle, sat around in a circle and watched tensely as the adversaries fought for honour, a Kingdom, and to settle intensely personal scores.

Bheema thought of Duryodhana's attempts to kill him while they were still children. He remembered the fiery hell that was Varanavata and the feel of death as it brushed close to him and all those he loved best in the world; the game of dice; the loss of their Kingdom; and above all, he dwelt on the humiliation of Draupadi, his beloved wife. She might be their common wife but she knew that he, Bheema, loved her more than his brothers did, great though their love was. The memory of her tears snapped open the bars that had barely held in the monster that was his anger.

Duryodhana in turn, thought of the loved ones he had lost to Bheema's fiendish wrath. The hundred sons of Gandhari had been killed mercilessly by that accursed son of Kunti, till only one remained. Duhshasana had been his favourite, a beloved brother, loyal friend, trusted confidant and fellow conspirator. The Pandava brute had actually torn open Dushasana's chest and quaffed his blood. Duryodhana's eyes swam with tears of grief and rage as he recollected that terrible deed. On this day, he would fight for all he had loved and lost, and finally revenge would be his.

The cousins charged at each other, spurred on by the intensity of their mutual hatred. It was a contest for the ages. The viewers watched breathless with admiration as the two men raised the level of combat to a standard the world had never seen before and never would again. The two men circled expertly, appraising vulnerabilities and lowered defences, before moving in to strike.

Blows were dodged and blows were struck while their blood and sweat mingled in a an unending stream.

Duryodhana began to edge ahead of Bheema, as his experience and skill began to tell. Any man but Bheema would have succumbed to the blows that landed like Indra's thunderbolt, but the second Pandava was the strongest man alive and his body withstood the punishment being meted out and kept him on his feet. But even his great strength could not last forever, and Bheema felt his iron constitution show the first signs of crumbling as fits of dizziness almost overpowered him. Sensing his advantage, Duryodhana moved like a whirlwind, striking Bheema repeatedly and so fast that Bheema felt his body under siege from all sides. The Kaurava leapt high into the air before striking, in order to gain the maximum impact. But Bheema continued to block the blows with renewed vigour as his survival instincts somehow spurred him on.

Watching the mauling of his brother by the abominable son of Gandhari, Arjuna turned to Krishna. 'Do you think Bheema can still win?' Krishna shook his head and said, 'Bheema's great strength keeps defeat at arm's length, but he will not be able to hold out for much longer. Duryodhana is too good with a mace. In a fair fight he will always prevail. I wonder if Bheema remembers his vow to break Duryodhana's thighs?'

Arjuna needed no further prompting. He stared at his brother, focusing his entire will on catching his brother's eye. Those piercing eyes penetrated the haze of blood surrounding Bheema and met his for a fleeting moment. In that moment, Arjuna tapped his thigh and Bheema saw all too clearly his only hope for victory and survival. He snatched at it.

Bheema waited for an opportunity and when Duryodhana again leapt up into the air, he brought his mace crashing down on his thigh and smashed it. Mortally wounded, Duryodhana collapsed to the ground, screaming in agony. The brothers and their supporters cheered their champion, even as he walked towards the fallen man and placed his feet on Duryodhana's head. 'This is for every wrong you have ever done us. This is your punishment for destroying so many lives. And most of all, this is for Draupadi! Feel the pain and repent for your misdeeds, you foul fiend!'

Yudhishthira rushed forward and pulled his brother away. 'It is finished now. There is no need for any more virulence. Nobody has won in this accursed war. We get a Kingdom but we have paid too heavy a price for it. At least Duryodhana will be joining his loved ones soon, while we will have to trudge on in this world, knowing that so many of our loved ones are gone forever!'

The words were uttered to comfort a fallen enemy, but Balarama was having none of it. He rose to his feet, quivering with the sheer force of his anger. Duryodhana had been his favourite pupil, and it galled him to see him on the ground, a broken man, vanquished by unfair means. He spat his fury at Bheema. 'That was the most shameful thing I have ever had the misfortune to witness! How dare you stoop to such despicable levels? I myself taught you the rules of fair combat, and you know that it is forbidden to attack beneath the navel. This will be the last time you flout the rules of combat and I shall personally ensure it!' With these words, Balarama snatched up the plough, his weapon of choice, and rushed at his former pupil, determined to end his life.

Krishna had to intervene and forcibly restrain his ill-tempered sibling. 'Control yourself, brother! This is but a tiny lapse in morality compared with your beloved pupil's transgressions. If I were to take the same view of the matter, I would have had to kill him many times over!'

Balarama allowed himself to be restrained, but he refused to be mollified. With blazing eyes he addressed the gathering: 'It is an ugly day for the Kshatriyas as Bheema's unforgiveable breach reflects badly on all of us. He is an unworthy champion and I will not condone what has happened today.' Turning his back on all of them, he got into his chariot and stormed off, leaving everyone in his wake chastened.

But as soon as Balarama's chariot disappeared, the men began cheering in earnest for Bheema. His brothers were besides themselves with joy and whooped with delight. They hugged Bheema in turn and staunchly informed him that he was truly the mightiest hero this world had seen. Krishna interrupted the celebrations and suggested they leave the spot as they had rendered their biggest threat ineffectual. The brothers departed with Krishna, feeling happy and content that the bloodshed had ended at long last. They heard the dying man they were leaving behind, utter the foulest words his agony could conjure, and they drove hard to put an unbridgable distance between themselves and that voice. With spirits buoyed up again, they felt it was right to be finally happy. None of them noticed Krishna's eyes. If they had, all their mirth would have been replaced by dark forebodings of despair.

19
Midnight Massacre

The Pandavas and Krishna made their way to the Kaurava camp to check for any signs of survivors. There were none. The men leapt down from their chariots for a closer look. Krishna alone tarried. Seeing that the others were at a comfortable distance from the vehicle, he alighted slowly. No sooner had he done so, than the chariot burst into flames and in a matter of moments nothing but ash remained. Seeing the gift Agni had given him destroyed so utterly, Arjuna was heartbroken. His chariot had been a part of him ever since Khandava and, in a strange way, he felt that it had fought with him and protected him almost as much as Krishna had. He tried to quell the tears that rose unbidden, and turned blindly to his best friend, as he always did, for an explanation.

Krishna provided him with the answer which resolved his doubt and confusion. 'As you know, in warfare, one of the means to render a foe vulnerable is to destroy his vehicle. Every warrior worth his salt wished to claim your life and they tried in vain to smash the chariot. The truth is, they were more successful than they or even you, realized. Drona and Karna went about it using their celestial weapons, and even your chariot was not a match for those. It was destroyed long ago; but my presence held it together. Now that you have accomplished all that you were meant to, I saw no further reason for it to remain.'

Arjuna nodded dumbly. His brothers stared at the burning wreckage and felt fear brush uncomfortably close to them with its clammy touch. The heroes of the battle of Kurukshetra trembled. Krishna smiled beatifically at them and said, 'Do not brood. It has been an exhausting day to say the least. I feel that it would be wiser to camp close by and return to our camp on the morrow, so that we are fresh and better equipped to deal with all the pending formalities.' The brothers listened to him and they stayed away from their camp. Thus did Krishna adroitly deliver them from certain death.

Shortly after Bheema had vanquished Duryodhana and left him to bleed to death at Samantapanchaka, he was visited by the trio who were all that remained of the mighty Kaurava army. Ashwatthama, Kripacharya and Kritavarma, stood around the fallen Prince and shed bitter tears for him. Ashwatthama was particularly affected; Duryodhana had befriended him from the start and had always stood by him. Tearfully, he addressed the man who had once ruled the world and was now lying bleeding in the dust at his feet: 'Truly, this is the blackest day in the history of mankind! Seeing you like this brings back to me all the pain I endured when my father was taken from me by foul means. However, the ache has been magnified a hundredfold. I am cursed indeed to lose my father and my friend, and just about everyone else I have ever cared for, in this accursed battle!'

Seeing Ashwatthama open the deluge of angst in his heart, broke Duryodhana's spirit in a way that Bheema's mace could never have managed. He spoke in shuddering gasps: 'It is so hard for me to believe that it ends like this. My best friend of unmatched valour is gone. All my brothers are dead. Men like the Grandsire and the Acharya, who I believed could never be defeated, have been vanquished. My mortal enemies, the Pandavas, whom I have hated all my life, are now in possession of the Kingdom that is mine by right and they still have each other and their sons by that whore, Draupadi. That vile witch who, using the tricks she learnt from some base den of inequity, finagled a promise from Bheema to kill Duhshasana and drink his blood. His blood! Can you imagine anyone capable of such evil?

And my friend Karna was killed by the treachery of Krishna and Arjuna. They were so eager for the victory they were not entitled to, that they stooped to killing a defenceless man who was in the act of freeing his chariot wheel. Did you know that Karna is the eldest son of Kunti, born of Surya? Don't look at me like that, it is true enough. The Grandsire told me the secret after his heroic death. The Pandavas do not know this, but Karna himself knew about his divine birth. Krishna made sure he knew as did that sinner, Kunti, hoping to turn him away from me. But my true friend Karna, did not go to join his brothers like they had hoped. He was told that death would remorselessly find him if he chose to remain with me, and yet he chose me over them, so great was his loyalty and love. Without him, life has no meaning for me.

Death is waiting in the wings and I am not long for this world. There is little solace for me, as the men responsible for killing so many of my loved ones will also usurp my throne. But, at least I will be going to the warrior's heaven. I have fought this war like a true hero and discharged every duty that is demanded of a Kshatriya. I will be reunited with Karna and my brothers. It is a great comfort to me, but at this moment, as life ebbs away, I wish there was some way I could make the Pandavas pay for what they have done; make them cry and lament the way I am doing now. Only then will I die in peace.'

The three men wept unabashedly, listening to the words of the crushed parody of a man who was all that was left of their beloved Prince. Ashwatthama felt that he was watching his father die all over again. At that moment, he and Duryodhana were kindred spirits, their souls conjoined in a shared hatred that was volcanic in its capacity to destroy. Ashwatthama spoke up, his voice turned harsh with the vehemence of the killing rage that had all but consumed the humanity in him. 'Duryodhana! I promise you that vengeance will be ours. If I am truly the son of my father, I will find a way to make them suffer and rue the day they swerved from the path of good conduct and common decency. The Pandavas and Panchalas will meet the inglorious death they so justly deserve, at my hands. Give me your blessing for the task I have undertaken and may victory be ours!'

Duryodana was greatly consoled by Ashwatthama's words which, in his utter desolation, gave him the hope needed to endure his last hours on earth. He sent Kripacharya for a vessel of water and sprinkling the sanctified drops on the head that had been commissioned to do murder, he installed Ashwatthama as Commander-in-Chief. Bidding farewell to Duryodhana, the three men then departed to make camp for the night and to discuss their plans for the morrow.

The trio retreated deep into a forest and decided to spend the night under a Banyan tree. Kripa and Kritavarma fell asleep almost at once, wearied by the happenings of that eventful day. Ashwatthama, however, could not sleep. He was too full of the turmoil that roiled through his innards, consuming all in its path with the inexorability of a corrosive acid in its quest to find an outlet. While he tossed about thus, Drona's son happened to glance up at the spreading branches of the Banyan tree and espied crows' nests that numbered in the dozens. The crows reposed peacefully with their wings spread protectively over the little ones in the nests. Their contentment made Ashwatthama resentful, and he glared balefully at the spectacle. Suddenly, a large owl flew soundlessly through the night and alighted purposefully on one of the branches. Swift and sure as a born assassin of the night, it suddenly attacked the sleeping crows, its talons merciless in carrying out its murderous task. Within minutes the place was littered with the carcasses of the slain crows. And the killer owl, pleased to have done a satisfactory night's work, seemed to look down at Ashwatthama as though conveying some message of portentous significance.

Ashwatthama, in a blinding epiphany, suddenly realised that the owl had shown him the path he should take if he was to successfully keep his fell promise to Duryodhana. It was obvious to him that in order to triumph where Bhishma, his father, Karna, and Shalya, had all failed, he had to rely on deviousness and entirely abandon the moral high ground. In order to triumph against the Pandavas, aided and abetted as they were in their unscrupulous ways by Krishna, he too, had to think like them. As he mused thus, an ugly smile spread over his features, twisting them out of shape, leaving him looking like a monster escaped from the fantasies of a madman.

Anxious to put his plan into action, he woke his companions and related his experience to them, concluding with the words, 'Like the owl that prevailed over its natural foes though they outnumbered it, we too, must mount an attack while the Pandavas sleep, and so do away with them once and for all. Tonight they will answer for their actions and I am the instrument of the Gods. Their punishment will be at my hand!'

Kripa and Kritavarma stared at him, unable to contain the horror and distaste they felt. Kripa had always considered his sister's son to be a decent enough lad, even if he chose to keep undesirable company; but the virulent creature standing before him was barely recognizable – with eerily hollow eyes that had lost their humanity. Kripa, therefore said hesitantly, 'Ashwatthama, surely you are not serious? What you are suggesting is without doubt the most foul deed ever contemplated and I dare not repeat it. As the Commander of an army of three, it is not unnatural that you should become desperate, but there is a right way to prevail over one's enemies. And it does not include killing men when they are sleeping and utterly defenceless.'

'I am not talking about killing men but monsters that would practice deceit and shirk the laws of fair combat, so that they may get their grasping hands on a Kingdom!' replied Ashwatthama.

Kripa tried again to deactivate the poison that had blackened his nephew's soul. 'We are all too tired and emotional tonight, let us discuss this in the morning with cooler heads. You are young and your blood runs hot with the terrible things you have witnessed. It is not wise to act while your mind is in such a state of tumult.'

But Ashwatthama had made up his mind and would not even think of turning back from the path to hell that he had chosen. 'I will not prevaricate. It is my firm belief that the owl was a messenger from the Gods. Now is the time for action, not for feeble speeches. Thinking too much is the enemy of action and I for one refuse to allow anything to hamper my resolve!'

Kripa was aghast and thought of the sweet little boy he once carried on his shoulders when his sister and Drona came to stay with him.

Feeling sure that he was watching the prelude to perdition unfold before his very eyes, he made another feeble attempt to talk sense into the boy who had grown up to become a cold-blooded killer. 'If your father were alive, it would have broken his heart to hear you talk of taking the lives of sleeping men. Think of him, of all the lessons he taught you, and desist from pursuing this evil plan of yours.'

It was the wrong thing to say. At the mention of his father, Ashwatthama once again felt all the pain and anger that was pushing him towards vengeance rise up within him in a tidal wave of emotion. 'My father died of a broken heart! Those sons of a wanton whore, the Pandavas, told that noble soul that his only son was dead – all for the love of a Kingdom which their father had lost, along with his life, because of his preoccupation with carnal pleasures. And my father was tricked into laying down his weapons, for his heart had burst asunder with sorrow. Yudhishthira knew what he was doing when he repeated the lie to my father. And Dhrishtadyumna beheaded my father when he, having dropped his arms, sat in yogic meditation! If that were not enough, Bheema cheated in his fight with Duryodhana and left him in the dust to die. A Royal Prince! Do those curs deserve better than my noble father or my good friend? I will not stand here talking uselessly when there is so much to be done. The two of you may join me or leave as you please, but if you try to stop me, I will be forced to fight and kill you!'

Ashwatthama stormed off in the direction of the Pandava camp with predatory intent writ large on his face. Kripa and Kritavarma stared at his retreating figure, and for a moment they were irresolute. Then, feeling powerless, like pieces of driftwood unable to fight the tide, they allowed themselves to be carried away by the surging, implacable wave that was fate.

It was an evil hour, and the blackness of that night was complete. Ashwatthama's prey were fast asleep, tired from their victory and unrestrained celebrations. The men had not only been a part of the greatest war the world had seen, but they were the victors! What stories they would have to tell their grandchildren! Great glory and fame had been achieved. The survivors feasted late into the night and drank themselves senseless. They laughed with the joy of being alive and wept for the ones who had not been fortunate enough to see victory. All were anxious to return to their homes, where they would be welcomed with the respect due to conquering heroes. There was singing and dancing, and above all else, there was the animated throbbing of life – but not for long.

Ashwatthama had reached the camp. He walked towards the entrance and stopped short, for it was guarded by a towering monster, clothed in the skin of slain beasts. Its eyes were bloodshot and flames poured from its mouth and nostrils. The creature barred his passage. Lesser men would have dropped to the ground, dead with fright, but Ashwatthama was unafraid, for that night there was none in the three worlds as dangerous as he.

Reaching for his bow, Ashwatthama sent weapon after weapon lancing through the dead of night to kill the thing that stood in his way. But the creature could not be harmed, and simply swallowed all his weapons and licked its lips tauntingly. But Drona's son was undeterred and decided to seek divine intervention. He started a sacrificial fire and began offering prayers to Shiva, the Destroyer. Weird beings emerged from the flames, stinking of mortified flesh and putrefaction. The smells intoxicated Ashwatthama and he sensed that the Lord was near. So great was his ecstasy that he offered his body to Shiva, by stepping into the flames. The Destroyer God stopped him and smiled down at him saying, 'I know what is in your heart, and you will soon achieve what you have set out to do. This camp was under my protection because Krishna is my dearest follower; but the time has come for the inhabitants to depart this world. Go and do what you must and be prepared for the outcome of your actions!'

Ashwatthama was euphoric, and within seconds he had succeeded in entering the camp. He made his way with unerring instinct towards the tent where the man who had killed his father slept. He woke the King of the Panchalas with a hard kick to his kidneys. Dhrishtadyumna rose groggily and found himself dragged to the floor by an assailant who had grabbed him by the hair. The last remnants of his wine-induced stupor slipped away as he found himself staring into the implacable eyes of Drona's son. But Dhrishtadyumna was a hard man and did not flinch in the face of certain death, even as Ashwatthama's well shod feet crushed his ribs like dried twigs. He barely gasped as they tore holes through his viscera. He looked at his killer square in the eye and uttered his last words: 'Not like this! I deserve a warrior's death. Pick up your sword and slay me with it.'

The last thing he heard was Ashwatthama's terrible laughter and the cruel words, 'You killed your *Guru*, and you will get what you deserve – to be crushed under my feet like the vermin you are!' And he pounded the life out of the wounded King lying at his feet in agony. Leaving the bloody pulp that was all that remained of the great Panchala warrior who had emerged from the flames, born from a father's humiliation and destined to be the victim of a destroyed friendship, Ashwatthama went out to finish the gory mission he had started.

The sleeping inhabitants of tent after tent were sent in rapid succession to follow Dhrishtadyumna down the dark path that was life after death, as Ashwatthama made his way round the camp, stamping out all traces of life. The battle of Kurukshetra had been witness to an avalanche of violence that the world had seldom seen before, but the vilest of atrocities the great battle had unspooled could not equal the methodical and relentless slaughter that took place in the Pandava camp that night. Mighty warriors who had celebrated the gift of life a few hours ago, lay dead, not having the good fortune to return from the limbo world of sleep to the land of the living. Dhrishtadyumna, Shikandin, and the five sons of Draupadi, known as the *Upapandavas,* were all victims of Ashwatthama's nocturnal massacre.

Kripa and Kritavarma had reached the spot and they set fire to the camp from all sides, because at that moment it seemed the most logical thing to do by way of an auxiliary offensive. Having performed their act of arson, they stationed themselves at the exit and knifed down anyone who tried to escape. They did their job with mechanical efficiency and shut their ears to the agonised sounds of the people dying within as the flames consumed them, as surely as a bereaved son's hatred had done.

When the sun rose the next morning, Ashwatthama had finished his task. All the survivors of the war had been killed and the camp lay smoking and in utter ruin. The stench of burning flesh, warm blood, and excreta, hung over the place, forming an infernal miasma. The overwhelming silence was broken when Ashwatthama, Kripa and Kritavarma, began their revelry, screaming themselves hoarse with an exultation that bordered on hysteria. They had done a thorough job.

They rushed to tell the dying Duryodhana the good news. The Prince had little time left. He smiled through his pain as Ashwatthama related what he had done. With the exception of the Pandavas themselves, Krishna, and Satyaki, the rest of their army was gone. Duryodhana was pleased with this final blow that he had managed to strike from his deathbed. 'Ashwatthama, you have succeeded where Bhishma, Drona, Karna, and Shalya, failed. I now die content. But it is too bad they were killed while they were sleeping...' and the Prince departed the world of the living.

The three killers paid their respects to the departed soul of their Prince and then began preparations for their own departure. Kritavarma decided to return to his Kingdom and the loved ones who awaited him. In their arms lay his only hope of succour, if not salvation. Kripa wished to retreat to a quiet place and perform penances to cleanse himself of the offal that now clogged his soul in having aided and abetted in a deadly sin.

Ashwatthama hugged his uncle and watched him leave. He was alone now and apprehensive. His mind refused to ponder the consequences of his killing spree, but fear loomed large and left him trembling, for he was afraid of dying. He had not been afraid to take lives, but now, at the thought of his own life being taken, he was terrified. Taking to his heels, he ran towards Vyasa's *ashram*, hoping to find sanctuary there and safe haven from the wrath of the Pandavas when they discovered what he had done.

Another man was rushing in the opposite direction. He was Dhrishtadyumna's charioteer and the lone survivor of the horrors of the night. Even he did not understand how he had made it past the gaping jaws of death that had consumed so many. Weeping and distrait, he somehow made it to the temporary camp the Pandavas had set up, and hurling himself at Yudhishthira's feet, choked out his tragic tale. The King, who had conquered the entire world, blanched on hearing the charioteer's words and almost fell to the ground in a fainting fit. His brothers and Satyaki rushed to him and they clung together, lending what support and solace they could muster, to each other.

When they arrived at their destroyed camp in a daze, fresh sorrow coursed through them when they saw the scene of the massacre. Yudhishthira was the worst affected and was simply inconsolable. Throwing himself face down on a huge mound of ash, he wailed, 'A few hours ago, I exulted because I had destroyed my enemies and won back the Kingdom that was stolen from me, as honour and *dharma* demanded. Even then my happiness was tempered with grief, as thoughts of all those who had died for our cause flooded my mind. My only consolation at the time was that it was finally over. The river of blood that flowed freely over Kurukshetra had finally been dammed. And yet, still more blood has been spilled on my account. The falsehood I uttered has been the cause of all this ruination. My beloved friends and sons are all dead, never to return... What will I say to Draupadi? How much more must she endure?'

While Yudhishthira gave vent to his grief thus, Draupadi arrived on the scene with Nakula, who had been sent to fetch her. Seeing the huge piles of ash that was all that remained of her sons, she collapsed. Bheema rushed to her side and tenderly held her as she lay unconscious in his arms. But even in that state, fiery anger surged through her, pushing the grief and despair aside and bringing her back to her senses. She shoved away Bheema's arms and glared at her five mighty husbands. The five men who had proved to be the scourge of their enemies, quailed beneath that scorching gaze.

When she spoke, her voice alone could have flayed the skin off their backs. 'I hear that I must congratulate all of you for winning back your Kingdom – while letting your sons and friends be killed in their sleep. As fathers you shall remain unmatched through eternity! You did not perform your duty to them while they lived; do so now, and avenge their deaths. That cowardly murderer, Ashwatthama, must be brought to his knees and it must be done immediately. I will not move from this spot till I hear the welcome news of his death.' So saying, she sat down on the ground, with her feet drawn up in the *Padmasana* or Lotus position.

Yudhishthira tried to calm her, for what she had asked was impossible. She wished them to incur the dread sin of killing a Brahmin. He tried to talk her out of it saying, 'Ashwatthama has gone into hiding, and must be deep in the jungle by now. It will be well nigh impossible to ferret him out.'

But Draupadi withered him with her scorn. 'Then I suggest you get started, for I will know no peace till he is killed. Search for him through all that is left of your lives on this world, if that is what it takes; but he must be found and made to pay for his crime. He killed my five sons and my noble brother, in their sleep! I want him to suffer the way he has made us suffer. Bheema! I entrust this task to you – do not let Yudhishthira deter you with his discourses on *dharma*. Find that assasin and kill him! And when you have done that, bring me the jewel he wears all the time on his head and I will know for certain that the deed is done.'

Bheema could never resist her and he turned at once to do her bidding. His brothers were about to follow him, galvanised into action by the passion of her hatred and need for blood to quench her overwhelming grief. As they hurried towards their chariot, Krishna approached Yudhishthira. 'We must hurry! Bheema must not be allowed to fight Ashwatthama alone. The man is more dangerous than you think!' Ushering Yudhishthira and Arjuna into his chariot, Krishna invoked his powers, raised the chariot, and sent it soaring across the heavens in pursuit of Ashwatthama, hoping to forestall Bheema.

As the chariot flew towards its destination, Krishna told the duo a story about Ashwatthama. Arjuna had been taught how to invoke the powerful *Brahmashira astra* by Drona, when he had rescued his *Guru* from the jaws of a crocodile. Ashwatthama, who had been watching sullenly from a distance, asked Drona to teach it to him as well. His father hesitated briefly, but as always where his son was concerned, he gave in. Having taught him the craft, he told his son, 'Ashwatthama, always remember that the *Brahmashira* must never be used against mortals. It must be invoked only to counter the forces of evil. Also, the user must have the purest of intentions. To do otherwise is a grave crime against humanity and the consequences will be most dire.'

Drona emphasised these points repeatedly, until Ashwatthama lost his patience. 'I understand what you are saying, father. But what I do not comprehend is why you taught Arjuna the secret chant first, while I, your only son, was left out. And as if this was not humiliating enough, you feel the need to continuously reiterate the need for ethical consideration while using the *Brahmashira,* whereas Arjuna just received a mild warning. Can it be possible that you think more highly of him than of me? Do you love him more?'

'I love nobody and nothing in this world more than you, my son,' Drona replied with tears in his eyes. 'But I cannot help but worry about you. Duryodhana is an evil man and yet you are close to him, and think the world of him. The company you keep seems to bring out the dark side in you. The Pandavas are good men, and if you persist in joining Duryodhana in hating them and wishing them harm, I very much fear that you will lose your way and stray from the path of righteousness!'

Hearing the disappointment in his father's voice was more than Ashwatthama could bear. He fled from him, ignoring his entreaties. Overcome by sadness and dread for the future, Ashwatthama wandered aimlessly like one who had reached the outer limits of his sanity. He wallowed in self-pity and pushed away the nobler sentiments from his mind. Slowly, he felt rage and hatred gain the upper hand. He hated Arjuna for usurping his father's regard. He hated the fact that his father had made his rival the better warrior. At that point, Ashwatthama wanted nothing more than the means to kill Arjuna.

The years rolled by and Ashwatthama thoroughly enjoyed bringing the Pandavas down in the world, and their exile absolutely delighted him. While the brothers were away, he made a trip to Dwaraka, to catch Krishna alone. Finding him in a secluded spot, he approached him, and using his status as a Brahmin, demanded that Krishna give him his discus, the famous *Sudharshana Chakra,* in exchange for the *Brahmashira.*

Krishna smiled at him, but it was entirely devoid of goodwill. 'What need do I have for a missile? You may keep the *Brahmashira* but I will let you have any weapon of your choosing that I own. Choose wisely, for some of my weapons might prove to be too much for you.'

Ashwatthama sensed the scorn in Krishna's voice and bristled. Holding his head high, he said he wanted only the *Sudharshana Chakra*. Krishna smiled again and told him to take it. Ashwatthama felt beads of sweat snaking their way down his spine like a clammy river. Trying to still his shaking fingers, he reached towards the great discus, hoping to pick it up and leave as soon as possible, away from that smile. But try as he might, he could not lift it. Again and again he tried, and again and again he failed. Finally, he sank to his knees in exhaustion. 'There is none fit to wield this weapon but you, O Lord!' he cried.

'What made you persist in this foolish quest, Ashwatthama? Nobody in the three worlds has dared to try and take the *Sudarshana Chakra* from me. Nobody has even thought of owning it. It seems to me that you possess a certain quality that sets you apart completely from all the mortals in this world. I wonder if that is a good thing...? So what were you planning to do with my weapon, Ashwatthama? Perhaps you would have used it against me? Surely you would have worshipped me first? And having done so, you would have faced Arjuna with great courage, is that right? But, for you, I am afraid it will always go against the grain to fight your enemy face to face.

Do you know that I would be doing the world a great favour by severing your head right now? I am tempted to do so, but two things have stayed my hand. You are a Brahmin; and also, fate has decreed otherwise. Go now, and when the time is right, let fate show you the way!'

This was the story Krishna narrated to the brothers. 'Ashwatthama is a sly one and there is something rotten in him, which no force on earth can expunge. If he sees Bheema, he will definitely use the *Brahmashira*. We must hurry!'

The chariot in the sky caught up with Ashwatthama, who was sitting with the *rishis* in Veda Vyasa's *ashram*. The Pandavas and Krishna rushed towards him. Sensing their approach, Ashwatthama felt his hatred and anger uncoil within him. He picked up a blade of grass and suffusing it with the power of the *Brahmashira*, released it.

Arjuna responded by invoking the *Brahmashira* himself, hoping it would counter Ashwatthama's. Seeing the celestial missiles rush towards each other, Vyasa and Narada derided the two men soundly for being stupid enough to release the two missiles which had the power to destroy the entire world. Arjuna revoked his missile immediately, since he was pure of mind and had no wish to harm the innocent. But Ashwatthama would not and instead, directed it towards Uttara's womb.

Krishna stepped towards him, radiating divine fury. 'Ashwatthama, that was most wickedly clever of you. From killing sleeping men you have stooped to the level of attacking babies, not yet out of the womb. But I will not allow the child to die; I will personally ensure that his soul is not separated from his body. He will grow up to rule the world for many a year and great glory will be his.

I have rid the world of many evil men, but since you are worse than all of them put together, your fate should be befittingly distinct. You shall roam the earth for ages, alone and despised by all who set eyes upon you. All your rage and bitter hatred will erupt as sores and ulcers on your body. And the foul odour of corrupted flesh and suppuration will envelop you, making dogs bite you and men stone you. Pain will be your constant companion. You will be relieved of the gem you keep hidden within your hair – the one you were born with, and which protects you from hunger, pain, and attacks from demons. The wound it leaves will bleed, putrefy, and never heal while you are alive, which will be forever. You will yearn for death with every ounce of your being but it will never claim you!'

Ashwatthama was reeling under the mighty impact of the terrible curse when Bheema grabbed him and proceeded to lop off his hair. Finding the glittering gem within, he ripped it out with all the force he could muster. Blood gushed out in copious bursts even as Bheema thrust him aside. Scrambling to his feet, Ashwatthama took to his heels, praying already for his heart to burst asunder.

Following his departure, Vyasa commended Krishna for saving Uttara and Abhimanyu's unborn child and for fulfilling his promise to Bhishma to keep the Kuru line intact. Having said their farewells, the Pandavas and Krishna hurried back to show Draupadi the gem. They told her the entire story, and she was content. She even forgave Yudhishthira for his initial lack of enthusiasm to avenge his dead sons, and presented him with the sparkling gem.

In course of time, when Uttara went into labour, the Pandavas and Krishna waited outside the women's chambers. As they had feared, the baby was stillborn. The women wailed in despair. The Pandavas wept. Draupadi alone refused to grieve. She came out to the grieving men and ignoring them all, asked Krishna to step into the birthing chamber. Leading him to the disconsolate Uttara, she commanded, 'Stop that crying at once! Krishna is here and while he is with us, there is no need to fear. He promised us the life of this child and his words can never be false.'

Expectant silence filled the room. Krishna closed his eyes and said, 'This child shall come alive if I have always stayed true to *dharma* and my duty.' The last syllable of his utterance had still not faded away before the child's cry rang out and filled the room with its life-affirming cadence. Flowers rained down from the heavens on the newborn child, who would inherit the world. Krishna's divine form shone with ethereal radiance. Everyone cheered the Lord, clapping their hands like children. Arjuna hugged his friend and wept unashamedly onto his chest. They all felt the same; it was as if Abhimanyu, the boy they had all loved, had come back to the world of the living.

The newborn boy was named Parikshit, for he had survived through divine intervention, as the lone descendent of a great lineage. The blessed child, as predicted by his divine-resuscitator, Shri Krishna, would go on to be a noble and mighty King, who would rule the Kuru kingdom for sixty years.

20
Restitution

With Duryodhana dead and Ashwatthama taken care of, the battle of Kurukshetra finally ended. Dhritarashtra, Gandhari, Kunti, and the other women of the royal household, heard the news and lost no time in hurrying towards the battlefield. The Pandavas went out to meet them. Arjuna had never felt so heartsore in his life. The death of the *Upapandava*s and so many dear friends, haunted him. He felt the loss of Abhimanyu like a stab wound, and the pain was a permanent fixture in his chest.

As he rode with his brothers and Krishna's reassuring presence ever by his side, all he wanted was the sight of Kunti's dear face. Arjuna felt like a small boy again. The years melted away and he was once again a frightened boy who had discovered that his father was dead. The youngster had turned to his mother and she had been strong for his sake; and he had drawn his courage from the deep wells of her inner fortitude. Now he needed Kunti again.

As the distance closed between them, Arjuna could see Kunti clearly. She stood a little behind Dhritarashtra and Gandhari, and her face was wet with tears. Her eyes were scanning the battlefield restlessly and Arjuna knew she was thinking of Abhimanyu, and the sons of Draupadi. He longed to comfort her and be comforted in return, but he knew that Dhritarashtra and Gandhari had to be addressed and appeased first, as protocol demanded. Yudhishthira threw himself at Dhritarashtra's feet and Arjuna felt the blind old man's resentment for his brother like a body blow. The King blessed him, but the hollowness of the gesture was all too evident.

It was Bheema's turn next, and Arjuna wondered about the reception he could expect from the father of his mortal enemy, whom he had killed recently. Suddenly, he saw Krishna do something peculiar. He elbowed Bheema out of the way and thrust an iron statue into Dhritarashtra's expectant arms. The blind man embraced the statue with a vice-like bear-hug, and with a shattering noise the iron statue crumpled like an eggshell in front of the stunned onlookers.

Dhritarashtra stood still for a moment and then dropped to the ground in a keening fit, as the horror of what he believed he had done consumed him. Krishna supported him gently and said, 'Fear not. You have done many things, but fate has decreed that you will not be guilty of killing your own nephew. Bheema lives. I divined your intentions and arranged for the statue of Bheema that Duryodhana used to practise with, to be brought here. It is the statue you destroyed with your mighty arms and not the man you should have treated as your own son but never did.'

The ageing monarch wept with mingled relief and guilt on hearing Krishna's words. 'I deserve every word of your reprimand, for it was my weakness and foolishness that has caused so much harm. Even I am aware that Duryodhana was most unfair to his cousins, but I loved my son and his death is more than I can endure. But I will make my peace with the loss of all my sons, for clearly it has been ordained to happen for the greater good. And it is my wish that my brother's sons inherit the Kingdom and restore wellbeing to the people.' So saying, Dhritarashtra embraced the Pandava brothers and blessed them. Only this time, he actually meant it.

Despite everything, Arjuna felt sorry for the old man. He caught Bheema's eye, knowing that his brother felt differently. Shooting him a look of warning, Arjuna followed Yudhishthira, as he walked towards Gandhari. The normally dignified Queen looked forlorn in her benumbing grief, and the mighty Pandavas were scared to approach her. Even Bheema trembled as he stood before the noble lady. Her eyes beneath the cloth she always wore, having forsaken the gift of sight for her husband's sake, roved over the five men who had killed every one of her sons. Rage built within her, springing forth from the depth of her loss, and she would have cursed them all. But Vyasa intervened and bade her hold her tongue. The great lady listened to the sage, but she could not stop herself from giving utterance to the bitterness in her soul. In a stirring indictment, she berated the Pandavas for depriving her of all her sons. 'It is thanks to you that I stand today without a single son to call my own, when I was the proud mother of a hundred fine sons. My husband and I are old and we have nobody to support us. Why did you have to kill them all? Surely you could have spared at least one of my boys?'

In a quavering voice, Yudhishthira spoke up. 'I will devote my last breath to ensure that you know no discomfort mother, for I am yours to command. It will be an honour to serve you in the place of your sons and I beg you to grant me this.'

Gandhari softened on hearing the sweet tone of genuine compassion; but then her eyes alighted on Bheema, and her pent up feelings flared again as she rounded on him. 'How could you kill Duryodhana by resorting to cheating? My firstborn child lies dead because of your perfidy. And I could not believe that you overstepped the bounds of common decency and drank Duhshasana's blood! You have behaved like a ravening beast and I am ashamed of you! How dare you show your face to me after all the terrible things you did to my sons?'

Too stung to pay heed to the repressing stare Arjuna threw his way, Bheema replied, 'I was fighting for my life, and I could not mull over ethics with your son prancing around raining blows on me from all sides, hellbent on killing me. It was only natural for me to do whatever it took to survive. As for Duhshasana, I can assure you that I did not actually drink his blood since it did not pass my lips. I was only fulfilling the vow I took on the day he dragged Draupadi into the assembly room by her hair! It is not befitting a Kshatriya to go back on his word. I believe that you know deep down that I only did what I had to and that your sons only got their just deserts for the wickedness and evil intent with which they always treated us.'

Being a woman of conscience, Gandhari could not disagree, but his words fanned the flames of her anger and mingled with the deepest sorrow. She took refuge in a fit of intense sobbing and the sound of her weeping fell on the Pandavas in a relentless crescendo, berating them more effectively than her words had done. While she wept, she caught sight of Yudishthira's beautifully formed feet, and their unmarked perfection infuriated her, buffeted as her mind was by images of her dead sons lying on the battlefield, reduced to nothing more than carrion for scavengers to feed on. So great was Gandhari's fury that it was transmitted through her lidded and blindfolded gaze and scorched Yudhishthira's toenails, burning and disfiguring them painfully.

Arjuna, who had been watching all this with uncharacteristic apprehension, felt more like a frightened child than ever. He hid himself behind Krishna, deciding that after all the bizarre events of the battlefield, it would not be surprising if the apparition in front of him burnt them all to cinders like Shiva did to Kama, when he opened his third eye. Gandhari caught the movement, and she was filled with a sudden tenderness. She had always liked Arjuna the best among Kunti's sons. Yudhishthira, despite being virtuous, had been an obstacle to her son's ascension to the throne and therefore, she could not help having mixed feelings about him. Bheema had been her son's hated adversary, and Gandhari could not love one who was her son's worst foe. But she had always liked Arjuna. It had been impossible for her not to like the handsome, talented boy who had grown to be such a fine specimen of manhood. She called him to her and hugged him gently to reassure him and even mussed his curls. As though sensing his desolation and need, she handed him over to Kunti, the way she would a mewling infant. At that instant, in his mother's arms, Arjuna knew that though he could never hope to be whole again without Abhimanyu, the healing process had begun and he would recover. It was a strangely depressing thought, but comforting as well.

Seeing her boys after what felt like eons, and holding Arjuna in her arms, Kunti cried fresh tears of grief, for she knew that her boys had lost an essential part of themselves on the battlefield of Kurukshetra, which they could never hope to recover. She wept for their loss and hers.

Gandhari consoled Kunti and Draupadi, who had also lost her children. The ever-dignified Queen scanned the battlefield with her divine vision and the extent of the devastation shocked her. She turned to Krishna, who was watching her intently and the words rose unbidden to her lips: 'You! You could have put an end to all this carnage, but you did not – and an entire race has paid the price for it. All the blood that has been shed is on your head. For that I curse you and your Yadava clan. Thirty-six years from now, the

Yadus will turn on each other and destroy each other, caught in the throes of the same killing frenzy that infected the Kurus and your race will be destroyed. Your women will know the bereavement we are suffering now. You will bear witness to all that and your passing will follow shortly after, to join the ranks of the departed, alone and without glory!'

Arjuna heard these words with horror, hoping that Krishna would somehow be able to deflect the curse, but his beloved friend smiled, his serenity unaffected. 'Everything you said will come to pass as I have always known it will. Despite what you think, I am powerless against destiny. The Yadavas cannot be destroyed by men or the Gods; so their destruction at the hands of their own has been preordained, and your curse will serve that purpose. In the meantime, you should control your anger and refrain from lashing out at everybody around you, especially since you know well that if anybody deserves blame, it is Duryodhana and his parents, who did not restrain him when they could have. What is done is done, and it is only in acceptance of providence that you will find the strength to move on. Curb your anger, for it does not befit someone of your wisdom and nobility.'

Krishna's gentle reproof left Gandhari deflated and she fell silent. Dhritarashtra came forward at this juncture, and requested Yudhishthira to make funeral arrangements for the fallen warriors. He said that the final rites should be administered without waste of time and it was the duty of the survivors to do this last service for all the unfortunates who had met their end.

Glad to have something to do, the eldest Pandava turned to Vidura and enlisted his aid to begin preparations for conducting the last rites for their fallen relatives and comrades-in-arms, since nobody knew these things better. The remains of the dead that littered the battlefield, were carefully gathered and long rows of funeral pyres were set up. The closest relatives of the fallen men then went around performing the heart-breaking task of lighting the pyres. Once the Fire God had consumed the remains, the ashes were gathered. Dhritarashtra and Yudhishthira led the procession to the banks of the river Ganga. Arjuna was carrying the ashes of Abhimanyu, and he held the clay urn close to his chest. The sombre procession was accompanied by the wretched sounds of bereaved women ululating in abject grief. Arjuna wished silence would fall.

On reaching the banks of the sacred river, the royal procession waded into the waters and allowed the sanctifying waters to cleanse and carry away the ashes of the dead. Ritual donations of gold and fine cloths were made and oblations for the souls of the deceased were offered. The Pandavas stood together and chanted the Vedic hymns for satiation of all they had lost. As this mournful session slowly wound to a close, Kunti spoke in a voice that could barely be heard. 'Wait! There is one more person for whom you must offer prayers! You cannot forget him!'

The brothers looked at her in silence. To the best of their knowledge, they had certainly not forgotten anyone. 'Mother, I think I have offered oblations for every single person who gave his life for me on the battlefield. Who have I have left out?' Yudhishthira asked her gently.

Kunti drew in a shaky breath and revealed her terrible secret in a torrential outpouring. 'There is one who deserves your prayers more than anyone else who has left us. He was a lion among men and famous for his courage, kindness, generosity and loyalty. Some say he was the mightiest warrior this earth has seen. This giant among men was the only one who had the valour and fortitude to oppose Arjuna in battle. He was none other than Karna, who was born to me of Surya, when I was still a maiden and unwed. I abandoned my baby to save my reputation and that of the proud family I was wed into. The child was found by Adhiratha, the good charioteer, and his wife, Radha. This boy grew up to be Karna, the self-made Kshatriya exemplar. A nobler soul or a truer, braver man, this world has yet to see. He was my firstborn, and I am proud to have borne him. Honour your brother and love him in death, even if you could not while he lived!'

The brothers stared at her – struck dumb by shock so great that it was quite some time before they could recover their faculties of speech. The pure-hearted Yudhishthira took the news the hardest as the realization dawned on him that he was guilty of the sin of fratricide. He looked at Kunti beseechingly, praying that it was all a monstrous lie and asked one question: 'Did you tell him the truth?'

It was Krishna who replied. 'Karna knew before the battle started that you were his real brothers. Kunti, Surya, and I, all spoke to him and revealed the secret of his birth. But he could not and would not abandon his friend Duryodhana, whom he had pledged to support. He made the decision to fight against you. But he promised Kunti that he would not hurt Yudhishthira, Bheema, Nakula and Sahadeva, though he would try to kill Arjuna, as his service to Duryodhana. He knew he had chosen death but refused to baulk, and it was his wish that the truth not be known to you. Yudhishthira would have offered him the throne and Karna would have given it to Duryodhana. In the end he did the right thing for the glorious hero that he was born to be.'

This was too much for Yudhishthira, who waded into the waters of the river with the air of a man hoping it would swallow him up. He cried long and hard even as he said the prayers for the brother he had never really known. He thought of how Karna had spared Bheema, Nakula, Sahadeva, and himself, though he could have killed them all; of how he had once been struck by the resemblance of Karna's feet to his mother's, on the day of Draupadi's humiliation. And he wept.

Arjuna stood by, watching him, too drained for tears. His mind refused to accept that Karna was his eldest brother. They had hated each other with a passion and been sworn enemies from the start. He remembered how Karna had singled him out as an adversary during the tournament and humiliated him. The insults they had traded and the million, hateful things they had done to each other, swirled around in his head and he felt sick with a mixed emotion he knew not what to name. Was it remorse? Karna was his brother; and he had known the truth! Arjuna was suddenly furious at the dead man.

Karna had known the truth before the battle and had sworn to leave the brothers unharmed, with the exception of Arjuna himself. Krishna said that Karna had known death was coming and was willing to embrace it. Could that be the reason Karna had had a hand in killing Abhimanyu? Did his fore-knowledge of his death at the hands of the third Pandava lead him to avenge himself beforehand, by taking something that was more precious to Arjuna than life itself? At that moment, Arjuna was almost glad that Karna had lost his birthright and suffered the way he had. Besides, no real brother would have treated Draupadi the way Karna had, he reasoned to himself.

Sensing the direction of his thoughts, Krishna drew Arjuna aside. 'Don't hate him Arjuna, he does not deserve it. He was a noble, if woefully misguided, soul. It was true that he was jealous of you, but that is not surprising because he always felt that you had stolen something from him. As it turned out, he was justified in feeling that way, even if you were not to blame in any way. By throwing in his lot with Duryodhana, he did some shameful things, such as that incident with Draupadi, but he himself told me that he regretted the whole miserable affair deeply. You see, he fell in love with her and when he was on the verge of winning her hand, she rejected him on account of his lowly birth and then chose you.

It is natural for you to hold him to blame for his part in Abhimanyu's death, but you are judging him harshly. In the heat of battle people do terrible things. You know that, for you have also let yourself be carried away despite your innate nobility and my guidance. Forgive him for everything, and even if you cannot bring yourself to love him, at least honour his memory for your brother lived and died like a true hero.'

Listening to Krishna's benevolent words, Arjuna's eyes filled with tears. 'I am grieved that it had to be this way between us. If only things had been different... If only fate had not chosen us as its playthings! What a miserable story this is! My mind refuses to conjure up anything pleasant associated with Karna; there is nothing but hatred and anger. I used to think that in future brothers would learn to live with one another, taking us as role models. Alas, now they will simply know us as the maniacs who killed their own brother. What a despicable example we have set for posterity.'

Arjuna's best friend soothed him and called together the other brothers. Krishna told them that by performing certain penances, they could cleanse themselves of the sin they had committed in their ignorance. The Pandavas were hardly appeased, and Yudhishthira was particularly depressed. Bheema and the twins were deeply disturbed. In a bid to lighten the mood, Bheema gruffly suggested that fratricide would have been inevitable either way; because one would have certainly killed the other in childhood, given what could have been a deep-rooted sibling rivalry. His brothers looked the other way, and Arjuna shook his head at this ill-timed jest. Yudhishthira gave him such an uncharacteristically stern look that Bheema lapsed into silence. Accompanied by Krishna and the elders, the Pandavas left that desolate site and made camp on the banks of the river. It had been a miserable day, and all everybody wanted was to rest their weary eyes and escape into slumber to forget, at least for some hours, the enormity of their self-inflicted tragedy.

The Royal family made camp on the banks of the river Ganga and spent the duration of the mourning period there. Yudhishthira fell into a deep depression, as he felt that it was his desire for the accursed Kingdom that had resulted in so much pain. He decided that the only way to atone for his sins was to renounce the Kingdom and become a wandering hermit. His brothers, wife, Krishna, Vyasa, and some of the other sages, employed their collective powers of persuasion to dissuade him from such an anti-climactic course. By the end of the period of mourning, Yudhishthira was resigned to bearing the weight of the crown.

The Pandavas shed their mourning clothes and with them, a heavy load of the emotional baggage they had been carrying. Dressed in fine clothes and adorned with jewellery that was even heavier than the armour and weapons they were used to carrying, the Royals took their places in the ceremonial procession that would take them to Hastinapura, the city from which their glorious ancestors had ruled. Dhritarashtra, as the former King, was at the head.

Yudhishthira followed in a resplendent chariot fit for Indra, drawn by white bullocks. Bheema took the reins and said in his hearty voice, 'I can hear the people screaming for us all the way here. It finally feels like we won a war and are conquering heroes. All that gloom and doom was extremely hard on my stomach. The good times are finally here again!' And whooping with glee, Bheema urged the animals forward.

His brothers were also feeling better than they had in a long time. Arjuna was holding the ceremonial umbrella over his brother's head, and he felt at peace. The twins were fanning Yudhishthira with their *chamaras*, and their youthful laughter rang out like the peals of heavenly music and warmed everyone who heard it, as they basked in the glory of popular approbation.

The women of the Royal house followed their men. They looked absolutely lovely in their beautiful garments and jewellery; but Draupadi stood out that day. She looked better than women half her age, who were still in the prime of their beauty. The wife of the Pandavas stood tall and proud, deeply content that her husbands had triumphed over the men who had dared defile her person. The loss of her five sons had torn her heart to smithereens. That enduring sadness had robbed her of her alluring smile but somehow enhanced her beauty. Uttara, Abhimanyu's young widow, stood next to Draupadi, who held her protectively. Draupadi had already come to love Uttara's unborn babe as her own. The thought lightened the lines of sorrow etched upon her features and made her radiant.

Yuyutsu, the only son of Dhritarashtra, who had survived the battle, followed the Pandavas. Krishna and Satyaki were also part of the procession. The citizens of Hastinapura were ecstatic to see their beloved Pandavas again, and felt that all their troubles would disappear with Yudhishthira at the helm. It was a fresh beginning for them as well, and they welcomed their King with showers of flowers and voices that shouted their goodwill. Witnessing the jubilant expressions on their dear faces, Yudhishthira felt the last dregs of the sorrow and pain that had threatened to submerge him, fall away. He finally had the popular affirmation that he had done the right thing after all.

Arjuna entered the Kingdom which he had won for his brother and felt a sense of deep satisfaction. He thought of Abhimanyu, who should have, if there was any justice in the world, been by his side; but that was not to be. Ultimately, there was some consolation to be had from the fact that Parikshit, Abhimanyu's unborn son, would one day inherit the Kingdom that his grandfather had sacrificed so much to win.

On reaching the palace, Krishna placed the crown on Yudhishthira's head, while Draupadi sat by his side. The newly anointed King appointed Bheema as his heir. Arjuna became Commander-in-Chief of the army, the logistics of which, Nakula would take care of. Sahadeva, Yudhishthira kept by his side, as his personal protector and advisor, recognising his wisdom and intelligence. Sanjaya was made the Treasurer, and their indefatigable and indispensible uncle, Vidura, was appointed Chief Minister.

21
The Final Journey

The years rolled by as all concerned put the battle firmly behind them and began rebuilding their lives. Arjuna was now completely involved in helping his brother run the Kingdom. Yudhishthira decided to perform the *Ashwamedha* sacrifice, and Arjuna was more than happy to follow the sacrificial horse to new lands and bring all under the suzerainty of his brother, with the help of his formidable *Gandeeva*. Those were good years for the third Pandava. With the death of Karna, he was without a rival and was, without doubt, the mightiest warrior in existence. Men trembled and women swooned in his presence; fathers told their sons stories about Arjuna and tried to inspire them to be like him. With the *Gandeeva* by his side, he was invincible and nobody knew it better than he did himself. Arjuna derived a sense of deep satisfaction from having achieved everything he had set out to do in his life, and took to dwelling increasingly on his triumphs as it dulled the pain in his heart, lacerated as it was by loss.

Arrogance had always been Arjuna's weakness. Following his many successes in the war and thereafter, the self-conceit he had barely managed to keep at bay, once again swelled his head. Yudhishthira, busy with the burden of governing his Kingdom, did not notice or correct him as was his usual wont. Bheema, who himself enjoyed boasting a good deal about his superior might, saw nothing wrong with Arjuna's fine opinion of himself, especially as it was well deserved. He said as much to Sahadeva, who alone saw the change and mentioned it to Bheema.

If there was one thing Arjuna loved more than listening to a suitably dramatised recitation of his valour, it was spending time with Krishna. And so it was his habit to leave for Dwaraka whenever Yudhishthira could spare him. The two friends would hunt, meditate, or simply talk.

Arjuna was relaxing one day with his friend and recalling some of his finest moments, when a distraught Brahmin forced his way past the guards and came towards them, crying and beating his chest. Krishna barely threw a glance his way and instead chose to feed his pet parrot some special treats with a concentration that seemed rather too deep for so undemanding a task.

'What is wrong with Krishna? It is not like him to be so callous about the feelings of others,' Arjuna mused to himself. He rushed to the Brahmin and raised him to his feet, feeling very compassionate indeed. 'Tell me the problem and I assure you that I will take care of it!' he said in all sincerity.

The Brahmin then unfolded his woeful tale. Some malevolent force was clearly at work, because his wife had delivered nine healthy boys, only to see them die almost as soon as they uttered their first cry. He had repeatedly requested the King for protection, but none was forthcoming whatsoever. Now his wife was expecting yet another child, and it would break his heart if this one too, was to be snatched away.

Arjuna heard him out and said, 'Set your mind at rest, for now you have me and my *Gandeeva* as the protector of your next child. Send word to me when it is time, and I will send the God of Death back to his abode with a sharp arrow aimed so precisely at him that he will never bother you or your son again. And if I fail to do so, I will build a pyre and allow the flames to immolate me.'

The Brahmin thanked him fervently and left with only a touch of scepticism and renewed hope in his heart. When his wife was ready to deliver their tenth child, he came to fetch Arjuna. The famed warrior snatched up his beloved bow and hastily followed him, wondering again at Krishna's apparent disinterest.

On reaching the Brahmin's humble abode, Arjuna busied himself building a barricade of arrows around the hut to keep away all unwanted intruders, including the dark Lord of Death. The keening sound of a newborn was heard, only to be replaced abruptly by a hollow silence that was pierced by the wails of the distressed mother. The two men rushed inside, only to be told that the tenth child had gone the way of the others.

The Brahmin rounded on Arjuna. 'You promised me that you would keep him safe and you have gone back on your word. Bring back my child or forsake your life as you promised!'

Arjuna could not believe that he had failed. He jumped onto his chariot and went in search of the missing baby. He searched the three worlds, but his efforts were fruitless. Even Indra, his divine father, would not help him and suggested that he go to Krishna instead. But Arjuna was strangely reluctant to do this. Realizing with disbelief that he had failed utterly in an undertaking, he returned to earth to end his life.

For the second time since his ill-conceived vow to avenge his son Abhimanyu by killing Jayadratha or consign himself to flames, Krishna stopped him. In his chariot, he carried his friend to Vaikuntha, the abode of Vishnu. Many were the wonders Arjuna saw before an eerie darkness engulfed him – a darkness so complete that it came close to driving him to madness. Krishna released his *Sudharshana Chakra* to light the way by acting like a fiery comet blazing its way across the heavens.

Soon the friends arrived at the abode of the Protector of the Universe. Vishnu reclined on his serpent Shesha. The Brahmin's ten missing children were also present, playing at his feet and on Shesha's hood. Arjuna stared in wonderment at the Lord, and felt blessed and humbled by the effulgence of the divine presence he was privileged to see.

Vishnu blessed the two men paying obeisance to him and then said, 'It was my wish that you pay a visit here, Arjuna. I was beginning to feel that you perhaps thought that you had no use for the Divine Protector. The entire charade with the Brahmin was designed so that my will could be carried out. You may take the children with you, so that they might be reunited with their parents. I take it that henceforth you will know better than to use your arrows to keep me away.'

Arjuna was too astounded by his good fortune to have seen the Lord in his divine abode to feel grievously chastened; but he resolved not to be so arrogant in the future, for indeed, he was as nothing compared to the Divine Will. It was not the first time Krishna had enlightened him. Arjuna promised himself not to be blinded by his own vanity any more, especially since it had the unhappy result of his having come close to ending as a repast for Agni, the Fire

God. Krishna still said nothing, but he was happy that his friend had learnt the lesson, for it was the last he would teach him in this *avatar*.

True to Gandhari's word, thirty-six years after the battle of Kurukshetra, the Vrishni clan was extinguished almost down to the last man. A few years previously, the sages Vishwamitra, Narada and Kanva, had visited Dwaraka. They were treated with due respect by all in the Kingdom. But a group of irreverent boys thought it would be funny to get one over the old men, who seemed to be awfully close to senility and hardly deserving of the reverence the good people of the realm were showering on them. Shamba, Krishna's son by Jambhavati, was presented before the sages in the guise of a pregnant woman and the ill-advised youngsters requested the venerable guests of the Kingdom to hazard a guess as to the sex of the unborn child.

The omniscient sages flushed with fury and rounded on the miscreants. 'How dare you rascals try to make us look like fools? That is no woman, it is Krishna's son, Shamba. But he will give birth to something, make no mistake; an iron mace will be delivered by him and it is that offspring of your folly which will be responsible for the complete destruction of the Vrishni clan. Laugh now if you dare!'

Petrified, the youths fled from the rage of the saints. But there was no escaping the events they had inadvertently set in motion. Shamba did give birth to an iron mace. The loathsome thing was presented at court. The aged monarch, Ugrasena, consulted with his wise men and decreed that the mace be ground into fine powder and buried in the sea. His instructions were carried out almost to the letter – almost – because the sharp tip of the mace remained indestructible. Finally, it was decided that it should be discarded in the sea along with the rest of the mace, where it was swallowed by a huge fish. The tide brought the powder back to shore and a virulent, green patch of reeds grew at the spot. As for the sharp tip of the mace, a fisherman found it and sold it to a hunter named Jara.

Feeling that catastrophe had been thwarted, the people went about their business. Life cannot go on just brooding about the prospect of death. But when thirty-six years had elapsed after Gandhari had pronounced her fateful words, ill omens were seen all over the Kingdom. Krishna realised that the time had come for his people to depart the world.

Krishna gave the order that the people should get ready to visit Prabhasa and offer prayers at the Shiva temple there. In those days, such pilgrimages were a huge event and generated a lot of excitement. People gathered *en masse* and the long trek began. Once the *puja*s had been performed and the Lord worshipped, the enterprise which had begun with proper religious fervour, deteriorated into licentiousness and uninhibited revelry. A drunken orgy commenced on the grounds some distance from the temple, at the place where the River Saraswati merged into the sea. Food and drink were consumed in vast amounts and folk were in a state of inebriation, their good sense drowned in intoxicants as all the primeval passions normally restrained by rigid self-control, came bursting forth.

No good drinking session was complete without a detailed discussion of the great battle fought at Kurukshetra. As the men gave their opinions about the key events in the great war, Satyaki gave vent to his long suppressed fury over the dastardly act committed by Kritavarma, Ashwatthama and Kripacharya, in the dead of the night, when the Pandava army had been slumbering. In strident tones, he said, 'I saw many terrible things happen on the killing fields of Kurukshetra, but none as base as the dastardly act of Kritavarma and his fellow assasins in taking the lives of sleeping men. The world has yet to see cowardice and evil of such magnitude. Could anyone have taken the life of Dhirishtadyumna – that fine warrior born from the sacred flames – if he was on his feet? Or the valiant sons of the Pandavas? This basest of creatures had to resort to treachery, along with that snake Ashwatthama and the weakling Kripacharya.' At the end of his tirade, Satyaki hawked up phlegm and spat it out in Kritavarma's direction, just in case he had not made his contempt clear.

The object of his ire responded in kind. 'What right do you have to talk about cowardice and treachery in others? I remember how you killed Bhurishrava while he sat in meditation with his fighting arm lopped off by Arjuna. It is my recollection that he had defeated you in fair combat, and you lay on the floor and put up the same resistance as a whore would to a rich customer, while he stomped on your head. You would have been dead if Arjuna had not come running to your rescue. That sordid episode is proof enough that you have no right to judge others.'

Seeing a few of the onlookers shaking their heads in agreement, (although it was equally likely that they were merely trying to clear their heads from the fumes of total intoxication), Satyaki lost control completely. 'Enough of your inane talk; it is time for me to pay back the murderer of Dhrishtadyumna in kind!' And with those words, Satyaki lopped off Kritavarma's head with one sudden stroke of his curved scimitar.

The dead man's relatives immediately pounced on Satyaki and tried to tear him to pieces with their bare hands. Krishna's son, Pradyamuna, jumped into the murderous fray, determined to rescue Satyaki; but to no avail as the duo were engulfed by wave upon wave of drunken and bereaved kin. They managed to take down as many men as possible before they succumbed to the blows of the furious mob.

Seeing the dead bodies of his favourite son and beloved friend, Krishna grabbed the evil-looking reeds close at hand and they immediately became a formidable mace in his hands. With this, he smashed the skulls of Kritavarma's relatives and left piles of corpses behind him. Others followed his example, tugging out tufts of reeds and finding themselves armed with powerful weapons. Krishna had moved away from the frenzy of mass killing all around him and stood to one side, watching in silence as his entire clan looked all set to extinguish themselves down to the last man. Shamba, his son, and Aniruddha, his grandson, went down as blows were rained down on their heads by blood relatives. Krishna continued to watch till there was nothing left to see save a river of blood and more carcasses than one could count.

Only Daruka, his faithful charioteer, and Babhru, a Minister of the Yadava court, escaped the carnage. Krishna sent Daruka to inform Arjuna and the Pandavas of what had transpired. Babhru was assigned the task of keeping the women and children who had been left in Dwaraka, safe. Krishna had barely issued the instructions, when an arrow came out of nowhere and decapitated Babhru. A moment elapsed before Krishna went in search of Balarama. He saw his beloved brother at the seashore, deep in meditation. A white serpent escaped from his lips like a sigh that had taken shape. And Krishna knew that Balarama had departed the mortal world.

Thinking of everything and nothing in particular, Krishna wandered into the forest and reclined under a tree, carefully sticking his feet out. The hunter, Jara, who had become the proud owner of the indestructible tip of the fatal mace, saw the divine feet and mistaking them for an animal, let his arrow fly. It pierced the heel of Krishna, which was the only weak spot on his person. When Jara realized what he had done, he wept and beat his chest, begging Krishna to forgive him. The Lord smiled at him and said that he had done a great service in releasing him from a mortal's life and that a place in heaven would be his after his own end. Having blessed Jara, Krishna bade him leave. The Lord then closed his eyes and severed his spirit, which flew to Vaikuntha, to once again become part of the essence of Vishnu, the Preserver of the Universe.

Daruka reached Hastinapura and informed the Pandava brothers about the destruction of the Yadava clan, as foretold by Gandhari. Arjuna did not bother to talk things over with his brothers. He called for a chariot and ordered the charioteer to ride in great haste to Dwaraka. As he always did in times of great turmoil and sorrow, Arjuna simply desired to be with his best friend; with Krishna by his side, everything somehow became easier. But this time he knew that Krishna would not be there; and he also knew that he himself would shortly follow him down the dark road of death to rejoin him on the other side.

Arjuna could hear the wailing of the women of the Palace a long way off. He walked in and though he was a veteran of heartbreak, the sea of sorrow he encountered proved too much even for him, and he sank to the floor in a dead faint. He was helped onto a couch by the piteously few members who remained of the magnificent clan. When he revived, he went at once to meet his maternal uncle, Vasudeva. The old man told him everything that had transpired and the two wept fresh tears. Arjuna marvelled that he himself still lived when his friend had departed the world. Vasaudeva said, as though reading his thoughts, 'It was time for him to pass on, Arjuna. He had achieved every single thing he was born to do. The destruction of so many *asuras,* who were crushing Mother Earth to death with their evil ways, was possible only because of Krishna. Kamsa, Shisupala, Jayadratha, and countless other villains, were destroyed by him, either directly or through his Divine Will; many were the miracles he performed and wonders that he wrought. Deeds that would ordinarily take a thousand lifetimes to fulfil, he accomplished in one glorious birth. We are blessed indeed to have known and been loved by him. But the age draws to a close and it is time for all of us to leave this world behind and reap the fruits of our labours here. Be calm and prepare yourself for the inevitable, Arjuna. Do not be so forlorn. Krishna will never be far from his beloved friend.'

Hearing the soothing words uttered by his noble uncle, Arjuna felt as though Krishna himself had put the words in the old man's mouth. He bestirred himself and began preparations for what needed to be done. He summoned the remaining Ministers and issued orders for the week ahead. They were to make preparations to leave Dwaraka. It was his intention to take the survivors to Indraprastha, where Krishna's great-grandson, Vajra, sired by his son Aniruddha and the *asura* Princess Usha, would be crowned.

Arjuna spent a sleepless night, unable to believe that he could not make the final journey from this life to the great beyond, with Krishna by his side. He drew some comfort from the fact that his beloved brothers and Draupadi were still there with him, and that they would remain together to the very end. Vasudeva passed away during the night and a saddened Arjuna personally performed the last rites for his uncle. Later, he went to the spot where the Yadava clan had met its end. Once more, he performed the last rites and rituals for all those who had passed away on that spot, victims of the combined curses of Gandhari and the *rishi*, and their preordained fate.

Having completed this onerous task, and when the traditional period of mourning for seven days had passed, Arjuna shepherded the survivors in the direction of Indraprastha. *En route*, the little retinue came under attack from a vicious group of bandits. Arjuna snatched up his infallible *Gandeeva*, but to his dismay, his memory failed him completely and he could not remember any of the *mantras* to summon the celestial weapons he had so painstakingly accumulated over a lifetime. Refusing to watch helplessly as the innocent folks dependent on him died in large numbers, attempting to protect their paltry possessions, he tried to fight with ordinary weapons. But soon his supposedly inexhaustible quiver became empty and his bowstring snapped. When he tried to restring the bow, his fingers refused to perform the task they had performed to perfection all these years. Arjuna finally gave up; partly because there was no other choice and partly because he had decided to stop fighting fate. The robbers departed as quickly as they had arrived, carrying away their precious booty and leaving many lifeless bodies behind.

Heartsick and finally feeling the full weight of his long years, Arjuna gathered together the dwindling number of survivors and hastened to Indraprastha. Once there, he installed Vajra on the throne before anything further could happen to that beleaguered clan. Deciding that Krishna would have been happy with his actions, Arjuna then made his way towards Hastinapura.

The third Pandava decided to take a detour and visit his ascetic ancestor, Veda Vyasa at his *ashram*. There he poured out his grief over the loss of Krishna and his inability to come to terms with life without him. 'How could such a thing happen? I cannot imagine a force strong enough to actually snuff the life out of Krishna, who could have crushed the three worlds to smithereens with just his fingers. And mighty Balarama is also gone! Satyaki, Pradyamuna... so many people I loved like my own brothers have left me for good. The entire Vrishni race has been decimated. My celestial weapons are lost to me; the power of my *Gandeeva* seems to be failing; and I am incapable of protecting those under my care. How could such a thing happen to Arjuna, the hero of the battle of Kurukshetra? Why does it have to end like this? Krishna is not here to explain all this to me and I cannot bear it!'

The venerable sage then spoke wise words to him. 'Arjuna, you know the answers even as you ask the questions. But your mind is so impaired by emotional turmoil that you refuse to acknowledge the truth to yourself. As you have said, Krishna would not have stood by and watched the Vrishnis kill themselves if it had not been ordained by all-powerful providence. His passing was also something that had to be, as he had done all that was expected of him and more. Krishna submitted to fate with typical grace and calm acceptance. He would certainly expect the same from you. The Pandavas have also carried out the task entrusted to them at birth; which is why your weapons fail you now. They have served their purpose and there is no need for their usage. All is as it should be. Deep within, you know it too. Let go of your passions. Talk to your brothers, and together you must prepare to leave this world and enter the heavenly abode you so richly deserve.'

Arjuna listened like an obedient child, and touched Vyasa's feet before leaving. On reaching Hastinapura, he told his brothers all that had transpired. The Pandavas then made a solemn decision. Yudhishthira, with the help of his brothers, completed any pending tasks regarding the governance of his beloved subjects, and began arrangements to place Arjuna's grandson, Parikshit, on the Kuru throne. Yuyutsu, humble and wise, was appointed as successor to Vidura. And finally it was time for the Pandavas and Draupadi to leave.

They left the palace quietly, unwilling to make their last journey with anyone other than themselves. A dog decided to walk with them, and meeting with no resistance, joined the solemn group. Having traded their royal robes for bark, the Pandavas and Draupadi set out with the vague design of visiting holy places, but their feet seemed to know where to take them. On and on they walked, crossing rivers, plains and mountains.

The brothers carried nothing of worth with them, but Arjuna held onto his *Gandeeva* and the quivers Agni had presented him. They were practically a part of him, and he was not ready to sever them from his being. But in the course of their journey, Agni met them, and he instructed Arjuna to return both the bow and the quivers to Varuna. The third Pandava acquiesced, but could not help thinking that now he knew exactly what Karna had gone through when his divine father had relieved him of his celestial armour and earrings.

Resuming their journey, the Pandavas and Draupadi came to the foothills of the Himalayas, and began the perilous ascent up the icy slopes with their bare feet and scanty clothing. Arjuna looked up at the majestic range and a wonderful sense of calm filled his soul.

With every breath he took, he felt more and more detached from his human self and he noted the progress of his brothers and wife as if from a distance that kept increasing. And yet he had never seen them more clearly.

Draupadi, who had found the going rough, suddenly lost her balance and plummeted to the depths below. Her husbands continued ahead without stopping. Arjuna felt Bheema's anguish – he had loved her more than the other four brothers. The second Pandava inched closer to Yudhishthira, wanting to know from him why Draupadi, who had borne so much, had to be the first to die. But Arjuna knew that it was because in the innermost recesses of her heart, she had always loved him, Arjuna, more than the others. He had known it, but had chosen not to acknowledge her love for him in full and given his deepest devotion to Subhadra. It was not a conscious decision, but Arjuna knew that he had done the right thing, for otherwise the Pandavas would have been torn apart by their forbidden love. But with Draupadi gone, he finally allowed himself to realise that he had loved her back in equal measure – always.

Sahadeva, wise and true, the family baby and Kunti's favourite, followed Draupadi shortly after. Arjuna watched him disappear into the foggy mist of nothingness below. A keener intellect the world had seldom seen, he thought to himself. Yudhishthira had disapproved of Sahadeva's vanity, and was explaining to Bheema that it was the reason for his passing, but Arjuna himself felt there was nothing wrong with being proud of the truths about oneself, especially since Sahadeva had used his intelligence to help others all he could. Moreover, he had been fiercely loyal and always striven to be the best that he could be in every aspect of his life.

Nakula, who could not bear separation from his twin for long, went down after him almost immediately. Arjuna thought, as he had many times in the past, that Nakula was the most handsome man he had ever seen. The fourth Pandava had even more lady admirers than Arjuna himself, or Krishna for that matter. Yudhishthira had cautioned Nakula as well, about the perils of taking inordinate pride in one's personal appearance. But Nakula's ability to bring laughter and warmth into their lives had been a precious gift to them all and Arjuna wanted the world to remember his little brother's generous heart, rather than a trivial foible called vanity.

Yudhishthira had always reserved his lengthiest sermons on humility and modesty not for the twins, nor for Bheema, who loved to boast about his inhuman strength, but for Arjuna. And with good reason, Arjuna thought to himself, as an inner smile lit up his noble visage and made him look more beatific than ever. His all-too-evident pride in his unmatched prowess with the bow and arrow, may have seemed like a shortcoming to many, but Arjuna himself did not see it that way. The *hubris* that was so characteristic of him, had helped him weather the roughest storms and the darkest days of his life. It had spurred him on to achieve everything he had ever wanted to. This imperfection which people kept pointing out, was an integral part of his aggregate persona. It was the same for Draupadi, and the twins, who had gone before him; and for Bheema, with his gluttony and vainglory, as well as for Yudhishthira, whose little white lie was perhaps the only black mark on an otherwise unblemished soul, but which nevertheless shifted the balance in favour of all that was good and noble in the world.

As for himself, at the end of it all, Arjuna could say, and rightfully so – that he was Arjuna, the best there ever was, and the best there ever would be. This last thought accompanied him as he fell into the chasm of nothingness. His embodied soul freed itself and soared heavenwards to where Krishna, Abhimanyu, and all those he had loved best, stood waiting to receive him.

Select Glossary

Acharya: Honorific for a *Guru* or teacher
Agniastra: Missile with the destructive power of Agni, the Fire God
Agneya: Fiery weapon of Agni, the Fire God
Akshahridaya: *Mantra* which endows winning expertise in gambling
Akshauhini: Consists of 109,350 infantry, 65, 610 cavalry, 21, 870 chariots & 21, 870 elephants
Amaravati: City of the Gods
Amrita: Nectar of immortality
Antardhana: Weapon of Kubera, the God of Wealth
Apsara: heavenly nymph
Arani: Flintwood used to start sacrificial fires
Astra: Celestial weapon of great power
Ashrama: Hermitage
Ashwamedha: Horse sacrifice
Asuras: Demons; evil counterparts of the *Deva*s
Avatar: Incarnation of God
Bhargavastra: Missile of Parashurama, the Brahmin-warrior God
Bibhatsu: One of Arjuna's 10 names, meaning 'one who is fair and ethical in conduct'
Brahmastra: A celestial weapon of unstoppable power, forged by Brahma, the Creator, himself
Brahmin: Uppermost in the Hindu caste hierarchy – it was considered an unforgiveable crime to kill a Brahmin
Brahmashira: Divine missile famed for its matchless destructive power
Chakravyuha: Complex wheel formation used by Drona at Kurukshetra
Chakra- shakut vyuha: Carriage wheel-shaped battle formation
Chakshushi: Secret science of the *Gandharva*s that gave them divine vision, enabling them to perceive whatever they wished in the three worlds, thereby elevating them to the status of the Gods

Danavas & Daityas: Evil creatures who were destroyed, along with the *Asuras*, in the famed clash between the *Devas* and the *Asuras*
Danda: Yama's weapon – the divine noose
Devadatta: Arjuna's conch
Dharma: Code of ethical conduct that upholds morality & righteousness
Dhananjaya: One of Arjuna's 10 names, meaning 'one who brings prosperity wherever he goes'
Dhanurveda: Skill with weaponry
Devas: Gods
Dvapara: In Hindu tradition, *Dvapara yuga* (age) is characterized by a marked deterioration/erosion of moral values, leading to an increase in death, strife and misery
Gandeeva: Arjuna's bow, gifted to him by Agni, the Fire God
Ganga: Holy River Goddess
Guru: Preceptor
Gurukula: Place of learning
Gurudakshina: Preceptor's fee
Hrishaba: Musical note
Jishnu: One of Arjuna's 10 names, acquired when he took a deadly oath
Kalakeyas: Inhabitants of Hiranyapuri, a *Danava* stronghold made arrogant by a boon of invincibility granted by Brahma; eventually destroyed by Arjuna
Karma: Hindu philosophy refers to the consequences of actions in past & present lives, that determines the good or bad of present & future lives
Kavacha & Kundala: Armour & earrings
Kiriti: One of Arjuna's 10 names, given to him when Indra presented him with a golden diadem
Kshatriyas: Warrior caste, ranked after the Brahmins in Hindu hieracrchy
Lingam: Phallic representation of Shiva, the Great God
Lokapalas: Indra, Varuna, Kubera & Yama – revered as Guardians of the Universe
Madhava: Powerful celestial weapon

Maharathi: Accomplished warriors were accorded this honourable title
Maharishis: Great sages
Mantra: Sacred chant
Nagas: Serpent people
Nishada: A lowly caste tribe whose chief pursuits were hunting & fishing
Paashupata: Shiva's favorite weapon, which conjured up weird, unearthly beings, capable of annihilating entire armies
Padmasana: Yogic lotus position
Panchajanya: Krishna's conch
Partha: One of Arjuna's 10 names, derived from *Pritha,* his mother Kunti's other name
Phalguna: One of Arjuna's 10 names – so called as he was born under the star, Phalguni
Pratismriti: Powerful means of accomplishing one's heart's desires – if one is worthy
Prayavrata: Vow to refrain from food & drink unto death
Prayopaveshana: Sanctified way of giving up one's life by fasting
Rajasuya: Sacrifice that enables the performer to call himself Emperor
Rakshasas: Demons
Rishis: Revered sage
Sabha: Grand hall or assembly room
Sairandhri: Maid skilled in the cosmetic arts
Sammohana: Missile capable of inducing deep sleep
Samsaptakas: Considered suicide squads, these warriors would take a deadly oath to conquer or die trying
Sanjivani: Secret art of bringing the dead back to life
Saptarishis: Seven great seers: Bhrigu, Angira, Atri, Gautama, Kashyap, Vashishtha, and Agastya, renowned for their great deeds, accomplished through the power of meditation
Sarpasatra Yajna: Sacrifice to destroy snakes
Savyasachi: One of Arjuna's 10 names, meaning 'ambidextrous'
Shakti: One of Indra's weapons of unlimited power

Sthanu: One of Shiva's names, meaning 'stoical'
Suchi-vyuha: Needle-shaped battle formation
Sudharshana Chakra: Vishnu, the Protector's divine discus & weapon of choice
Suta: Lowborn
Sutaputra: Son of one who is lowborn
Swetavahana: One of Arjuna's 10 names, meaning 'rider of a divine chariot'
Swargalokha: Heaven – abode of the *Devas*
Swayamvara: An ancient tradition wherein suitors assembled in a grand hall and the bride would choose her husband from amongst them
Tapas: Severe penance
Teerthayatra: Pilgrimage of purification
Vahana: Vehicle
Vaishnava: Sacrifice of great power once performed by Vishnu, and also by Duryodhana, while the Pandavas were in exile
Vaishnava: Missile imbued with the power of Vishnu, which none could withstand
Vajra: Indra's favorite weapon, shaped like a thunderbolt
Varunastra: Missile imbued with the power of Varuna, presiding deity of the water bodies
Varunapasha: Weapon of Varuna, God of the Waters
Vavavya: Weapon imbued with the power of Vayu, God of Wind
Vijaya: One of Arjuna's 10 names, meaning 'undefeated'
Vishosana: Divine weapon of great power
Vishwaroopam: Cosmic form of Lord Vishnu
Vyuha: Battle formation
Yajna: Sacrificial rite
Yaksha: Demi-God who submits to the authority of Kubera

Select Bibliography

Bonnefoy, Y. (1993). *Asian Mythologies*. (W. Doniger, trans.) Chicago: University of Chicago Press

Chaturvedi, D. K. (2006). *Tales from the Mahabharat*. New Delhi: Diamond Pocket Books

Chinmoy, S. (1988). Tales from the Mahabharatha. Citadel Books

Devadhar, CR. (2006). *Vikramorvasiyam of Kalidasa*. Mumbai: Motilal Banarsidass

Dhand, A. (2008). *Woman as fire, woman as sage: Sexual ideology in the Mahabharatha*. Albany: State University of New York Press

Iyer, N.S. (2007). *Musings on Indian writing in English*. (Vol. 3). New Delhi: Sarup and Sons

Katha, A. C (2010). *Mahabharata (Set of 3 volumes)*. Bombay: Amar Chitra Katha Pvt. Ltd

Lang, A. (2006). *Custom and Myth*. Na: Bibliobazaar

Mani, V. (2002). *Puranic Encyclopaedia: A comprehensive work with special reference to the epic and puranic literature*. Delhi: Motilal Banarsidass

Menon, Ramesh. (2006). *The Mahabharata: A modern rendering*. Lincoln, NE: iUniverse

Rajagopalachari, C. (2006). *Mahabharata* (47th ed.). Bombay: Bharatiya Vidya Bhavan

Roy, P. C. *The Mahabharatha of Krishna Dwaipayana Vyasa*. (Vol. 1). Kolkata: Oriental Publishing Co

Sarma, B. (2008). *Vyasa's Mahabharatam*. Kolkata: Academic Publishers

Subramaniam, N. (2009). *Mahabharata*. Chennai: Young Kids Press

Uberoi, M. (1996). *The Mahabharatha*. Delhi: Ratna Sagar P. Ltd

Vogel, J.P. (2005) . *Indian serpent lore or the Nagas in Hindu legend and art*. Whitefish, MT: Kessinger Publishing

Vyasa, K.D. (2008). *The Mahabharata of Krishna Dwaipayana Vyasa*. (K.M. Ganguli, Trans.) Middlesex: Echo Library

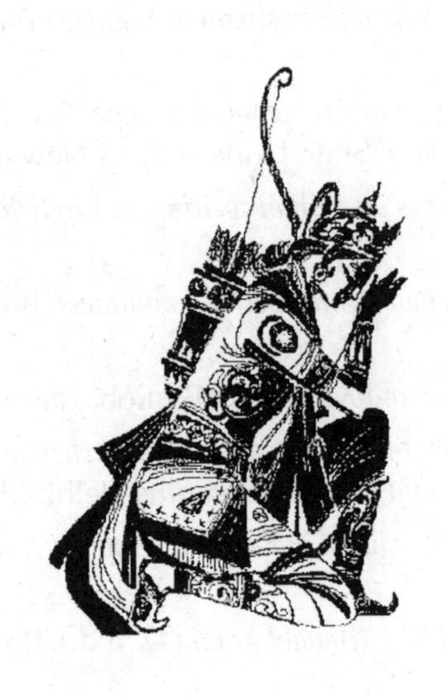

TITLES AVAILABLE

MORE TITLES FROM
LEADSTART PUBLISHING

THE SPEED OF TIME
Poplular Science For The Reader With Little Or No Background In Physics
SHARAD NALAWADE

As you read this book, you realize that he world you live in is stranger than fiction... Did you know that you exist in different places at the same time? Are the trillions of atoms that make you, nothing but vibrations in 10 dimensions? Is it true that we are all connected with each other? Can you go into the future to change the present? Why do scientists and philosophers struggle with the concept of Time? Can science explain consciousness through physics? Is nature hiding the best kept secrets which can never be unravelled by humans? The Speed of Time approaches the most complex and esoteric theories of science in lucid, clear and simple language – like a thriller leaving you wanting more...

HEALING THE BLUE PLANET
An informed Consent
BANE SINGH

What ails Mother Earth? The answer can be found in the propensities of Man, her most gifted but also her most prodigal son. The world today may look to be the oyster to modern Man, with his faculties of creativity, inventiveness and enterprise. But all this has come at a grievous cost to nature that we, in our reckless quest for 'progress' and comfort, have inflicted on the mother planet. Climate change; global warming; rampant exploitation of non-renewable fossil fuels; greenhouse gases; retreating glaciers; pollution; ozone depletion; dwindling forests; e-waste – are stark symptoms of the inexorable degradation wrought on a once-pristine environment. We seem to be heading mindlessly toward our collective doom of a sixth extinction, this time caused by human-induced climate change. Time is running out, but all is still not lost. The symptoms, the diagnostics and the line of cure, are all presented here.

Available at all Leading Bookstores and Book Selling websites
or by direct order from
LEADSTART PUBLISHING PVT LTD
Unit 122, Building B/2, Near Wadala RTO,
Wadala (E), Mumbai 400 037
T 91 22 2404 6887 **W** www.leadstartcorp.com